P9-CDS-593

Blood Ties

What would it be like to break this little demon with kisses and bend her will to his?

"I thank you, Brother," Tristan said, nodding, as gracious as a king in spite of the guards who held him fast. "Now may I kiss my wife?"

"You would kiss me?" Siobhan laughed. He hated her; he had shown her nothing but contempt. But suddenly she saw something else in those cold, green eyes, something wicked she had never seen before in the gaze of any other man.

"Oh yes," he answered, his mysterious smile making her blush. "I would."

Praise for Lucy Blue's previous
Bound in Darkness novel
My Demon's Kiss

"A stellar story . . . the first stunning book in the alluring new medieval series, *Bound in Darkness*. Blue compellingly sucks readers into a bygone but thrilling world of knights and vampires, romance and terror. . . . Utterly captivating. . . . An absolute must for fans of paranormal romance."   —www.roadtoromance.com

"A fine medieval vampire romance. . . . *My Demon's Kiss* [is like] taking Angel and placing him mostly in eleventh-century England. The story line is action-packed . . . and never slows down."

—www.thebestreviews.com

ALSO BY LUCY BLUE

My Demon's Kiss

The Devil's Knight

LUCY BLUE

POCKET BOOKS

New York London Toronto Sydney

The sale of this book without its cover is unauthorized. If you purchased this book without a cover, you should be aware that it was reported to the publisher as "unsold and destroyed." Neither the author nor the publisher has received payment for the sale of this "stripped book."

An *Original* Publication of POCKET BOOKS

 POCKET BOOKS, a division of Simon & Schuster, Inc.
1230 Avenue of the Americas, New York, NY 10020

This book is a work of fiction. Names, characters, places and incidents are products of the author's imagination or are used fictitiously. Any resemblance to actual events or locales or persons, living or dead, is entirely coincidental.

Copyright © 2006 by Jayel Wylie

All rights reserved, including the right to reproduce this book or portions thereof in any form whatsoever. For information address Pocket Books, 1230 Avenue of the Americas, New York, NY 10020

ISBN-13: 978-1-4165-1195-3
ISBN-10:   1-4165-1195-4

This Pocket Books paperback edition March 2006

10 9 8 7 6 5 4 3 2 1

POCKET and colophon are registered trademarks of Simon & Schuster, Inc.

Cover art by Franco Accornero; handlettering by David Gatti

Manufactured in the United States of America

For information regarding special discounts for bulk purchases, please contact Simon & Schuster Special Sales at 1-800-456-6798 or business@simonandschuster.com.

For Blue, who likes this hero better

Acknowledgments

Endless thanks to Timothy Seldes, a dear man and a truly magnificent agent, and Lauren McKenna, brilliant editor and friend. I'd love them even if I didn't need them so much. More thanks than I could ever express to my family (the Addisons and Sorensons forever included) for everything—no writer has ever been given better, more constant support.

And finally, thanks to Michael Hemlepp, the best lawyer in the history of time.

The Devil's Knight

Prologue

Siobhan scrambled through the thorny brush at the foot of the hill, the Norman knight hot on her heels. "You'd best hope I never catch you, poppet," he shouted, hacking away at the vines and brambles with his sword. "You'll be begging me to kill you."

Siobhan wished she was already dead, that it had been her head cleaved off in the first shock of the attack instead of her father's. The Norman king's men hadn't even bothered with a royal proclamation this time. With no warning at all, they had poured into her father's village in the middle of the night, setting the wooden walls aflame. She and her mother had run from their burning manor house just in time to see her father's head fall from his shoulders in the narrow street and roll into the gutter, his angry face still moving. If Siobhan should somehow survive this night and live to be an old woman of a hundred years, she would never forget the sight, the way his eyes had blinked and his mouth still moved as if to curse them all.

But she couldn't stop to think about it now. She

dropped to her knees to crawl under a thicket, the thorns tearing at her back as she reached the bare face of the druid's hill. She had never thought she would have to run so far; she had assumed the Norman knight would give her up when she reached the thick of the woods, where his horse couldn't follow. But no such luck.

"I will catch you, poppet!" he promised from behind her, closer now. She huddled in the briars, hoping he had lost her trail, but his voice grew closer still. "Where will you go now?"

She straightened up against the rock, a long thorn tearing at her cheek. The steep hillside was completely overgrown, a natural defense for the ancient tower on its summit. When the king had issued his first proclamation, her mother had wanted to come here, to give up their cozy manor house for the cramped stone tower. "We can defend the druid's keep forever," she had insisted. But her father would not be moved. The old king had given his father these lands in his treaty with the Saxons, making Da a noble lord the same as the Norman bastard the new king meant to replace him. He had made a formal protest, written in his own beautiful hand, and had insisted that would be the end of it. But maybe young King Henry couldn't read.

"Come back here now," the knight who was chasing her called out, stopping at the worst of the briar thicket. "Come back, and I won't hurt you."

Siobhan looked back and snorted—did he think she

was stupid? She had seen what his friends had done to her mother before their captain had shown her the mercy of cutting her throat; she knew what this one had in mind for her. She might be only eleven years old, but she wasn't stupid. She turned back to the rock face and started looking for a way to climb.

"Little bitch," she heard him grunt, struggling through the thorns, and her heart raced faster with panic. What would Sean do? she thought, kicking off her shoes. If her older brother had been there, she was convinced that none of this would have happened. He would have reasoned with their father, made him run or at least put up a better defense than noble right and pride. But Sean was far away, learning how to be a knight himself.

"Come down here, you little monkey," the Norman said from behind her, laughing. He was very close now. "Where do you mean to go?" He was right, of course. The rock face before her was too high and steep; she would never have the strength to make it all the way to the top. Even if she managed to climb out of his reach, he would only have to wait for her to come back down again or fall. But she couldn't just give up and let him have her.

She saw something shiny in the rock a foot or so above and to the right of her hand, a bit of quartz, perhaps, and she moved toward it just to give herself a goal. Glancing down, she saw the knight break free of the thicket and touch the rock face just below her, cursing the brambles as he came. She looked away, refusing to be distracted.

Her hand closed over the glimmer in the rock, and the cliff gave way around it like sand. The stone was not a stone at all; it was metal, a handle. Clinging with her other hand and feet, she pulled, drawing something from the rock. It was a sword, barely half as long as her father's but perfect for her, gleaming dully in the moonlight.

"Got you!" The knight grabbed her ankle and yanked her down from the wall so abruptly she fell, scraping both knees and her nose and spraining her wrist. But she didn't let go of the sword.

"Aren't you the pretty little thing?" He had taken off his bucket-shaped helmet somewhere in the brush, and his face was shiny with sweat, a round white cheese in the moonlight. "That was quite a chase." He towered over her as she straightened up, one fist planted on the wall by her head, the other hand already fumbling with his hose. "You'd better learn how to behave."

She brought the sword up hard into his stomach, clutching the hilt in both hands. If he had been wearing chain mail, she couldn't have given him more than a scratch—she wasn't very strong. But the night was hot, and the battle hadn't been much; the knight had left his heavy armor in his tent. The blade pierced him straight through the gut.

He clamped a hand around her throat, and for a moment Siobhan was certain they would die together. She twisted the sword, dots of color appearing in front of her eyes, and his eyes glazed over. His fingers loosened, and she wriggled free and stepped aside as he crashed to the ground.

"Murder," she whispered, still clutching her weapon in her fist. She held it up and saw the Norman's blood gleaming scarlet on the dull silver blade. "I have done murder." A cold tremor shook her in spite of the warm summer night, but she smiled. Tucking the blade into her belt, she bent down to look for her shoes.

1

Tristan sat on the battlements of his half-finished castle with his daughter in his arms. "Were they bad men, Papa?" Clare asked, pointing toward the gore-streaked trophies mounted on the gatehouse just below them.

"Yes." He tugged one of her braids, turning her face to his. "Very bad men." He cuddled her closer, kissing the top of her head. "That is why they died." Five years old was much too young to understand the brutal politics of Henry's England or to witness their effect. In truth, five years old was too young to be living in this wilderness at all. But in both matters, this little one's father had no choice.

"Are there more bad men in the woods?" she asked, laying a hand on his cheek.

"Yes." That was the problem. No matter how many of these brigands he managed to capture and punish, more always seemed to appear. And now Henry had taken all but five of Tristan's knights and more than half his soldiers to sort out some dispute in Brittany— only by begging and promising to lead a force in the next war had Tristan escaped having to leave his new home to fight himself. "But our castle is nearly finished." He looked down at her and smiled. "That will keep the bad men out." Assuming he could finish it at all, he thought, looking down on the darkening forest. He had already spent every penny of his meager inheritance; if he didn't start collecting rents from the villagers soon, he and his household would starve, little Clare included. But the peasants in this godforsaken border country were already itching to revolt. If he couldn't somehow prove he could protect them before he put them under tax, they would throw in with the brigands completely, and he, like his predecessors, would fail no matter how many he killed. And now he had no army to speak of to defend him. He swallowed a sigh, cuddling his daughter close. His cousin the king was determined to put a friendly fortress here on his border with Scotland, and Tristan had been glad to take the title Lord DuMaine to help him. But neither of them had expected it to be so hard or that it would take so long to do it.

"Are all the people bad, Papa?" Clare said, sounding worried for the first time in their conversation. She had many friends among the children of the peasants being held here, and she was very fond of her nursemaid, Emma, a local wench as well.

"Of course not." Below them in the bailey, his master of works, Silas of Massum, was paying his craftsmen their wages. "Most of the people are good." Three carpenters and two master masons had been murdered since work on the castle began, their throats cut while they slept. "But they are afraid of the bad men in the woods," he said. "One man in particular, their leader, Sean Lebuin." A woman would say he shouldn't be telling a child such things, he knew, giving her bogeyman a name, any more than he should let her see the trophies of his righteous executions. But he wanted his Clare to know the truth, to be ready for whatever evil the world might hold and to know he would always protect her. "All of the good people are afraid of him," he told her, caressing her hair. "Every time King Henry sends a knight to protect them, Sean Lebuin tries to kill him."

"Oh, no!" She leapt down from his lap. "Will he kill you?"

"No." He cradled her cheek in his hand and smiled. "He will not kill me." No one in his life had ever cared so much if he should live or die. Perhaps that was the only real reason he loved this child so much, this odd habit she had formed of loving him. "I promise he will not."

Silas turned away from his assistant for a moment to find young Emma, nursemaid to Lord Tristan's daughter, hovering behind him in apparent distress. "What is it, dear one?" he asked her with a kindly smile.

"Master Silas . . . you . . . thank you," she stammered. "You've always been so kind."

"Have I?" he asked, bemused, as he finished his notes. After twenty years as a master mason and a dozen English castles built at his direction, he must be an old man at last. Pretty wenches now mistook all his flirting for kindness. He rolled the scroll and tucked it into the money box. "What is wrong?"

"Nothing, really." She sounded genuinely distraught, and he looked at her, surprised. But then she smiled. "I just . . . it's time the little one was put to bed."

"Ah, I see," he nodded, understanding. "You're afraid to disturb Lord Tristan." He looked up at the battlements, where the lord of this new castle was surveying his domain, and smiled. He had served some of the most powerful men in England, King Henry included, but Tristan DuMaine made him a little nervous, too. "Come, I will go with you."

Little Clare ran to her nurse as soon as she saw them. "Emma!" she said, hugging her as the girl picked her up.

"My lord," Silas said with a nod as the knight stood up, struck as always by the sheer size of the man. Many of these French-born nobles were tall by English standards, but DuMaine was broad as well, as thickly muscled as any of Silas's own masons. His dark hair was streaked from the sun and longer and much less neat than was the current noble fashion, adding to his barbaric appearance, and his blue-green eyes had a disconcerting tendency to pierce the very soul of anyone unfortunate enough to find themselves under his gaze. No wonder poor little Emma was afraid of him. "Mistress Emma was concerned that Lady Clare might be missing her bedtime," he explained, giving the nursemaid a wink.

"We were looking at the bad men," the little one explained, pointing toward the grisly display on the gatehouse.

"Indeed," Silas said, trying to hide his shudder. He did not dislike his current master by any means. But he did think Lord Tristan's skills as a parent left a bit to be desired.

"Take her, then," Tristan said, giving the older man a scowl of impatience as he took his child back into his arms for a moment. He liked Silas very much and had nothing but admiration for his learning. But his delicacy could be rather annoying. "Go straight to sleep," he told Clare, giving her a kiss.

"No, Papa," she corrected. "Prayers first."

He smiled. "Aye, then, as you will." He handed her over to Emma. "Prayers first, mistress, then sleep."

The wench looked for a moment like she wanted to smile back but couldn't quite make herself do it. "Yes, my lord."

Watching Tristan watch them go, Silas saw he was not the only one to appreciate Mistress Emma's ample charms, and he smiled. "Lady Clare is quite beautiful, my lord," he remarked when they were gone. "Does she favor her mother?"

Tristan rewarded this jibe with a smile. "She must," he answered. "Though in faith, I don't remember."

"Who was she?" Silas asked, intrigued. He had asked the same question of many of Tristan's men in the months they had spent at Castle DuMaine, but none of them would surrender so much as a word of their lord's private business.

The young knight did not seem offended or surprised by the question, just not terribly interested. "No one," he answered with a shrug, leaning against the stone wall. "Some woman . . . a minor baron's widowed sister." He frowned as if searching his memory. "Amelia, I think her name was. Or Alice." He shrugged again, dismissing the problem. "Maybe it was Anne."

"My lord!" Silas scolded, genuinely appalled. "You truly don't remember?"

"I truly do not." The old scholar looked so disapproving, Tristan couldn't help but smile. "I met her at her brother's house on my way to a campaign," he explained. "When I returned, they said she had died giving birth to my child, Clare, and the baron seemed to resent the inconvenience of another mouth to feed. So I took her with me."

"Did you grieve for the mother at all?" Silas asked. "Did you regret her loss?"

"She was never mine to lose," Tristan answered. "If she had lived, I would likely have made her my wife, but she did not." Silas's reproach was beginning to annoy him. "She was just a woman, Silas."

"Aye, my lord. She was." The master of works could see his noble employer was fast losing patience with this topic, but he couldn't resist one more jab. "Your

Clare will be one as well. I hope no man ever dares to forget her name."

Tristan opened his mouth to reply and stopped, his attention caught by a sudden flash of fire in the woods. "En garde!" one of the guardsmen shouted from his post atop the gatehouse as a flaming arrow soared over the wall.

"Silas, get down!" Tristan knocked the older man flat to the stone walkway as a full volley of fiery missiles sailed just over their heads. In less than a moment, the wooden palisade that still protected the unfinished parts of the bailey wall was blazing, along with the thatched roof of the stable. Swearing the worst oath he could think of, Tristan leapt back to his feet and sprinted for the stairs.

"Protect the house!" he shouted into the chaotic throng of his guardsmen. "Wet down the roof—and take my daughter to the tower on the motte!"

"Aye, my lord," his captain answered, gathering a detail to obey.

"My lord!" his squire, Richard, was shouting, running toward him leading Daimon, his horse. "Will you ride out?"

"Of course not," Tristan said impatiently, taking the reins from the boy as the horse reared in fury and fright. "The gates will hold them, fire or not."

"No, my lord," Richard answered, his face ashen under smears of soot. "The gates are breached."

"Impossible." The front defenses were solid stone;

the gates were banded oak and iron. A full-on siege with proper equipment couldn't have broken through this quickly, much less a mob of brigands armed only with arrows and rocks.

"We are betrayed," his squire said, his youthful voice cracking in panic. "The peasants . . . at the first arrow, they attacked the gatehouse from inside."

"The peasants?" he demanded, anger becoming full-blown fury. He was trying to defend these people, to protect them and make their lives easier and safer. Why should they betray him? "Lebuin," he muttered, swinging into the saddle. Drawing his sword, he galloped for the gates.

The battle should have been over quickly. The Normans had never expected treachery from within, and Sean's brigands outnumbered them at least two to one. But DuMaine's reputation as a warrior was well founded. He managed to get what was left of his knights on horseback before the stables collapsed and the rest of the horses were released by the brigands to flee. This mounted force was small, but fierce, cutting through the outlaws like reapers through wheat, their lord ever leading the way. If they could cross the wooden bridge to the castle motte and burn it behind them before the outlaws, the fortress could still hold, the attackers held at bay by the deep ditch around the motte.

Siobhan stepped back into her archer's stance and took careful aim, shooting one of the riders straight through the throat as he raised his sword against Evan, her brother's closest friend. The Norman knight fell backward, blood spewing from his lips, and Evan turned and saw her.

"Thanks much!" he called out with a grin, waving. Then he dragged the dying knight to the ground to commandeer his horse.

Tristan wheeled Daimon in a circle just in time to see his captain fall. The bowman who had killed him was no more than a boy and a skinny one at that, but his aim was deadly. He wore the green and black that marked him as one of Lebuin's own kin, somebody's squire, no doubt. Another brigand now mounted on the fallen captain's horse was bearing down on Tristan, and he turned to meet him, broadsword raised. But with his other hand, he drew the dagger from his belt and flung it at the boy.

Siobhan felt the blade pass through her shoulder and staggered, gasping in shock. Blood poured from the wound as her arm went cold, her bow falling out of her grip.

"Siobhan!" Sean ran toward her, bashing a Norman foot soldier's skull with his sword hilt as he came. He caught her as she fell, dropping his weapons to hold her.

"I'm all right," she insisted, wrapping a fist around the dagger's hilt. The devil's knight had missed her heart, but her arm was all but useless.

"You're fine," Sean agreed with a shaky little laugh, pressing a kiss to her brow. Clasping his hand over hers, he yanked the dagger from her flesh, holding her close as she screamed.

Her head swam for a moment, the world going black, but she didn't faint. "Go, Sean, hurry," she ordered, pushing her brother away. "I will be all right."

Tristan dispatched the brigand who had meant to challenge him to a joust so easily, it was almost laughable. Whoever he was, he rode well enough, and he probably fought well enough on his feet. But doing both at once was obviously beyond him. Tristan broke his left arm with a single glancing blow as he bent low over Daimon's neck to avoid the clumsy swing his opponent was making with the heavy pike in his right. Then as the outlaw swore in pain and let the reins fall from his hand, Tristan swung about and kicked him squarely in the chest. The brigand slipped sideways in the saddle, losing the last of his control over his mount, and Tristan struck him in earnest, splitting his skull with his sword.

"Evan!" he heard a woman scream, and he turned to see the little bowman he had meant to kill still standing on his—no, her—feet. She was staring straight at him in horror, and the man beside her turned to stare as well. Sean Lebuin. The outlaw leader saw his man fall beneath Tristan's sword, and his blue-painted face twisted in fury. Grabbing for his own horse, a pure white mare with an unkempt silver mane, he leapt onto its back, ready to fight.

"Sean, wait!" Siobhan cried, taking up her brother's

sword and running to hand it to him, her own pain forgotten. DuMaine had slaughtered Evan like he might have been a child playing knight on a pony. They had fought many noble knights in their quest to free their people, but she had never in her life seen a man move so quickly or maneuver his mount with such skill, not even Sean himself. "Do not challenge him alone," she shouted over the din, but her brother wasn't listening. Taking the sword, he kicked his mount and charged into the fray. "Sean!" DuMaine was smiling, she realized, a devil indeed with the flames of the palisade behind him. He wasn't the least bit afraid.

"My lady!" Someone was grabbing at her wounded arm, trying to get her attention, and she turned impatiently. "My lady, help me, please." The woman was about her own age, dressed like a peasant, and her face was vaguely familiar. Siobhan had seen her before, probably in one of the villages where the brigands had been given sanctuary. Clutched in her arms was a child, a small blond girl wearing a pink silk gown. "Lady Clare is only a baby," the woman said. "Please, you must help me protect her."

"Lady Clare?" She took rough hold of the little one's chin, turning her face to the light. She had green, almond-shaped eyes that regarded Siobhan in solemn fear, but she did not make a sound. "This is Tristan Du-Maine's child?" She looked back at the battle, and her heart leapt into her throat. Both horses were reared up on their hind legs, flailing at each other with their hooves, and blood was already pouring down Sean's face from a gash in his forehead.

"Yes, my lady," the peasant woman answered. "But she is innocent."

Siobhan turned back to them in a panic and saw the child still watching her. Tristan DuMaine's only child. "Here," she said, holding out her arms. "Give her to me."

For the first time since he'd realized his gates were breached, Tristan felt hope. If he could kill Lebuin outright in single combat, there was every reason to believe his followers would surrender. And he was very near to doing that exactly. The rebel leader fought more skillfully than Tristan would ever have expected him to do, but the death of his companion had blinded him with rage even before Tristan's sword had blinded him with blood.

Tristan pulled Daimon alongside the brigand's mare and slashed at him again. Lebuin managed to twist and dodge the worst of the blow, but he lost his balance in the saddle. More skilled by far than his man had been, he shifted his weight and rolled to the ground by his own will instead of falling, using the horse as a shield between Tristan and himself. But on the ground, he was done for. Daimon kicked out at him, knocking him flat on his face, and Tristan leapt out of the saddle and pinned him to the ground.

"Stupid bastard," he muttered, grabbing the brigand by his hair and yanking his head back, ready to release it from his neck and end his own troubles forever.

"DuMaine!" It was the woman's voice again, the unnatural creature who had killed one of his five precious knights with a single arrow. Looking up, he saw her coming toward him and froze, his blood running cold. She was holding Clare in her arms, a dagger pressed to his little one's throat.

"Release him!" Siobhan's heart was pounding from shame as much as fear. Brigand she might be, but it was not in her nature to murder an innocent child. "Release him, or she dies!" *What if he doesn't care?* she thought, her mind racing wildly. *What if the lack of feeling he had shown for the people he imprisoned and enslaved extended even to his own flesh and blood?* She wanted to look at Sean for reassurance, but she didn't dare for fear of losing her nerve. She made herself look at DuMaine instead, straight into his cold green eyes.

"Devil," Tristan said softly, feeling sick. He could see now that the woman standing over them was beautiful, even under the garish blue paint, with wide sapphire eyes and jet-black hair that glistened in the firelight even in disarray. But she was a devil, a beast in woman's shape. What true woman with a gentle woman's heart could threaten the life of a child?

"Let my brother go," she ordered, her voice like ice. She pressed her dagger more tightly against Clare's throat, and the little girl gasped, breathing in hard through her nose, her eyes wide with fright. "I will not ask again."

For one long, terrible moment, Siobhan was sure he

meant to call her bluff. Then slowly he rose to his feet, letting go of Sean and letting his broadsword fall.

Sean leapt to his feet and held his sword point to the Norman's throat. "Tell your men to surrender," he ordered.

"Let my child go first," DuMaine answered, still staring at Siobhan. She had seen such fury only once before, when Sean had cut out the heart of the man who had murdered their father.

"The child will not be harmed," Sean said impatiently. "I swear it."

"Not you," DuMaine answered. "Her." His jaw was clenched so hard, a muscle twitched in his cheek. He was handsome, Siobhan suddenly realized, as finely made a man as she had ever seen. But there was no mistaking the hatred in his eyes. "I would hear her swear."

"I swear it," she answered. Another of their men came forward to bind DuMaine's hands behind his back, and when he did not resist, she let her dagger fall. "She is safe."

Tristan nodded, still watching as she put Clare into Emma's arms again. Had the nurse been part of the plot? Did all of them hate him so much? "Papa!" Clare screamed when she realized Emma meant to carry her away. "The bad men!" For the first time, she started to cry. "The bad men!" She was still sobbing as they disappeared.

"Enough!" Tristan shouted, a roar to overwhelm his

grief, and those few men still fighting the outlaws to reach him dropped their swords. His knights were already afoot, noblemen captured by rabble, betrayed by the weakness of their lord. Looking away from the evil beauty before him at last, he turned to Lebuin. "This castle is yours."

2

Siobhan raced across the wooden bridge to the motte, pushing past the soldiers that loitered in front of the door to the tower. "Sean!" she shouted, clattering down the steps.

Her brother was standing in the middle of the open hall. "Sean," she repeated, running to his arms.

"There you are," Sean said, half laughing as he hugged her close. "How is the south wall?"

"Broken," she answered. "Some of the men are cutting timber to rebuild it now." She drew back and looked at him. Blood still trickled from his forehead, but he was smiling. "Are you all right?"

"Of course." She touched the gash, showing him the blood. "It is nothing," he promised. He gave her hair a tug. "What of your shoulder?"

"Less than nothing." A thin, bearded man in a velvet cap was sitting on a stool to one side, guarded by two of their men as if he might have been dangerous. "Who is this?" she asked.

"Silas of Massum," Sean answered. The man was

staring at her as if she might have sprouted horns, and she scowled at him. "He is the one who has built you this beautiful castle."

"Not for me," she muttered. The stranger's eyes widened for a moment, and she blushed, turning away.

"You didn't care for Lord Tristan?" Sean teased.

"No," she answered, smiling at his tone. "I think he's a murdering bastard."

Another patrol came down the steps, leading the girl from the courtyard with the little girl still in her arms. "The bad man!" the child shrieked, pointing at Sean. "He is Sean Lebuin!"

Siobhan saw her brother blanch, his smile fading at once. "Hush yourself," she ordered the little one brusquely. "You, lass—keep her quiet."

"Forgive her, my lady," the nursemaid stammered. "She is only a child."

The man Sean had called Silas stood up. "Bring her to me," he ordered, giving Siobhan a disapproving look. "Come, Emma."

The peasant girl glanced over at him, then looked back to Siobhan. "Go on," Siobhan told her, feeling silly. Why should this girl fear her? Had they not come to free her, for pity's sake?

"Master Silas," the girl said, hurrying to the old man's arms. "I'm so sorry . . . I never thought."

"Hush now," he soothed her. "It will be all right." Over her shoulder, the child watched Siobhan with fierce green eyes. "I promise, little one." The old man took the child himself and held her close, and after a moment, her little arms wrapped around his neck.

"Yes, for God's sweet sake." Gaston had come in with this latest patrol, much to Siobhan's dismay. The baron of Callard's man had become her brother's shadow, a dark blot that followed wherever he went. The weapons and horses he had brought from his master for the attack had been welcome enough, she supposed. But the man himself could drop dead from a pox, and she, for one, would not mourn him. "Let the old man keep the brat." He laughed, coming close to where she stood between Sean and the prisoners. "This pretty one has better work to do." He reached for the nursemaid, Emma, twining a hand in her hair.

All the tension of the night seemed to snap like a twig inside Siobhan. "Leave her," she ordered, slapping him hard across the face with one hand as she drew her dagger with the other. He turned to her in fury, and she pointed the blade at his crotch. "Take care, Sir Bull," she said, smiling at him with deadly menace. "I will make you an ox where you stand."

"You dare?" he said, his eyes narrow with rage.

"She's right, Gaston." Sean moved between the angry courtier and Emma, putting a hand on Siobhan's shoulder. "This wench is one of ours, a child of this land. She is not to be abused." Gaston backed off slowly, his eyes still locked to Siobhan's. She raised an eyebrow at him, sheathing her dagger as Emma retreated behind the old man. "Go and find the friar,"

Sean told Gaston. "The chapel is still burning; he must be hiding in the manor house."

Gaston didn't care to take orders even from Sean, she noticed, but he didn't dare defy him, either. "As you wish," he answered, forcing a smile. He gave Emma a final wink before he turned and left.

"Bastard," Siobhan muttered, and she heard the old man mumble something similar under his breath.

"You don't know that," Sean joked, ruffling her hair.

"I can guess," she retorted. "The sooner we are rid of him, the better I will like it."

Before Sean could answer, another of his most trusted men, Michael, had come in. He had been close to Evan, the man DuMaine had killed, and was likely heartsick with grief. But his manner gave nothing away. "The knights are being held in the courtyard," he said, giving the prisoners a glance. "All of them." DuMaine included, his eyes seemed to say.

"Very good," Sean nodded. "Master Silas, we will speak again in the morning." He turned to the waiting guards. "Take them upstairs, to the back of the tower." His eyes met the old man's. "Keep the child away from the windows."

The old man went pale, but he nodded. "Yes . . . I will." He started toward the stairs with the child still in his arms.

"No!" the little one demanded, suddenly struggling. "Master, where is my papa? I want to see my papa."

Suddenly Siobhan wanted nothing more than for

this night to be over, to go back into the forest and find some cool, safe place to lie down and sleep under the stars. But their project was barely begun. The child began to weep, and Siobhan's own eyes filled with tears in spite of her resolve. She remembered that pain so clearly; she knew just how the little one felt. But she could not stop to weep with her, could not afford this pity. She turned her back as the child was led away.

"Come," Sean said, putting an arm around her shoulders as the guards led the prisoners upstairs, the child still watching her, tears on her cheeks. "Come with me."

He led her out of the tower and across the bridge to the courtyard. Tristan DuMaine had been bound hand and foot to a wooden scaffold at the center of the courtyard with a thick gag in his mouth. But even so, he was magnificent, the most powerful-looking man she had ever seen. On his feet, he must have stood a full head taller than Sean, and his arms were thick and gorgeously muscled, straining at his bonds. As she and Sean watched, his four remaining knights were led out from a shed, chained in a line, with a boy no more than twelve or thirteen following behind them. "Who is that?" she asked her brother.

"DuMaine's squire," Sean answered, his own expression grim. "I all but begged him to swear loyalty to us, but he refused." The boy stumbled, falling into the knight before him, and DuMaine let out a roar behind his gag that made her blood run cold. Michael hurried forward and helped the boy back to his feet.

"What will you do with him?" Siobhan asked. DuMaine was silent again, but he was watching her, his green eyes boring through her. "Sean?" A great wooden block had been set up, she suddenly realized as another of Sean's rebels came across the courtyard with an axe. "Sean, no . . . not the boy." She turned her back on DuMaine, taking her brother with her. "Please . . ."

"Siobhan, we have no choice." Sean's grip on her arm was almost painful, and the look on his face showed he felt as horrible as she did, if not worse. "The common soldiers who survived the battle will be spared—we will buy their loyalty with mercy. But we have nothing to offer these knights. If we let them live, they will go to their king—"

"I know," she cut him off. "But the boy—"

"The boy is badly wounded." He looked over her shoulder at the prisoners, and she looked back herself. Michael was still supporting the boy, an arm around his shoulders, speaking urgently in his ear, but the boy was shaking his head. "He would not survive the night even if we spared him," Sean said.

"Then what would be the harm?" she asked. She laid a hand against his chest. "Sean, please. He's just a child."

He smiled grimly. "As you were when our father died," he answered. "Were you spared, my love?"

She smiled back. "Not by choice," she admitted. "But let us be better than our enemies."

He closed his eyes in resignation, his smile twisting broader for a moment. "As you will, my lady." He pulled her to him and kissed her forehead. "You are your father's daughter." Still holding her hand, he moved forward. "Release the boy!" he ordered. "Lady Siobhan would spare him."

Another man joined Michael to unlock the boy's shackles. "No," the squire protested, trying to fight, but it was obvious his strength was all but gone. "I will not . . ." He made as if to strike out at Michael and collapsed into his arms.

"May Christ bless you, my lady," one of the other knights said, falling to his knees. But Tristan DuMaine still glared at her, more furious than ever. "Bless you for your mercy."

"Keep your blessing, Norman dog," she answered, making her voice cold. "I have no mercy for you." Sean was right. If these men were allowed to escape, they would run to their king like children frightened by a storm. All of her and Sean's great plans would be for nothing; all of their friends would have died in vain. She made herself think of her cousins, their heads mounted on DuMaine's stone wall, and of Evan, cut down by Du-Maine's own sword before her eyes. "You sicken me," she said to the man on his knees, but her eyes were on DuMaine. "I will not watch you die." She turned away.

"Go inside and make ready," Sean said softly for her ears alone as Michael and the other soldier carried the boy toward the manor house. "We will join you soon."

"Henry will see your master hanged in pieces and the rest of you fed to his dogs!" she heard one of the knights shout as she left the courtyard. Perhaps it was the one who had blessed her for her mercy, she thought with a smile. He was a lying Norman, after all. The friar was waiting in the doorway, and she took a deep breath. One more trial still awaited her before this night was done.

Tristan's mind was buzzing as he was dragged, still bound and gagged, into the great hall. Lebuin had put all four of his knights to the axe, reading sentence against them as "traitors to England and the will of God" as if he might have been king, bishop, and sheriff all in one. The first knight had used his last breath to curse his captors and promise the vengeance of the crown, but the others had staggered to the block like men in a trance, their eyes fixed on Tristan. They had followed him from France; many had served his father before him. And for their loyalty, they had been slaughtered like sheep. He looked now at Lebuin, standing at the dais in the hall that a few short hours ago had been his. You will die, he thought, picturing it in his mind. Your head will feed the crows.

A fair-sized crowd of brigands and peasants was gathered, and he looked around frantically for Clare. But luckily his child was nowhere to be seen. Standing near the open hearth was the castle friar, looking as if he would have rather have been standing at the gates of hell itself. As Tristan was dragged toward him, he met his eyes for a moment in sympathy.

"God's faith, Sean." A woman laughed from behind him. "You still have him gagged?" Coming down the stairs was the rebel girl, Siobhan. She was dressed now in an obviously costly but rather wrinkled gown of dark blue silk with her hair loose on her shoulders.

"It seemed best, my lady," Lebuin answered, looking her up and down with obvious approval as she reached them. Tristan met the woman's eyes with his own, glaring pure contempt, and she raised her delicate eyebrows.

"Oh, yes?" she said, still amused. The woad and soot was gone from her face, revealing flawless porcelain skin. "What did he say?"

"My lord, this is most irregular," the friar protested to Lebuin. The young priest had never been overly fond of Tristan or his rule. When Tristan had given the order that the peasants were to be held within the castle walls, Brother Thomas had lodged a formal complaint, had even threatened to leave his post. But surely he could not be in league with these rebels. "I mean to say, he cannot be married if he cannot speak."

"Of course he can," Lebuin answered. "It isn't what he says that matters, Brother Thomas, only what he writes back to his king."

For a moment, Tristan was so shocked, he couldn't quite believe what he had heard. Married? They meant to marry him to this creature? He began to struggle, flinging one of the men who held him aside with a sharp jab from his elbow and butting the other in the chest with his head, making him fall to his knees. Three more rushed forward to subdue him, including Lebuin himself, who drove a fist into his jaw, making him see stars. He staggered, almost falling, and heard a delicate snort of laughter. As his vision slowly cleared, he saw Siobhan was watching, her pretty mouth turned up in a wicked smile. She had pled for Richard's life, he thought. But she had threatened Clare. Where was Clare now?

"Yes, but . . . how will he write, my lord?" the friar ventured.

"He has written already," Siobhan said, taking a scroll from the pocket of her borrowed gown. She was tired of this farce before it had even begun—everything about it was ridiculous. She hadn't worn a proper gown since she was a girl of twelve, and then it had been plain linen, not such frippery as this, and the slippers that went with it must have been made for an infant or a pixie, they were so small. I should have worn my boots, she thought, watching the scowl on her reluctant bridegroom's face as Sean and the others dragged him back to her side.

She had to admit that Sean's plan did make a certain sort of sense. If King Henry believed his cousin had made peace with the rebels through marriage, he wouldn't send more troops right away, even if that cousin should die in a freak accident mere days after his wedding. If she had her way, by the time the truth was discovered, the castle would be razed, the peasants relocated, and the rebels themselves long gone. She just wished she could have drawn a different part in the performance.

"All we need is his seal," she finished explaining to the friar as she handed over the scroll. She had been practicing DuMaine's handwriting for weeks now, copying letters the rebels had intercepted on their way to London; she knew the match was perfect.

"Sweet God," the friar muttered, wiping his brow. He was Saxon-born himself, the only son of a free farmer starved out of his inheritance by the Normans and driven into the church. When Sean had asked him for his help in expelling DuMaine and his knights, he had reluctantly agreed. But she doubted he had counted on this.

"Think of the people, Brother," Sean said urgently.

"Yes," the friar answered, nodding, but his gaze was fixed on the floor.

"Still, it does seem hard that we should keep him gagged," she said, turning back to the Norman lord. Standing so close, she was awestruck again by the size of him—he towered over her as if she were a child. His green eyes narrowed as he looked down to meet her gaze, and she felt a shiver in her stomach. What must he be thinking? "I hear tell he is a pretty thing." Remembering her audience, she traced a hand across the Norman's cheek in a mocking caress. "I want to see his face." She thought of her father, murdered like a dog before his house, and her mother, raped and slaughtered, as she met this Norman's eyes. Let him speak, she thought. Let him show the good friar what he is again.

Tristan jerked away from her touch as the brigands laughed and hooted, a few of them shouting encouragement. He heard familiar voices in the crowd, the peasants he had been charged by his cousin to protect. How could they have hated him so much without his knowing? He tried again to look for Clare, silently praying these savages would at least spare her this horror, but Lebuin jerked him back toward his bride.

"Whatever you wish, little sister," the brigand leader said. Sister? Tristan thought, surprised. He had thought the girl must be the brigand's lover, some common wench he had picked up in his travels and made into a rebel for his cause. But apparently she was his sister, a lady of at least some noble blood. His shock must have shown in his eyes, because Lebuin smiled, sharing a wink with the girl. "Cut his gag, Gaston."

Siobhan watched as the gag was cut, waiting for DuMaine to start shouting curses as his knight had done. But he did not. "Many thanks, my lady," he said softly, with sarcasm so bitter she could almost taste it. With the gag removed, he was even more handsome, with strong, well-sculpted features and a sensuous bow of a mouth. But there was nothing of the lover in his manner, no mistaking his feelings as he looked her up and down. "How fares your shoulder?"

"Well enough," she answered, smiling sweetly. "Your aim is not the best."

"Too bad," he answered, smiling back.

"Is it?" She moved closer, looking him over with the same insolence as he had shown her. "Did you wish to see me weep?"

Tristan turned as she circled him. "In faith, I would not mind it." Lebuin watched the girl with jealous eyes, he saw, as she moved around him, his guards making way for her. "You are a woman, after all," he said over his shoulder, meeting her eyes with his as she faced him again. "I should like to think you have a woman's heart."

"In faith, I do, my lord." She thought of this Norman bastard's trophies displayed upon his gates, of the carnage his predecessors had wrought. "I have wept for your crimes long ere this." She looked up into his handsome face, still so arrogant even in defeat. "I wept for my cousins, murdered by your hand." She had meant only to taunt him, but as she spoke the words, rage rose up inside her, powerful enough to make her forget the farce she was meant to be playing, this travesty of a wedding. "For my father, rightful lord of these lands, cut down like a dog by the king he trusted to protect him. He is worthy of grief, think you not?" He did not even flinch, she saw. He felt nothing for the people of this land, for her people. "But you? Nay, my lord." She stepped back from him before she was moved to kill him outright, Sean's fine plans be damned. "I will never weep for you."

Tristan's blood ran cold to see the rebel fervor burning in her eyes. "If you have my letters and my seal, you should kill me now." He looked her up and down again, his lip curled in a sneer. "I would take it as a mercy."

To her surprise, she felt her cheeks flush hot. "Would you indeed, my lord?" she said. She took the dagger from her belt and traced its point along his jaw. "I could oblige you, I suppose." Still he showed no sign of fear. How could she frighten him? If he faced death so bravely, what could make him flinch? In his place, what would have broken her? "But faith, DuMaine, I find you quite the prize." She traced the blade along his lower lip, remembering the lust she had seen once in a Norman soldier's eyes. "I don't think I'm quite finished with you yet."

"Enough." The friar cut her off, his face flushed red as a berry. "Sheath your blade, my lady." He turned to look at Sean. "Or I will not continue."

"As you wish, Brother Thomas." She put the dagger away, still standing close enough to DuMaine to feel his breath. "By all means, let us be done."

Tristan looked down at her, standing so close, he could feel her heat. "Lady Siobhan, will you have this man for your husband?" the friar said, fumbling with his book.

"Oh, aye," she answered. She smiled up at Tristan with an expression so sweet, the desire to wring her neck with his bare hands was like a fever in his mind. *Where is my child?* he wanted to ask her. *What have you done with her?* "'Til death may take him from me."

"Will you love him?" the friar went on over chuckles from the crowd.

"At least once, with great vigor," she answered, repeating the threat she had implied before. Tristan smiled coldly. Not a chance, he thought.

The friar cleared his throat. "Will you honor him?" he asked.

"Absolutely, Brother." She laid her hand on Tristan's chest, her smile fading into a scowl. "I will piss on his grave every Sunday."

The crowd roared with laughter again, but inside, Siobhan was shaking. For the second time that night, she was bluffing, playing a part for this man, this Norman they would kill. What could he be thinking? She could feel his heart beating under her palm, not racing with fear but powerful, the heart of a lion. "God will not bless you for your impertinence, my lady," the friar was saying, his voice seeming distant as her own blood pounded in her ears. "Answer truly, as if in fear of God. Will you obey your husband?"

"Not once." This time she did not smile, and no one laughed. She did fear God; she feared his wrath at what she did this night. But not DuMaine. She would not fear this Norman, would not let him think she was afraid of him, not for a moment. She faced him, her eyes locked to his. "But you may pretend I said yes."

The friar paused, taking a deep breath. "And so I shall." He turned to Tristan. "And now for you, my lord." His face went pale at his scowl. "You . . . do you . . . ah, well." He looked to Sean Lebuin. "Perhaps you should make his vows for him."

"No." Again, Tristan spoke quietly, but the menace in his tone reached to every corner of the hall. "I will make my vow. Just one." The men who held him tightened their grip, but he did not need to move closer. His bride could hear him well enough. "You say that you will kill me, sweet, and chances seem fair that you will." The girl did not back down from him or change expression, but he saw her cheeks turn pale. "But know this, my lady. I will do you the same service." A gasp whispered around the hall. "This grave you mean to piss on will not hold me. I will return from hell itself to punish you for all your dear transgressions." She opened her mouth as if she meant to speak, but he spoke first. "I will kill you, darling," he finished. "That is my wedding vow to you."

Siobhan was trembling all over, more and more intensely as his words went on, and even Sean looked pale. Fool, she scolded herself in her head. This threat was no worse than she should have expected, no more plausible than the curses she had heard from his kind a hundred times before in battle. She should laugh, she knew. But those men had sounded frightened or angry; they had known they were cursing the wind. Tristan DuMaine believed every word he had spoken. "Fool," she whispered aloud to him this time, and her new-made husband smiled, a knowing, bitter smile that mocked her for doubting his promise.

"Finish, Brother," Sean said, no longer laughing. "Declare them man and wife."

Tristan barely heard him or the words the friar spoke. The church's word was meaningless, their ritual a farce. The truth was between this Siobhan and himself, the vows they had spoken from the black depths of their hearts. That was their marriage, the power that would join them. She was shaking now, a properly fearful little bride, and a new sensation seized him. She had called him her prize, had said she meant to use him once before she killed him. For a single moment's madness, he imagined he would let her do it, imagined how it would feel to take this wicked little rebel into his arms. He smiled down on her, the lazy smile that had made Clare's mother take him to her bed even when he had told her she would never be more than a diversion. What would it be like to break this little demon with kisses and bend her to his will? "I now declare you man and wife," the friar was saying.

Siobhan saw her bridegroom's eyes change as he smiled, and she reached for her dagger again, expecting him to try to escape. But he did not. "I thank you, Brother," he said, nodding, as gracious as a king in spite of the guards who held him fast. "Now may I kiss my wife?"

"You would kiss me?" She laughed. He hated her; he had shown her nothing but contempt. But suddenly she saw something else in those cold, green eyes, something wicked she had never seen before in the gaze of any other man.

"Oh, yes," he answered, his mysterious smile making her blush. "I would."

"I think not," Sean said with a laugh that sounded forced.

"Wait," she said, holding her brother back. "Why not?" She drew her dagger and held it to Tristan's throat. "Let him go." This was another challenge, she realized; the Norman meant to shame her, to prove she was a fraud. But he would not. Still holding the dagger between them, she leaned up and kissed his lips.

For a moment, she thought she had called his bluff indeed; he seemed ready to withdraw. Then suddenly his hands came up and closed around her arms, and his mouth on hers turned hard. Stop it! she wanted to shout as his tongue teased her lips, warm and sweet. He was her enemy; how dare he touch her so? No man had ever dared to kiss her this way, even when she'd wanted it; no man had ever made her knees go weak. The kiss broke for a moment as he pulled her body closer, lifting her off her feet to mold her form to his, his lips barely brushing her own. Then his mouth turned hard again, demanding, and her will seemed to dissolve. The hand that held no weapon clutched his shirt front, and her mouth opened to his.

"Enough!" she heard her brother shout, and his fist crashed into Tristan's head, knocking him away from her. Of all the men who might have done it, Gaston was the one who caught her as she fell back from her Norman husband's arms.

"Are you quite well, my lady?" he said with a mischievous grin as Sean punched Tristan again, catching his jaw to send him reeling backward.

"Of course," she said, pushing him away. Tristan had fallen into the rushes, and half a dozen of her brother's men had rushed forward to subdue him.

"Take him from my sight," Sean ordered, furious. "Take him outside and kill him."

"No," Siobhan said, moving forward. Tristan was smiling up at her, triumphant even as they held him down, blood trickling from the corner of his mouth. Hot fury made her feel faint. "Not yet." He had sealed their vows of murder with a kiss, had meant to make a prize of her in front of her brother and his men, to prove she was a helpless maiden after all. But she would show him his mistake. "Take him to his bedchamber and bind him to the bed." She made her lips draw back into a feral smile. "As I told you . . . I am not quite done."

3

As soon as DuMaine was taken out, Sean led Siobhan up the stairs, out of the sight of the crowd. "Are you all right?" he asked.

"Of course," she answered, determined that it should be true. "Why should I not be?

He smiled. "My brave girl." He hugged her close, and she felt her heart grow calmer. "You did well."

"Many thanks." She would have liked to have been held a little longer, but he was already letting her go. "DuMaine is a bastard."

"Aye, love, he is," Sean agreed. "But you gave no ground." He touched her cheek. "I was proud of you."

"I should hope so." Just down the hall, she could hear the guards scuffling with her bridegroom, following her instructions. "Normans don't just smell, you know. They taste horrible."

"I don't doubt it." The sounds from the bedroom grew louder, and someone yelped in pain before shouting a curse. "So do you mean to bed him?"

"Of course not." She moved behind a column where

she was still hidden but could see down into the hall. "But I will let him think I will for now." Gaston was standing by the hearth, talking to one of his own soldiers, but she noticed he kept glancing toward the stairs, smirking his nasty little smirk. "Let your friend, Gaston, think it as well."

Sean followed, a hand on her shoulder. "Why Gaston?"

"So he can tell his master," she answered. "Our own men care nothing for DuMaine's nobility or marriage; that wedding was no more than a mummer's play for them. But Gaston . . ." She stopped, choosing her words with care. She hated Gaston, hated Sean's alliance with his master, the baron of Callard. But they needed it, at least a little longer. "Gaston is a Norman," she said at last. "He is your friend tonight, but if other Normans should come here demanding proof of this marriage, will he lie for us?" She turned back to her brother. "I doubt it."

"Gaston has just as much reason to hate DuMaine as we do," Sean insisted, rejoining the same debate they had been waging for weeks.

"Not so, brother. At least, I do not believe it." What she believed was that Gaston—or rather, the baron of Callard—would be as happy someday to have Sean out of his way as DuMaine. But she had learned already that this was a theory her brother did not wish to hear. "If Gaston thinks I have bedded this Norman, if the friar thinks it; if we have sheets stained with blood—"

"No one will say you and DuMaine were never really

wed," he finished for her. Two of the men who had brought DuMaine upstairs came out of the bedroom, both of them looking worse for wear. Catching sight of Siobhan, one grinned, holding a rag to his bleeding lip.

"He is yours, my lady," he called.

"Lucky bastard," the second one muttered, making his companion snicker.

"Enough," Sean said with a scowl. "Go downstairs and find Bruce and Callum. Tell them I want them." Chastened, the men nodded, barely glancing at Siobhan as they passed on their way to the stairs.

"Why Bruce and Callum?" she asked Sean, curious. The two men he mentioned were hardly his most skillful soldiers, nor were they pleasant company.

"Never mind," he answered, watching until they were gone. "How long do you suppose this consummation should take?"

"Not long, I shouldn't think." For a single moment of madness, she found herself remembering DuMaine's kiss to seal his vow, imagining what it might be like if she truly meant to do as she had promised. Would he want her, given the chance?

"Fine," Sean nodded, the sound of his voice driving this foolish thought away. "Go find someplace out of sight—"

"No," she cut him off. "I have to go in." She thought again of Tristan's smile of triumph after he had kissed her, and her face flushed hot with rage. She thought of the Norman knight who had chased her the night her parents were murdered, the first man she had ever killed. She could still smell his breath, still had nightmares of what he would have done if he had caught her. But now she was a woman grown. Now she would have her revenge. One of the castle serving women, Cilla, was coming up the stairs with a tray, and Siobhan smiled at her. "Come, Cilla," she said, heading for the door. She stopped and touched her brother's arm. "I won't be long."

Sean caught her gently by the wrist. "Don't do anything foolish," he ordered. "Fright him if you will, but don't let him touch you."

"Don't worry," she promised. "I won't."

Tristan fought his captors like a man possessed as they bound him to the bed, so wildly that when his limbs abruptly stopped flailing, they assumed he was well and truly caught. Two of them left the room while two finished tying off his bonds. "Where's your cousin now, my lord?" one of them said as he finished. "Where is your royal blood?"

"Leave him be," the other answered, stepping back. "Can't you see he's beaten?" He smiled. "My lady will have no trouble with him now."

Tristan smiled back, surreptitiously testing the slack in his bonds all the while. One good, strong jerk, and he thought he might break free. "Your lady, as you call her, is a slut."

"Bastard!" the first brigand shouted as the second drove his fist into his face.

"That was bravely done," a woman's voice said from the doorway. Both brigands turned as Siobhan came into the room, followed by an old woman Tristan recognized from his kitchen. "Striking a man when he is bound like a pig for the slaughter."

"He is a pig," the man who had struck Tristan answered. "He called you—"

"I heard what he said." In the dim light of the bedroom, her dark blue eyes looked almost black, and her skin glowed like moonlight. The shadows suited her, his demon of a wife. "And we will slaughter him." Her eyes met Tristan's for a moment, her mouth curling slightly in an almost-smile. "But not yet." She nodded to the old woman, and she came forward to the bed, carrying a tray.

"You see, old dame?" Tristan asked her as she set it down. "You see what your people have brought into your home?"

"Not my home, my lord." She wiped the blood from his face with a wet towel, her mouth set in a frown.

"Not your lord, neither, mother," one of the brigands piped up.

"Leave Cilla in peace," Siobhan ordered. "Both of you, go, attend my brother outside."

Neither of the men looked pleased, but they obeyed without questioning her. Siobhan gave Tristan a smile, then turned away to admire herself in his mirror.

"They will not leave you in peace," he said softly to the woman tending his wounds. With her help and the soldiers gone, he might still escape this trap. "They will raze this castle to the ground, destroy your crops, abduct your daughters—"

"And how will that be new?" She cut him off. He heard Siobhan laugh softly, her back still turned. "When have your king's men not done the same and worse?"

Across the room, Siobhan waited tensely for his answer. "When have I done worse?" he said at last, his voice so sad and gentle, she could hardly believe it was him speaking. She turned to find him looking up at Cilla, silently pleading. Realizing Siobhan was watching, her old nursemaid looked away, hurrying to fill a cup with water.

"I will pray for your immortal soul, Lord Tristan," the old woman said as he drank. "I will grieve for the little one you leave behind." She looked back at Siobhan again. "But I will not weep for your castle."

"Nor should you, Cilla," Siobhan answered, smiling at her. "Save your tears for my noble father, your rightful lord, murdered these twelve years past."

"Aye, Mistress Cilla, do," Tristan said, all the gentleness she had heard in his voice turning instantly to ice. "Had I known him, I might weep for him myself." His eyes met Siobhan's.

For a moment, she almost doubted herself, doubted the right of this man's death. He had not known her father; in truth, he could have been little more than a child himself when her home was attacked and destroyed. Then she thought of her cousins, their heads displayed to feed the crows, not by some long-dead stranger but by this man himself. For all his pretty words to the serving woman, he would have done no differently than the men who had murdered her father, given orders from his king. "Leave us, Cilla," she said, drawing her dagger and making herself smile. "My bridegroom is ready for me now."

"Yes, my lady." Glancing one last time at DuMaine as she picked up her tray, Cilla left them alone.

"What now, my lady harlot?" he said, the lazy drawl of his Frenchman's tongue seductive and mocking at once. "You should have had them strip me, think you not?"

"Not so, my pig shit lord," she answered. He still doubted she meant to do as she had promised, and in truth, he was right. But she wasn't ready to let him be so certain. "I think I can manage well enough." She cut the lacings on his tunic with her dagger, laying it open with the point.

"You do that well, sweetheart," he said, his sneer making the endearment worse than his insults. "You must have had much practice."

She smiled, refusing to rise to the bait. "Not so much as you might think." She laid the knife aside to unlace his hose by hand. "I am still a virgin, after all."

His breath caught short as if he were trying not to gasp outright. "The hell you are," he answered through a scowl.

"Do you doubt me?" His reaction pleased her, she

found. He sounded almost frightened. "I am wounded to the heart." She let her eyes move over him as she had seen her brother and his men look over likely wenches, smiling without thinking as she did it. He was the prettiest man she'd ever seen, a carving of an angel made of flesh—those green eyes had likely seduced thousands in his day. Now they were watching her, bright with fury—wicked brilliance burned behind those eyes. His nose was over-large and slightly crooked, as if it had been broken once, and a tiny scar turned down the corner of his mouth. But these flaws only made him seem more handsome.

"What ails ye, love?" she asked him, aping the tone of a seducer herself. She opened his shirt, running a palm over his stomach, lean and beautifully muscled. "I thought you Normans liked this sort of thing."

"What sort of thing is that, Siobhan?" he asked, his voice roughened to a growl.

"Brawling and tupping at once." The sound of his voice speaking her name gave her a queer little shiver in her stomach. She traced a long, white scar across his side, the leavings of a wound that must have nearly been mortal. Her enemy was a great warrior, for all he was a whoreson dog. "I thought rape was the great sport of your king and his retainers?"

"Aye, petite, it is," Tristan answered bitterly, fighting for his voice. If this seductress was a virgin, Henry was the pope. "But we prefer to be on top."

She smiled. "I see." She had rarely kissed a man in

all her life, but now she leaned down and kissed the livid bruise her brother had left on his cheek. "Alas for you." She kissed another swollen bruise along his jaw, her hands sliding over his chest, and he muttered a curse, jerking his head away.

"Answer me one question," he demanded, fighting for control.

"Only one?" She raised her head to look at him, pure deviltry gleaming in her eyes. "By all means."

He made himself smile back, his brain casting about for some insult that would hurt her. "What perversity made you wear that gown?"

To his surprise, she laughed. "You do not like it, then?"

"I like the garment well enough." Such a beauty must surely be poisoned with vanity, he thought. Surely he could wound her through her pride. "On a proper lass, it would be lovely. Its rightful owner likely looked quite fetching in it."

"In faith, she did not." She sat back on her haunches beside him on the bed with her skirt pulled up over her knees, a shocking, unladylike gesture made more seductive by its very lack of grace. "She had thin hair and a face like a horse."

"Still, I imagine that it fit her." She was like some wild creature from an ancient tale, he thought, some nymph made to ruin the righteous. "It hangs upon you like a rag."

She frowned, looking down at herself. "My shape is not very womanly, is it?"

"A kind of woman's, I suppose." He let his gaze drift up and down her form, his mouth set in a sneer. "Does my plain speech offend you?"

"Your life offends me, husband," she answered, recovering her smile. "But you will mend anon." She leaned down, her face level with his. "I promise." She kissed him softly on the lips, drawing back as he moved against his will to kiss her back.

"Devil," he rasped as she sat up.

"So you have said." Her voice trembled, but her heart was cold. "But I think that the devil is you." She kissed him on the lips again, opening his mouth with her tongue as he had opened hers when they were wed. He truly thought she wanted him, the fool, that she would give herself to him, her enemy. She thought that he would fight her kiss, would try to turn his head away, but he didn't even do that. His mouth rose up to meet her kiss, becoming the aggressor, and she felt him go hard against her where she straddled him. " 'Swounds, sweet husband," she said as she broke the kiss. "Methinks you might want me after all."

He smiled, the hateful sneer she had learned to expect in the few short hours she had known him. Had he sneered that way at her cousins before he put them to the axe? "You forget I am a soldier, Siobhan. I can fuck anything if I must." She opened her mouth to answer, and his hand came up and clamped around her throat, the rope that held it snapping like a thread. "Sadly, I don't have the time."

She tried to gasp for breath but found none, her air cut off completely as she tore at his fist with both hands. She tried to grab the dagger she had left on the table, but she couldn't reach it, and bright points of light danced madly in front of her eyes. No! she roared inside her head, more furious than fearful. But in truth she couldn't make a sound.

"Playtime is over, petite," he said softly, squeezing harder, his thumb pressed over the pulse in her throat. "Time for lessons." He worked his other wrist free of its bonds, his skin raw and bleeding. " 'Tis a pity you won't live to profit from them." She fought against the darkness, swinging at him blindly with her fists, but his arm was much longer than hers. He grabbed the dagger easily with his free hand and held its point under her nose. "Shhhh . . ." Still holding her tightly by the throat, he cut the bonds on his ankles, then leaned closer, driving her stumbling backward as he stood. "What shall I do with you now?"

His grip was loosening; she was beginning to breathe. "Go to hell," she tried to curse him, but the words came out a whisper. He had crushed her throat; her voice was gone.

"With you in my arms, little wife." He leaned down and kissed her forehead, breathing in her scent. He should kill her, wring her neck and leave her while he had the chance. She had sent the guards to her brother; he might even still escape. But somehow he couldn't seem to let her go.

"My brother will kill you." Every whispered word was like a jagged shard of glass ripped up her throat, and still no voice would come. "You cannot escape." She grabbed for the dagger, and he clenched his fist again, the world going black as he tossed the knife away.

"I require no blade, little devil." He sounded drunk, he realized, his words slurring together. She had bewitched him somehow, stolen his reason. But he could still be free. "I will rip you apart with my hands."

She felt his grip unclench, becoming a caress. "My beautiful Siobhan." The same queer thrill she had felt before shivered through her as he raked both hands up through her hair, lifting it to let it fall through his fingers. "Like silk."

"Stop it!" She tried to slap his hands away, and he caught her by the wrists, driving her back against the wall. "Let me go!"

"Let you go?" he echoed. "But I thought you wanted to play." He brought his mouth down to hers slowly, holding her fast as she struggled. She could not fight him; she could not escape. He kissed her, and her knees went weak, her strength dissolving. His tongue pushed tenderly inside her mouth, warm and alive, and she allowed it. She welcomed it; she kissed him back, feeding on his mouth.

"Siobhan . . ." He spoke her name like a caress, as if they might have been lovers indeed. He was too strong for her, her murderer; she had no weapons left. He let go of one wrist to touch her cheek, and she tried to punch him in the face. But he was too fast for her as well; he caught her fist before it could make contact, covering it completely in his palm. "Little devil," he whispered with a smile. He should be trying to escape, she thought. Why did he not run? He was right; he could kill her easily. Why had he not done it?

"No," she whispered as he moved close to kiss her again, his lips barely brushing her own before they moved to her jaw. "Sean . . ." She gathered her strength, holding her breath to use it in a single, tortured scream that felt like her throat was being ripped away. "Help me, Sean!"

Tristan's eyes went wide for a moment, then he scowled, grabbing her hard by the shoulders and bashing her hard against the wall. But Sean and the others were already there, the door flying open with a crash. In an instant, her brother had struck the man who held her hard across the skull with his sword hilt, dropping him unconscious to the floor.

"Sean, I'm sorry." She slumped to the floor beside her fallen husband, her legs melting beneath her. "I'm so sorry . . . I don't know how he got away."

"Hush, love," Sean answered, barely looking at her. "Take him out of here, to the courtyard," he ordered the men. "He is done—and keep Gaston away."

"Forgive me," she said softly, staring at the floor. She had failed them; she was weak, a woman after all. "I let him escape."

"You did not." Her brother draped her shoulders

with a blanket as Tristan was carried out, his body life-less as a corpse. "Is he escaped?" He drew her gently to her feet and smiled. "You did well enough." He drew his jeweled dagger, a trophy taken from the man who had murdered their father. "But now let us be done." He started to cut his own arm.

"Wait." She reached for the knife. "Let me do it." She sliced the blade across her palm and let her blood drip onto the sheets.

At dawn, she went out into the courtyard. Bruce and Callum were already on horseback, and two other men were trying to control DuMaine's own horse, a beauti-ful white destrier. Tristan himself, or what was left of him, lay sprawling on the ground.

"Fair morning, husband," she said, every word still painful and barely more than a rasp. But Tristan had suffered much worse—in truth, they had beaten him so badly, she would hardly have known him, could hardly believe he still lived. But at the sound of her voice, he started to move as if he were trying to stand. "I have come to say good-bye."

He made it to his knees, braced on all fours like a dog. But his eyes as he looked up at her were very much a man's. The proud devil inside of him lived on. She steeled herself for him to speak, determined not to give away the anguish she was feeling, fool that she was. He was her enemy, the murdering oppressor of her people. She must rejoice at his pain. But looking down at him, she thought of his kiss, the sound of his voice as he whispered her name. Why had he not run? He looked up at her now like nothing would please him so well as to see her dead.

But when he spoke, his words were not the curse she knew she deserved. "Please," he said, a rasping whisper as he knelt before her. "My child . . . my Clare." She took a step back in horror, and he caught her hand, his grip firm but not threatening, his green eyes locked to hers. "Promise me, Siobhan."

"Let her go," Sean ordered, raising a hand to strike him.

"No!" Siobhan said, holding up her free hand to hold her brother back.

"Promise me," Tristan repeated, apparently oblivious to anyone but her. "Swear she will be safe."

If Henry's men had given him the chance, would her father have pled for her this way? Aye, she thought, he would have. Let us be better than our enemies, she had said to Sean when he would have beheaded the young squire. Surely little Clare deserved as much. "I swear it." She returned his grip for a moment. "I will guard her with my life."

"Enough, little sister," Sean said, putting a hand on her shoulder.

"Yes," she answered. She drew her hand from Tristan's, and he allowed it, dropping his gaze as well. "More than enough." She bent and touched Tristan's bruised and bloodied cheek. "Good-bye, husband. Wait for me in hell." She stepped back, and Sean and his men scooped up Tristan and flung him over the destrier's back. The horse stopped prancing at once, as if he knew his rider even in such a sorry state. Biting so hard on the inside of her cheek she tasted her own blood, Siobhan watched them bind him to the saddle. Then Bruce and Callum led his horse away.

"There," Sean said as they passed through the broken gates. "It is finished."

"Yes." A strange, sharp ache was clenched around her heart, and her cheeks flushed hot with shame. "At last, it is done." She looked up to find her brother watching her, studying her face. "So what now, captain?" she said, making herself smile.

Sean smiled back. "Victory," he answered. "Come, love. I will show you."

4

Tristan no longer felt pain in his flesh. He had lost so much blood, he could feel very little sensation at all. But he felt fury. He felt hate.

Siobhan had bewitched him. Somehow, even with her throat clenched in his fist, she had managed to distract him long enough to stop him from escaping. She had stolen his reason, his will, with her beauty, then summoned her minions to finish him. And he had allowed it. For a kiss, he had squandered not only his life but his quest. Entranced by the beautiful devil's blue eyes, he had forgotten all else—his commission from Henry, even the safety of his child. He deserved the death that awaited him and eternal damnation behind it. But not yet. He had promised Clare that the bad men would not murder him, and he would keep that promise. He had promised Siobhan that no grave would deny him revenge.

He would keep that promise, too.

They rode for what seemed to be days—he vaguely noticed the world going dark, then light, then dark again, but he lost count of how many times. He heard the voices of the brigands speaking to one another, but he made no effort to find meaning in their speech. All his strength and will he focused on staying alive. Twice the larger of the outlaws came and grabbed him by the hair to turn his face up where he could see it. "Dead yet? No? As you will." But neither of them touched him further or took any more notice of him than they would have a bag of grain they were carrying on a pack mule behind them.

It was dark again when the big one said, "Turn off the road." Daimon stopped, and Tristan tried to concentrate at last, to test what strength he might have left and start to make a plan. "We have brought him far enough." Once they stopped, they would finish him, he knew, unless he killed them first. But how was he to do it? One of his arms was shattered, he knew, and dislocated from the shoulder, and several of his ribs were crushed—he had been tasting his own blood for hours now.

"We should see if there is a house nearby," the second brigand said as they stopped in a clearing in the woods. "We do not want him found."

"Why not?" The big one brought his horse alongside Daimon, drawing his knife as he came, and Tristan tensed, twisting in his bonds. "Who will know him here?" Instead of slitting Tristan's throat, the brigand cut the strap that held him bound to Daimon's saddle and kicked him in the side, letting him slump to the ground. "Farewell, Lord Tristan DuMaine," he said, spitting on him. Could they really be so stupid? Surely they would make certain he was really dead before they left him.

"Aye, my lord, farewell," he heard the second brigand laugh. "We will enjoy your castle."

Come closer, Tristan thought, willing his body to move.

Suddenly a great, black shape sprang out of the shadows—a tremendous wolf that pounced upon the largest brigand and knocked him from the saddle. "Damn me, Christ!" the brigand screamed as the beast's fangs tore into his throat, and if he could have found the strength, Tristan would have laughed in sheer joy at the sound. It was as if some sympathetic demon had conjured his rage into flesh and set it on his captors, so just did the wolf attack seem. Using the last of his strength, he turned his head to watch what the beast would do next. It seemed to be feeding from the brigand's throat, drinking his blood, oblivious to his struggles. When the man stopped twitching, the beast let out a sound that began as a howl but quickly changed to something else, something human. As Tristan watched in disbelief, the wolf stood up, his form melting into the shape of a man.

The brigand's horse reared up and screamed, and the man drew back and snarled, baring long, white fangs that gleamed white in the moonlight. He was young, no older than Tristan himself, with long black hair and eyes that glowed green for a moment before fading into brown. He was naked to the waist, but he wore the hose and boots of a noble knight. The horse reared back from him again and broke into a run, dragging the dead brigand behind it, his foot still caught in the stirrup.

"What the devil are you?" the second brigand stammered, aiming his crossbow at the demon knight. The demon smiled, wiping the blood from his mouth with his arm.

"You guessed it already," he answered, reaching up to grab the brigand by his tunic. The man fired the crossbow, sending a bolt through the demon's shoulder, but he didn't seem to feel it. He snatched the bolt from his flesh as he dragged the man down from his horse, then used it to stab him in the throat. Once again he bent to drink from the fountain of blood. Tristan watched the ripple of the muscles in his back as he fed, fascinated and appalled.

"No!" the demon knight suddenly shouted, flinging the man he held against a tree like he might have been a child's toy. The brigand's head lolled on his shoulders as he fell, obviously dead, and the demon knight sank to his knees. "No . . . I am not," he mumbled, and Tristan heard the lilt of Ireland in his voice. "I am done."

What are you? Tristan thought, trying to focus on the creature's face. As if to oblige him, the demon knight leaned closer, gazing intently into Tristan's eyes, his nostrils flaring slightly as if to catch his scent. He

touched Tristan's cheek with his fingertips, and Tristan
tried to flinch away. But his strength was gone. He was
dying. He tried to close his eyes, to shut out the
demon's searching gaze, but even that power was lost.
The demon knight slid a hand behind his neck, lifting
him toward him with great tenderness, and Tristan
saw great sorrow in his dark brown eyes. Then he
bared his fangs again and sank them into his throat.

No! Tristan thought, a shout inside his head, and his
body lurched upward, fighting back in spite of his
weakness, pure fury giving him strength. He struck at
the demon with his unbroken arm, bashing a fist into
the side of his head over and over again. The demon
sank his fangs in deeper, holding him fast.

In desperation, Tristan turned his head and sank his
own teeth into the demon's bare shoulder, tearing at
the flesh like a dog. The demon howled in pain as blood
poured from the wound, and without thinking, Tristan
bit him harder, sucking at the blood.

Feeling rushed back into his body, the pain that had
left him returning in an instant, making him shudder
as if in a fever, then instantly fading away. Warmth and
joy washed over him, a kind of drunken ecstasy, and he
fed harder, desperate for more. The demon struggled in
his grasp, his fangs still clamped to Tristan's throat, but
the pain was nothing; all that mattered in that moment
was the blood. Visions rose before his eyes of a golden
hall, a hundred demons battling around him, corpses
piled around his feet as he struck them back with his

sword. Strength flowed hot into his veins, the strength of the man in his vision, and he clasped the demon to his breast, feeling the fangs in his own mouth growing longer.

"No!" the demon shouted, flinging him away as he had flung his other victim. But Tristan was not dead. He moved his limbs, flopping like a fish upon the shore, and the warmth spread outward to his hands, strength and health returning to his muscles—more, much more than he had ever felt before. All his fear and all his pain were gone. All that was left was the fury, the healing fire of his righteous rage. The demon knight climbed to his feet, backing away, saying, "No."

Tristan sat up, the night breeze cool and soft upon his face. Turning toward the demon, he sprang to his feet in a crouch, reaching for a sword dropped by one of the brigands. "Stay back," he ordered, raising it toward the demon, his voice strong as it had ever been. His broken arm was mended; he could feel it tingle, and his ribs no longer even ached.

"Stop," the demon knight said, holding out a hand to him. The wound Tristan's teeth had torn in his shoulder was healing itself; as Tristan watched, the skin was knitted whole. "You don't understand what has happened—"

"I live," Tristan answered. "That is enough."

"But you do not," the demon said, taking a step closer.

"You killed them." He looked back at the dead brigand slumped against the tree, his eyes staring blank.

This creature had killed him with no effort at all, had taken a bolt from a crossbow in the shoulder with barely a flinch. "You killed them both with no weapons," he said. "I saw you." He raised the arm that should have been shattered but that was whole, holding a sword, ready for battle. "Will I now kill in this fashion?" With such power, he could scourge Lebuin and his rebels from the earth like the vermin they were. Siobhan's power would be nothing; he could kill her in an instant, without thought.

"You can," the demon admitted. Now that he was no longer feeding, he looked like any other man except for the fire in his eyes.

Tristan smiled. He would even look like himself. "That is all I need to know." Daimon was still standing behind him, nervous but faithful even so. With a demon's speed, he leapt onto the horse's back, urging him onward and galloping into the night. He heard the demon knight behind him swear an oath, heard him crashing through the trees, giving chase. Once he glanced back over his shoulder and saw the wolf, racing over the ground. But he was no match for Daimon. Bending low over the horse's neck, Tristan urged him onward, leaving the wolf-knight behind.

Once he knew he had lost his pursuer, he slowed his mount and looked around, trying to get his bearings. He had ridden over most of Britain as part of King Henry's retinue before receiving a holding of his own, but nothing he saw here was familiar. When the forest on either side gave way to a clearing, he saw he crossed a great, flat plain—could they have ridden so far south? He tried to think back and count over the days since they'd left his captured castle, but it was impossible. Worse, the magical sense of well-being he had first felt after biting the demon knight was fast giving way to the most painful hunger he had ever felt, a yawning, empty ache. He would have to find someone soon who could tell him where he was and give him something to eat.

He turned off the main road onto a narrow track as the open plain turned into forest again. He had ridden many miles from the deserted spot where his captors had fallen to the demon; surely he must be near a settlement of some kind. He slowly became aware of a strange sound in his ears, a kind of thrumming drumbeat in the distance, barely audible over the clop of Daimon's hooves on the hard-packed earth. Without thinking, he urged the horse into a faster trot, and the hunger in his belly turned sharper, making him wince. His last meal had been at his own table hours before the attack; 'twas no great wonder he was hungry. But he had starved before on marches at war and never felt such pain. His thoughts were losing focus; he could barely remember his purpose on the road, why he was there or what it was he sought. All that seemed clear was the burning need to feed.

A rough wooden hovel seemed to hunker by the road ahead, and as he drew nearer, the sound of drumming grew louder. A heartbeat, he thought, mildly horrified. That is a heartbeat. What sort of monstrous creature could be making such a sound? It seemed to be coming from the hovel, but surely that was impossible—such a beast must surely be too large to fit in such a shelter. But some instinct stronger than reason led him onward, closer and closer to the sound. He stopped his horse a few feet from the hut and staggered toward it, feeling drunk, and the very worst of the fury he had felt in the hands of Lebuin and his men seemed to return full force, as if his enemies themselves were hiding in the hut.

"Who is there?" he demanded, pounding the door with his fist. "Come forth and fight!"

"My lord?" The peasant who opened the door was a fair-sized man, but certainly no monster. "My lord, what offense—?"

Tristan fell on the man just as the demon knight had fallen on his captors, his new fangs tearing into the man's bearded throat. Without a thought, he drove him back into his hut, slamming him against the wall, oblivious to his screams of pain and terror or the huntsman's knife he stabbed into his arms and chest. He drank deeply, the blood that should have sickened him delicious on his tongue. Nothing seemed to matter but the blood.

Reason came back to him slowly, the horror of what he had done creeping back into his consciousness as the man in his grasp went limp. The terrible hunger was gone, replaced by an equally terrible remorse. He had murdered this peasant in cold blood, attacked him like some ravenous beast . . . Appalled, he let the body go, watching it fall dead to the floor. He was an animal, a demon. He looked down at his hands. His sleeves were slashed and torn at the forearms from the peasant's knife, the edges stained with blood. But his flesh was whole.

He touched his face, his jaw that should have been broken, his nose that had been smashed. All felt whole and sound; he felt no pain at all. The demon had cured him with his blood. He had made him like himself. *I live*, Tristan had told him. *No*, he had answered. *You do not.*

"What am I?" he said softly, falling to his knees on the dirt floor of the hut. "Sweet Christ—" His tongue burned as if a fire had exploded in his mouth as he spoke the oath, and he brought a hand to his mouth, expecting to see blood. But the burning stopped at once as soon as he fell silent. He looked down at the dead man before him and saw a wooden cross hanging from a cord around his neck, a peasant's charm against evil. He reached for it slowly, holding his breath. As his fingertips made contact, he felt more searing pain, saw smoke rising from his burning flesh as he snatched his hand away.

"Cursed," he mumbled, watching as the skin on his fingers healed itself from the burn. "I am cursed." He should have been horrified, sickened at the thought.

But another, more powerful thought possessed him. He took up the peasant's knife and plunged it into the flesh of his arm, wincing at the pain. But as soon as he withdrew the blade, the wound closed up again. "I cannot be killed." He thought of Sean Lebuin, slaughtering his knights like cattle, noble men whose only crime was obedience to their lord. He thought of Siobhan, his beautiful pretended bride, bewitching him to ruin. He looked down at the rough blade in his hand and smiled. He would keep his promise, cheat the grave. As this damned demon, he would have his just revenge.

He dragged the body out and buried it in the soft forest loam, his guilt but a little. If the man was righteous, he was now in his heavenly reward. And if he was not, a demon at his doorstep was no worse than he deserved. When the chore was done, he went back into the hovel and rummaged through the dead man's possessions, finding clothes to replace his own. The leggings and tunic were rough and unrefined, but they were clean, and he found he barely felt the cold.

But as the night began to fade and the sun began to rise outside the open door, he found he felt tired, so sleepy he could barely hold his eyes open. He would have to make camp as soon as he was clear of the scene of his crime. Looking for provisions for his journey, he opened a clay jar and found cheese, but the smell of it sickened him—everything in the hovel stank of death. Buckling his own belt around his hips, he stuck the peasant's knife into the sheath that had once held a silver dagger and the fallen sword he had taken from one of his dead captors into his scabbard and started to leave the hut.

Pale sunlight struck him like a wall of fire, making him scream out in pain. He fell back into the shadows of the hovel, his blood boiling in his veins, smoke rising from his skin. He scrambled back from the light, kicking the door shut, but even the tiny beams that filtered through the wooden walls were agony, burning through his cursed flesh like rods of molten iron. He snatched a leather blanket from the peasant's narrow cot and huddled under it, curled up in a shadowed corner like a rat. "What hell is this?" he murmured, furious and frightened. But even in his fear and fury, the strange weariness grew stronger, making his body grow heavy and his mind grow numb. Almost before the words were spoken, he was sleeping, waiting for the dark.

Gaston had served the baron of Callard since they were both of them boys, and he had no doubt of his greatness. But to his mind, superstitious nonsense was likely to be his undoing. He had ridden all night from the wreck of the castle DuMaine to report with no sleep, no food, and no woman to reward him for his efforts. But now he must cool his heels and wait while his master consulted a witch.

"Your history is dark, my lord," the crone muttered over her bones. Gaston suppressed a snort of laughter. Any child of five within these walls could have said as much with no magic to guide him. The baron fixed his faithful servant with a glare to make his blood run cold before returning to his own study of the bones. Crouched on the floor beside the baron's chair was his latest mistress, a redhead in a noblewoman's gown. She looked up at Gaston as well, and he saw the mark of an iron brand on her cheek. *On your way out then, sweetest?* Gaston thought, giving her wink.

"I know my history, old dame," the baron said. "Tell me of my future." He gave Gaston a friendlier glance. "Tell me if my plans will fail."

"No, my lord," the witch hastened to assure him. Her clothes were rough and wild, and she spoke English with the porridge-thick brogue of the Scots. *How far had some poor patrol been forced to ride to find this one?* Gaston thought with an inward sigh. "You will succeed." She tossed the bones again, leaning close over the table. "You have won already."

Gaston nodded to his master, and the baron's smile widened. "Your powers are great, old dame," the baron said. "Now tell me something my own man could not."

"Your enterprise will give you power beyond reckoning, my lord," the witch answered, an obedient toady's response. But she didn't speak as one currying favor; her voice was hushed with awe, her rheumy eyes wide. "You will cheat even death . . . but no." A toothless smile broke over her face. "Not you." She looked up and met the baron's eyes. "You are nothing."

Gaston held his breath as the familiar flush swept

over his master's face, and the girl on the floor let out a whimper, clinging to her cruel lover's leg as if for shelter from his wrath. "You dare," the baron breathed.

"One will come to take possession of your fate," the witch said with no sign she felt afraid or noticed his anger at all. "His evil is beyond your darkest dreams." She smiled again. "He is a devil indeed."

"Liar." The baron struck her with his fist, knocking her aside into the rushes, then flung the heavy wooden table over after her. "Take her from my sight," he ordered his guardsmen. "A week in the stocks will make her visions true."

"But . . . my lord," one of the guards said as the crone on the floor began to chant in her own tongue, the Gaelic that always put Gaston in mind of a cat trapped in a thicket. "This creature is a starving ancient—she will not live a day—"

"Mayhap her devil will save her." The thought seemed to calm him; the flush faded again. "If he should come, let me know." He rose from his chair, giving the young woman still clinging to his leg an impatient look. She withdrew, but Gaston noticed she looked up, exchanging a glance with the merciful guardsman.

"Yes, my lord," the guardsman said, moving with his fellows to obey. The crone was still laughing and chanting as she was carried away.

" 'Tis glad I am that I made haste, my lord," Gaston said as he followed Callard to the window. "I would have hated to have missed the show."

"Your wit will be your murder, Gaston," the baron answered, but he smiled. "Tell me of DuMaine."

"Dead as Judas Iscariot, my lord, along with all his knights," Gaston promised. "Or did you mean the castle?" He watched the baron's mistress retreat back into the shadows. Should he tell his master what he guessed about her and the guardsman? No, best to save that for a more profitable moment.

"The castle fell, I presume," the baron said, interrupting his thoughts.

"Yes," he answered quickly. It was not wise to lose one's focus in the presence of the baron, particularly when he'd already had a disappointment. "But it was barely damaged. And Silas of Massum survived."

"Well done, Lebuin," Callard said with a slight, musing smile. Outside the window, the ancient witch was being chained into the stocks, still chanting. "The peasant prince is as clever as you said, then."

"Aye, my lord," Gaston answered. "But no more clever than you would wish him to be."

The Baron closed the shutter. "And the girl?" He turned back toward the shadows where his mistress hid. "Tell me again about her. She is beautiful, yes?"

"Exquisite," Gaston agreed. He thought of the little bitch threatening him for daring to insult a peasant wench, and a wave of affection swept over him for his master. "The most beautiful I myself have ever seen, with no vanity to speak of. But she is . . . spirited, my lord." Callard raised an eyebrow. "She had DuMaine bound to his bed and used him like a doxy before she would let him be killed."

"Did she?" the baron laughed, delighted. "Good for her. I'd say we were well matched." A pair of strong men had come in to set the table on its legs again, and a pair of women were bringing in breakfast. "Breaking her spirit will be . . . amusing, I think."

"Aye, my lord," Gaston answered, his stomach rumbling and a general good humor lifting up his heart. "I dare say it will be."

5

Silas had passed the most difficult night of his life. Sometime after midnight their guards had taken him, little Clare, and the nursemaid, Emma, into a room on the second floor of the manor house and left them. The child and her nurse had cried themselves to sleep eventually, but Silas had watched out the window all night, watching the brigands celebrate their victory, watching them brutalize DuMaine for sport. But he had noticed they did not damage DuMaine's castle. All of the fires that had been set were quickly put out, and guards were set along the castle walls, just as if a Norman lord were once again in residence. These were not common thieves and outlaws, he realized, not certain whether to be glad or horrified. These people had a plan.

At dawn, he watched the girl, Siobhan, bid her husband farewell with a final insult before what was left of him was carried out the castle gates, slung over his own horse. She had not been present for the beatings, at least, he had noticed. Nor did she seem entirely happy as Tristan was taken away. But she was not grieving either.

As she and her brother turned back toward the manor house, she looked up and saw the scholar at the window. Freezing in her tracks, she gave him a look of such loathing, his blood turned thick in his veins.

A few moments later, the door to the upper room opened. "Come," one of the brigands said, motioning to him. Another bent over Emma and shook her gently awake.

"Bring the little one, darling," he said, and Silas saw the girl smile as if she knew the man. "Sean wants to see them both."

Lebuin was waiting in the great hall below. Breakfast was being served as usual; all that had changed were the faces at the trestle tables as it was eaten. Siobhan was pacing near the open hearth, dressed in her boy's clothes again with her hair bound back in a braid. Silas saw the blue-black print of five fingers bruised into her throat.

"Good morning, master," Lebuin greeted him, motioning him to a chair. "Have you slept?"

"No," Silas answered, standing where he was.

"Who could sleep?" Siobhan said. She glanced at Clare, who was yawning, holding Emma's hand behind Silas, but her eyes darted quickly away.

"Things have been rather unsettled," Lebuin said. One of the women set a trencher before the brigand leader and returned his friendly smile. "But I expect they'll soon return to normal. Your workers are waiting, Master Silas."

"Waiting for what?" he asked, hiding his shock.

"Waiting for you to show them how to finish this damned castle," Siobhan answered before her brother could speak. "Sean wants it done at once."

"In Silas's good time," Lebuin corrected. "But before the harvest, yes. Can it be done with the workers you have?"

Looking around, Silas saw his own master carpenters and masons sitting together at one of the tables, watching him. They looked nervous and unhappy, but unharmed. "You mean to stay at DuMaine?" he asked.

"I mean to stay here, on my ancestral lands," Lebuin answered, a hard, angry look flickering briefly in his eyes. "This is my sister's castle now. She is widow to Du-Maine." Behind him, Silas heard Clare let out a little hiccup and Emma shush her gently. "More importantly, this manor belonged to our father long before DuMaine set his Norman boots on English soil."

"No," Clare raised her little voice above her nurse's murmur. "My father is not dead!"

"Poor lamb," Lebuin said with a sigh.

"Stop it, Sean," Siobhan answered, giving him an impatient look. She came and knelt down in front of the little girl, and Clare drew back from her in fear. "How do you know he is not dead?" the brigand woman asked her, her voice surprisingly kind.

"Because he promised," Clare answered. "He promised me the bad men would not kill him."

"The bad men," Siobhan repeated, looking back at

her brother with an enigmatic smile. "Aye, love, he promised me the same." The child was sad, but she was not pitiful, she thought, looking into the wide green eyes so like DuMaine's. She was no poor lamb. "Perhaps he will still keep his promise." Somehow she would have to live, this little one. Somehow she would have to go on without her papa, just as Siobhan had done herself, and she had no brother to help her, to teach her how to fight. "As God be my judge, child, your father was alive when last I saw him."

"Siobhan," Sean said behind her.

"But he has gone away," she finished, paying him no mind. "He had to go away and leave you with Emma and this Master Silas to look after you."

Clare looked up at Silas, silently begging confirmation, and he smiled. "It is true, my lady. This lady is Siobhan, and she is your stepmother. But Emma and I will stay."

"I am glad to hear it, master," Lebuin said. "Now, what will you need from me to finish this castle in time?"

"Sean, for pity, leave him be," Siobhan said, standing up. "He already told you, he has had no sleep. Your castle can wait one more day." She looked around at the assembly. "Where is Gaston?"

"Gone," Lebuin answered, his good humor showing cracks, Silas noticed. "He has gone to report to his lord."

"His lord," Siobhan repeated softly, her bitter disapproval impossible to miss. "Would that he would stay there." She looked back at the scholar. "Come, master," she said to him. "I have had no sleep this night myself." She reached out to touch Clare's cheek, but when the child recoiled, she smiled. "Sean, I beg your patience."

"Not at all," her brother answered. Watching these two brigands, Silas felt more confused than ever. There was obviously great love between them, even kindness in their hearts. So how could they have done such evil? "I leave the Lady Clare in your protection—'tis right that she should be. Will you take Master Silas to his room?"

"I will," Siobhan nodded, smiling. "Come, Master Silas."

The scholar kept his peace until Emma and the little girl were settled into the child's own room. But when Siobhan moved to leave him at the door of his own chamber, he caught her by the sleeve. "Forgive me, my lady," he said when she turned on him, annoyed. "But what is to become of Lady Clare?"

"Why should I care?" she asked. "That will be for my brother to decide."

"Why should that be?" he countered. "Is she not your daughter now?" When she didn't answer, he moved into the room and motioned for her to follow. "Please . . ." With a scowl, she gave in, closing the door behind her.

"Your only concern is the castle," she began, turning to him.

"You told the child that Lord DuMaine still lived," he cut her off. "Was that true?"

The old man would not be put off, she could see. He

obviously cared for the little girl, and she could hardly blame him for that. But she had no time for this, nor patience either. "I told her DuMaine was alive when last I saw him, and he was," she answered. "But he is dead by now, Master Silas. That, I promise you, is true."

"Is it?" he answered with a strange smile.

"I told the child what I did to give her hope," she said, feeling an entirely inappropriate blush in her cheeks. "She has lost her family, lost everything she has ever known in a single night." She returned his smile with another just as cryptic. "I remember how that feels."

"So it's true, then," he said, turning away. One side of the room was dominated by an immense oaken table covered with scrolls and a lot of queer instruments whose purpose she couldn't possibly have guessed. A single armchair was pulled up beside it, and the scholar collapsed into it, obviously exhausted. "You and your brother once lived on these lands."

"Not once, master. Always." He wasn't at all as she would have expected a great builder of castles to be. There seemed to be no arrogance about him, none of the snobbery she expected from those who lived within the royal circle. "We have never left this forest, ever, nor will we. Our father was lord here by birth and by title."

"And now his son will have his castle," he answered. "Or his daughter, rather."

"My father cared nothing for castles," she retorted. "He cared only for his people and their welfare. He was born here; his line dates back to long before the Saxons came, to the days of Arthur. He was not some stranger come to milk a fortune from the earth and the people who work it before returning to France."

"Still, it was kind of DuMaine to pay for a castle," Silas said with his strange little smile.

"He paid for nothing," Siobhan retorted. "His king—"

"His king can barely pay for his own troops," the scholar interrupted with a laugh. "No, lady, I assure you. Tristan DuMaine paid for this fortress from his own coffers. He sold his own ancestral lands in France to do it." Her eyes narrowed in disbelief. "When you and your brother burned the first planting, he used the last of his inheritance to buy more, lest his people starve come winter."

"His people," she scoffed. "His slaves, you mean."

"His people," he repeated. "Those he built this castle to protect."

"He built it as a prison!" she said, almost shouting. "Spare me your lies, old man. A Norman castle serves nothing and no one but the Norman king."

"And yet you and your brother wish to have one," he answered. "Enough to do murder to get it."

"I did not murder DuMaine," she said, trying to shut out his words.

"Did you not?" he countered.

"No." She should end this conversation now; it could only make her angry. "But why should you care? You've been paid your commission, and we have allowed you to live. Why should you care who lives here when your task is done?"

"I am not accustomed to having my survival a question of doubt," he answered. "And I do not enjoy being confused. I thought Lebuin wanted this castle to fail. Three of my masons were murdered in their sleep—your brother's work, I thought."

She smiled, drawing the dagger from her belt. "Not my brother's, master." She took a step toward him and was gratified to see him recoil, his mild eyes wide with shock. "If I had my choice, this castle would be taken down to gravel, and no other would ever be built in its place. This is not a Norman holding; our people are not slaves."

"The king is a Norman, my lady, whether you choose it or not," he said, his tone surprisingly gentle, as if she might have been his pupil. "This manor is in England, and England is ruled by the Norman nobles. All who live here do so by their leave."

"Not me," she retorted. "Not my people." She still held the dagger in her fist, and for a moment, she had the wild thought that she could kill him, end this madness with a single stroke. With no engineer to finish his castle, Sean would have no choice but to abandon his plan, would have to dissolve his idiot alliance with the baron of Callard, this stranger hiding in the shadows, giving out weapons and offering advice. She even took another quick step closer, the dagger held out before her.

But she could not do it. She could kill in battle, but this would be cold-blooded murder. And besides, Sean might never forgive her, and then where would she be? Who would she have if Sean abandoned her? "I am very tired, Master Silas," she said, sheathing the dagger. "I think that I should go."

"Lady Clare needs you, my lady," he said. "She needs your strength to protect her, your woman's kindness—"

"I have no woman's kindness, sir." She cut him off. "The child will have my protection because she is an innocent. But do not ask me to be kind." She stopped at the door and looked back at him, this strange man who was neither knight, farmer, nor priest. "I do not know how." Before he could answer, she left him, slamming the door behind her and breaking into a run.

She threw herself across the bed that had once been Tristan's, the only place she could be certain she would not be disturbed. The blooded sheets had been removed and put away, but the broken bonds where her husband had been tied still hung from the posts. She picked up the ends of the one he had broken, marveling at his strength. The strap was leather, the thickness of a horse's rein, yet Tristan had snapped it in two. She thought of his hand around her throat, her own fingers straying unconsciously to the bruises on her skin. She thought of him pinning her hard to the wall, of his hand covering her fist. She thought of his kisses, possessive and tender, the power of his arms around her as he held her fast. Devil, he had called her, damning her to hell, but he had spoken her name like a prayer. Siobhan, he had whispered, running his hands through her hair.

"No," she said aloud, turning her face to the pillow. "I won't think about it anymore. He is dead." Tears burned her eyes, and she let them come, too tired to fight any more. "Tristan DuMaine is dead."

As the sun was setting, Tristan woke inside the peasant hut. When darkness fell, he ventured out into the moonlight and found he could face it quite well. The warm, fierce joy he had felt with his first taste of blood had returned, along with a weaker shade of the hunger he had felt. He would have to feed again, but not for some time yet. He could not face the daylight anymore, but he could walk the night.

Daimon was still waiting, grazing on the turf behind the hut. "Come," Tristan said, and the horse obeyed, a bit more slowly than he might have when his master lived, perhaps, but quickly enough. Through the open door of the hut, Tristan could see the bloody rags he had discarded, all that was left of his fine, knightly clothes. Now he was dressed as a peasant with a nobleman's sword, like one of Lebuin's own men. He smiled at the thought, climbing into the saddle. "Come," he repeated, turning his mount on to the forest path. "Let us go and find Siobhan."

In his broken, dying state, he had known he'd been carried some days away from his home, but apparently it had been nearly a week since the castle had fallen. Lebuin's men had brought him all the way from the northern border to the southern plains, lands he knew very little. But why? he thought, emerging from the forest onto the broad road again. Why bother to carry him so far away to die? He vaguely remembered one of the brigands mentioning not wanting his body to be found, but surely the woods around DuMaine Castle would have hidden his grave well enough. Why not just murder him outright? He found himself remembering Siobhan, her face as she had begged her brother to spare Richard's life. Was Richard still alive? Why had she cared? Had her feelings been the reason Lebuin had sent him here to die? She had tormented him, bewitched him, and betrayed him. But she had sworn on her life to keep his daughter safe.

"Devil," he muttered to himself, and Daimon turned his ears back to listen. "It's nothing, my friend," he promised, stroking the horse's neck. The woman was a mystery to him; nothing about her made sense. If he had captured her before, when his castle still stood, he might have passed an interesting few days or months holding her prisoner and learning all her secrets. But she had captured him instead, brought down his wrath upon her, wronged him much too sorely to ever be forgiven. And besides, he had no time.

The night before, he had moved as if in a trance, the strange events that had spared his life more like a dream than truth. But now, riding alone in the moonlight, he thought them through again—the wolf-knight whose blood had apparently both healed his wounds and damned him from the light; his flight through the forest and murder of the woodcutter; the burning of the sun and the name of the Christ on his tongue. He was no scholar nor penitent either; he had used his time in more useful pursuits than studying old texts or listening to clerics. But he seemed to remember a bard at Henry's London court telling tales of ancient Saxon warriors who walked this island after death, seeking vengeance on their murderers. Somehow their very rage kept their bodies wakeful after their souls had fled to hell. Perhaps he was like one of these; surely he had cause enough. The bard had never mentioned how these creatures came to be; perhaps they were made by one another, as he had been made by the wolf. Such a monster would be made for darkness, he thought, would be outside God's grace. A godly man would never be so called; his corpse would rest, waiting to be reborn in Paradise. But Tristan was not a godly man, nor had he ever been. He hadn't had the time or patience for it. God's heaven was a pretty thought, but the ugly earth was here and now and needing his attention. The closest thing to heaven he had ever touched was his child, his Clare. If he had finished his castle as he had hoped and built the home he had wanted, he would likely have even come around to God in his own time—his father, someone had told him, had given a great sum to the church on his deathbed and bought his way out of his sins. But Lebuin and his brigands had not given Tristan that chance.

Within the hour, he began to see others on the road, peasants mostly, making their way in a broken procession in the opposite direction. Most of them looked at him curiously, a man dressed as they were with the horse and arms of a noble, and some of the men smiled and nodded as he passed. But it was miles before anyone actually spoke. "Be ye of Sir Reese's men?" an old man carrying a pitchfork asked.

"Just the same," Tristan answered as if he knew Sir Reese from Adam. "Where are you folk bound so late?"

"Home," the old man answered. "And better we had stayed there in the first place."

Following along for a mile or so, Tristan discovered all of these people had come from seeing a traveling pardoner in the seaside village of Kitley, and he understood what the old man had meant. A pardoner was the very bottom of the clerical hierarchy, not even a priest. Most were clerks who wrote out dispensations for the wealthy and delivered their penance to the bishop, usually skimming a bit off the top for their own expenses. Some supplemented this scavenger's income with various schemes, preying on the common folk whose scant few pennies would not impress the true church enough to buy an indulgence. This one said he had a holy relic, a veil that had once belonged to the Virgin Mary. For a price, he had offered to let these common folk touch it to cleanse their souls of sin and heal their bodies of pain. "Did it work?" Tristan asked the old man.

"Nay, lad," he answered, bent over his stick. "Do you not see me here?" He smiled a toothless, bitter smile. "He said I was not penitent enough."

"Pride is a deadly sin," Tristan agreed, returning his smile.

"Aye," the old man answered. "That it is." He looked back over his shoulder at a wagon following some distance behind. " 'Tis no great matter to me," he said with a sigh. "But you see those there? 'Tis the family of a young woman struck with a bloody flux after her child was born." His wrinkled face twisted in a frown. "The little snake said she must have been unfaithful to her husband," he said, lowering his voice as if loath to be overheard. "She died in the yard of the inn."

If Tristan had still been a noble lord, he would have seen this pardoner clapped into the stocks. But since he was not . . . His demon hunger was growing stronger, he thought, and Kitley wasn't so far out of his way. Perhaps he would seek a bit of absolution of his own. "Safe journey, gaffer," he said, turning his horse around.

The pardoner had already put on his nightgown when Tristan knocked on his door. "Begone with you," he hissed through the tiniest crack he could peer out of. "Come back in the morning."

"The morning will be too late." Tristan pushed his way inside, forcing the door open with the skinny man still clinging to the handle. "I hear you have a holy relic. I would see it."

"And who are you to make demands?" The man looked like a freshly plucked chicken, but he had the manner of Caesar reborn. "Begone, I say." Tristan took a step closer, scowling, and the man took a step backward. "Who are you?"

"A sinner." Watching him, Tristan could just imagine his disdain for the woman he had sent away to die, and a demon's sort of righteous rage began to simmer inside him. "I hear you can sell me salvation."

" 'Tis . . . 'tis not so simple as that." Fear flickered in his close-set eyes, and sweat broke out on his brow. He took a sidestep toward the door, and Tristan grabbed him by the front of his nightgown. "I would have to hear your confession!"

"Why?" He leaned down to inhale the man's scent, listening to his heartbeat, quick and thready as a rabbit's. "Are you a priest?" This time he could feel the fangs growing sharp against his tongue, feel the hunger growing in his belly. "Show me this holy thing you say you have," he said, his voice deepening, becoming coarse and thick as if he had been drinking too much wine. "Perhaps it will protect you."

Using both hands to free himself from Tristan's grasp, the pardoner lurched backward toward a chest, his face pale with fear. "It is here." He took out a yellowed length of linen. "The veil of the Blessed Virgin Mary."

"How impressive." In truth, if the mother of Christ had worn all of the garments Tristan himself had seen attributed to her, she must have changed her clothes three or four times every day and never worn the same bit twice. Remembering the way the peasant's cross had burned his fingertips, he cautiously reached for the veil.

"Isn't it beautiful?" the pardoner agreed, obviously encouraged. "Many is the time I have caught a whiff of her sweet scent still clinging to the folds."

Tristan's fingers closed around the cloth . . . nothing. Whatever it was, it was not blessed. He met the pardoner's eyes with his own, a sardonic smile twisting his mouth.

Suddenly a blade flashed through the false relic, a dagger the skinny fraud had hidden in its folds. He jabbed it hard into Tristan's stomach. "I warned you," he said, trembling all over as his heartbeat pounded in the air. "I told you to begone."

"You did." Tristan pulled the blade from his flesh, feeling a moment's pain before the wound healed itself with a hiss. "How many others did you send away?" He thought of the peasant husband weeping for his dying wife, defending her innocence from sin, and rage consumed him. "How many did you declare beyond forgiveness?" He caught the man by his skinny shoulders, lifting him off his feet. "You who cannot look down on a maggot—how many good folk did you condemn to hell?" Without waiting for an answer, he tore open his throat.

Later he walked out into the dooryard of the inn where a crowd of peasants had already gathered, waiting for dawn and their chance to be duped. Sickened by their very innocence, he opened the leather pouch he had taken from the pardoner's corpse. "Save your confessions for a true priest," he advised them, speaking barely loud enough to be heard, before scattering coins into the crowd. "There is no salvation here." Watching them scramble for a moment, he turned away and disappeared into the night.

Siobhan walked out into the courtyard, breathing in the cool night air, her eyes stinging with tears. Above her was the castle motte, its tower black against the yellow moon, and she found her eyes drawn to it, something nagging at her memory. It was obviously brand-new, the latest advancement of ugly Norman architecture. But something about it was familiar.

"Where have you been?" Sean demanded, coming across the courtyard to meet her. "It's after midnight."

"The boy, Richard," she answered. He frowned. "DuMaine's young squire." He nodded. "He is dead."

"Ah." He put an arm around her shoulders. "Poor lad." He turned her face up to his. "Are you all right?"

"Of course." Her brother had begun to show an alarming tendency to treat her like a woman, and she didn't care for it one bit. The boy had been a soldier, after all; his death was a good one. Why should she want to weep for him? "He was no one to me," she said, shrugging away from him before he could say more. "Sean, that tower . . . why does it seem so familiar?"

He smiled. "You haven't guessed?" he said, obviously as glad as she was to let the other matter drop. "It's built on the old druid's mound."

Her eyes went wide. "You jest."

"In faith, I do not." He seemed to find this sacrilege amusing. "Silas said that when they first cleared the land for the castle, they were quite pleased to find a natural hill in just the spot DuMaine wished to place his motte. Taking down the old ruin on top of it was no great matter at all—they did it in a week."

"They took down the druid's tower?" In her father's day, most of the common folk would not even approach the tower for fear of the power it contained. No wonder they had been so eager to see DuMaine defeated.

"To the ground," Sean agreed. "Then paved over the floor and built their tower over it."

"Holy Christ," she murmured, a rather incongruous oath for such a crime. "Sean, we cannot stay here—"

"Don't be ridiculous." He cut her off. "Our blood is safe here, whatever DuMaine might have done."

"Not if we shame the ancient places," she protested. "You know what Mother always said—"

"Mother's superstitions did not save her husband, did they?" The angry light that drove her brother ever onward in his quest flashed for a moment in his eyes. Then he smiled. "Tomorrow I want to start moving your things into the tower."

"What? Sean, no—"

"The manor house is overrun with soldiers," he said, cutting her off. "It isn't safe there for your little Lady Clare and her nursemaid. Soon it may not be safe even for you."

"I can take care of myself," she said.

"I know." He laid a hand on her head, so like Papa for a moment she could have cried. "But you are all the world to me, Siobhan. I need you to be safe. And we need the child as well." He let her go, taking a step back as another patrol emerged from the manor house. "I will put my quarters in the ground floor, with Silas's office above and you and the women on top."

"I have to sleep in the room with the brat?" she protested.

"No, no," he promised, smiling and shaking his head. "There are two rooms on the topmost floor. They are already well furnished for a lady, I think. DuMaine must have been planning to take himself a wife."

The smile she was learning to conjure on her face whenever Tristan's name was mentioned twisted her mouth without her thinking, a bitter, reckless smile. "And so he did," she answered.

"And so he did," Sean agreed. He gave her braid a gentle tug. "Are you done soldiering tonight? Will you come inside and sleep now?"

"In a moment." She wasn't sleepy, just tired, and the thought of the manor house's crowded, smoky hall just made her feel more so. "Go on, brother. I will follow you."

He nodded, barely touching her cheek one last time. "You fret too much, Siobhan." Before she could think of an answer, he had gone inside.

She looked back at Tristan's folly, the inner fortress he had thought would keep him and his little girl safe, built on the mound of ancient magic. When she was a little girl herself, her mother had told her stories about the druids, how they had come to the people of this forest and joined their blood with theirs, giving them a portion of their power. Their magic had saved the old ones from the Saxons in the time of Arthur, magic from Merlin, the last of their race. She and Sean were the last descendants of this ancient line; their blood was tied to the mound and the tower that had stood upon it.

She drew the short sword she still carried from her belt. The blade of her first kill. She could have managed a much longer weapon now and had more than once. But this sword was a gift from the druids, or so she believed, no matter how much Sean might tease her.

"What is that?" a small voice said from so close beside her, she nearly jumped out of her skin. Looking down, she found little Clare, dressed in her nightgown.

"What does it look like?" she asked, irritated. The child had a nursemaid; why was she wandering the courtyard in the middle of the night?

"A sword," Clare answered, unperturbed. "But it's too small."

"It is too small," Siobhan agreed. She stuck the sword back into her belt. "Why aren't you asleep?"

"Because I am not sleepy." By all rights, the child should have been terrified of her, but she didn't seem to be. In truth, after her first fit of grief, she had betrayed no fear of any of them. Her father's daughter, Siobhan could not but think.

"Where is Emma?" The child shrugged, spreading her hands, but her guilty look told the true tale. Emma had a sweetheart among the soldiers. "I see," Siobhan said with a sigh.

"She thinks I am asleep." Clare looked off in the direction of the tower just as Siobhan had done. "Sean Lebuin said we were going to the tower."

"Yes." The little one called Sean by both his names, like a priest might say Jesus Christ. Or Lucifer the Damned. "He thinks you will be safer there."

"My papa said I would be safe inside the tower." Siobhan hid her flinch. If the child should ask again about her father, she wasn't certain she could lie. She had sworn to Tristan to protect his daughter, a simple oath to make. She had no desire to hurt an innocent child or to allow anyone else to do it. But how would she protect her from the truth?

"He was right," she answered. She squatted down beside the little girl, putting their faces level. "You see the drawbridge?" she said, pointing. "We will be able to pull it up if anyone attacks, so they can't climb the cliffs to reach us. And if they try, our men will be able to shoot arrows down at them and kill them. Do you understand?"

"I understand." The wide green eyes were serious and clear as they took in the drawbridge.

"No one will be able to hurt us," Siobhan promised.

The child turned her gaze back on her. "You did," she answered. "You and Sean Lebuin came inside the castle."

"Yes, but we didn't reach the tower, did we?" Siobhan answered. "If you and your papa had been inside the tower, we would never have been able to reach you." Clare nodded, her eyes clouding as she thought this over. "You see this sword," Siobhan went on, drawing it again. "Do you know where I found it?"

"You know I don't," the child answered.

"I found it in those cliffs," Siobhan said, smiling. "When I was just a little girl myself, not very much older than you." She held the hilt out to the child. "Go on and touch it." Clare obeyed, her fingers barely making contact with the leather cover of the hilt. "When you are old enough, I will give it to you." The child's eyes widened in shock. "Yes, I will," Siobhan promised. "I will teach you how to use it." She stood up again.

The little girl stared up at her, obviously puzzled. "Why would you do that?"

"Because you are my stepdaughter," she answered. "I am sworn to keep you safe." She slid the sword back into her belt. "I will teach you how to use this sword so the next time your enemy comes, you can fight him." She thought of the way Clare said "Sean Lebuin," thought of her own hatred for the Normans who had killed her mother and father. "Whoever he might be."

Understanding broke over Clare's face like sudden sunlight. "You are sworn," she echoed. "You are sworn to Papa."

The strange, unwelcome pain Siobhan had been fighting twisted in her chest, and she wanted to do something hateful and selfish to push it away, something to prove she didn't care. But Clare was innocent. She didn't deserve the fate she had been given, and Siobhan was all she had left. "Yes," she answered, making herself smile. "I am sworn to your papa." She held out a hand to the child. "Come. Let us go inside and go to sleep."

Clare hesitated for a moment, chewing her bottom lip. Then she put her hand into Siobhan's. Feeling another shiver of guilt, Siobhan led her back into the manor.

6

Over the next few nights as he moved north, Tristan discovered that being a demon could be damned inconvenient. His new aversion to sunlight gave him only the short midsummer nights for travel, and he had to feed first. Finding prey was not quite so difficult as he might have imagined. Every settlement he came to seemed to have its own villain who needed to be sent to hell for the good of the righteous, and the woods were full of bandits and thieves. But if for some reason he couldn't find a suitable victim, he found he could put off his hunger for a single night only. Any longer and he found himself in the same dire distress that had driven him to his first kill, a desperate desire that overwhelmed every other thought.

It was in this state that he discovered he could change his shape. He had been riding without feeding all night long in hopes of getting out of a knot of towns and villages where his face might be known, and had finally reached a thick, unbroken forest. He tethered his horse in a tiny clearing near a cave where he could sleep through the day—another function of his new world that he found most irritating. "Wait here," he murmured pointlessly to Daimon. That was another problem, he thought. He had never been known for his charm, but he was still accustomed to fairly constant company. In truth, he had been alone more in the past week than he ever had in his life before. Much longer, and he might run mad as well as cursed.

Putting this happy thought aside, he went out into the woods to hunt, moving silently along the narrow paths in search of some other lone traveler whose life would not be missed. For hours he searched, his demon hearing straining for the drum of a human heartbeat, but he heard nothing, and his body had begun to sense the coming of the dawn. If he did not feed that night, he feared he truly would wake up a madman at the next sunset, so far beyond reason he might slaughter any creature that came near him, even his own horse. Then how would he ever get home?

Any creature, he thought, his mind drifting as he started to run. Could the blood of any animal sustain him? As if in answer to his thoughts, a heartbeat rumbled back to him, low and powerful as distant thunder. Following the sound, he ran faster, and his vision blurred and changed. The stag sprang up from a thicket, his great head turning to look back for barely a moment before he fled. To Tristan's eyes, the beast was nothing but a blur of light, a shape in flame with a burning, scarlet heart. He followed, his reason whispering the chase's folly—no man could catch a stag on foot. But he was not a man. In a single, fluid moment, his perspective changed. He was running low to the ground, faster than a man could ever have dreamed, and all sense of weight or constriction from his clothes and the weapons he carried was gone.

He overtook the stag and took it down, leaping up to reach the animal's thickly muscled throat. Holding the beast beneath him with massive paws, he drank deeply, the blood less rich than that of men but sweeter—mead instead of wine. The creature shuddered, and he felt a vibration inside his own chest, heard his own low, thrilling growl. But as his hunger lessened, he felt a new sensation, a sense of pity he had never felt as a demon. The stag was innocent, his brother in the wild. Why must he die in fear?

He lifted his head from the animal's throat, licking the blood from his mouth. He was a dog, he realized, some huge, square-headed breed like a mastiff, with golden fur the color of his hair. The stag struggled, weaker but still strong. "Go," Tristan ordered, the word coming out as a yelp. The creature twisted, looking back at him, its eyes still wild with terror, paralyzed within the demon's gaze.

Gathering his reason, Tristan stood, his body changing, melting back into the shape of a man. He stepped back from his prey and turned his head away. "Go," he repeated, still hoarse but with a man's voice. The stag struggled to his feet, its antlers tearing at the loamy ground. In an instant, it was gone, thundering into the forest.

The wind was rising around him, the beginnings of a summer storm. Suddenly he seemed to feel a presence just behind him, some dark spirit watching his kill. He turned quickly, his hand on his sword. "Who is there?" he shouted into the night. But he saw nothing, only the empty forest. He turned back, and he heard a voice, a whisper behind the rustle of the leaves. "My son," it breathed. But his father was long dead and rotted to dust, had been since he was a boy.

The other demon, he thought. Surely it must be the demon who had made him, pursuing him in secret. Now that he thought about it, it only made sense; he had tried to stop him that first night. But why did he not show himself? He hadn't seemed particularly shy before. "Come out!" he shouted, brandishing his weapon. But no one came to confront him, and the voice died away with the wind. He stood there for several more minutes until the storm broke and the rain began. But still he saw no one.

Over the next few nights, he felt the presence often, always after a kill. But no one ever came.

At last he reached the edge of the northern woods that separated his own estate from that of the baron of Callard, a minor noble whose father had done some dark service for Henry's father and who Tristan himself had never met. He had fed well just at sunset on a thief who had tried to rob him as he slept; with luck, he might reach his own borders that night. Whistling a little under his breath with satisfaction at the thought of bringing his quest to an end, he decided to risk being seen for the sake of speed, turning Daimon off the narrow forest path and onto the broader road.

A mistake, as it turned out. He had been riding for less than an hour when he came upon a carriage, leaning precariously to one side, one of its two lead horses lying on its side, panting in the mud. As Tristan reined in, a man in livery and two armed soldiers came around the carriage and blocked his path.

"You there," the coachman ordered. "Climb down and assist us."

"I am no healer of horses," Tristan answered. In truth, even if he had been, he doubted he could have been much help. The beast on the ground had a broken leg, the bone protruding from the flesh, and a long, jagged wound down one side. The idiot had apparently tried to drive the carriage straight through a pile of deadfall and brush blocking the road.

"Did I ask your occupation?" the man said in a fury. "Who is your master?" He was looking frantically from side to side as he spoke, like a rat trapped in a corner.

Tristan almost said "Henry of England" without thinking; then he remembered his costume. "I serve no one," he answered instead.

"A brigand," one of the soldiers said, drawing his sword. "We might have guessed as much." The coachman blanched and retreated as the soldiers moved forward. "Give us the horse, villain," the soldier said.

"Never, by my life," Tristan answered, smiling a little at the joke. He was fairly certain he could dispatch all three if he had to, but he was worried about his horse. Daimon's loyalty had already been tested to all reasonable limits by his own condition; putting him in the midst of such a fight might frighten him away for good. "But I will climb down and have a look at yours."

The soldiers smiled, exchanging a look. "Very well," the first one said, taking a step back.

Tristan moved quickly to the poor beast on the ground. "Idiot," he muttered, fixing the coachman with a glare. "There now, dear," he spoke softly to the fallen horse, stroking her foam-specked muzzle. "The worst is over now." With his sword, he quickly cut the suffering animal's throat.

"You will pay for that!" the second soldier said.

"No." Tristan straightened up, his sword still drawn. "You will."

They both rushed him, obviously expecting he would fight like a brigand berserker, but of course he did not. He crouched slightly, waiting, then cleaved the first one's head from his shoulders with a single, graceful arc of his sword. The second one slashed at his back as he turned, cutting his flesh to the bone in a strike that would have dropped a mortal man. But Tristan barely flinched. Whirling like the fiend he was, he brought his sword up, point-first, into the soldier's belly.

"No," the coachman protested, breathless with fear.

"You cannot . . . we are the baron of Callard's men, you fool!"

"What of it?" Tristan said, moving toward him. He was not hungry, but something in the coachman's look of horror brought out the demon's killing rage inside him even so.

"Lebuin will hear of this," he warned, stumbling backward. "The baron will see you hang."

"In faith, sirrah, I doubt it." The wind whispered softly through the trees, and for a moment Tristan thought he heard a laugh. He jerked his head around to look, but there was no one.

"Doubt if you will," the coachman said as Tristan turned back to him. His throat worked nervously as his hand went to his own sword, the jerky reflex of a man unaccustomed to battle. "But your captain will not save you."

"I have no captain." Again, he scanned the woods on every side for some sign of someone else. But there was nothing; no other heartbeat whispered to him from the dark. In the instant that his gaze was turned away, the coachman attacked. Almost by reflex, Tristan caught him, dropping his sword as he went for his throat.

Straightening up from the kill, he again felt the presence of another, the same prickle of foreboding on his skin. He whirled around, taking up his sword. "Show yourself!" But just as before, there was no one.

He looked down at the dead man at his feet. He knew he should bury him and his companions, or better yet,

burn them. This was a main road; someone would find
them. But he didn't have the heart. Wiping his mouth
with his sleeve, he turned away. He released the second
horse from its harness and gave it a gentle swat, sending it trotting down the road. "Daimon, come." His
own horse trotted to him, head lowered as if in salute.
Tristan sheathed his sword and swung into the saddle.
Turning aside from the broad road again, he galloped
toward Castle DuMaine.

All was quiet for a long, still moment. Then the
corpse of the coachman shuddered, the flesh of the
face contorting as if at some new horror. The eyes
snapped shut, then open, once, then again. The mouth
twisted into a smile. "My son . . ." The voice seemed to
echo through the clearing on the wind, swirling
through the trees, until it came again. "My son." This
time the dead thing's mouth formed the words, and the
voice came from the ruined throat.

He sat up awkwardly, a puppet on a string. He lifted
the sword, a clumsy arc so wide he nearly cut his
throat before he stopped. He let it fall, then lifted it
again, more slowly this time, and the set of his shoulders was softer, more natural. More alive. He smiled
again, a gruesome, clownish leer. Leaning on the
sword, he staggered to his feet. Using the sword as a
crutch, he limped away into the forest.

Tristan found a shelter in the forest, a man-made
cavern dug into a hillside, probably made by Lebuin
and his bandits in the days when they were still a minor

annoyance and he was still a man. He slept fitfully throughout the day, his rest tortured by dreams of his daughter and Siobhan, the beautiful demon who called herself his wife.

Sometime near sunset, the dream turned darker and more familiar. He was standing in a golden hall, dazzled by torchlight dancing on jewel-studded columns. The floor was strewn with corpses, pale men in English armor, their throats all torn open. He saw the demon who had made him, the young knight with long black hair, standing near the dais of the hall, his bloody sword in hand. A dark-haired woman crouched before him on her knees, her hands raised up, entreating him for death. "No!" a little man cried out, rushing between them.

"My son." He heard the voice from behind him just as he did when he was awake, a whisper on the wind. He turned as quickly as he could, his body heavy and sluggish in the dream, and this time he saw the man who spoke. He was tall and thin, dressed in a robe of gold embroidered all over in scarlet, queer symbols like nothing Tristan had ever seen. His pale red hair was long and lank over his shoulders, and his mustache and beard trailed to his chest. "My son," he repeated, opening his arms as if he thought Tristan would embrace him. "You are magnificent."

"Who are you?" Tristan demanded. Behind him he could hear the others speaking, but he could not make out what they said. He reached for his sword but found he had none, no weapons of any kind. "What am I?"

The tall man in the robe just smiled. "I will come to you," he promised. The shape of his body began to change, shrinking shorter and broadening at the shoulders. The long, pale hair turned darker and short, the face clean-shaven and young. Something about this new figure was familiar, as if he might have seen him in passing in a crowd. "You will understand."

"Tell me!" He tried to take a step toward the men, but his feet wouldn't move. "Tell me now!" But the dream was fading, dissolving into mist.

He opened his eyes to find the young demon who had made him looking down on him, holding a stake of wood. "You!" he roared, lunging up to seize him, the two of them rolling as one across the earthen floor of the bunker. His maker tried to drive the stake into his chest, but Tristan grabbed his wrist and twisted, wrenching the weapon away. "Who are you?" He raised the stake himself and saw a flicker of fear in the other creature's eyes. "What did you do to me?"

Moving fast as lightning, the demon struck the stake aside with enough force to knock it from Tristan's grasp. "What did I do to you?" he echoed with a laugh. "Idiot!" Tristan reached for his throat, and he grabbed his arms and tried to pin him to the floor, sending them rolling again. "I tried to release you—"

"To kill me, you mean." Yanking free, Tristan punched him, making his head snap back. But before he could press this advantage, the demon recovered, baring fangs like Tristan's own and lunging for him again.

"You were already dead," he said, rising to his feet and dragging Tristan by the tunic with him. Standing, he was half a head shorter than Tristan and much more slight of build, but in strength he was apparently his match.

"Not quite," Tristan retorted. He drew the dagger from his belt and slashed the other demon across the face.

"Bastard!" the demon swore, his Irish accent more pronounced as he drew back in pain. The wound was deep, but it barely bled before it began to heal itself.

"Likewise," Tristan snarled, grabbing his opponent by the shoulders and shoving with all his strength until he pinned him to the wall. "Who are you?"

"Your brother, idiot." The Irishman made a token effort to free himself, but he seemed more amused now than angry. "Whether either of us likes it or not."

"I told you," a voice said from the shadows. The small, bearded man Tristan had seen in his dream stepped into the pool of moonlight falling through the narrow door. "I knew you couldn't just destroy him."

Tristan was fast losing patience. "I have no brothers," he answered, yanking the other demon toward him, then bashing him against the wall again. "Who are you?"

His opponent frowned, then drove his forehead full force into Tristan's, making him see stars, demon or not. "Son of a bitch," he muttered, rubbing his forehead, and Tristan, sitting on the floor again, was inclined to agree with him. "Pax, boy, for pity . . ." He offered his hand. "I am Simon, duke of Lyan."

"Duke of Lyan?" Tristan knew the name, a mostly useless manor of the crown in Ireland. But he had never heard tell of its master being a monster.

"For the moment, anyway." When Tristan had first seen him, he had seemed half wild, a creature of the dark. Now he looked like any other noble knight, albeit prettier than most with his long black hair and wicked grin. "And this is Orlando the wizard."

"Wizard?" The ache in his head was fading, but he still felt just as confused. He looked back and forth between them, remembering his dream. "Where is the girl?"

The other two exchanged a look. "What girl?" Simon said slowly.

"The girl who wanted you to kill her." He climbed back to his feet. "I saw her with you in my dream." His sword was still lying beside where he'd been sleeping, and he silently calculated how quickly he could reach it.

"I told you," the man called Orlando told the demon knight, Simon, again. "He was an accident, but he is not for killing."

"An accident?" Tristan echoed.

"I didn't mean to make you," Simon explained. "I meant to kill you."

"Ah," Tristan nodded, nonplussed.

"It was nothing personal," Simon promised, his mouth quirking up in a grin.

"We need him," Orlando pressed on as if they hadn't spoken. The graybeard stood barely waist high to his companion, and he wore the mottled clothes of a fool. But he was obviously accustomed to ordering this Simon about like a child with the manner of a giant and an emperor combined. "He has a place in your quest."

"I thank you for your kindness, sirrah," Tristan said sarcastically. "But I have a quest of my own."

"Your quest is salvation," the little wizard answered, turning his airs on Tristan now. "The destruction of evil—"

"What makes you think so, wizard?" Tristan cut him off. "Why should I give myself to such things when I believe in neither?" He turned back to Simon. "Tell me who I am." He picked up his sword. "Tell me what you made me, accident or not."

"A vampire," Simon answered. Tristan frowned, and he smiled. "The word means nothing to you, I know— it meant nothing to me either."

"So what is it?" He had no time for riddles. His child was left to the mercy of his enemies; he had problems enough of his own. "What is a vampire?"

"A child of evil," Orlando said. "A mortal possessed of a demon that gives him a demon's strength but denies him the light."

"I know that much already," Tristan retorted. "How is such a creature made?"

"You know that as well," Simon answered. "I am a vampire; I drank your blood; in the struggle, you drank mine. That made you a vampire, too. The matters of the soul are more complex, but that is the most practical explanation."

"I care nothing for matters of the soul," Tristan scoffed.

"Have a care, boy," Simon said, making Tristan bristle. In truth, Simon didn't look as old as he was himself. "Do you love this demon's life so much you wish to keep it forever?"

"Why not?" Tristan said with a careless smile of his own. "Am I not immortal now?"

"No." Simon drew his sword so quickly, Tristan never saw him move until it was poised at his throat. "Not really," he went on. "If I should take your head or drive a stake through your heart, you would die, and your soul would be damned." He let the sword fall and sheathed it.

"So that is what you meant to do just now before I woke?" Tristan said, turning to him. "Send my soul to hell?"

The handsome demon's eyes went wide for a moment. "I suppose," he admitted. "In truth, I hadn't really thought of that. I knew I was not meant to make another vampire, so I meant to correct my mistake . . ." His expression seemed truly contrite. "I am sorry, Tristan."

"Is that why you were following me?" As much as he wanted to hear the truth about what he had become, he was more concerned about his own business. These two seemed all wrapped up in some fool's crusade of God and souls and demons, nothing that was any use to him.

"We picked up your trail a week or so ago," Simon said. "In truth, it wasn't hard. You weren't exactly discreet in your murders." He grinned. "The sheriff was an interesting choice."

"He was a pig," Tristan said with a frown, remembering the man. "I saw him procure three different farmers' daughters for ruin in the space of one night. I doubt he'll be much missed."

"There was quite a celebration," Simon admitted. "But are all of your victims such villains?"

"Just lately? Yes," Tristan answered. He thought of the brigand he had drained the night before and smiled. "You say I am your brother. Why have you called me your son?"

"I have not," Simon said with a frown.

"I heard you," Tristan said. "Not three nights past when I had killed a coachman." He thought of the man he had seen in his dream and the way he had changed his appearance. But Simon had been in the dream as well, as himself. "I dreamed of you just now," he said. "That's why I asked you about the girl; I saw you and Orlando and a woman in a hall of gold with columns covered in jewels."

"Sweet saints," Simon muttered, and the wizard mumbled an oath as well in a language Tristan didn't understand.

"There was another man as well," he went on, watching their faces. "Tall, with long red hair. He called me his son."

"Kivar," Simon said. "The vampire who made me. His spirit must still haunt my blood—"

"Not so," Orlando cut him off. "You know that is not true." Both of their expressions were grave. "He lives."

"He said that he would come to me," Tristan said. "He said that I would understand." The details of the dream were fading as he spoke of it; he was losing the face of the man he described. "You say he is another vampire?"

"He is more than that," Orlando said.

"A vampire can be killed, just as I told you," Simon explained with a bitter smile. "I've killed Lucan Kivar twice already."

"His demon soul is released from his body," Orlando said, as if this were supposed to make sense. "He can possess the dead, take on any shape he likes until his quest is done."

"When you drank my blood, you became as I am, but you are still yourself," Simon said. "At the moment of death, you were transformed to something else, from mortal man to vampire. Kivar used to be the same, I think—he made me just as I made you, except that he acted on purpose. But now he attacks corpses, men already dead. He takes possession of their bodies and pilfers their minds." His scowl darkened as if some memory pained him very much. "He can see their memories; he knows what they wanted, what they thought. But the spirit in control of the body is Kivar."

Tristan's own flesh crawled with horror at the thought of such a thing, but he refused to show it. "So Lucan Kivar is evil," he said, keeping his tone flat. "But you are not."

"I am," Simon answered. "But not by choice."

"Simon is sworn to destroy Lucan Kivar," Orlando said. "Now you must help him."

"I must?" Tristan said, arching an eyebrow.

"Orlando has made a study of Kivar for many years," Simon explained. "He believes that he can be destroyed with a holy relic from the time of his making, a Chalice." Tristan's doubts must have shown in his face, because the other demon smiled. "I did not believe it either," he admitted. "I used to be a Crusader; I have seen enough of holy relics to know their uses well, and destroying true evil is not one of them."

"But you believe in this one?" Tristan said, still skeptical.

"I have seen it." Again, his expression clouded as if at some remembered horror. "More important, I have seen Kivar's reaction to it. Whatever the Chalice may be, Lucan Kivar wants to possess it, and I know enough of him to know that whatever he wants, I do not."

"So you mean to have it first." Tristan had served with knights of chivalry since he was ten years old; he had heard every fairy story about the Grail ever devised and believed not a single one. But watching his so-called brother's face, he could not doubt he believed in this chalice, or that he would do anything to win it.

"The Chalice is salvation," Orlando said. "For Simon and for you as well. If the two of you find it, you can be restored to mortal life."

"And why in hell's name would I want that?" Tristan laughed. He needed answers, instruction in the powers this vampire had passed on to him, not some myth of evil spirits and magical cups. "You witnessed the end of my mortal life, Simon—did it seem so grand I should want to relive it?"

"I don't know you," Simon admitted. "I know you had been treated badly, that the men with you meant to see you dead. I smelled the evil in their blood; 'tis why I was drawn to them in the first place."

"You know nothing," Tristan scoffed. "The men you killed were nothing, no more than messengers. My true enemy still lives, a common thief who has stolen my castle, my title, even my child. You say you are sworn to this quest, and may all good go with you, but I am sworn as well. To my king, to hold these lands for the crown. To my child, to protect her from evil."

"What is your king compared to the power of the Chalice?" Orlando said disdainfully. "How can you protect your child as a creature of evil yourself?"

"Tristan, I know what it is to seek vengeance," Simon said in a much more sympathetic tone. "I know the sacred honor of a knight, sworn to the service of my lord, and I know what it is to love. But Orlando is right. So long as you are a vampire, you cannot serve your king or save your child. You can only bring them darkness and can only give them pain." He took a step closer. "Kivar has come to you in dreams. You have heard his voice. If you do not fight him, he will destroy you and all that you love."

"Kivar is a dream, a fantasy," Tristan answered. "Sean Lebuin is real."

"Oh, Kivar is real enough," Orlando said bitterly. "You should pray you do not learn too soon how real."

"I do not pray," Tristan retorted. "Nor have I ever done." He met Simon's dark eyes with his own. "You speak of holy relics, of salvation. Even as a man, I held no hope in such things. You speak of this demon we carry as if it were a curse, but for me, it is a blessing. I have no love for killing, but I have never feared it, have never hesitated to kill to achieve what I wanted or the glory of my king. This power you would be rid of is all that I could wish, all I need to see my justice done."

"Your justice?" Simon said with another twisted half-smile.

"Aye, sirrah, my justice," Tristan said. "You search for this chalice so you might escape damnation for your sins. Believe me when I tell you, I am already damned."

"And what if you succeed?" Simon asked. "If you have your vengeance—your justice, you call it—what then? Will you take this child of yours into darkness? Will you play lord of the castle as a demon?"

"Do you not?" Tristan countered. "Your grace?"

"Nay, sir, I do not." Pain darkened his eyes. "I know what evil Kivar holds for me and for my love—may you never know as much. I will not rest until I know he is destroyed." He met Tristan's gaze with his own. "And neither should you."

"I will not join you," Tristan answered, refusing to be moved. He could not afford to be distracted. "When my castle is secure and my daughter is safe, if you still want me, I will consider it. But for now, you must forgive me."

"Madness," Orlando fumed. "Stupid, arrogant—"

"Enough," Simon stopped him, putting a hand on his shoulder. "I do forgive you, Tristan, and I will trouble you no more unless you ask it." He offered his hand, and Tristan clasped it, thinking this the strangest offer of alliance he had ever heard tell of in his life. "I just hope you do not find you cannot forgive yourself."

"I will risk it," Tristan answered. He looked down at the little wizard, still fuming but silent. "But I thank you for your hopes." Nodding once more to his strange brother in blood, he left the hillside hovel and whistled for his horse.

Simon watched him ride away, shaking his head. "It's not fair," he muttered. "Ten years before I found a mount who would bear me, yet this one . . . Why should his horse not fear him?"

"Because he knows he is an idiot," Orlando muttered. "What now, warrior? You cannot kill him."

"No," Simon agreed. "But we can follow." He looked

down at his friend with a bitter smile. "Kivar will be along."

Over the next few days, Sean made good on his promise to move them all into the tower. When Siobhan came into the lower chamber looking for her brother one afternoon an hour or so before sunset, she found it buzzing with activity, ready to serve as the castle's new main hall. Several of the trestle tables from the manor had already been carried in and set against the walls, and a huge tapestry Sean had taken in one of their forest raids was being hung behind a newly raised dais along the back wall. "Quite passable," said a passing servant who had once served Tristan DuMaine, obviously pleased. "Wouldn't you say so, my lady?"

She made herself smile as she glanced in his direction. "Very nice." In truth, she felt sick, the shiver of dread she felt every time she passed the threshold of this tower writhing in her stomach. Sean could say what he liked about the sin being DuMaine's; she knew better. They had no business living here, not in this new tower. This hill belonged to the Old Ones, and it always would. If they did not mean to honor them, they would do well to leave it alone. "Where is my brother?"

The servant frowned. "I don't know." A chair with ridiculously ornate carvings on its back and arms was being carried in by two men she barely knew—soldiers of Tristan's old garrison. "He was here half an hour ago."

Their answer quickly came. "The baron's man is dead, Lebuin!" Gaston was raging, following Sean down the stairs. "Another is likely the same, and the third will not live out the week—from what the messenger said, he could be dead already!"

"I feel the baron's grief, Gaston," Sean answered, sounding tired and annoyed. "But what is that to me?"

"The survivor said the man was yours," Gaston insisted.

"Then he was mistaken." He caught sight of Siobhan. "I have no more men in the forest."

"Then where did this brigand come from?" Gaston glanced at her as well and hesitated before he went on. "Who else would attack the baron's coach?"

"I couldn't say," Sean said mildly, the expression on his face telling his sister he was reaching the end of his patience. "What does your survivor say about it?"

"He raves," Gaston muttered. "He swears the man attacked the coachman and tore out his throat like a dog, but the coachman was gone when we found them."

"Perhaps the coachman did the killing," Sean suggested. Siobhan joined them, and he smiled. "Or perhaps it was some lunatic run off from his people or set loose in the woods."

"A lunatic who took down two of the baron's best soldiers with a sword?" Gaston was sweating, she saw—how marvelous. "The baron is furious, Lebuin. He will want answering—"

"And I will answer." Her brother fixed the courtier

with the glare that could make the rowdiest brigand quake in his boots. "Come, Siobhan." He held out his hand, and she took it.

"The baron is coming!" Gaston insisted. "He is coming here—"

"And we will welcome him." He turned his back on Gaston and led Siobhan up the stairs.

He took her to the topmost chamber of the tower. A workman assembled a huge cabinet bed on one side of the room. "Come and see your view," Sean said, taking her to the window. "You can see all the way to the river."

"We should station a guard here, then," she answered. Tapestries depicting girls petting unicorns and other such nonsense had been hung around the walls, and a heavy oak wardrobe stood open to reveal the gowns hanging within. "What was he talking about, Sean?"

"Some of the baron's men were attacked in the forest," he answered. "Never mind; it has naught to do with us."

"But he said the baron was coming here." A delicate screen had been set up in the corner of the room. "What is that?" she muttered, peering around it.

"A privy closet, little heathen," he answered with a laugh. "Surely you haven't forgotten."

"I'm perfectly capable of using the necessary on the wall like everyone else," she grumbled.

"In the dead of night, you mean to walk all the way

down the stairs, across the courtyard, and up onto the wall?" he teased. "That's quite a voyage."

"Better that than to expect someone else to carry my piss out in the morning," she retorted.

"Don't say piss." He looked her over with a frown. "What have you been doing?"

"Practicing my bow," she answered. "And I'll say piss if I bloody well feel like it, thank you. Stop changing the subject; why is the baron coming here?"

"You have no need to practice anymore," he said, still frowning. "You are the Lady DuMaine now, remember?"

"The hell I am." Her head was starting to hurt, the oppressive air of the tower closing in around her. "Sean, enough. Why is the baron coming? What manner of madness are you plotting now?"

"It isn't madness." His eyes slid from hers. "Gaston should not have spoken of it before you."

"No, he shouldn't have. You should have told me yourself." He reached for her arm, but she shook him off. "Since when is that puffed-up popinjay your confidante? Am I nothing now?"

"Siobhan, you are everything." He took hold of her shoulders, holding tighter when she moved to shrug away. "Everything that has been done has been for you, for our family. How can you doubt that?"

"Because our family now is you and me," she answered. "And half of us don't know what the plan might be from one moment to the next."

His eyes narrowed as he frowned. "You think that I would bring you harm?" he said, letting her go.

"No, never," she answered at once. "You would protect me with your life, I know." This time it was she who reached out for him, laying a hand on his arm. "But I think perhaps you mean to protect me too much."

He smiled, some of the tension leaving his face. "Perhaps you are right," he admitted.

"Am I not your soldier?" she asked him, pressing the moment. "Have I not proven time and time again that I am strong, that I can do what must be done to win our cause?"

"Yes," he answered. "Too often." A strange shadow seemed to pass over his eyes. "I have asked too much."

"Never," she insisted.

"Yes." He touched a lock of her hair that had escaped her braid, drawing it down along her jaw. "I should have taken you away from here when you were still a child, moved heaven and earth to give you the life you deserve."

"You have given me all that I wanted." She took his hand and clasped it tightly. "You gave us both our revenge."

"But at what cost?" He's frightened, she suddenly realized, a horrifying thought. She had never seen Sean look worried. Even in their earliest days as brigands in the forest with a hundred Norman soldiers riding hot upon their heels, he had always seemed so certain they would escape, that somehow they would win. But now he seemed haunted, even desperate. Could he fear this baron of Callard? But why? "I know you think I am a fool to try to hold this castle," he said.

"No," she promised. "Not a fool—"

"But if we don't, what then?" He looked down at her hand, still clasped in his. "I would gladly hang from a gibbet to avenge our father's death and make his people free, even for a moment." He looked up again with tears in his eyes, a terrible, heart-rending shock. "But not you." He framed her face in his hands as their father might have done. "I cannot let you die."

"Sean, no one will hang from a gibbet," she insisted. "We can leave this place, disappear into the forest—"

"It's too late for that, Siobhan." He let her go. "We killed the king's cousin, or have you forgotten?"

"No," she answered. "I have not forgotten."

"If we should try to run, we will be admitting our guilt." He turned away from her, going back to the window. "We have to stay here, stay with the plan. We must make them believe that DuMaine died in an accident, that you were his wife in truth."

"And so we will," she promised. "We have the sheets, and the people will say whatever we ask them to say—"

"The word of peasants will not sway the crown," he cut her off. "And who knows what they will say come winter, when Henry finally finds the time to make his inquiry?"

"They are our people," she protested. "They hated DuMaine." But was that true? her mutinous mind seemed to whisper. Since they had come to the castle, she had heard no one say they regretted the death of DuMaine. But no one had said they had hated him, either. She had found no evidence of his oppression, heard no tales of cruelty or torture. In truth, he had apparently been quite tolerant for a Norman lord. "We have freed them," she finished, pushing those thoughts away.

"And ruined their crops in the process," he answered. "Have you seen the stores, little sister? We will be hungry, come Christmas. DuMaine and his rule might not seem like such a hardship then." A bitter smile twisted the corner of his mouth. "A slave can be contented if his belly is kept full."

"You don't believe that," she said.

"Do I not?" He looked down on the courtyard. "We need help, Siobhan. Someone with a noble title who can vouch for your claim to the king, someone who can help us feed our people."

"The baron of Callard." A cold despair seemed to cover her like a wet blanket. If Sean was losing hope, what chance did she have of keeping hers?

"Gaston is a villain and a toady besides," he said, turning back to her. "But his master is not. The baron's father was a Norman, but his mother was English, a child of these forests like our own. He was born here and has never been to court."

"Then how can he help us?" she said, trying not to sound sullen.

"His father was a powerful ally of King Henry's father," he explained. "The king has often offered the baron his favor, lands in France, even, but the baron has no wish to leave his home. He hates the Normans almost as much as we do, for all his father was one of them. He believes as we do that the people of these forests are not born to be serfs but free men."

"He has no serfs of his own?" Sean sounded so hopeful, she hated to dispute him. But his patron sounded a bit too good to be true. Particularly when his own man, Gaston, seemed to be terrified of him.

"Yes, but not as DuMaine and his ilk would have them, not as slaves to be exploited and abandoned," he answered. "They serve him because he protects them, and no man is forced to stay. He treats them with justice, and they are loyal in return, just as the people here once were loyal to our father." Her doubt must have shown on her face. "What did you think would happen, Siobhan? If we had simply done away with DuMaine and abandoned these people, what do you think would have happened to them?"

"I don't know," she admitted. She had often wondered just that, but she had never allowed herself to dwell on it. She had always just assumed that Sean knew what he was doing, that he would have a plan that would make good on all his promises. Was this alliance the plan? she wondered now. She had always known the baron was Sean's ally, that they had met together in secret even from her, but she had never realized how important his brother believed his help really was.

"The king would have sent another courtier just like DuMaine to take his place, a Norman lord who would likely have punished them for DuMaine's death by burning every cottage he could find and hanging every able-bodied man he could catch," he went on. "Is that what our father would have wanted?"

"Of course not." The sun was setting, painting the walls of DuMaine's white castle shades of purple and red. In the courtyard below, she could see Master Silas and his masons gathering their tools to put them away for the night. The wooden palisade she and the others had burned so easily with their flaming arrows was almost completely gone, replaced with stone. By the first snowfall, the castle would be finished, just as Sean wanted. "If Tristan's castle is finished when the king's man comes, he will be more likely to believe he died by chance," she said, understanding at last.

"Exactly so." She turned to find Sean smiling. "Now do you see I am not mad?"

She still wasn't so sure. "If this baron of Callard is the man you say, of course we are glad to have his help," she said. "But why should he come here?"

"To be here when the king's man comes, I hope," he answered. He seemed to hesitate, as if deciding just how much he should tell her. "But even if he is not . . ."

"What?" she prompted.

"The baron is not married." He cradled her cheek in

his hand. "He is a young man, and handsome, and you are beautiful. If you were to marry the baron; if you could make him love you—"

"You mean to marry me off again?" she demanded, recoiling.

"Only for love," he insisted. "If he loved you, he would use all of his power, all of his influence to keep our people safe, and he could do it, Siobhan. I'm a brigand, a criminal; what can I do? But he could."

"Sean, this is madness." He couldn't be saying these things; surely she must be dreaming. He could not want to use her as a woman-pawn again, a thing to be bartered away.

"He could keep you safe, you and our people," he said. "If you were his wife, no one would dare to threaten you, not even King Henry himself."

"You can't be serious," she scoffed. "Why should the baron want to marry me? My last groom was bound and gagged at the altar, you'll recall."

"This would be completely different." He drew her over to a mirror that was propped against the wall. "Look at yourself, Siobhan. Even dressed as a brigand, you are fair. Imagine how beautiful you could be if you let Emma or one of the other women help you—"

"Shall I paint my face as well?" she demanded, jerking free. "Shall I wear bells upon my feet and gambol like a monkey?" She could gladly have slapped him silly; her palm was fairly itching to do it. "If you need a whore, brother, the camp outside the castle walls is full of them, all more than willing to do as you bid. I am a soldier—"

"You are a woman," he retorted. "A lady born of noble blood, fair to look upon. As a soldier, you will never be better than adequate, another bow to fill the gaps, expendable. As a lady, you might rule the world."

"That's a lie!" Tears stung her eyelids, but she would not let them fall. "I am the best archer you have, and you know it."

"I have no more need of archers." He softened his tone. "Yes, little sister, you have fought well, much better than I ever could have hoped. But I should never have put you in such a position; I should never have risked your life. What would our father say if he should know it?"

"He would be proud," she insisted. "We have avenged him and our mother. We have saved their people."

"Not yet, we have not," he answered. "But you can."

"No," she said, shaking her head.

"Listen to me." The desperate fear she hated had come back into his eyes. "I do not ask you to play the whore for Callard or any other man. If you do not like him when he comes, leave him be, and I will not dispute you. But what harm could there be in thinking on the match? What will it cost you to wear a proper gown and be a proper woman for once in your life?"

"You don't know," she answered. *What perversity made you wear that gown?* Tristan had asked her. *Bound to the bed, knowing she meant to see him dead,* her enemy had known her. He had wanted her, not as a pawn, not dressed up like some pretty painted doll, but as herself. As much as he had despised her, he had died to kiss her lips. "You could never understand," she told this brother that she loved with all her heart. "And I could never tell you." Before he could answer, she had turned and run away, pushing past a line of servants on the stairs to escape the tower.

7

Tristan stood at the edge of the woods as twilight fell, not certain he believed his eyes. He had expected to find his castle a broken ruin, the villagers scattered to the winds as they had been when he first came here. But if he hadn't known better, he would have sworn the events of a fortnight before had never happened. The castle was perfectly intact, the only sign of damage a freshly thatched roof on the gatehouse. Guards patrolled the high stone wall—his guards, many of them. The drawbridge was closed, but a boy waded at the edge of the moat, catching fish or tadpoles in a little net. Where was Clare? he thought. Was she still inside?

From behind him came the bay of hounds and rumble of hooves—a hunting party. He faded back into the thicker shadows as they passed, the leader blowing his horn to signal the guardsmen above. The dogs snuffed the ground, catching his scent, perhaps. He smiled, baring his teeth at them. Now he had a plan.

The sun was gone by the time Silas had finished shutting down construction for the night, its last light fading above the castle walls. As he gathered up his plans and the money box, he heard the portcullis opening. Turning, he saw a party of hunters coming over the drawbridge, raucous with success. Of the half a dozen men, only two had come to the castle with Sean Lebuin, he noticed. A month ago the others had been soldiers of Tristan DuMaine and had seemed, to him at least, to be happy to be so. But now they hunted with their master's killers. With a sigh, he turned away, willing himself to think on it no more. He was a scholar, not a noble; the vagaries of politics should not be his concern.

But for some reason, he found his eyes drawn to the dogs. Most of them trotted behind the hunting party toward the kennels, their tongues lolling out from the long day's hunt. But one, a great golden mastiff, barely seemed to be winded, and it did not follow the others. As the hunters dismounted and the other dogs danced around their feet, eager for attention, this one ignored them, slipping fearlessly between their horses to disappear into the shadows near the wall.

A dog, he thought, shaking his head again. Now I am fretting over a dog. Tucking his scrolls under his arm, he followed his crew into the hall.

As Silas disappeared from the courtyard, Tristan rose up in his human form in the shadowed corner of the high stone wall. Inside the castle was even more at ease. The courtyard buzzed with perfectly normal activity, the household settling in for the night. He might still have been master here for all the difference his absence had apparently made.

"Hello!" he heard a woman's voice cry out, and he shrank back against the wall, his hand half-consciously clenched into a fist. Siobhan was coming toward the hunting party. "Did you find success?"

"Aye, my lady," one of the hunters answered—Donnell, Tristan's own master of the kennels, he realized with a painful shudder of rage. Had they all betrayed him?

" 'Tis amazing how much easier it is to find game when you're not being hunted yourself," another one laughed—one of Lebuin's brigands. Siobhan laughed with him and clasped his hand in greeting. "Where is Sean?" the brigand asked her now.

"In his precious tower." She was dressed like a ragamuffin squire again, her glossy black hair braided down her back. But in the dim light of the torches, her skin glowed like pale gold, and her wide blue eyes looked black. Even now, Tristan found himself remembering the way her skin had felt beneath his hands, the taste of her tongue in his mouth.

"Come, love," the brigand said to her, putting an arm around her shoulders. "Join us in the hall." He led her away toward the manor house, and Tristan took a half-conscious step forward before he could stop himself. No, he thought. Not yet. Fading back into the shadows, he turned and headed for the tower.

He moved between two mounds of broken stone that had been heaped behind the castle chapel—pagan cairns for the traitors he had executed. The brigands had honored their own kin, but the chapel itself was still a half-burned ruin. The bailey wall was finished, as was the second drawbridge leading to the motte—the fatal flaw that had finished him corrected. Sean meant to make a defense. But what of Silas? He had caught a glimpse of him as he'd come in with the dogs, so he was still alive, and the progress on the construction showed he was still working. But under what sort of duress? The master mason knew the truth of what had happened at this place, and Tristan couldn't believe Lebuin could have swayed his loyalty. He might not be a warrior, but Silas had honor, nonetheless. If Lebuin truly meant to rule these lands as lord, he couldn't mean to leave Silas alive for long.

Luckily, he thought, Lebuin would soon be dead himself.

"You there!" A man was coming across the bridge to the motte. "Where are you supposed to be?" he demanded.

Tristan smiled, recognizing him. This was the captain who had put his knights to the axe. "Right here," he answered, moving into the light.

Recognition flashed in the brigand captain's eyes, and his face went pale. "You . . ." He turned as if to flee, and Tristan lunged, driving him flat to the ground. "Help!" the brigand tried to cry out, but it was too late.

In a single moment, Tristan's fangs tore open his throat, silencing him forever.

He let the empty husk fall to the ground and straightened up again. Above him on the motte, the tower windows flickered with candlelight. Licking the last of the blood from his lips, he waited, watching the guards on the other side of the drawbridge. They were relaxed, passing a bottle back and forth—easy duty. The guards on the castle wall were the ones who had to be watchful. Any fool could see the tower was safe.

Tristan looked down into the rocky ditch that separated the spot where he stood from the motte. A man could never have crossed it without the drawbridge, not without being cut to ribbons by archers from the tower above. But a dog could do it.

He leapt into a crouch, changing his form as he went. The steep bank crumbled under his paws as he scrambled to the bottom, but the ground below was solid, as was the motte. It was a natural cliff, a steep-sided hill that he and Silas had hardly believed could be real when they had found it, so perfect was it for their purpose. He bounded fast around the foot of the cliff, darting in and out of the thorny brush. Anyone watching from above would think he was chasing a rabbit.

But when he had reached the back of the tower, he stood up again as a man. Looking up once more to make certain no one saw him, he began to climb.

•   •   •

Siobhan caught the bottle that was being passed around the hearth and took a long swallow before she passed it on again. "Careful, my lady," Michael warned.

"Aye, love, be careful." Sam, the leader of the hunting party, laughed. He had been with Sean from the beginning, had served their father years ago. "You don't want to get yourself so drunk you bruise your pretty arse."

"It wouldn't be the first time," she retorted, laughing with him. But very few in the circle seemed happy to join them, she noticed.

"Yes, but things are different now," another of the men protested, glancing at the new ones, the men who had once served DuMaine. "You are the widowed lady of DuMaine." The girl in his lap pressed a kiss to his cheek, and he turned from the discussion to squeeze her close.

"And what is that?" Siobhan scoffed, blushing in spite of herself at this display. In the woods, no man would have dared bring his doxy to the fire for fear of putting the lass in danger. But now, she supposed, they were safe.

"Leave my lady be, ye milksop," Sam ordered, drinking again himself. "What is it to you what she might do? Nothing, that's what."

"Exactly," Siobhan said, taking back the bottle. She had always been fond of Sam.

"Nothing now," Michael said quietly. "But when the king's man comes to hear what happened to his cousin, it might mean a great deal." His eyes met hers in warning. "To all of us."

"God's might!" she swore, leaping to her feet. "Will you not leave me in peace?" Did of all them know more of her brother's plans for her than she did? she thought. She looked at the peasant girl, so pretty in her kirtle, and her stomach writhed in horror. Was that what she was meant to be, some pretty pet for a noble instead of a brigand? She thought again of Tristan, his bitter but beautiful smile as he'd called her "little wife." But Tristan was dead. He had despised her for a lowborn brigand, but he had wanted her. Would the baron be the same? "I can't," she said aloud. Her eyes met Michael's for a moment as she turned and fled the hall.

Tristan climbed the iron ladder hidden in a fold of the tower to the narrow escape door above. With luck, the brigands wouldn't have discovered it yet.

Slipping inside, he found himself in the narrow gallery above the first floor hall—unguarded, he noted with an inward sigh of relief. Lebuin apparently meant to make his great hall here. The room that had been little more than bare walls during Tristan's residence was now fully if haphazardly furnished with tapestries and trestle tables. But it was all but empty. Lebuin was standing near the dais, with one other man seated on a chair before him. "Get out," he ordered, obviously angry. "Get out, Gaston."

"Are you certain?" the stranger said. "We still have much to discuss."

"We have nothing to discuss," Lebuin said with a nasty snarl. "Get out."

The other man shrugged. "As you will." He took a cup from the table and drained it before he left the hall. Tristan moved back against the wall as he went out. Now was his chance. He opened the hidden panel behind him and moved quickly down the tightly spiraled wooden stairway beyond, emerging in an alcove hidden behind a tapestry. He and Silas had planned this route as a final escape for any trapped within the tower, but it worked just as well as a secret way inside.

Lebuin was still sitting at the table with his back to the alcove. His head was bent over, and his shoulders were shaking. "God, please forgive me," he said aloud just as Tristan was emerging, making him freeze in his tracks. But the brigand did not turn. Apparently he meant to speak to the Almighty, not the man he had murdered in cold blood. "The sin is mine," he went on as Tristan moved closer, his soft boots silent on the bare stone floor. "Not hers. Never hers. My God, you know she is a child." Tristan stopped again, his hand on the hilt of his sword. "Everything she is, I have made her." The rebel leader's voice was ragged with tears, and he thought himself alone. This could be no trick. But why should Tristan care what he prayed or if he prayed at all?

"Every evil she has done has been at my command."

Was he not a demon now? Tristan thought, his grip tightening on the sword. Why should he feel mercy toward this man he meant to kill? "Do not let her suffer, please, my God," Sean begged, breaking down completely. "Please God, let me keep her safe." He dropped his head to his folded arms and wept.

Tristan let go of the sword, disgusted but resigned. He could not kill the man at prayer, not even for revenge. If nothing else, Lebuin did not deserve to die with a prayer on his lips. He stood over him for a moment, barely a step behind him. If he should turn or even look over his shoulder, he would see the demon. He would cry out—a curse, no doubt. Then Tristan would have him. He would strike him dead.

But Sean did not look back. His tears slowly subsided as if he had fallen asleep. Tristan moved closer still, reaching out to touch the hilt of the jeweled dagger Sean wore in a sheath at his belt. He drew it slowly, waiting for the brigand to stir, but he did not. He looked down at the knife, a lethal but beautiful object—Italian-made, would be his guess. Only the richest and most arrogant of nobles would carry such a weapon. He wondered where Lebuin had stolen it.

"I will come to you again," he said softly, tucking the knife into his own belt. "Perhaps before the dawn." The brigand moaned as if in troubled dreams, and Tristan smiled. Disaster was upon him; why should he sleep well?

He heard voices from outside the door, the men returning to the hall. Smiling again at the thought of what was to come, he turned and headed for the stairs.

Siobhan passed through the doors of the tower sometime after midnight. She had walked the castle wall for hours until her head felt almost clear again. But her heart was still in chaos; she needed to be alone. At least in her new room in the tower, no one would disturb her.

The lower hall was quiet, the men who slept there already bedded for the night. Sean himself was sleeping at one of the tables, his head down on his folded arms. She almost went to him and woke him, but after a step she stopped. What could she say to make him understand how she felt? She didn't understand herself. Since she was twelve years old, she had believed that they were partners in their quest for freedom for themselves and for their people. But it was not so. Sean was the knight with a quest. She was no better than a pawn.

The room he had made for her was dark but for the glow of the moon outside the window. Someone had leaned a spotted mirror against the wall opposite the door, and she gazed at her shadowy reflection. This was the prize Sean thought could win a baron's heart? She could almost laugh. Her handed-down tunic was worn as a rag, frayed at the neck and split up one sleeve, and her leather breeches were worn soft as linen, she had kept them so long. Even for a boy, she was a disgrace. Her face was clean, but one cheek was smudged with a familiar fading bruise from her bowstring's recoil.

And she bore other bruises as well. On her neck were five distinct round marks, made by the grip of her dead Norman husband. Four had faded to a dull yellow-green, but the one over her pulse was still almost black. He could have killed me, she thought as she touched it, remembering the fury in his blue-green eyes. "Tristan DuMaine," she whispered, barely making a sound as her lips formed the shape of his name. The devil's knight, her enemy; the Norman they had murdered. He had called her beautiful.

She untied her braid and loosened the waves of her hair on her shoulders, blue-black in the tender light. Like silk, he had said it was when he touched it. She drew her own hands through it just as he had done, letting it fall through her fingers. He had been desperate to escape. He had known they meant to kill him; she had never let him think anything else. She had only touched him to humiliate him, to prove she was a brigand like the rest.

But when he had escaped his bonds, he had not fled; he had held her. He could have killed her in an instant and escaped, but he hadn't. He had kissed her mouth. Her own hand strayed now to touch her lips, remembering the taste of him, the way his tongue had felt. She had been so angry to be bested, so afraid of what he meant to do. But his kiss had been soft, almost tender, drawing her to him even as she fought. She had never doubted that he hated her, even when he took her in his arms. He had never pretended anything else, had not tried to flatter her or charm her into helping him escape. But he had held her to him and kissed her. He had called her beautiful and spoken her name like a prayer. For the first time since that moment, she let her waking mind drift into foolish fancy, the madness that haunted her dreams. She imagined how it might have felt to be his love indeed. A warm, sweet flush spread through her, making her feel drunk again. She thought of the power of him, his strength as he held her, his arrogant fury. What would it be to possess such a man, to know him as her own?

She caught her own gaze in the mirror and scoffed, disgusted at her foolishness. She was a warrior, not a woman, whatever Sean might think. She would forget Tristan and his kisses; she would not marry again. She was a soldier, and Sean would have to accept it.

A sudden movement in the mirror made her start, her hand going by instinct to her sword, though she knew it must be one of the castle servants, come to put her into bed like she might have been a child. "Go away," she ordered, turning toward the door. "Leave me in peace."

"In peace?" The voice came from the shadows by the window, and it made her blood run cold. "Why should you have peace?" A shape emerged in the darkness, a man built like a mountain, and the voice went on, mocking and familiar. "Murderers belong in hell."

"Tristan?" Her tongue felt dry in her mouth. She could barely form the word. He moved into the light at last, and she felt her knees go weak. "No . . . . you are not here." She was still drunk, seeing phantoms.

"Where else should I be?" His face, so bruised and bloodied when she'd seen it last, was whole again, the skin pale but perfect. The thin streaks of gold in his dark brown hair gleamed in the moonlight, and his green eyes glittered with malice. "Is this not my castle?" His mouth curled in the smile that haunted her memory, cruel and sweet at once. "Are you not my wife?"

"You are dead." He held no weapon she could see, but she trembled even so. He towered over her, his shoulders twice as broad as hers—he could cover her fist with his palm. Even now, in terror and shock, she could remember the strange sensation she had felt when his hand closed over hers, a fearful thrill. "They took you away, Bruce and Callum. You were dying."

"Are you certain?" Tristan mocked her, moving closer. This was the moment he had dreamed of in a fever, the moment he would finally kill Siobhan. He had meant to let her see his face, to frighten and torment her for only a moment before he wrung her neck or bled her dry. Even when he let her brother live, he had never doubted he would murder her on sight. But now that he was here at last, a moment just wasn't enough. "Did your friends ever return?" Her huge blue eyes were wide with fear, but she did not look away. Any other woman faced with the husband she had helped to murder would have had the decency to scream or faint, but not his beautiful monster. She might turn pale and tremble, but her hand was on her sword. "These men you sent to hide your crime, where are they now?" She drew the sword with a sharp rasp of metal, her eyes defiant, and he smiled. "Shall I tell you, sweeting?" He took another slow step closer. "Would you care to guess?"

"You could not have killed them," she insisted.

"You might be amazed." She was inching backward toward the door. "I can kill whomever I like." In a moment, she would make a run for it, he knew. His little warrior could sense she was outmatched.

"You were dead!" she shouted, her voice's sudden rise in pitch giving away her fear. "I saw you."

"You saw I was dying." He should kill her now and let himself be done. But somehow he could not. "You should have made certain, my love." He raised the dagger he had stolen from her brother's belt. "Sean should have made certain."

"No, I just saw him," she said, shaking her head. But the knife was Sean's. She had seen him in the hall below, sleeping, slumped over the table. She had almost gone to him . . . An icy fear swept through her. Surely he had only been asleep. She looked up into Tristan's eyes. "You can't have killed him—"

"Can I not?" He wanted her to say what she had done, to hear her say again how she despised him. Then he could let it be over between them. Then he could take his revenge. "I have not killed him yet, Siobhan," he said, moving closer. "But I swear to you I will."

"No!" she screamed, her terror forgotten in fury. She struck him with the sword, a blow that should have sliced his arm from his shoulder. But he barely flinched. He grabbed her wrist, wrenching the sword from her grip, and she heard a small sound, like steam on an ember. Looking down, she saw the sleeve of his shirt was ripped open, its edges stained with blood. But the flesh beneath the rip was whole. "Holy Christ," she whispered, feeling faint.

"Be careful, love," he teased her as the tension in her arm went slack in his grip. "You might not want to call Him." He held the dagger to her throat, tracing its tip down her skin much as she had done to him the night that they were wed. "Blasphemy is mortal sin. But then, why should you care?" Her heart was beating faster; he could hear it. At last she was truly afraid. "What is an oath to you?" He let the dagger scratch her flesh, teasing himself with her blood, and she gasped, a sweetly feminine sound. But in her eyes he saw as much fury as fear. Even now, if he allowed it, she would murder him. "You swore before God's altar to love me, to obey me, remember?" he taunted. "You laughed as you said it, knowing it was a lie." He took a step closer, and she struggled again in his grip, tearing at his fist around her wrist. "Or have you forgotten, sweet wife?"

"No," she answered, struggling to make herself be still. She knew now what he wanted; he wanted her to be terrified, to hear her beg for mercy. But she would not. "I have not forgotten." She made her free arm fall to her side, taking a deep breath. Then she looked up into his eyes. "I wanted you to go away."

"You wanted me dead," he said, glaring down on her with such rage, she thought she might die just from his eyes. How could he be here? *The grave will not hold me*, he had sworn at their mummer's play wedding. *I will return from hell.* "But you are a coward, just like your brother."

"Why did you come here?" she demanded, her voice barely shaking with fear. "Why could you not stay in France where you belonged and leave our people be?"

"Your people?" he scoffed with a laugh.

"Aye, my lord," she retorted, his mockery making it easier to be brave. "My father's people, born to this land as Sean and I were born to it, born to freedom—"

"Freedom to starve, you mean," he said, laughing again. Even now, looking death straight in the eyes, the little fool would not give up her cause. "If I should let you live, if I should leave you be, as you say, what then? What will your people say to you this winter, now that their crops are destroyed?"

"You know nothing of this land." *He sounds like Sean*, she thought, almost laughing herself in pure madness. *A slave can be contented if his belly is full*, her brother had said, and she had hated him for it. "You know nothing—"

"And what do you know, little monster?" he retorted.

"How to fight and to fuck like a man." His smile cut through her like a knife. "What good will you be to your people?"

"Good enough," she swore, flushed hot with rage. "I will finish you." She lunged for him, grabbing for the hand that held Sean's dagger, and she felt the blade swipe across her cheek. But he hadn't been expecting her attack; she had momentum. She forced the dagger back into his shoulder just above his heart.

His eyes widened for a moment, then he smiled. "Well done." Still holding her fast by the wrist, he yanked the dagger from his flesh. As she watched in horror, the gash she had made closed over, sealing itself with a hiss. "At least this time, you tried to kill me yourself." He pressed the dagger's hilt into her free hand. "Would you care to try again?"

She slashed him this time, across his throat and down the muscles of his chest, ripping through his shirt. Again the wound opened, but no blood came out. A few scant drops welled at the edges of the wound, then the flesh was healed.

"What ails you, love?" he teased her. "You look as if you see a ghost."

"Demon," she whispered, looking up into his eyes. "You truly are a demon." She let the dagger fall.

"Yes." She tried to back away a step, and he caught her by the shoulders, his smile melting into a scowl. Now was the moment for revenge, he thought. She was terrified; her heartbeat thundered in his ears. He let his palms slide up her arms, and she shivered, now too frightened to resist his touch. His hands encircled her delicate throat, and she gasped, biting her lip. No brigand mob could save her now. No one would even hear her scream. "Did I not promise you I would return?" She closed her eyes against him, her lashes black against her death-pale cheek. She was his now for the taking, just as he had dreamed. One last, swift movement of his wrist, and her life would be snuffed out forever. "I am your husband." One tear slid down her delicate cheek, glistening in the moonlight. "Is that not so?" he demanded roughly, hungry for her voice, to hear her speak once more.

"Yes." His touch was almost tender, more a caress than a threat. She had dreamed of this moment for night after night, the terrible sweetness of his touch if somehow he should return. She had told herself it was a nightmare, that it would fade in time, but she had never truly believed it. No man had ever touched her the way Tristan did; no man had ever dared. But now he did not mean to touch her but to kill her. His hands and voice were cold. "You are my husband," she said.

"Then kiss me." Her eyes flew open, and he smiled, his bitter devil's smile. "Kiss me good-bye."

He was mocking her, tormenting her before her death as she had taunted him. She slid her hands over his shoulders, rising to her toes to reach him. He seemed surprised; his green eyes widened, then she closed her eyes and touched her mouth to his. A thrill raced through her stomach as his arms enfolded her, a sudden, senseless desire more potent than fear. "Siobhan," he said against her mouth, the voice she had heard in her dreams. She clutched the rough wool of his tunic, dizzy as he crushed her closer, deepening the kiss. Alive, she thought. This was no dream. Her husband was alive. His mouth on hers was brutal, demanding surrender, his tongue pushing inside. She could fight him; she must fight him, but she knew he would not let her go. She tore her mouth away from his to look into his eyes and saw a flash of demon's fire burning in the green. Hell itself could not keep him away. Just the thought of it made her feel faint.

He bent and scooped her off her feet, and the trance was broken. "No!" she cried out, thrashing in his grasp, flailing like a lunatic to get away. "Stop it!" She tried to punch him with her fist, and he flung her over his shoulder like a sack of grain. "Let me go!"

"Will you scream for Sean again?" he asked, wicked laughter in his tone. "Please, call him to save you." He tossed her onto the bed, throwing his weight over her to press her flat to the mattress. "Watch me rip his heart out." She slapped him hard, still writhing underneath him, and he grabbed her wrists and pinned them. "My bride's gift to my love."

"Your love my ass," she swore, arching upward. He was too strong; she couldn't escape him. "Leave Sean alone!" He covered her completely; she could hardly move at all. "Please, Tristan . . ." The image of Sean sleeping in the hall below made tears rise in her eyes. They had quarreled; he probably thought she hated him. And now she might never see him again. "Please, leave him alone."

Tristan had bent to kiss her cheek, but the sudden change in her voice made him freeze. She was pleading, soft and sweet, but not for herself. Leave him alone, she begged. Even now, she cared for no one but her brother, the whoreson who had meant to murder him. Jealous rage like nothing he had ever felt before burned through him.

"Aye, sweet love," he said softly, his open mouth against her skin. She twisted her hips, trying to thrash her legs free, and his cock, already throbbing with desire, pushed hard against her thigh. "I will leave Sean alone." He nuzzled her throat, his tongue finding her pulse. "Every friend he has will die." With demon's fangs, he tore a long gash in her flesh, making her cry out in pain.

"No," she whispered, breathless, hating the weakness she knew she would hear in her voice if she spoke the words aloud. "Tristan, stop . . ."

"Tell him, Siobhan," he ordered, his voice thick and deep in his throat. "Tell him I will take all that he loves." She could feel the rumble in his chest as he spoke, but no heart beat in his breast. "Tell him I will come for him when all his loves are lost." His tongue swept over the wound he had made in her throat, and a strange tremor swept through her, making her gasp for breath. "Tell Sean you are mine."

She felt his teeth tearing deeper, and she screamed in pain. But there was something else as well, more frightening than painful. His mouth was pulling at her flesh like a suckling babe, drawing her blood down his throat. She heard a sigh she'd never meant to make escape her lips, and a sweet, hypnotic want possessed her, making her body seem to melt in his demon's embrace. His hands moved slowly down her arms, the palms hard and calloused against her skin, but she couldn't seem to fight him, could only preen under his caress.

"Tristan," she repeated, his name coming out as another pleading sigh. His hand cradled her breast through her tunic, a tender lover's touch, and she clenched her jaw, desperate to resist the desire she felt. She moved to push his hand away, wrapping her hand as best she could around his wrist to pull him back, but she couldn't reach around it. "Tristan . . ." Just knowing she could not undid her completely, made her hold his hand against her instead, lacing her fingers with his. One of his legs was between her own as he crouched over her, and she arched up against the hard muscle of his thigh, moved by instinct, reason lost. And still he fed upon her throat, her lover returned from hell. She heard him moan, a sound despairing as her sigh, and his arm entwined around her waist, holding her to him as her body weakened. Her muscles were failing, turning slack and heavy, and suddenly she felt cold. "No," she whispered, entwining a hand in his hair but too weak to pull. She was dying. "Please . . . my love . . ."

Tristan felt her heartbeat slowing to a crawl, its pounding faded to a gentle flutter he could barely feel through her thin tunic. He tasted vengeance in her blood, sweeter than his dreams, but there was more. Drunk with his own desire for her, he tasted yearning in her blood, yearning for him. She had wept for him, he realized as he drank from her heart; she had grieved for him, dreaming of his kiss. Drawing back from her throat, he looked down on her face, the beauty he had sworn he would despise, but he could not. Even now he was bewitched by her. Bending down, he kissed her lips, the lightest brush to taste her breath the same as he'd tasted her blood. "Who are you?" he whispered, tracing the curve of her cheek with the back of his hand. "What do you want, Siobhan?"

You, she thought and would have told him if she'd had the strength. Just you. But surely that was wrong; she hated him, wanted him dead. He was her enemy, sworn to destroy her, to enslave her people. He had sworn to murder the brother who loved her, the only soul left she could love—even now, he meant to kill her, too. To want him was treason, a betrayal of all she held dear. The devil had bewitched her on purpose, stolen her mind with his cruel demon's kiss. He would steal her soul before he took her life. "No," she whispered again, forcing her eyelids to open. Bending over her, his face was beautiful, a cruel devil's trick. The devil should be ugly, she thought, should come in the shape of a beast, not a beautiful knight she could love. "Leave me now," she ordered, fighting for her voice. He smiled, his arrogant nobleman's sneer. "Begone . . ." He brushed his lips across her brow. "Demon . . . begone."

"Shhh . . ." The sight of her too weak to fight him was more than his pride could resist. He kissed her throat, the lurid bruise his teeth had left over the vein, the mark of his grip where he had held her as a man. She was his, and he would not give her up, not even to damnation. She sighed as he pressed kisses down her jaw, her body arching upward, betraying her zealot's resolve, and he smiled. But he would not take her in this state, as much as she deserved it. He wanted her strong, able to fight back when he conquered her completely. "I will come back to you, darling," he whispered, his mouth close to her ear. "What was it you said to me in the hall at our wedding? I am not done with you yet." She turned her face away as he moved to kiss her mouth, giving him her tender cheek instead. He kissed it with the reverence of a penitent kissing a saint, holding her fast as she struggled. Then he let her go.

Moving fast along the narrow corridor that led to the stairs, he heard a voice coming from the second room, the weeping of a child. Clare . . .

For a moment, he considered going on without stopping, the wisest course if he did not mean to finish this tonight and take her away with him. But she was his beloved child, and she was crying. Demon or not, he could not just leave her alone.

He slipped into her room, the door handle turning

easily. Emma was nowhere to be seen. "Clare," he said softly, approaching the tall, posted bed.

"Papa?" She turned toward him as he reached her, her eyes wide with hope and shock. "Papa!" She threw herself into his arms.

"Shhh," he murmured, holding her close. "Hush now, precious love." Tears of his own spilled down his cheeks. "Please don't cry." He kissed her silky golden hair, forcing himself not to squeeze her so tightly he hurt her. "I promise, it's all right." But that was a stupid lie—he was a demon, cursed by God. How could he care for a child?

"I knew you would come back," she said.

He smiled, holding her back to see her face. "How did you know?"

"You promised." She frowned. "Papa, you're bleeding!"

He touched his own cheek where she pointed. The tears he shed were blood. "It's nothing, petite," he promised. He drew her close again, her tiny weight in his arms comforting him even now. "Are you well?" he asked her. "Is your Emma taking care of you?"

"Yes," she nodded, settling against him. "She and Siobhan."

"Siobhan?" he echoed, surprised. The last time he had seen his child, Siobhan had been holding a knife to her throat. "Lady Siobhan takes care of you?"

"Yes." She held his man's hand between her little ones. "She promised she would teach me how to fight. She makes them keep the dogs out of the hall so they can't scare me." She looked up at him. "She said she promised you." She frowned again. "Is she really your wife?"

"Yes." He had almost killed the one person who seemed able to protect his child. For a moment, he could hardly speak, just thinking of it. He barely remembered Siobhan's promise in the courtyard, he had been so close to death. But Siobhan remembered. She had kept her word. "She is my wife—your stepmother." Saying the words, he felt confused, all his plans for vengeance shaken to the core. "She will keep you safe." He heard movement on the stairs, his demon's ears able to detect voices even so far away. Emma was coming back. "Siobhan will protect you until I come home."

"No," Clare protested, clinging to him. "I want to go with you."

"Not yet." He took her precious face between his hands and smiled. "I cannot take you with me yet, sweet love." Tears glistened on her cheeks again, breaking his heart. "But I am with you, I promise." He kissed her forehead. "I will come again." He hugged her close for one more moment, loath to let her go. Emma was speaking to someone, a man—soon they would be too close to avoid. Only the thought of Clare watching him do murder induced him to release her. "Go to sleep, sweet love." He tucked the blankets under her chin and slipped away into the night.

Siobhan struggled to sit up, her body still heavy and cold. She rolled onto her side, one leg hanging over the side of the bed, her eyes struggling to focus in the gloom. Across the room, she could make out the shape of her reflection in the mirror. Tristan was gone, a demon on the loose. "Get up," she muttered, gritting her teeth. The wound in her throat burned like a brand, and her limbs ached as if from bone-freezing cold. "Get up, Siobhan." Her sword lay on the floor where she had dropped it, and she focused on the blade, gleaming silver in the moonlight. She lunged for it, holding a hand to her throat, catching herself on her knees. Her hand closed hard around the hilt and she dragged it toward her. Her head was swimming, the tower room spinning around her. But Tristan could be anywhere. She had to stop him, to save Sean and the others. Leaning on her sword, she staggered to her feet.

8

Lilith had survived as mistress to the baron of Callard for almost six months, a privilege of her noble birth, perhaps. But now her time was drawing to an end. Setting the tiny packet she held aside for a moment, she studied her face in the mirror, the brand he had burned into her cheek. The mark had been made a fortnight ago, long enough for the flesh to heal into an ugly purple scar. If what the servants had confessed to her was true, she had no more than a night or two left to live. Unless she killed him first.

She poured the pinch of coal-black powder into the bottom of the pewter cup and put it back on the tray just as she heard his footsteps coming up the hall. "Good evening, my lord," she said, bobbing a curtsey as he came in, followed by two of his guardsmen. He barely even glanced in her direction as he went to his chair.

"Bring me my letters," he said brusquely to one of his footmen as the other knelt before him to unlace his boots.

"Will you drink, my lord?" she asked, pouring the wine. One of the guardsmen was named John. He had promised to help her; had delivered the message from her aunt that held the poison; had promised to spirit her away as soon as the baron was unconscious, before his body could be found. Don't look at him, she ordered herself inside her head as she carried the cup to the baron. Don't look at John. She made herself smile as she bent low before her lover, offering the cup.

"What is this?" Callard muttered as he took it, but she didn't answer. She had made the mistake of teasing him once, giving him a saucy retort to such a question. When she'd come back to herself three days later, she had learned to keep her peace. He took a sip and nodded, releasing her to rise. She trembled, freedom so close she could taste it. He took another deep swallow as he turned his attention to his letters, and she risked a glance at John. He looked pale as milk, but there was triumph in his eyes.

"Would you like for me to sing for you, my lord?" she asked.

"I would like for you to shut your mouth," Callard answered, sounding drunk. He frowned, giving his head a shake, and she had to bite down on her cheek so hard she tasted blood to keep from smiling. The poison was working, just as her aunt had promised. "Leave me," he ordered. "All of you—get out!"

"May I not stay?" she asked. She wanted to see him die; she needed to be certain. "I will be quiet—"

"Go!" He rose, swaying slightly on his feet, but strong enough to strike her to the floor with the back of his hand. She huddled on the floor, seeing stars. "Keep this creature away until I call her," he ordered the guardsmen, sitting down again. Lilith started to rise, but he kicked her down again. Cheeks burning with shame, she crawled to the door with the guardsmen behind her. The last time, she promised herself. This is the last time.

As soon as the door was safely shut behind them, John sent the other guard away. "I can keep an eye on this," he said, nodding toward Lilith. "He won't call her back tonight."

"No," the second guardsman agreed. "I won't be far if you need me."

They waited in silence for more than an hour, John standing sentry at the door, Lilith sitting in the corner on the floor, each pretending the other was not there. They must not give themselves away, not until they were certain he was dead. Once they heard a small thud, as if Callard had dropped something, and both of them tensed, Lilith half-rising from her perch. But still they waited.

"Go," she said at last. "Go and see."

John's eyes went wide, fierce soldier that he was. "Me?"

"He will kill me," Lilith pointed out.

Before he could answer, the outer door opened. "Who goes?" John demanded, raising his pike.

Anthony, the coachman who had been presumed to

be killed with his guards in the forest, walked in, his livery torn and stained with blood and dirt. A thick roll of cloth that looked like it had been ripped from his mantle was wadded around his neck. "I must see the baron," he said.

"God's head, man," John swore, appalled. "What happened to you?"

The coachman smiled, a wide, sunny grin that was eerily unlike him. "You'd never guess." He turned his head to look at Lilith, his movements jerky, like a jester's doll. "The baron?" he asked again, measuring her with his eyes. "Where is he?"

"Inside," John said. "Have you seen the captain of the watch? Where have you been?"

The coachman walked past him without answering, headed for the door.

"Wait, you," John ordered, grabbing his arm. "You . . ." His face went pale. "Sweet saints, you stink . . ."

"Let him go," Lilith suggested. Something in Anthony's expression was making her flesh crawl. He was still smiling, but his eyes were dead. "My lord will deal with him."

"Yes," John answered, letting the man go. He wiped his hand on his tunic as the coachman went inside, closing the door behind him.

After a moment, they heard someone laugh, a high-pitched cackle that sounded like neither of the men they knew inside. Then nothing. "He's found him," Lilith said, rising to her feet. "Callard is dead."

"Hush," John ordered, but he offered her his hand. "Come." Leading her with one hand and drawing his sword with the other, he went into the room.

Callard was lying on the bed, his tunic half removed, one bare arm hanging over the side. "Where is Anthony?" Lilith said softly.

"I don't know." The air in the room was thick with the stench of an open grave, strong enough to make the soldier gag. "Holy Christ . . ." The coachman's clothes were lying in a heap before the fire, crawling with maggots and flies. Lilith screamed, and John caught her close for a moment, covering her mouth with his hand.

"What is it?" she demanded, barely louder than a whisper, when he let her go.

"Why should I know?" John let her go and moved closer to the pile of filth, poking at it with his sword. A rat scuttled out of the rags and over the blade, making Lilith gasp again, catching her own scream this time. He heard a noise behind him and turned as the woman beside him melted to her knees.

Callard was rising from the bed. "No," Lilith whimpered, reaching for John's leg as if she might hide behind it. "It cannot be."

"What a mess," Callard said with a sigh. His voice was just the same, but his inflection seemed different, as if he had a foreign accent. He pulled his tunic the rest of the way off and looked down at himself, touching the hard muscles of his torso as if he had never noticed them before. "Oh, yes," he murmured, smiling to himself. "This will do well." Another rat scurried close by Lilith, and she screamed, leaping to her feet.

"Forgive us for disturbing you, my lord," John said, shaking her off as she tried to cling to him. "Anthony insisted he must see you . . ." He looked back at the pile of rotting clothes, his mind searching for some lucid explanation.

"Come here." Callard was still smiling, the beatific grin that strangers found so charming. "Bring me your sword."

"No," Lilith said, grabbing hold of the guardsman's arm. "Don't do it." But the guardsman shook her off again. "John, no . . ." He held out the sword to Callard, who took it. Still smiling, he raised it and cut off the guardsman's head.

"No!" Lilith screamed. She wanted to run, but her legs wouldn't seem to move. John's body crumpled to the floor, his head rolling toward the hearth, and Callard stepped over him as if he barely noticed. "Leave me alone," she demanded, her voice breaking in a shriek. "You are dead!"

He raised the sword again, staring down at his own arm as if in awe. "Not so much, my dear." He let the sword fall from his grip and turned his gaze on her. "For which I must thank you." She tried to speak, but her voice dried up as he moved closer. "In truth, I wish I could show mercy." He caught her by the neck and dragged her to him, kissing her mouth. She felt her legs turn weak, the taste of his tongue revolting as he pushed it past her teeth. She wanted to bite him, but the very idea made her sick.

He caught her hair up in his fist and yanked her head back, a gesture she knew from him only too well. "Let me go," she pleaded, writhing in his grasp. His free hand moved up her rib cage to her breast, cradling her softness in his palm, a far less familiar caress. Then suddenly, his head fell back, and she saw his teeth had changed, the canines long and curved like the fangs of a poisonous snake. "No," she breathed, unable to scream, as he clamped down on her throat.

Siobhan stopped just inside the stable door and leaned against a post to catch her breath. The gash in her throat hurt her a little, but it was no worse than any number of other wounds she had suffered in her years as a brigand. But no other wound had ever made her feel so weak. She closed her eyes for a moment to shut out the light of the torches, their flickering making her dizzy. Tristan had disappeared from the castle. Somehow, she would have to saddle her horse and ride out. She straightened up, feeling stronger for her moment's rest. Apparently none of the grooms were about, which should make escaping easier. A groom would have asked questions; he might even have alerted Sean. But now she would have to saddle her own horse.

"Make haste," she murmured, urging herself on. "You've done it a thousand times before." Her little mare was already having her supper and didn't take kindly to having her feed bag removed. "Pray pardon, mam'selle," Siobhan teased, scratching her behind the ear to make it up. The mare's last mistress had been a Norman maiden on her way to seek asylum in a convent, the first owner of Siobhan's best gowns as well. She had cursed Sean for the devil incarnate in a voice like a cat stretched on a rack and had declared Siobhan an unnatural monster. "Ah, well," she said now, remembering. " 'Tis likely she was right."

"Who was right, dear heart?" She turned at the sound of his voice, and for a moment, he could have sworn she almost smiled. "Where are you going, Siobhan?" Tristan hadn't gone at all. He was watching her from the shadows, his arrogant smile on his lips.

"To find you." She drew her sword. "I have to kill you." She lunged for him, and he caught her easily, holding the wrist of her sword arm captured in his fist.

"Do you want to kill me?" Tristan had been amused to see her coming after him, and something more, a darker feeling like his hunger for her blood. Speaking to her now, he felt a strange new power in his voice, a hypnotic rumble in his throat like the purr of a lion to its prey. "Tell me the truth."

"No," she admitted. She couldn't help herself; she felt entranced. While she gazed up into his eyes, nothing else in the world seemed to matter, as if he were her love indeed. But this power was unnatural, a demon's trick like his power to heal. She did not want to tell him the truth of her heart; she didn't want to tell him anything. But she couldn't stop. "We did wrong you, Tristan." His eyes went wide, his sensual mouth turning hard, ready to sneer. "But I would do the same again."

"Why?" He caught her by the shoulders, making her face him, and she dropped the sword. "Why, Siobhan?"

"Because you are my enemy." She saw pain in his eyes, fury at the sheer injustice of her words. "You think it was all Sean, but I swear it was not. It was me, too. Even if Sean had died in the siege, I would have killed you myself." His grip tightened painfully, his fingers bruising her flesh. "Why will you not kill me?"

Even now, under a spell of his own making, she called him nothing but her enemy, gazing up at him with those wide blue eyes that would haunt him forever, immortal or not. "Do you want me to kill you?" he demanded, tempted to shake her like a rat.

"No." She didn't even want to run anymore, she realized. She had no more will to escape him. "I only want to know why you will not."

His answer was to kiss her. Still holding her hard by the shoulders, he bent slowly forward, his eyes locked to hers, and she faced him, her lips slightly parted, her own eyes open wide. He barely brushed her mouth with his, and she shivered, swaying slightly backward in his grasp. "I will kill you, darling." He kissed her more firmly, open-mouthed but soft. "Just not yet." He kissed her in earnest, lifting her up to reach her. He tasted her tongue, heard her sigh as she melted against him, her hands clutching his shirt. He set her on the railing of the stall, putting her face level with his. "You are mine," he murmured, framing her jaw in his hands as he kissed her cheek.

"No." He kissed her eyelids, first one then the other, so tenderly she almost felt like crying. No one had ever treated her so tenderly in her life as this Norman who promised to kill her. "I am my own, myself." His tongue swirled softly in the crevice of her ear, making her tremble. "Please . . . I want to be myself."

"Yes," he promised, smiling as he kissed the corner of her mouth. "I would want nothing else, little demon." He had thought that he wanted her to fight him, that he needed her fury to take her and be satisfied. But this strange surrender moved him more, he found. He kissed her mouth again, crushing her sweet lips, his cock going hard enough to hurt him. "You shall be damned as you are."

She barely heard him anymore; his words meant nothing. All that mattered was his touch. His arms enfolded her, so strong she knew he could hold her forever. She pressed her cheek to his, nuzzling his skin, thrilling to the stubble of his beard. He was a man, as rough and strong as any brigand she had ever known, with the arrogant will of a king. He had no fear, no doubt in the rightness of his course. Above all else, in spite of all, he wanted her just as she was.

"Tristan," she murmured, half pleading, her fingers tangled in the softness of his hair. He kissed her throat, barely touching the wound he had left there, and a thrill raced through her, burning and sudden as lightning. Her body arched upward of its own accord as if to beg for murder, but his kiss moved on, trailing softly down her throat to her shoulder. His hands unlaced her tunic as his eyes met hers, a wicked half-smile daring her to protest. "Demon," she cursed him, smiling back, her palm against his cheek. She should fight him, try to get away, to slay him as she knew she must. But in this moment, she could not.

"Brigand," he answered in kind. Somewhere outside the warm dark of the stable, vengeance waited, all that he was sworn to do. But all that mattered now was her, his beautiful enemy, Siobhan. He held her hand against his cheek, turning to kiss her wrist. Her pulse was still weak from his bite, but her skin was warm with life.

He drew her to him, moving closer, and she wrapped her legs around him. "Wanton," he scolded, eyes wide, and she laughed.

"So you have said." She ran her hands over his shoulders, molding the muscles of his arms. "So cold," she murmured, kissing the side of his neck, nuzzling under his shirt. "Why are you so cold?"

"Because you murdered me." He caught her face between his hands and made her look at him, remembering the word Simon had used. "Because I am a vampire."

"Vampire," she repeated. That was the name of the

demon he had become. He kissed her, pushing forward, and she caught him by the shoulders to stop herself falling over backward. His hands slid underneath her tunic to the lacings on her breeches, and she smiled. "I am barely a woman, remember?"

"You are a woman," he answered, his voice turning rough as a growl. His kiss moved to her breast, its softness cupped so gently in his palm to bring the nipple up over her open blouse. The cool wet of his mouth made her shiver, her skin breaking out in gooseflesh, but the chill was sweet. He suckled tenderly, his demon's fangs barely bruising her skin, and she gasped, nearly falling again as her thighs went weak with pleasure. "This is a woman," he promised, kissing the valley between as he moved to the other breast.

He put a hand between her legs again, his other arm around her waist to hold her as she rose up off the rail. He yanked the breeches down and off with a speed and skill that made her gasp. "God's faith, my lord Norman," she teased him, turning her face away as he rose up to kiss her. "Methinks you have unpantsed a lad before."

"Peace, woman," he warned her just before he bruised her mouth with his. He put himself between her thighs, his hands molding her hips. He gathered her close to him, his sex brushing hers for a moment, and she thought she might swoon at the shock of it, hard cock behind rough wool against her tender flesh. Then he backed away, bending again to her breast. His hand moved slowly to her sex, lazily exploring.

"God's faith, my lady brigand," he mocked her, twisting her curls around his finger. "Do all your lovers make you turn so wet?"

"Nay, sirrah," she answered, fighting for her voice as tremors rippled through her, making her feel weak. "Not all." His fingers barely curved into the cleft to press the sensitive button of flesh at the crest, and she gasped, clutching his shirt. "Your needs must be quite proud," she managed to murmur, bending her head to his shoulder.

He smiled, turning to kiss her cheek. "I am." He kissed her mouth, drawing her lower lip into his mouth as his fingers pressed further, finding resistance. "But you lie." He raised his head to look at her. "You have no other lovers."

"Nay, I told you not." She draped her hands around his neck to draw him closer, arching up against his touch. "Does it matter, demon?"

Innocent or not, he had never seen such an exquisite little wanton. "No, brigand." He guided the tip of his cock to her entrance, teasing them both. "It does not." Her lips parted, panting breath, a sight to drive him mad. Unable to hold back another moment, he drove himself inside her.

She cried out, clinging to him as if for comfort as her body opened to his thrust, sharp pain dissolving into pleasure such as she had never felt. She had touched herself before and found release, but she had never felt another flesh inside of her, filling her up. The very strangeness of it shook her to the core. For a moment, he was still, cradling her close and kissing her cheek as she held him so tightly her arms began to ache. Then slowly he began to move, drawing back and pushing forward, delving deeper with each stroke. His hands were braced against the rail, and his eyes were closed, his brow drawn deep in concentration, making her long to kiss him. She wrapped her legs around his hips, one arm still curved around his neck. With the other hand, she traced the muscles of his arm, thrilling as ever to the brutal power she could feel beneath his skin. His green eyes opened, meeting hers, and the gentle waves of pleasure she had felt lapping through her swelled into a single, gorgeous flood.

"Tristan," she whispered, and he smiled, the arrogant sneer that she had tried to despise but that turned her flesh to flame. He quickened his rhythm, and she melted, trusting him to hold her as her head fell back. The wave inside her exploded, ecstasy drowning her completely, and still he was pounding, making the wave roll on. Only when she thought she must surely be dying did she feel him come as well, a last powerful thrust to touch her soul.

He gathered her into his arms, lifting her off the rail. She sighed, as soft and pliant as a newborn lamb, and he kissed her, feeling drunk. "Sweet demon," he soothed her, lowering her to a soft nest of straw. She tried to hold him as he moved to let her go.

"No," she insisted. "You must not . . ." She sounded

as lost as he felt, and her poor little body was exhausted. But still she would fight him; she was reaching for her sword.

"Hush, my lady." He caught her hand and kissed the palm, pressing it to his cheek for a moment before he let her go.

"No one," she said, seeming to fight for her voice. "No one else must die."

He smiled, caressing her hair. "As you will." He traced the shape of her mouth, entranced himself. "You need not seek me out to kill me, love." She looked up at him, her blue eyes haunted by the same strange agony he felt. "I will come again." He bent and kissed her one last time before he let her go.

The old groom had heard his young mistress sighing with her lover and had kept his distance, not wishing to disturb her. Such beauty deserved to be loved. But when he saw the man who emerged from the stable, he thought he must be dreaming. "No," he muttered, fading back into the shadows lest he be seen. "It cannot be." He crossed himself for mercy as Tristan DuMaine disappeared into the night.

Tristan rounded the corner of the stable and melted into canine form as a pair of figures parted near the wall. One was a stranger who skulked toward the gates. The other was Gaston, the courtier he had seen with Lebuin, moving openly toward the tower.

When they were gone, he went to where they had met and found a dead man lying on the ground. His eyes were open and staring, his lips drawn back in a grimace of rage and horror. He was Tristan's enemy, part of the force who had taken his castle and his life away. But looking down on him, the vampire felt no satisfaction in his death. *No one dies tonight,* Siobhan had insisted, and he had agreed. I can swear but for myself, sweeting, he thought, turning away. Your friends are another affair. The sky was still pitch-dark, but he could feel the dawn approaching—another new talent of his demon nature. If he meant to reach his shelter in the forest, he must go. One of his own hunting hounds came around the corner and stopped to sniff at the corpse. She looked up at Tristan, a question in her liquid eyes. Then she turned away and headed for the shelter of the kennels, a cozy little nest at the foot of the tower, well protected from the sun. Smiling inside his magical disguise, Tristan trotted after her.

9

Siobhan heard voices, people shouting from somewhere far away. Sunlight was falling in filtered beams through the thatch of the roof. She had slept through the night.

"Siobhan!" She heard Sean's voice, and relief swept through her. He was alive.

"Here," she called out, sitting up. Her clothes were pulled askew—good lord, she was still half-naked. "Sean, I'm here!" She scrambled into her breeches just as her brother burst in.

"Sweet Christ," he mumbled, falling to his knees beside her. "You live." He gathered her into his arms.

"Of course." She felt so tired, so cold . . . she couldn't think. Tristan had returned. "Sean . . ." He held her close for a moment in a blissfully warm embrace.

Michael came running in and stopped when he saw them. "Oh no . . ."

"It's all right," Sean said. He drew back and saw the gash in her throat. "Who did this to you?" he demanded.

"I . . . ," she began and stopped. *Tell him,* Tristan said inside her head. *Tell him I have returned. Tell him you are mine.* "I don't remember," she lied. "I didn't see."

"We've found a second body," Michael said. "Angus, the captain, thrown into the ditch."

Siobhan felt the breath rush out of her, but she could not make a sound.

"Like Sam?" Sean said, gently touching the wound in her throat.

"Worse," Michael answered. "His throat is torn so badly, he's nearly beheaded. But there is no blood."

"Sam?" She felt sick; the stable seemed to be spinning around her. Angus had never been one of her favorites, but he was one of their men, a brigand who had been with them from the beginning of their quest. And Sam . . . "Sam is dead?"

"Aye, love," Sean said, caressing her hair. "His body was found near the castle wall this morning. When you weren't in your room . . ." He drew her close again.

"Sean, listen to me." As dearly as she wanted comfort, she pulled away. "I have to tell you something."

"Michael, have Silas brought to the hall," Sean said, his eyes meeting hers. "And Gaston." He stood up and scooped her off her feet with a slight groan.

"I can walk," she insisted, but in truth, she wasn't sure she could. Sean hadn't picked her up since she was a child. But Tristan had, as if it were nothing at all. Had Sam been dead already? He had promised no one else would die. She could believe he had murdered them all for vengeance, but she could not believe he had lied.

"I will," Michael was saying. "And I will send Cilla to tend you, love." He gave her hand a squeeze as he left, and she sank against Sean's shoulder, her arms draped limp around his neck as he carried her out into the courtyard. At the far end, she could see a patrol lifting Sam's corpse from the ground, and rage and fear swept over her, making her feel sick. His clothes were soaked with blood, his eyes staring blind, his lips drawn back in a grimace. "Sweet Christ," she murmured, hiding her face against Sean.

"Hush," he answered, kissing her forehead again. "It will be all right." Siobhan could feel him tremble and hear the fury barely restrained in his tone. His reputation as a brigand notwithstanding, Sean's temper was slow to rise, but when it flamed, it could rival hell itself. But for her, his fear was worse. And he was right to be afraid. *Tell Sean I will take all that he loves*, Tristan had told her as he held her to the bed. He had killed Bruce and Callum on the road, Angus and Sam inside the castle walls. He meant to kill them all.

She closed her eyes as they crossed the bridge, trying not to think of anything until they were alone. She had betrayed her people, her own blood, for the kisses of a demon who despised them all. And now Sam, a brave, true warrior who had loved her well, was dead.

"My lady!" She opened her eyes as they passed into the hall and saw Emma running towards them. "Captain, what has happened?"

"Bring the little one, Lady Clare," Sean answered her. "She must go upstairs with Siobhan."

"Sean, no," Siobhan protested, coming to life in his arms. "I have to speak with you alone." How could she tell him Tristan was a monster with Tristan's own daughter at her side?

"I will find her," Emma said, nodding. "We will follow you."

"It will be all right," Sean murmered, kissing her hair as he started up the stairs.

He carried her into her room and kicked the door shut behind them. "It's all right now," he said, laying her on the bed. "You're safe."

"No," she said urgently, shaking her head. "I am not—none of us is safe." He sat down beside her on the bed, and she took his hand. "Sean, listen to me." There was no time; Emma could come in with Clare any moment. "It's Tristan. Tristan DuMaine has returned."

His eyes widened for a moment, his face going pale. "Sweetheart, that's impossible," he said, shaking his head. "Tristan DuMaine is dead."

"Yes," she nodded. "He is . . ." She thought of the sound his flesh had made when it healed itself after her attack, a hiss like water on hot coals, the flash of fire she had seen in his eyes as he kissed her. "I think he must be," she finished with a shudder. "But he was here."

"Siobhan—"

"He bit me." It sounded ridiculous, she realized, but

when it was happening, it had all made a weird sort of sense. "It's like he has become some sort of demon. Sean, I slashed him with my sword, a blow that should have killed him, and he barely flinched—I saw the wound heal itself, saw it close up in barely a moment. I struck him with my dagger . . ." She stopped, another thought occurring. "He had your dagger." He was staring at her, obviously appalled. "He showed it to me; I thought you must be dead, but he said not."

He reached for the sheath at his side. "Siobhan, I swear," he began, then stopped. The sheath was empty.

"He took it." She made herself sit up. "He said he would kill all of your men. He wanted me to tell you . . ." *Tell him you are mine,* her memory whispered again.

"Siobhan, this is madness. Enough." He stood up, backing away from her. "Dead men do not come back."

"He said he would." In his heart, he believed her; she could see it in his eyes. "He promised me he would come back from the grave to punish me. Don't you remember?"

"I remember what he looked like when he left here," he said angrily. "I remember my instructions to Bruce and Callum before they took him away."

"And did they ever return?" she countered. "I have not seen them if they did."

"Siobhan, I said enough!" His words were furious, but his face looked green with fear. "Tristan DuMaine was not inside this castle last night. Tristan DuMaine is dead—and gone. He cannot come back." His expression softened. "Poor child . . ." He came back to the bed and took her hand. "It's all right." He bent and kissed her forehead. "It was just a dream."

"A dream that almost murdered me?" she answered. If she'd had the strength, she would have slapped him. "If I am a liar or a child who cannot tell her dreams from truth, what bit me?"

"Nothing," he insisted. "You were attacked in your sleep with a blade of some kind—"

"Then where is the blood?" she asked "Who killed Angus? Who murdered Sam?" She squeezed his hand. "Sean, you must believe me. We must leave this place." He will find me, she thought, unable to stop the thought from coming. "Whatever Tristan has become, we cannot fight him—I could not even wound him last night. You could not believe how strong he has become—"

"Aye, lass," he cut her off. "I don't believe it." He stood up again, his tone as cold as his expression. "Listen to me, Siobhan. You are a woman, with a woman's heart, and your guilt has driven you mad."

"Guilt?" she demanded, breathless. She didn't have the strength for this. He was her brother; he should believe her, not treat her like some raving lunatic child.

"Your guilt about DuMaine," he said. "I never should have let you be a part of this, love. I'm sorry."

Cilla came in before she could answer, her old nursemaid looking frantic with horror. "My poor, sweet lady," she cried, hurrying to the bed. Michael followed close behind her, carrying her basket of supplies, and Emma and Clare followed him. "What has happened to you?"

"Someone attacked her in the night," Sean said before Siobhan could answer. "The same person who killed the others, I would think."

"Who was it, my lady?" Emma asked as Michael helped Cilla unpack her bandages and little pots of herbs and salve.

"She doesn't remember," Sean answered for her again. He laid his hand on her brow, his eyes meeting hers in a narrow frown that bade her to keep silent. "But I mean to find out." Caressing her cheek with the back of his hand for a moment, he turned and headed for the door. "Come, Michael." With a final look back, they were gone.

"Sean!" she tried to call after him, but Cilla was pushing her back on the bed.

"Hush now," she soothed. "Still and quiet, love, that's the way."

"My papa killed those bad men." Clare was standing at the foot of the bed, watching Siobhan with Tristan's eyes. "My papa has returned." She smiled. "Just as he promised he would."

"My lady, hush," Emma scolded. "Why would you tell such a lie?"

"I am not lying," the little girl said. "Am I, Siobhan?"

"That is quite enough," Cilla said. "Emma, take this child away."

"I cannot," Emma said, looking back and forth between Clare and Siobhan and turning pale. "The captain has bolted the door and set a guard for my lady's protection."

"It doesn't matter," Clare said. "My papa will still come."

Clare has seen him, too, Siobhan thought, feeling dizzy. "Yes," she answered, turning her face to the pillow and closing her eyes. She was so tired. "Yes, he will."

"Hush now, all of you," Cilla scolded. "Lady Siobhan is ill; she needs her rest." She patted Siobhan's cheek. "A good, long sleep, and some good, strong broth, and she'll soon be better."

No, Siobhan thought, *I will not.* But she had no more strength to protest.

Silas had been comforting young Brother Thomas in the half-ruined chapel when Lebuin's guards had seized him and led him to the tower hall. Gaston was already there, his hands bound behind him. "You're mad, Lebuin," he was saying, obviously ready to combust with fury. But the rebel leader was paying him no mind.

"Gather all of DuMaine's original garrison in the lower hall," he was telling one of his own captains. "Only use force if someone resists, but no one is above suspicion."

"Yes, my lord," the captain nodded. With a final contemptuous glance at Gaston, he led his patrol away, leaving two men to guard the doors.

"Lebuin, what is this?" Silas asked mildly. "Why have you brought us here?"

"Can't you guess?" Gaston said. "He thinks one of us murdered his men—an old man or his nearest ally."

"Siobhan is my nearest ally," Sean said, turning on him. "And now she lies near death."

"Lady Siobhan was attacked as well?" Silas asked, horrified.

"Not so sorely as Angus or Sam, but yes," Sean answered, still glaring at Gaston. "She will live."

"How was she wounded?" Silas had seen the body of the man, Angus, when it was brought up from the ditch. The very idea that any young woman could have suffered the same was appalling.

"In the throat," Sean said, turning his eyes on the scholar at last. "A pair of jagged tears in the flesh, just here." He pointed to a spot on his own throat just over the thickest vein. "An ordinary assassin would have simply cut her throat."

"What reason would either of us have to kill the girl?" Gaston demanded. "Or your bloody captain, either one?"

"Siobhan hates you, Gaston, and you know it," Sean answered him coldly. "Perhaps Angus tried to defend her."

"So I ripped his throat out with my teeth?" Gaston asked, quite reasonably, Silas would have been forced to admit if he were asked. "I dragged his bloodless body down the stairs and dropped it into the ditch? The man outweighs me by a stone, at least." He looked over at Silas. "Or did Master Silas carry him for me?"

"Do we know Angus was killed by a man?" Silas asked. "I saw his wounds myself; I would have said they were made by some manner of beast, and from what I have heard, the other man was the same."

"No beast could have scaled the castle wall," Sean pointed out. "No beast could have attacked my sister."

"What does Siobhan say?" Silas said.

"Siobhan does not remember," he answered, but a lie flashed in his eyes. "She must have been sleeping."

"Unless she did it herself," Gaston said. Sean turned on him, sword drawn, before the words were out, but the other man did not flinch. "You're right, Sean; the chit hates me. But she was none too happy with you last night either." He glanced at Silas for a moment as if not certain he should continue before him. "Did you not say your plans for her future did not please her?"

"So you're too much of a weakling to have murdered Angus, but my sister did it?" Sean said bitterly.

"She could have set those dogs of hers on him," Gaston answered. "She's made it quite plain she considers DuMaine's kennels to be hers and no one else's."

Dogs, Silas thought, his mind wandering for a moment. He had seen a dog last night, the golden mastiff that had not seemed to be part of the pack. But that was madness.

"But why, Gaston?" Sean was asking. "Why should Siobhan want to kill Angus?"

"Who knows?" Gaston retorted. "Why did she attack one of your soldiers' sweethearts last night in the hall? She was drunk out of her mind—and with your friend Sam, I might add."

"Siobhan attacked another woman?" Silas said, disbelieving.

"Attacked is much too strong a word, from the way I hear it," Sean said brusquely.

"But she was not herself; your own men have said it," Gaston pressed on. "Perhaps she thought if one of your best men were mysteriously slaughtered, you would give up your plans, give up this castle. Is that not what she wants?"

"You're mad," Sean answered, but Silas thought he heard the faintest trace of doubt in his voice as he said it. "Siobhan cares for every one of our men as much as she does for herself; she would never have done anything to harm them."

"Not knowingly, perhaps," Gaston said. "But drunk, angry, and frightened as she was last night?"

"Why should Siobhan be frightened?" Silas asked.

"Who knows what tricks her woman's mind might have played upon her?" Gaston went on, ignoring him. "Perhaps that's why she made those marks on her own throat; perhaps she meant to kill herself out of remorse."

"No!" Sean roared, his patience at an end. He drove Gaston back against the wall, his sword poised under his chin. "My sister is not mad." Gaston opened his mouth as if to argue, then seemed to think better of it. "She would rather die than let any of our men be killed, especially Sam. She was attacked by someone else." He leaned closer, his blade cutting a tiny slice in Gaston's throat remarkably close to where Siobhan was said to be wounded. "Any man who dares say otherwise will wish he'd been born without a tongue."

"Kill me, then," Gaston answered. "Then explain to the baron of Callard how your sister is a saint."

For a moment, Silas was certain the brigand leader would take the man at his word. Then he backed away. "Cut his bonds," he ordered the nearest of the guards, sheathing his sword. "Release him."

"Aye, my lord," the man nodded, moving to obey.

"But watch him," Sean continued. "If he tries to tell his lies again, arrest him and bring him to me."

"Aye, my lord," a second guard said, coming to help. "He will keep his peace." He fixed Gaston with a glare of his own. "You may depend upon it." He took him none too gently by one arm while his comrade took the other, both of them hustling him quickly out the door.

"What of me, Lebuin?" Silas asked when they were gone. "Am I to be released as well?"

Sean didn't answer for a moment. "You liked Tristan DuMaine, did you not?" he said at last.

"Yes," Silas answered. "I thought he was an honorable lord."

Sean smiled bitterly, shaking his head. "And my mercy means nothing, I suppose."

"Your mercy is temporary." The rebel knight's blue eyes widened. "Is it not?"

"You think I mean to murder you?" Sean seemed genuinely shocked.

"What else can you do, sir knight?" Just then, the fierce young rebel looked very young indeed, he thought. "If you release me, do you think I will keep your secrets?"

"My secrets?" he echoed. He smiled again. "Mayhap you will not. But will you keep Siobhan's?" Silas's shock must have shown on his face, because Sean laughed. "She is very beautiful, isn't she, Silas?"

"Exquisite," the scholar agreed.

"Imagine what she might have been . . ." His voice trailed off, his smile fading to an expressionless mask. "Silas, do you know aught of what happened in her room last night?" he asked. "Do you know what murdered my men?"

For a moment, Silas thought again of the dog he had seen. In all his months working on this castle, he was almost certain he had never once seen it before. But a dog alone could hardly have done so much evil. "No, Sean," he answered. "In faith, I do not know."

Sean watched him for another long moment, then nodded. "Aye," he said, turning away. "You are released."

10

After a nap, Siobhan felt much better, but her mind was still in a whirl. She watched Clare and Emma playing with Clare's dolls as the night played over in her head . . . Tristan in this room, alive but a monster. Tristan in the stable, her demon lover in her arms. He had murdered Angus and Sam; he must have. He had sworn to murder everyone Sean loved. But not her. *Tell him you are mine.*

She opened the cask of letters she had collected before the castle siege, Tristan's letters stolen from his couriers on the road. For months, she had practiced his script until she could produce a perfect forgery. But she had never really paid attention to the pith of what he wrote.

"Dear Uncle," he began in a long missive to some minor baron in France.

I also regret that you find yourself unable to assist me as I had hoped. I believe you know I would not have troubled you so on a whim. But since you have obliged me with advice in lieu of silver, allow me to respond.

The course of action you suggest would perhaps be to my benefit if I intended to remain here only so long as required to complete this fortress and secure the district. However, I intend to make DuMaine my home, to live out my days and rear my daughter in the midst of these peasants. To that end, I hesitate to place the burden of my debts upon their backs, particularly now with the rebels so active and so many of my troops away at war. While you are no doubt correct in your assertion that their poverty is due at least in part to their support of these self-same rebels, I believe that my ultimate interests will be better served by mercy in this matter than punishment by whip or taxes either one. Having observed your management of your own lands, I know you will disagree and consider me a fool—you need not bother to respond to tell me so.

In short, my lord, I thank you for your counsel. If you should find your situation different and wish to reconsider making me a loan, I will be most grateful and swear that you will quickly be repaid with whatever interest you deem fair.

Your obedient servant and kinsman,

Tristan DuMaine

When she had first heard this letter, Sean had been reading it aloud, making Tristan sound like the worst sort of spoiled, sniveling fop. "No doubt he has gambled away his inheritance and now means to milk our people dry to recoup it," her brother had scoffed, and Siobhan had agreed. But now that she knew the man himself, she read it very differently. Hearing the words in his voice in her mind, she could well imagine the pain it had cost him, begging money from a man he obviously did not respect. That he had not only done so once but accepted the old man's scolding to repeat his suit was a testament to . . . what? His determination to finish his castle, yes, but also to spare the common people of the district taxes they could ill afford to pay. The people she and Sean were so convinced he cared for not at all. Silas of Massum had told her Tristan had paid for the castle from his own purse, had bankrupted himself to reseed the fields after they were burned. At the time, she had called the old scholar a liar, but this seemed to suggest he was not. Sean spoke of his ally, the baron of Callard, as a Norman overlord who cared for his people. Could Tristan have been the same? And if he was, what were his murderers?

This thought was put off by a knock on the door. "My lady?" Silas said from outside. "May I come in?"

"Of course." Her guard unbolted the lock and let him in. "In truth, I was just thinking of you."

"Of me?" He studied her, obviously concerned. "I was much disturbed to hear that you had been attacked." He sat down on a rug-covered chest near her chair. "Your brother said this morning you did not remember your assailant. Has your memory returned?"

Sean would have had to lie, she knew, but to hear it still gave her a shiver. "No," she answered. "I remember no more now than I did when I awoke."

Silas smiled slightly, a question in his eyes, as if he recognized this for the evasion it was and would like to guess the truth. "Thank God it was no worse," he said.

"Yes," she nodded. Michael had said Angus's throat was torn out as if by a wolf . . . Tristan had done that. "Master Silas, you are a learned man," she said. "You have many books."

"Yes, of course."

"Do you have any books about demons?"

Of all the things she might have asked him, he had expected this the least. He glanced at Clare and Emma, but they seemed engrossed in their game. "Demons, my lady?" He was shocked by her pallor, but she seemed quite lucid—or had, at least, before this. "Do you have need for such a book?"

"A curiosity," she answered. "Why, do you think a woman should not think of such matters?"

"In truth, I believe no one should," he admitted. "I believe far too much ill in this world has been blamed by the ignorant on superstitious nonsense."

"So you do not believe such a thing as a demon could exist?" Again, she sounded merely curious, but her interest could not be so idle, not with men being slaughtered in the night.

"I am more likely to believe in a man turned to evil," he answered.

"Or a woman?" she replied with a soft but wicked smile.

"Yes," he said. "Or that." Could Gaston be right? he thought. He thought of her confessing it was she who had murdered his masons, or ordered their murder, at least—boasting more than confessing. Could she have set her dogs upon her brother's men to push him into giving up his quest? Watching her now, so delicate and pale, he could hardly believe it. She was like an angel. But she was a soldier as well.

"So you do not possess any such book?" she asked. He was watching her so strangely, she would have feared to ask him what he was thinking.

"I do." Even if she could have killed those men, how could she have hurt herself? he thought. The wounds on her throat were appalling; just to see them made him feel faint. "What hurt you, my lady?" he asked, speaking gently as if to a frightened child. "Was it a demon?"

"As Sean said, I do not remember," she answered. She could not bear his sympathy, the kindness in his eyes. If she let herself, she could dissolve into tears and tell him all that had happened. For a moment, she considered it. He was a learned man; he was a friend to Tristan. Perhaps he could help her.

But no. Sean did not trust him. She could not either.

"A demon seems a likely explanation," she went on, making her tone light. "But perhaps you think I am ignorant to say so."

"No," he promised, returning her smile. "I will find you your book."

"Thank you, Master Silas." She stood up too quickly, and her legs gave way beneath her.

"My lady!" Emma cried, rushing to help Silas catch her.

"I am all right," she insisted, feeling a fool. "Just a bit dizzy." She gripped Silas's arm as he and the girl led her back to the bed. "The book, Silas." Clare was watching again, and the look in her eyes made Siobhan shiver. "You won't forget?"

"No, my lady," Silas said, patting her arm. "I promise I will not."

An hour before sunset, Silas sent a book to the tower by one of Lebuin's men and wandered out into the courtyard. "So you do not believe a demon could exist?" Siobhan had asked him. An odd question, to be sure. "A demon seems a likely explanation," she had shrugged when he asked why.

The courtyard was swarming with brigands as it had been all day, but none of them seemed to have any clear idea what it was they should be doing. He had heard that the lieutenants among DuMaine's former troops had been taken prisoner for questioning. No doubt there would be more beheadings soon if the cul-

prit responsible for the murders could not be found.
Gaston had suggested Siobhan had set her dogs on the
dead men, but Silas had seen little evidence that she
cared much for the kennels. She seemed kindly toward
the beasts when they came near her, but she rarely
sought them out. And would a pack of dogs murdering
a man not have raised an alarm among the guards? No,
some other power was at work here, either from the
lady or another. "A demon seems a likely explanation,"
she had said. Likely to whom? Why should she think of
such a thing?

One of the dogs Gaston would label a deadly weapon
was sunning itself in the grass, scrubbing its back on
the ground with an air of ecstasy that made Silas smile
in spite of his worries. DuMaine had been fond of his
animals. Indeed, he had taken as much interest in the
design of the stable and kennels as he had in his own
quarters; this was one of the reasons Silas had liked
him so well from their first meeting. In the scholar's
mind, no man who treated dumb beasts with such con-
sideration could be truly cruel, no matter what his reputation might be.

Another dog emerged from the steps that led down
into the kennels, sniffing the air. Usually the entire
pack roamed the courtyard until nightfall, but today he
saw only these two. Perhaps they, too, could sense the
tension in the air. Still, it was strange. As he watched,
the second dog squatted in the grass to do its business,
then trotted back to the kennels.

"Master Silas?" His chief assistant was coming toward him, carrying the money box with a scroll under his arm. "Some of the masons have been questioned again," he said as he reached him. "What shall we do?"

"Just answer honestly," Silas answered. He gave the young man a smile that he hoped was encouraging. The first dog he had seen got up and went back to the kennels as well. Were they hiding? "We have nothing to hide." His mind drifted again to the dog he had seen the night before, the way it had looked back at him, meeting his gaze like a man. "Go, tell the men to stop work for the day," he ordered. "I will be back."

The kennels were dark and cool, a pleasant place that smelled of straw and earth, not filth. DuMaine's dog boys had been charged most sternly with keeping the animals clean, and Lady Siobhan had kept up the practice, insisting the bedding here be changed as often as the rushes in the hall. A few of the brigands with dogs of their own for hunting or fighting still kept them near to hand out of habit, but most had joined the castle pack, mutts mixing with the purer breeds in a near-platonic peace their masters would be hard-pressed to emulate. Usually by this time of day, they would all have been awake and outside. But today they were all sleeping, gathered in a cozy ring around a central figure—a man who slept in their midst.

Silas crept closer, not trusting his eyes in the dim light. Surely he must be mistaken . . .

"My lord?" he said softly, hardly daring to speak. The

man was Tristan DuMaine. His clothes were poor, a peasant's garb, and his face was rough with beard. But there was no mistaking it was him. He slept on a makeshift bed of straw, his favorite hunting hound tucked in bliss against his side, its head on his chest. All of the dogs seemed eager to be near him, even the brigands' mutts, as if they knew their true master had returned. Watching in shock, Silas was happy beyond measure to see his friend alive. But for some strange reason he couldn't have named, the sight gave him a chill.

"Lord Tristan," he said, raising his voice a notch as he moved closer. The hound raised its head from Tristan's chest and blinked at him, his tail thumping the floor. "Tristan . . ." With pounding heart, he bent and touched the young man's shoulder.

His eyes snapped open, glowing green, and Silas recoiled in horror. Tristan grabbed him by the wrist as he sat up, his demonic eyes showing no sign of recognition, and his lips drew back in an animal snarl, showing long, white fangs. "Y-you," Silas stammered, too shocked to struggle. "It was you . . ."

Holding the scholar in a grip of iron, Tristan fought for clarity, to see beyond the drunken haze that was his daylight world. "Silas . . ." The fear in his friend's eyes was almost comical—he must look a perfect horror. "You can't . . ." Even his voice was slurred, and he was speaking much too loudly, trying to be heard over the living man's heartbeat, like thunder to him. He had never fed the night before, he suddenly remembered. Silas was in danger, friend or not. "You must not come upon me without warning, Silas, not in daylight, at least," he said, consciously speaking more softly. "I am . . ." He smiled a bitter smile. "I am not myself."

"I see that." Silas smiled as well, his heartbeat slowing down a bit. As soon as Tristan had spoken, the worst of his fear had abated in spite of his monstrous appearance. Monster or not, he was still DuMaine. "Welcome home, my lord."

Tristan smiled in earnest. "Many thanks." He released Silas's wrist, feeling rather foolish. He still felt thick, and the hunger was still there. But seeing Silas so calm made him feel calmer himself. The man was frightened, but he wasn't hysterical. He still knew Tristan for the man he had been, the man he still was at heart, and that was a greater comfort to him than he ever could have guessed it would be. He was not quite so alone after all. He offered his hand and smiled as the scholar clasped it. "I am glad to see you, Silas."

11

Siobhan awoke again, this time from a nightmare. "My lady?" Emma said. "Are you well?"

"Fine." Her mouth felt dry, and her skin was still clammy with fear. "I am fine."

"Master Silas sent you a book," the girl said, handing over a weathered, leather-bound tome nearly as big as a tabletop. "Michael brought it up."

"Wonderful," she said, opening it at once.

After a few pages of the horrors written there, she thought she would never sleep peacefully again. Her Latin was not the best, and the text was written in the common vernacular of a soldier of the days when Rome still ruled and the language was still spoken in the streets, not the formal diction of the contemporary letters and religious texts she was accustomed to reading. But even understanding only half of what was written was enough to make her hair turn white. The incubus, the succubus, the fire-breathing worm-gods of the Irish pagans—if the writer was to be believed, he had encountered every scaly, fanged beastie hell had ever spawned. But so far none of them sounded remotely like Tristan DuMaine.

She got up from the bed, slowly this time, and went to the window. In her dream, she had been standing in this selfsame spot but in the ancient druid's tower, gazing at the setting sun. She couldn't remember any particular detail that should have frightened her, only words spoken by someone behind her. "The wolf has found us . . ." She had not recognized the voice, and now the words meant nothing. But the sense of dread she had felt inside the dream remained.

"Michael also brought more food," Emma said. "The guard would not even let me see him."

"I'm sorry, Emma." The poor girl had done nothing wrong; it was cruel that she should be punished. But there was little Siobhan could do. She took her book to the table to keep reading, and soon she heard the bed creak behind her. By the time she heard Emma snoring, she was lost in the Roman soldier's story once again.

The shadows had grown long and the room dim enough for her to think of lighting a candle when she happened upon what she wanted. "A sad, strange tale," the soldier began, or words to that effect.

We came upon a town where a witch was about to be stoned. She was a beautiful young woman, and our captain demanded to be told the evidence against her.

"She is the consort of a devil," the city fathers told

us. "Her husband who was dead has come to her."
They showed us marks upon the creature's neck,
saying the dead man had fed upon her blood, and when
the captain questioned her, she swore that it was so.
"She raised him up," the priest who had condemned
her said. "She has used magic to transform him to a
demon." "Not I," the woman wept, but none in the
town did believe her. Seeing no hope of discovering
more without causing a riot, the captain allowed them
to proceed, and the woman was stoned until dead.

That night as we camped on the green, we heard
a commotion from the church—a brawl, or so it
sounded. A patrol of us went to investigate and beheld
a sight such as I might hardly describe. The witch's
demon husband had returned in search of her and was
wreaking vengeance on the town. His shape was the
same as any normal man, but his eyes glowed like
embers in a fire, and in his mouth were the fangs of a
lion. The priest demanded he be gone in the name of
Holy God, and the demon was averted for a moment.
But when the priest did let the crucifix he carried fall,
the demon fell upon him, ripping out his throat.

We did attack the monster, but our swords were
all but useless. A hundred wounds we did inflict,
but none did harm him, all healing in an instant,
and I did smell brimstone in his blood. At last in
desperation, my sword broken, I did raise a stake
of wood against him, driving it straight through
his heart. With the howling of a thousand wolves,

he fell, never to rise. One of my comrades struck his
head from his shoulders, and the corpse did dissolve
into bile.

Since that time, I have told this story to a learned
monk of the mountains of the East. He told me that
this creature was a thing his people call "vampire,"
a man neither living nor dead, cursed forevermore
to walk the world of night. What should make such
a monster he could not tell, but I do not doubt his
word.

"Vampire," Siobhan said softly, touching the word
on the page. Somehow Tristan had become this thing,
vampire. She thought of his laughter as she tried to
cut him with her sword, the way his flesh had healed
itself with a hiss like blood in flame. "You cannot kill
me," he had mocked her. "But I can kill anyone I like."

"No one dies tonight," she had demanded of him,
and he had agreed—"As you will," he had promised.
But he had killed Sam just the same. Against her will,
she remembered his face as he kissed her, the sweetness
of his touch. He had bewitched her, but not just with
demon's magic. She had wanted him, longed for him
from the first time they met, the first moment he had
touched her. "I will return from hell itself to punish
you," he had sworn at their wedding, and so he had
done, just as he had promised. "I will kill you, darling."

"No," she said now, speaking to the gathering gloom
of the night. "I will kill you first." The very thought

made tears rise in her eyes, but she would not let them fall. Tristan was a monster, a vampire. A stake of wood could destroy him.

For a moment, she considered sending for Sean and showing him what she had read, but she quickly decided against it. *He would not believe me,* she thought, remembering the poor wife in the story, stoned for a witch. Had she loved her husband? Had she feared him in his demon's form?

"It doesn't matter," she said aloud. "He is evil. He must be destroyed."

"My lady?" Emma said, yawning as she sat up on the bed.

"Where is my sword?" She went to where she had left it and found nothing but the clothes she had worn the night before. "Where is it?" She opened her trunk and found it laid inside, the short sword she had found in the cliff as a girl.

"My lady, what is wrong?" Emma said, getting up.

"Nothing," she promised. "Nothing has changed." A sword alone was little use to her, she thought. She needed a stake as well. "Emma, I'm freezing."

"Freezing?" the girl said, aghast. It was midsummer; the room was sweltering hot.

"Yes," Siobhan said. "Go downstairs and fetch wood for the fire—lots of kindling. That hearth is old; it may not be easy to light." Clare was sitting up as well, watching her with green eyes so like Tristan's, their gaze made her shiver.

"Take Clare with you," she ordered. "Hurry—I'm chilled to the bone."

"My lady, they won't let me," the girl protested. "The guards—"

"Ho there," Siobhan said, banging on the door. "Open up at once." The door swung open barely a crack, and one of Sean's most trusted and least efficient brigands peered inside. "Where is my brother?" she demanded.

"Downstairs, my lady," he answered. "He said you were not to be left."

"Did he, in faith?" she asked, privately pleased. If she had to slip out, this boy would give her little trouble. "Did he say I was to be frozen?"

"No, my lady, of course not," he said, obviously confused. "But—"

"This girl is going to fetch me some wood," she cut him off, catching Emma by the wrist and dragging her to the door. "She is going to take the child with her to take her to the privy on the wall."

"The captain said—"

"The captain has not spent the day locked up with a fretful child," Siobhan interrupted again. "What is her crime, that she should be imprisoned?" Clare had come to stand beside her, and at this, she looked up, a tiny frown wrinkling her brow. "Take her yourself, if you fear Sean so much."

"I?" he stammered, appalled. "Nay, my lady, I could not."

"Then let Emma do it." The maid gave her hand a

conspirator's squeeze. "Hurry," she ordered, shoving her through the door.

"I don't want to go," Clare said, deepening her frown. "I want to stay with you."

"And so you shall," Siobhan promised. She would keep her promise; she would protect this child as if she were her own. "But for now, you must go with Emma."

"Come, my lady," Emma said, holding out her hand. "We will be back soon." With a final long, questioning look, the child obeyed, taking her nursemaid's hand.

"Do not linger, Emma," Siobhan said. "No more than a moment." She gave her a wink behind the guardsman's back. "I will be right here."

Orlando watched as Simon saddled his horse. "I don't suppose I should waste breath on objecting," the little wizard said wryly.

"You can if you wish," Simon answered with a grin. "But you cannot stop me." Malachi snorted as if eager to be under way, and Simon scratched under his chin. "I won't be long. The main road isn't far."

"What have you told Lady Isabel in your letter?" Orlando asked.

"Everything, of course." He swung into the saddle. "If something happens, I want her to know what became of us." He brought the horse around. "As soon as I find someone headed south who looks trustworthy, I'll give them the letter and ride back."

"As you will," the wizard nodded. Tristan, their new

comrade-at-arms, had not returned the night before; heaven only knew what mischief he had found at his castle. "You did send her my greetings, I hope?"

Simon smiled again. "Of course." In truth, he hesitated to leave his small companion alone, particularly with Kivar most likely on their trail. But Orlando had insisted he could not leave Tristan with no guidance at all, whether the new vampire wanted help or not. "I won't be long," he repeated, clucking to his horse. With a final wave, he rode away.

Silas entered the crowded hall with the golden mastiff following at his heel. The day's mad activity had done nothing to inform the castle residents of the nature of the evil that pursued them and little to assuage their fears. The so-called castle guard had been brigand bandits barely a month before; their discipline was somewhat less than perfect, and they were angry. "What are we supposed to do, then, Captain?" one of them was demanding of Sean as Silas and his companion came in. "Wait around for whoever or whatever it is that's killing us to pick us off one by one?"

"No one goes anywhere alone," Sean answered. "No man is to venture outside this tower or off the walls without a full patrol."

The discussion made it ridiculously simple for Silas and Tristan to pass unnoticed through the hall and out the other side.

At the foot of the stairs, they encountered Emma,

leading Clare by the hand. "Well met, mistress," Silas said, giving her a smile.

"Master," she nodded in reply. Clare shrank against her, obviously fearful of the dog. "It's all right, sweeting," the nursemaid soothed. "He seems tame enough."

"Quite tame," Silas agreed. "I think I can promise you, Lady Clare. This beast will never harm you."

The child edged closer, one hand held out before her as Siobhan had shown her to do. "He's pretty," she ventured.

"Magnificent," Silas said, smiling at Emma and trying not to hold his breath. The dog nudged Clare's hand, and she gasped, but she did not draw back.

"He likes me," she said with a smile.

"He certainly seems to," Emma agreed.

"I am sure of it," Silas said. For the first time since finding him that morning, the scholar began to have some sense of the agony his young friend must be suffering. He loved his child above all else in the world; how horrible it must be to be so near to her and unable to touch her or protect her.

"Hello, doggie," Clare said softly, reaching out to barely stroke the golden fur on the animal's neck. "Hello." She took a step closer as Tristan sat back on his haunches. "So soft." She knelt beside him and pressed her cheek against his neck, breathing deeply. "He smells like Papa."

"I hardly think so," Emma laughed. "Come, my lady. We are meant to hurry, remember?"

"Where are the two of you headed, mistress?" Silas asked, prolonging the moment as best he could.

"Not far," Emma answered. "My little lady has been shut up all day."

"I see." Silas suddenly remembered; Lebuin had kept the child locked up with Siobhan. But if Tristan truly meant to do as he said, the last place his daughter should be just now was in the tower. Hidden in the kennels, Tristan had explained how he had become the creature he was, this vampire, and Silas had told him all that had passed while he was gone, how Sean Lebuin had insisted the castle be finished, and of his alliance with this mysterious Baron of Callard. "Lebuin makes fine speeches and can be clever, moment to moment, but he seems to have no skill for planning on his own," he had explained. "The strategist is Siobhan."

"Bollocks," Tristan had scoffed with a laugh, scratching his hound between the ears.

"Not so, my lord," Silas had warned him. "She told me herself, it was she who arranged for the murder of my masons—she all but boasted of it. The peasants here look to her to protect them, not Sean." Tristan's expression of fury had been terrible to behold. "In faith, I doubt not it was she who convinced them to betray you."

"My darling wife." Seeing him smile as he said it, Silas could well have called him demon. And now he had come to take revenge. "Emma, will you do me a kindness?" he said now.

"Of course, master." She laid a hand on Clare's golden head, but she made no effort to pull her away from the dog.

"I have left some papers in my room in the manor house," he said, improvising. "But I mean to pass the night here in the hall—"

"Aye, master, you must," she said quickly "It isn't safe—" She broke off, glancing at the child. "I will fetch your papers."

"Thank you, mistress." He racked his brain for a moment. "They are . . . they are on my desk, of course. A bundle of scrolls—just bring whatever you find."

"I will." She held out her hand, and Clare reluctantly took it, rising to her feet. "Where will I find you?"

"I will be waiting in the hall." The dog that was his lord nuzzled the child's ear one last time, making her giggle. "Thank you, Emma."

"Not at all, Master Silas." With a final smile, she pressed the little one's hand between her own. "Come along, my lady."

Silas watched them go, disappearing through the archway that led to the hall. When he turned, Tristan stood beside him as a man. "God's light," he muttered, catching his breath.

"Forgive me, Silas." He laid a trembling hand on the older man's shoulder, steadying himself as much as Silas. "Thank you . . . I think I can manage from here."

"Are you certain?" Silas said, glancing fretfully up and down the curving staircase. "There will be guards—"

Tristan smiled. "Not to worry," he promised. "Go and wait for Emma in the hall."

*   *   *

As soon as Emma and the little one were gone, Siobhan bolted the door from the inside and fastened the shutters to the room's only window. She stripped off her kirtle and put on her breeches and boots with her underblouse, gathering her hair into a thong at the nape of her neck.

Someone was coming up the hall, muttering under his breath. She tucked the sword under the rug on the bed. "Aye, anon!" she called as someone pounded on the door. "Who comes?"

"It's me, my lady," a rough voice answered—one of the servants. "Joseph. I have brought your wood."

She unbolted the door and opened it. "Bring it in," she said, nodding again to her guard. "Just put it by the hearth."

The servant gave her costume a questioning glance. "Shall I make up the fire for you?"

"No," she said, shaking her head. "I . . . I have put on more clothes. My chill has passed."

He definitely thought she had lost her mind. "As you will, my lady," he said with a barely muffled sigh, heading for the door again with his arms still full.

"But leave the wood!" she ordered. "I might need it later—the nights are cold." In midsummer, she silently added, feeling a perfect fool.

He just stared at her for a moment with a half-smile on his face as if he thought she might be joking. "Of course," he said at last. He laid the wood on the hearth, his eyes never leaving her face. "Sleep well, my lady."

"Thank you," she nodded. "I shall try." She smiled at him as pleasantly as she could manage as he left, then bolted the door behind him.

None of the wood was quite what she wanted as a stake—the logs were too thick, and the kindling was too small. She picked up the most likely candidate and pretended to strike an imaginary foe, trying to imagine driving it into the heart of a demon vampire. Into Tristan's heart, she corrected herself, shivering in horror at the thought. "God save me," she said softly. "Give me strength to do it, for I swear I cannot."

More footsteps were coming up the corridor—could Emma and Clare be back so soon? She tucked the stake into her belt behind her back like she might hide a dagger and turned to face the door.

She heard the guard cry out sharply for barely a moment, then a thud against the door that shook it in its frame. "Owen?" she said, calling the guard by name. "Joseph? Is that you?"

For a long moment, she heard nothing, then the sound of something heavy sliding down the door. She heard the outside bolt slide back. "Who is there?" she demanded, her heart beginning to pound so hard it ached. The handle turned, but her bolt was still fastened, a heavy bolt of iron. "Tristan?" I will come again, he had promised. You need not seek me out.

Wait! she wanted to cry out, I am not ready! She was meant to destroy him; he had killed two of their men, killed Sam after he had promised he would not. In truth, he had killed young Owen just that very moment. If she couldn't stop him, drive the stake through his heart, strike his head from his shoulders, he would murder Sean and everyone else she held dear.

But he was her husband. It had begun as a joke, a taunt against her enemy, but somehow the vows they had taken had become the truth. How could she kill the man she had known the night before? He had bewitched her, but all that she had done, she had wanted. She wanted him, wanted to touch him, to be his just as he demanded. She was a woman, weak and foolish, just as she had always feared. "Go away," she ordered, a childish defense. "I will not let you in." The handle turned again, slowly, and the door rattled in its frame. "I said go away!" Please, Tristan, she begged inside her head. Please, don't make me kill you.

A thin, gray tendril of smoke curled up from the crack under the door. She backed away, watching as it rose and thickened, and a soft, pleasant scent filled the room, like new-mown hay at twilight, wet with dew. She reached behind her for the bed, her fingers seeking out the sword hidden under the rug, but she was clumsy and distracted, hypnotized by the mist as it writhed and turned solid. In a few dizzy moments, the sword was forgotten as her demon lover stood before her.

"You cannot banish me, Siobhan," he said, coming closer, his handsome face distorted with fury. "This is my castle." She moved as if to run, and he caught her by the shoulders. "You are my wife."

"How can a dead man have a wife?" she scoffed, taunting him as always, but this time he shook her, making her cry out.

"Tell me the truth," he demanded, not in the seductive demon's purr that had entranced her so completely the night before but in the rough, heartfelt voice of a righteous man betrayed. "Tell me you murdered the men who were building this castle, innocent workers who never wronged you or anyone else."

"What?" The night before, he had smiled at her, teased her, made love to her—why was he so angry now? "No," she said, shaking her head. "I didn't . . . not really. I didn't think—"

"Why doesn't that surprise me?" he said, mocking her.

"It was months ago," she protested. "I told Sam we would have an easier time making you go back to France if your castle could not be completed, and he . . ." Her voice trailed off as she looked up at him. "You killed him."

The accusation in her eyes was more than Tristan could bear—how dare she accuse him? Who in heaven's name was Sam? "You ordered those men killed," he said, aghast.

"I never ordered anything," she insisted. "I have no power to give orders—do you not see where I am now, a prisoner?" She couldn't think, not with him glaring at her so. Emma and Clare would be back any moment; she had to act quickly. But what was she going to do? "I did not mourn those men, but I did not kill them. I would have, but—Tristan, why are you surprised? You knew what I was; I never pretended—"

"Aye, lady, I knew," he said with a bitter laugh. "I knew the first moment I saw you, unnatural little beast, firing arrows at my men." A rage very different from the need for revenge he had felt on his way home was making him dizzy. "I should have killed you—"

"You tried, but you missed," she retorted.

"Then using an innocent child as a hostage," he went on, his voice thick with disgust. "Tell me, Siobhan—does Clare remember how you meant to cut her throat?"

"I would never have done it," she said angrily, confessing the truth without thinking. "I prayed to God you would not call my bluff—"

"As if I would have risked my child—"

"How was I to know that?" she demanded. "I didn't know you! You were a stranger, this Norman who was making slaves of my father's people—you had just killed my brother's best friend—"

"Who was trying to kill me, if I recall aright," he said sarcastically.

"You meant to kill Sean, and I couldn't . . ." An aching lump rose in her throat, all the grief she had been holding back so long, she barely thought about it anymore. She hardly knew what she was saying or even thinking; the words just came pouring out. "I couldn't let you kill him, Tristan; I can't . . . he's all I have left, and he loves me." Tears were blinding her; his chest as he held her by the shoulders was a blur before her eyes, and if he hadn't been holding her, she might have crumpled to the floor. "They killed Papa like a dog, cut his head off right in front of our house with me and Mama watching," she said, sobbing like the weakling girl she had sworn she would never be again. "Norman soldiers . . . we were nobles; the king had made Papa a knight. Sean was a knight . . ." Her vampire husband's face had changed; she saw pity in his warm green eyes, and pain twisted her heart like a fist. "They raped my mother, Tristan, all of them, over and over, because she was a woman, and she couldn't even fight. I couldn't fight . . ." She thought of the sword she had hidden behind her, found on that terrible night. "I watched them," she told him, cold to the marrow of her bones. "I ran away . . ." She bent her head and cried as he drew her against him.

"Hush now," he murmured, pressing her close. He barely recognized his own voice, could hardly believe the man comforting her was himself. He had never done such a thing in his life except with Clare, his own perfect, innocent child. Siobhan was none of those things—she was not perfect; she was hardly innocent; and she was a woman grown, old enough and strong enough to shoulder her own burdens, certainly. But like Clare, she was his, and he could not bear to see her pain. "Of course you ran away." He kissed her hair. "They would have murdered you as well, or worse."

"Yes," she admitted through a hiccup, clutching his tunic in her fists. She wanted so much to melt against him, to let him comfort her. He was so strong, stronger than any man she had ever known, and he held her safe. A moment before, he had wanted to murder her, but the sight of her tears made him tender—what manner of madness was that?

"Don't cry," he said gruffly, the lion's growl. In his mind, he could see her, a terrified child, running for her life from the men who had slaughtered her family and destroyed her home. 'Twas no great wonder she hated all Normans, Tristan himself included. "It's over now," he promised.

No, she thought. It is not. Not nearly. But looking up at him, she couldn't seem to say it. She wanted to tell him the rest, that she had killed a man that night, her first kill ever, that every night since she had seen the dead man's face haunting her dreams. She wanted to tell him she knew what he was, that she was more afraid of him than she had ever been of anything in her life. She needed to say it not to hurt him, but to make him comfort her, make him promise he would never hurt her, that she need not be afraid. But meeting his eyes with her own, she could not make the words come out. "Tristan," she whispered, sick at heart. The corner of his mouth quirked up, almost a smile, and she kissed him, unable to do anything else.

He gathered her closer, passion flaring between them in an instant. She wrapped her arms around his neck, crushing her breasts against his chest as she reached up for him, desperate to be closer still. He lifted her off of her feet, her legs entwined around his hips. "I should murder you," he murmured, breaking the kiss for barely a moment before kissing her again. "My love . . ."

"My love," she echoed, feeding on his mouth. "I love—"

"Tristan!" Silas was coming through the door, obviously out of breath. "Hurry—Lebuin!"

"Siobhan!" Sean's voice shouted, his footfalls heavy coming up the hall, followed by others. "Sweet Christ . . . Owen? Owen!" Then they were running.

Tristan put Siobhan behind him, keeping a grip on her wrist. He turned to the door just as Lebuin burst in.

"Siobhan!" he was shouting, but the name died on his tongue, his mouth falling open in shock. His face went white, and his eyes went wide.

"Did your sister not tell you I would come?" Tristan demanded with a smile, the brigand's fear all that he ever could have wished. Still holding Siobhan by the wrist, he advanced, fangs bared, ready to strike.

A blade of fire pierced his flesh, so unexpected he gasped. Looking down, he saw a sword point protruding from his chest for a moment before it was withdrawn, and pain like he had felt in the moment he was dying seemed to rip him apart. Turning in horror, he saw Siobhan holding the sword. Tears streaming down her face, she struck again, slashing at his throat as if she meant to behead him. He recoiled, knocking the blade aside, but not before it sliced through his skin, pouring blood from his throat. He grabbed for her, twisting the sword from her grip, but the wounds she had made were not healing. He was weakening. "No," he protested, touching her cheek, and her lip trembled as she reached behind her, drawing a stake of wood.

"Kill him!" Sean ordered, rushing forward, and Tristan turned, knocking him aside like he might have been a child. With a roar at the others, he lunged for the window, ripping the shutter from the frame.

"Tristan!" Siobhan screamed, rushing forward as he jumped. Her hands made fists on empty air as Silas caught her from behind. "No!" The vampire fell through the darkness, his white tunic like a ghost as it rippled in the moonlight until he crashed at last and disappeared into the brush at the foot of the ravine. "Oh, dear God . . ." She turned, tearing away from Silas. Sean reached for her, and she grabbed up the sword, still red with Tristan's blood. "Stay back!" Pushing past him and his men, she sprinted for the stairs.

"My lady!" Michael called as she ran across the hall. "A message—!" But she barely heard him, plunging out the door.

"Tristan!" She half-ran, half-slid down the steep, sandy bank. This was the site of her first kill, the place where she had found her sword. But all she could think about was finding Tristan; she did not even care what she would do when he was found or what he would most surely do to her. "Tristan!" Some of the thorny hedges were broken and crushed, and crawling underneath the thicket she could feel blood on the ground. But the vampire was gone.

*　　*　　*

In canine form, Tristan swam across the moat, struggling to keep his head above the surface. The bones he had broken in his fall had healed at once, but the wounds Siobhan had made still bled and burned; he was feeling weaker by the moment. Siobhan . . . how could she betray him now, turn from his kiss to his murder in a moment? The thought made him feel worse, so faint and sick, he could barely climb the bank when he reached it. He half-ran, half-staggered to the cover of the forest, collapsing in a thicket. Why was he not healing? Even hell itself had turned on him, it seemed.

By force of will alone, he transformed into a man and made himself rise to his feet. He whistled for Daimon, hoping against hope that the horse had not been discovered or wandered away after being left alone so long. After a moment, a great white shadow appeared in the trees, and he almost wept with relief. "Come," he ordered, and Daimon came closer, waiting patiently as he climbed into the saddle, pain making him see stars. "Good lad," he muttered, patting the horse's neck. Wrapping the reins around his fist, he let himself slump forward, trusting Daimon to find his way back to their shelter.

When Orlando heard hoofbeats, he assumed Simon had returned. He left the shelter, prepared to let fly with a lecture to frighten the birds from their nests. But the horse was white, and the rider looked barely able to sit up. "Tristan!" He rushed forward as quickly as his legs would carry him, reaching the horse just as it stopped. "What on earth . . . ?"

Tristan thought he was starting to improve. He didn't seem to be bleeding anymore. But the burning pain had turned cold, as if he were freezing from the inside out. "Well met, wizard," he muttered, the most he could manage to get out before tumbling unconscious to the ground.

12

Simon returned just before dawn, fully expecting Orlando to meet and scold him. When the wizard did not, he knew something was wrong.

"What happened to him?" he asked, coming into the shelter and seeing Tristan laid out on the floor.

"So now you turn up," Orlando said sarcastically, barely glancing up from rummaging through his pack. "I had to drag him in here by his feet. If he hadn't been in such sorry shape, he would have been mightily embarrassed."

"Why couldn't he walk on his own?" He crouched beside the pallet. Orlando had stripped off Tristan's tunic and cleaned his wounds, but both were still livid and open. If Simon hadn't known better, he would have sworn he was dead. "What could do this to a vampire?"

"Nothing, from all I know," Orlando answered. He pushed Simon aside and began to stitch the gash in Tristan's stomach. "A stake would have destroyed him. A wound from a blade should have healed."

"But these do not." After more than ten years being

sure he could not really be wounded, Simon found this rather upsetting.

"Actually, they are healing," Orlando admitted. "The gash in his throat was much worse when I first examined it—someone apparently tried to take his head."

"Someone who knew what he was?" Simon asked. "Someone who knew how to destroy a vampire?"

"I cannot guess, and Tristan did not say," the wizard answered. "He was conscious, barely, when he made it back here, but he said very little before he passed out." He finished his stitches and sat back. "We will question him more when he wakes."

"If he wakes," Simon said morosely.

"Don't take on like an Irishman," his small companion scolded with the tiniest hint of a smile. "He will wake. I suspect that by nightfall, he will be just as he was." He stroked his beard, frowning in thought. "But I do wonder how he was wounded."

"Aye," Simon agreed with a sardonic smile of his own. "So do I." He tossed Orlando the sack of food he had brought him, then closed and sealed the door.

"So where were you, then?" the wizard asked. "Did you have trouble finding a messenger?"

"Not at all," he answered, sitting on the floor with his legs stretched out before him. "I found a traveling minstrel as soon as I came to the main road. He was in rather a hurry to be gone from this region, and the idea of serving a duke and his duchess at Charmot suited him right well."

"So why was he in such a hurry?" Orlando asked, guessing the heart of the matter at once.

"He spent a day and night with the baron of Callard, some two days' ride from here," Simon answered. "Apparently he didn't like his welcome."

"The baron is not a music lover?" Orlando said, arching an eyebrow.

"I asked the same question." The sun was rising; he could feel the daytime need to rest creeping over him. "He said no, that the baron paid him well enough and wanted him to stay. But other matters in his hall were too . . . what was the word he used? Unsettled."

Orlando opened the jug of mead Simon had brought and sniffed it with a smile. "Indeed?"

"I tried to get him to say more, but he would not. So I made my own investigation." Tristan muttered something in his sleep—a good sign, Simon supposed.

"You paid a call on the baron?" Orlando asked, surprised.

"I didn't have to," Simon answered. "If the number of fled peasants I found on the road are any indication, his lands will be empty before the month is out. They say a strange plague has oppressed the baron and his household—a disease that causes the blood to dry up in a man's veins."

"And what has made them think so?" Orlando said, his interest more piqued.

"The fact that all who die from it are found with no blood in them at all," Simon answered. "I spoke to one old woman who had been a cook in the baron's own house. She was so frightened, she could hardly speak at all."

Orlando swallowed a healthy mouthful of bread. "But you persuaded her."

Simon smiled. "A bit. She said 'twas no sickness killing Callard's men but a great serpent." Orlando stopped chewing, and he nodded. "She said that she had seen the marks—two round gashes in the throat."

"A vampire," Orlando said. "Could Tristan have ventured so far?"

"He could have, but I doubt he would," Simon said. "His purpose is here, remember? Besides . . ." All traces of good humor left his face. "Some of the killings were done in daylight."

All color drained from the wizard's face. "You are certain of this?"

"Certain enough." He had settled back against the wall, but now he sat up again, fighting to stay awake until his tale was told. "Several of the people I questioned spoke of men being taken while working in the fields or hunting in the forest—alive in the morning, dead at night."

Orlando set his bread aside, no longer hungry. "Lucan Kivar."

"We know he was following Tristan." From the night he had made Simon a vampire, Kivar had survived by inhabiting the bodies of the dead, somewhat free to wander day or night. But he still apparently needed to feed on the blood of the living to maintain the illusion and keep the body he had stolen fresh. Simon had driven him out of his last mortal form with an enchanted stake found in the catacombs beneath the castle Charmot, the home of Simon's beloved, Isabel. But his spirit had escaped. "Perhaps when we found Tristan, he fled."

"He has no cause to fear us," Orlando said bluntly. He got up and checked the seal on the door as if fearful some evil might break in at any moment. "If Kivar is oppressing this baron of Callard, he has a reason for it." He looked down at Tristan, a frown of worry on his face. "I fear we shall know it soon enough.

By daybreak, Siobhan and a patrol of brigand guardsmen had searched every inch of the moat around the tower motte, and other patrols had searched every inch of the castle. But Tristan was nowhere to be found.

She walked back into the tower exhausted and filthy, her clothes torn by brambles and caked with mud. The hall was empty except for Sean, sitting on the dais, staring at nothing like a man in a trance. "Did you find the body?" he asked, turning to her as she came in.

"No." She took the cup Cilla offered her and drank.

"How is that possible?" Her brother sounded as if every spark of life inside him was gone, leaving a hollow shell. "You saw him fall. No man could survive a fall from such a height." His expression twisted in a snarl of rage. "Someone has hidden the body—"

"Sean, stop," she cut him off. "No one could have reached him before I did, even if they had been watching. There was no body to find." *I told you!* she wanted to shout at him. She might have if she hadn't been so tired.

Instead she went to him and put an arm around his shoulders, pressing a kiss to his forehead. He laid his head against her for a moment, squeezing her close as he repeated, "How is that possible?"

"Wait here," she said, pulling free. "I will show you." Silas was nowhere to be seen, she suddenly noticed, nor was Gaston. "I have a book upstairs."

"A book?" he repeated through a laugh that sounded like the nearer edge of madness.

"Just wait."

Her room upstairs was just as she had left it. The shutter hung loose from one nail in its top hinge, where Tristan had ripped it open. Tristan's blood stained the rug where she had stabbed him with her sword. "Forgive me," she whispered, making herself look away. The book still lay on the table, open to the page where she had read the tale of the vampire.

Sean's Latin was only a little better than her own, but he read the story quickly, his eyes growing wider with horror by the moment. "You see?" she said when it seemed he was done. "Tristan is a vampire."

He looked up at her. "You conjured him?" he demanded. "You called him up from the grave?"

"I called him . . . are you mad?" All that was written

on the pages, the nature of the demon his enemy had become, the only way to destroy him, and all her idiot of a brother could see was that a woman must have called him up. "No, Sean, I did not conjure Tristan from the grave." She shuddered with a sudden chill, remembering. "Unless it was at our wedding. He swore he would return to punish me, remember? Even from hell itself."

"Aye, I remember," Sean said, standing up. "I would have kept him gagged, but no. You had to torment him."

The sheer injustice of this charge was almost more than she could bear. "Aye, brother, I wanted to torment him. And you wanted me to marry him in the first place."

The angry energy drained from him in an instant. "Aye," he admitted with a bitter smile. "I did."

"The point is not how he came to be this vampire," she went on patiently. "The point is how we must defend ourselves against him."

He looked up at her, a strange sort of admiration dawning in his eyes. "You meant to kill him," he said, incredulous. "Last night in the tower . . . you were trying to cut off his head."

"Yes." Even now, the thought made her feel sick. But what choice had she had? What choice would she have when he returned?

"Forgive me," Sean said, reaching for her hand. "I thought . . . you cannot imagine what I thought."

"I don't have to imagine," she said tersely. "I know." And it's true, she thought but did not say. I do love him. If you had not come in when you did, I would have told him so. Her brother kissed her hand, and she smiled, tears rising in her eyes. For years, she had lived for Sean's approval. But now it meant nothing at all.

"Sean." Michael was coming in, looking as exhausted as she felt. "It's true—the message from the sentries was correct. Our scouts have confirmed it."

"Message?" she said, confused.

"A message arrived from our sentries on the road just as your husband was learning to fly," Sean explained with a touch of his old humor. "The king's agent and his retinue are almost here, less than a day away. The baron of Callard is with them."

"Callard has betrayed us?" she said. "Where is Gaston?"

"Gaston is in his rooms," he answered. "And no, we have no reason to believe the baron has betrayed us. Perhaps he encountered the king's man on the road."

"Tristan has received no new letter from the king," she pointed out, her mind racing in spite of her condition. "Why would he just send someone—?"

"It's not that hard to imagine," Sean insisted. "Du-Maine was—is—the king's cousin. Perhaps he wanted someone he trusted to see his new wife for himself."

"Perhaps." Sean wanted to believe his plan could still work, that all would still be well. If he thought his great ally, the baron, had abandoned him, he might despair altogether, and then where would she be? "When do the scouts believe the party will arrive?" she asked Michael.

"By nightfall at the latest," Michael answered. "Perhaps as early as midday."

"Lovely," she grumbled. So much for any of them having any rest. "Very well." She gathered her strength and her wits, refusing to dwell for so much as a moment on the consequences if her plans should fail. "Michael, where is Emma?"

"In the manor house with Lady Clare," he said, obviously confused.

Clare, she thought, her resolve threatening to fail. Poor child . . . what was to become of her? She had said she had seen her father; did she know what he was? Not now, she scolded herself. You cannot stop to think about that now. "Ask her to come to my room and help me," she said aloud. "And Cilla as well. I'll need a bath, and someone will have to do something with my hair. That gown I wore for my wedding is atrocious; I'll have to find something else." What perversity made you wear that gown? Tristan's voice mocked her from her memory.

"What are you saying?" Sean asked.

"I'm supposed to charm the baron, am I not?" He looked so surprised and pleased, she could almost have laughed at him. "I hardly think I can do it dressed like this."

"But what of DuMaine?" Michael said, meeting her eyes, obviously as doubtful as she was herself.

"Tristan has never appeared to me in daylight," she answered. "Perhaps he cannot." She took another deep breath, silently praying for strength. Please, God, just get me through this moment and the next. "In any case, there's naught we can do about him now."

"We will manage him," Sean promised, giving her a hug.

"Aye," she answered, making herself smile. He meant well, her brother; he deserved her loyalty the same as he had all her life. Why did she want desperately to punch him in the face? "We will manage." She drew back and looked up at him, willing herself to see him as she always had, the hero who could vanquish any foe and would always protect her. It was hard, but not impossible, and her smile became more true. "We always have before."

Once again, Siobhan regarded her reflection in the mirror. "You look beautiful, my lady," Emma said, standing behind her.

"Do I?" In truth, she could hardly believe the woman before her was even herself. Her thick black hair was combed perfectly smooth and pinned back from her face in a proper married woman's coiffure, crowned with a circlet of gold over a flimsy excuse for a veil of the finest linen. She wore a gown of blue brocade the color of her eyes over a white silk chemise, its delicate lace peeking out at the bodice, and the points of her sleeves were so long, she thought she would surely trip over them going down the stairs. On her feet were tiny slippers so delicate they would surely dissolve if she stepped in a puddle. Her skin was scrubbed white as marble, but her cheeks were flushed pink with anxiety, and her eyes were bright. "I do," she decided. But she was not herself.

"You look like a princess," Clare said, watching from the bed. The rug stained with her father's blood had been taken out and thrown away before she was allowed to come into the room, and she seemed to know nothing of what had happened the night before. "My papa will be pleased."

Siobhan turned to look at her, but before she could answer, the door opened, and Silas came in. His eyes when he saw her widened in shock. "Heaven shield my heart," he said, pressing a hand to his chest and smiling for a moment, though the worry never left his eyes.

"Your heart is safe with me," she promised, returning his smile. "Thank you for coming, Master Silas."

"I wasn't aware I had a choice." He glanced at Emma and winked, and the nursemaid laughed nervously before she looked away. "Your brother said it was urgent."

"Quite, I'm afraid." She went to Clare and caressed her little cheek, earning the sad little half of a smile that was the best she could hope for from her. "Will you go with Emma, please? I need to speak to the master alone."

"Yes." She rose up to her knees on the bed and

opened her arms, and Siobhan embraced her, burying her face for a moment in her golden hair. "You need not be so worried, my lady," Clare said softly for her ears alone. "Papa will be here anon."

Siobhan's heart flipped over like a jester in her breast, but she smiled as she let her go, and said, "I have no doubt."

"I must say, it's hard to imagine," Silas said when Emma and the child were gone. Siobhan raised an eyebrow. "That she should be so fond of you, my lady," he explained. "And you of her."

"Anyone would be fond of Lady Clare," she answered brusquely. "She is a beautiful, sweet-tempered little girl." She made herself stop wringing her hands and went to the window. "Why she is fond of me, I could not guess."

"Because you are fond of her." He flipped the book she still had open on the table. "Her father was not the most jolly fellow either, if you will recall, but she loved him very much."

"Loves him, Silas," she corrected, turning back to him. "She loves him very much."

He smiled, but his eyes were wary. "Yes," he agreed. "Tristan still lives." He looked her up and down again as if he couldn't quite believe his eyes. "No thanks to you."

"I meant to kill him," she admitted. "I thought . . . God's truth, Silas, I don't know what I think anymore, or even what I feel."

Before he could answer or she could lose her nerve,

she began to tell him everything, every detail of Tristan's return. She had to trust someone; she was not wise enough to manage the chaos her life had become all alone. Sean would never understand—he had already proven as much. Emma was sweet, but she was an innocent maid with less experience to guide her through such matters than Siobhan had herself. Michael would have done anything in his power to help her, but his true loyalty would always be to Sean, and she could hardly blame him. If she had not lost her mind, she would be the same. Silas, wise and kind and noble, was her only hope. "Your book is how I found out what Tristan is," she finished. "It tells about a demon called a vampire—"

"It tells about dragons in Scotland as well," he reminded her gently.

"And if Tristan had breathed fire at me, I would believe he was that," she retorted, returning his smile. Just having it out was like lifting a weight from her chest. "But he is not. He is a vampire."

He just stood there looking at her for so long, she began to feel foolish. Then he nodded. "Yes," he said with a weary sigh. "I believe he is." He offered his hand, and she took it, the simple comfort of the gesture making tears threaten her again. "Last night you meant to kill him," he said, brushing her hair back from her face, his eyes searching hers. "What do you mean to do now?"

"I don't know," she admitted. She could feel the

sword strapped to her leg under the gown, within easy reach, but the thought of using it again made her feel sick. "Everything depends upon this man the king has sent, and this baron of Sean's, and mostly . . . mostly on Tristan himself." She squeezed his hand before she let him go. "He tried to kill Sean last night right here in this room, holding my hand just as you do now, as if I should allow it." She let him go to turn away from him, pacing, her skirts tangling around her legs. How did anyone move in such a costume? she thought. "But I cannot, Silas."

"Of course you cannot." She turned toward him in her pacing, and he caught her gently by the arm. "When your brother sent me to you, I thought you meant to sentence me to death," he said. "With the king's man coming and me knowing the truth of Tristan's death, it seemed logical."

"Sean thought that, too," she admitted. "I convinced him to let me deal with you, that I would decide what was best." The very idea seemed horrible, she knew. "He isn't a bad man, Silas. You have to understand—"

"I do understand, my lady," he cut her off gently.

"But I swear, I will not allow him to harm you," she finished. "I fear I am no good brigand, Silas. I am done wishing anyone harm."

"May you stay so ever after," he said with a smile. "In the meantime, I will make you the same promise." He lifted her hand to his lips. "I will do you no harm, either. Whatever you decide, whatever you say to these men who are coming, I will not dispute you." He took her hands in his and looked her up and down again. "Now, let me teach you the manners to match your gown."

Tristan awoke to the gloom of the shelter feeling more himself. He made himself sit up, fighting his ordinary daylight stupor. He felt no real pain, just the sort of general ache he remembered only too well from the morning after battles as a mortal man. He looked down at his chest and found the gash where Siobhan had stabbed him all but healed. Neat black stitches such as a surgeon would make crisscrossed the spot where the wound had been, but the skin underneath was barely scarred. He touched his throat and found it healed as well.

Simon was sleeping on the other side of the room, flung out in every direction on a soft traveler's pallet. Tristan rubbed the back of his own sore neck and grimaced. His vampire brother was far better prepared for the life of a demon than he was. Not only did he travel with a wizard, he apparently had excellent provisions.

As if in answer to his thought, the door opened, making him flinch back from the light. Orlando came in quickly, closing it behind him. "Good," he said, dropping a basket of washing. "You are awake."

"So it would seem." He watched, bemused, as the little wizard settled down to sort stockings. "Are you the one who stitched me up?"

"Better me than Simon," he answered. "Are you healed, then?"

"I think so." He took the dagger from his boot and began to cut the threads, wincing as he pulled each one out. "I didn't think I could be wounded so."

"No more did I." With a frown, Orlando put aside his laundry and came to take the dagger. "I know more about vampires than I would care to tell you," he said, removing the stitches much more gently and efficiently. "But I have never heard tell of any weapon that could do so much damage and have it last so long. How did it happen?"

"Siobhan," Tristan answered. With a stab of pain far more intense than the prick of losing his stitches, he thought of his beloved's face as she attacked him, weeping and miserable. His beloved . . . she was that, he realized, his wild, reckless demon of a wife, more than any other more gentle or manageable lady ever could have been. But she had tried to kill him. She had wept to do it, but she had done it just the same.

"A woman did this?" Orlando said, interrupting his thoughts. "How is that possible?"

"Why should you ask me?" Tristan retorted. "You are the one who claims to know so much of vampires. I just happen to be one."

Simon grumbled in his sleep and rolled over as if they were disturbing him, and the wizard smiled at him in obvious affection. "What sort of weapon did she use?" he asked more quietly.

"A sword," Tristan answered. In truth, he would have preferred not to speak of it at all, to Orlando or anyone else. But he supposed he had no choice. "A small, thick sword, smaller than any I have ever seen." He was surprised at how clearly he remembered the weapon. "The metal was a dull silver color, not bright like steel, but the blade was sharp."

"Obviously." His brow furrowed in concentration, the dwarf went to his pack and rummaged inside, emerging with a scroll. He opened it and studied what was written there, muttering under his breath too softly for Tristan to hear what he said.

"Does your paper tell of such a sword?" the vampire guessed.

"It might." He showed him the scroll. It was not covered with writing at all but a drawing. Most of the page was occupied by a rough map of Britain. But at the top was a cup—the chalice he and Simon were searching for, no doubt. Underneath it was a cross made from what looked like a wooden stake and a sword very much like Siobhan's.

"A stake," Tristan said, remembering. "She had a stake as well, hidden in her belt. She stabbed me, then slashed at my throat. Then she drew the stake."

"Merciful gods," Orlando muttered. "Whoever this woman is, Tristan, she knows what you are. And she knows how to kill you." He pointed. "Is this the sword?"

"It could be," he said with a frown. "This woman, as you call her, is my wife, the daughter of a local man, a brigand. What would she know of vampires?"

"Wife?" Orlando echoed, shocked. "Your child has a mother?"

"Every child has a mother, wizard," Tristan answered with a twisted smile. "But no, Siobhan is not Clare's mother." Saying this, he felt another odd, sad pang. "She is the wife forced on me by the brigands." From outside, he heard Daimon whinny in alarm. "It's rather a long story," he said, standing up. "Did you hide the horse?"

"Do I look as if I could have hidden the horse?" Orlando said, rising to his own small height. "In truth, the beast would hardly let me near you." He led the way to the door, holding a hand out behind him as if to warn the vampire back from the light. "Simon came back after you; perhaps he did it." As if in reply, a second horse joined the protest.

"Wake up, brother," Tristan said, giving Simon an ungentle nudge with his boot.

"Careful," Orlando warned. "He doesn't always awaken so gently as you." As if to make his point, Simon sat up with a snarl, eyes glowing. "Calm yourself," the wizard told him. "Someone is outside."

"Stealing our horses," Tristan agreed, eyes narrowed in fury.

"Bastard," Simon said, apparently recovering himself in spite of the oath. He got up from his pallet. "Who is it?"

Orlando opened the door the tiniest crack and peered out. "One of Tristan's brigands," he said softly. "He must know his business; he already has both horses tethered together, and neither of them seems to be distressed." He stepped back, pushing the door shut as gently as he could. "He seems to be coming this way."

Tristan exchanged a bitter smile with the other vampire. "Good for him."

"Wait," Orlando ordered. "Let us question him before you kill him." He motioned them back as he snuffed out the single candle, and Simon immediately retreated into the shadows. After a moment, Tristan did the same.

Orlando stepped behind the door just as it opened. The man who came in was indeed one of Sean Lebuin's brigands. Tristan had seen him at the castle with Emma, Clare's nursemaid, a tall, well-favored young man with a pleasant, gentle manner at odds with his occupation. He was moving cautiously, sword drawn, as if he had noticed the hidden shelter had been opened recently. "Who is there?" he demanded of the dark.

"A traveler," Orlando answered, stepping into the light.

The young man's manner changed at once. "Well met, little master," he said, dropping his sword point. "What brings you here?"

"I travel with my lord, the duke of Lyan," Orlando said. "We come in search of Tristan, Lord DuMaine."

At this, the brigand tensed again, but it was too late. Simon lunged out of the shadows like the wolf he had been the first time Tristan saw him, grabbing the man by the shoulders as Orlando slammed the door behind him. The brigand dropped his sword at once, but his manner was defiant. "DuMaine is dead," he answered, meeting Simon's gaze.

"Not quite." As Orlando lit the candle, Tristan stepped into the light.

"Holy Christ . . ." The brigand crossed himself, his face turning white as milk. "I thought she surely must be mad, that somehow she had convinced Sean, but . . . we searched the ditch for you for hours . . ." Simon loosened his grip, and he fell to his knees. "Christ save us."

"He may yet," Simon said, obviously trying not to smile. Personally, Tristan thought his vampire brother had a rather perverse sense of humor. "What is your name, sirrah?"

"Michael," the brigand answered him, but his eyes never left Tristan's face. "What do you want?"

Tristan considered the question. He could kill this man, add one more death to his tally of revenge, but that seemed hardly worth the effort. "Information," he answered. "You are Sean's man, are you not?" Michael said nothing, but the sudden defiance in his eyes was answer enough. "I want to know exactly what your captain is planning, down to the final detail."

"Never," Michael said. "I cannot."

"Never is a very long time, Michael," Simon said, smiling in earnest. "And you can do whatever you must." His voice had changed, Tristan realized, had deepened to the hypnotic growl he had heard from his own throat the night he had seduced Siobhan. "Why have you come here?"

"The treasure," the brigand answered, his eyes wide in the trance. "The treasure in the tunnels." He pointed toward a pile of broken chests and dirty rags in a corner of the shelter. "The king's man is coming, and Lord Tristan is a monster. He fears he may have to flee with Siobhan." He frowned. "But she will not go. Surely he knows that."

"What treasure?" Simon pressed, sobering at once, and Orlando had tensed as well. "What tunnels?"

"The treasure we have stolen," Michael answered. "We hid it in the tunnels we found when we dug the shelter. Siobhan does not know." He frowned again as if this disturbed him. "Sean did not want her to see them. He said their mother poisoned her with superstition, made her believe the old tales."

"Show me," Simon ordered. "Show me the way to the tunnels."

The brigand's gaze strayed again to Tristan, his expression turning sad. "Siobhan wept for you, DuMaine," he said. "From that very first day when she thought you were dead. I heard her myself, standing outside the door to your chamber. She lay in your bed and sobbed like I had never heard her do before—it broke my heart to hear her."

"The tunnels," Orlando said urgently.

"Let him speak," Tristan ordered, not giving a damn for any tunnels.

"She weeps for you now, this very day," Michael went on.

"Then why did she try to kill me?" Tristan demanded.

"Why did you try to kill her?" the brigand countered. "She thinks you will destroy us all, that you are some sort of demon. She read something in a book."

"Of course," Orlando muttered.

"You said the king's man is coming," Tristan said, his mind racing, breaking through the torpor that oppressed him. The sun must be starting to set. "When?"

"Even now," Michael answered. "I must make haste. I must retrieve the treasure, make ready an escape." He looked back toward the pile of trash. "Sean thinks the tunnels may lead all the way to the castle, but it is a labyrinth."

"Move that rubbish," Orlando ordered, but Simon was already moving. He shoved the broken chests out of the way to reveal a trapdoor in the floor. "Have you not seen this?" the wizard demanded of Tristan.

"I didn't look." He took a step toward Michael. "Does Sean mean to leave before the king's man arrives?"

"No," the brigand answered. "He still has faith in Callard, at least as much as ever he did. But if Callard fails, he wants to be ready. All he cares about is saving Siobhan."

"Or so you believe," Tristan said bitterly.

"Nay, my lord," Michael said. "I swear it is true. Siobhan is the one who wanted the Normans driven out. Sean did it all for her."

Simon opened the trapdoor and peered inside. "There are tunnels," he said, dropping through the hole to stand shoulder-deep in the floor. "Hand me a light."

"And why would Sean do that?" Tristan asked Michael. If he was using his vampire's powers of persuasion, he didn't mean to do it, but the young man answered even so.

"She is his sister, his kin," he explained. "He loves her more than all the world. He wanted revenge for his father and mother, but he had it when the old baron died and he cut out his heart. The rest was all for the men who had joined him, outlaws who hated the Normans, and for Siobhan."

Simon emerged from the hole. "It's just like the catacombs at Charmot," he told Orlando. "There are even paintings on the walls. There were druids here."

"Druids, yes," Michael agreed. "Sean said his mother's line was descended from druids."

"The mother's line," Orlando repeated, meeting Simon's shocked gaze with his own.

"Another doorway," Simon said.

"Perhaps," Orlando agreed.

"You say these tunnels lead all the way to the castle," Tristan said impatiently, hardly caring what they meant. He still had little interest in his vampire brother's quest, but he needed his help for his own. Perhaps these tunnels would buy it.

"That was what Sean guessed," Michael answered. "But we never had time to find out."

"Tell me all you know of the king's man and this Callard." He looked at Simon. "With his grace the duke's assistance, I think it is time I went home."

13

Siobhan stood at the top of the tower and watched the line of riders and soldiers drawing ever nearer on the forest road. They had always known Tristan's royal cousin would send a proper delegation to inquire after him. But no one could possibly have expected anything like the army she saw now. There were at least three score men on horseback, and twice as many on foot.

"Christ on the cross," Sean muttered beside her. "Why should Henry send so many?"

"Perhaps he did not," she answered. "Perhaps some of them belong to your friend Callard."

"I'm sure they do," he said, but he didn't sound sure in the least. In truth, her brother had become steadily more nervous as the day had worn on. Now, as the day was failing into dark and the party they had dreaded was so close, if someone had clapped their hands behind him, he might well have jumped over the battlements.

"Captain!" a man shouted, coming through the arch. "The scouts have returned."

"Michael?" Sean asked, turning to him. "Is he among them?"

"No, Captain," the man said, glancing at Siobhan. Michael's disappearance was one reason Sean was so agitated. He had gone to scout the road some hours before, or so Sean had told her. Something in his face had made her think perhaps he lied. But that was madness. Sean would not lie to her, not now.

"What news?" she asked the man aloud.

"Ill, my lady," he admitted. "One of the men fell in among the foot soldiers for a mile or so, and we know now why there are so many Normans coming. They all belong to DuMaine."

Sean swore an oath under his breath, and she was inclined to do the same. "Are you certain?" she said instead.

"Aye, my lady," he answered. "Most of the knights ride under DuMaine's banner—the troops who rode to the king's war in France." He looked as greensick as she felt; Sean turned his back completely, shaking his head. "His whoreson Majesty has sent them home."

"That's it, then," Sean said, his tone dull as death. "We are finished."

"No." She caught his arm, making him face her. "Why should we be? What has changed?"

"DuMaine's knights know us, or have you forgotten?" he said with a bitter laugh. "They will know we took the castle by violence, that he would never have married you willingly."

"How will they know?" she demanded. "They have been away—perhaps he captured me. Perhaps I . . ." Her voice trailed off for a moment, but she made herself go on. "Perhaps he fell in love with me."

"So much so that he let me live?" Sean said. "Nay, love. You are a beauty, but no woman could do that."

"You don't know that," she insisted, though in her broken heart, she already knew he was right; 'twas the very root of her despair. "And even if you have the right of it, what else can we do? Our course is set; we can't flee now."

"We could make a defense," he said. "The castle is finished; it could withstand a siege."

"For how long?" she said, already shaking her head. "You said it yourself, the stores of food are nearly empty. And even if they were not, even if we were well supplied, how could we withstand a royal attack?" All day long, she had found herself remembering her villain's mockery of a wedding. Now she thought of it again, of Tristan's curse. *I will kill you, darling,* he had promised. *You'd best come along and do it, sweeting,* she thought in answer now, suppressing a lunatic's laugh. *Or the hangman may deprive you of your chance.* "You should leave," she said aloud. "Now, before they arrive—slip out through the south gate with what men you think might be recognized—"

"Are you mad?" he interrupted, aghast. "I will not leave you here to face the Normans alone."

"Even to save us both?" She took his hands, forcing

herself not to tremble, to be strong enough for herself and Sean and all their father's people. "With you gone, I can tell them I married DuMaine with some chance of making them believe it. Silas has promised to bear witness to my tale, whatever it may be, and he is well known and much favored at the royal court. Tristan's knights know him as well."

"No," he said, shaking his head. "I will not hear this—"

"You must hear it." She had no more time to argue, even to spare his feelings. Night was coming on, and Tristan's friends were returned. Heaven only knew what would come before the dawn. "Your plans have all but failed, Sean, but if you trust me, I can still make them come right. Silas will help me better than you could, and you know it. And if your friend the baron is true, he will help me as well. And even if he is not . . ." She broke off, the look of agony haunting her brother's eyes making her stop before she made him feel worse by slandering his great ally. "I am just a woman, Sean," she went on with a smile. "Those knights know you for their enemy, but they will see me as nothing but a prize. It will never occur to them that I could have plotted treachery against their lord—at worst, they will think I was your pawn. If I pretend to be the foolish twit they will see in me, I can make them feel pity, not anger."

"You could never play such a part, Siobhan," he protested. "It is not in you."

"I can do anything I like." She could feel him weakening, and the sensible part of her was glad. But the deepest, buried center of her heart ached to think he could leave her, even when she herself demanded that he do it. *Tristan would not leave me*, she thought, though she tried not to think it. *Not if he loved me. He let himself be damned to stay with Clare.* But her brother was not Tristan. "You taught me that, remember?" She took his face between her hands, feeling much too old to be his little sister. "I will make them believe that I am what they see," she finished. "Am I not a pretty thing, in faith?"

"You are beautiful." He held her hand against his cheek and kissed it. "Callard will protect you until I can return."

"I will protect myself." She moved into his arms and hugged him tight. How will he ever return? she thought, holding on with all her might. Even if she did as she boasted she could, what then? Did she mean to play the Norman lord's widow forever? Not likely, since her husband was technically alive, a vampire, sworn to vengeance—sworn to murder her, in fact. She stepped back and looked up at her brother for what felt like the last time. "You must not fret for me," she told him with a smile. At least Sean would be safe.

"I will come back for you—for all of you," he promised, kissing her on either cheek. "Our quest is not yet done."

Tristan stood in the shelter of the trees and watched the caravan pass by, Daimon's lead in his hand, Simon and Orlando on their mounts beside him. Henry had sent his knights back home; the French campaign was apparently done. He watched the men he had led into battle ride by him, his feelings strangely muddled. They were his sworn retainers, most of them his friends. He could call each one of them by name, from Sir William on his snow-white mare to the foot soldier Remus, who had stopped to take a piss in the grass beside the road and was running to catch up. They would know him as well, would rejoice to see him and serve him happily again. But he felt set apart from them by more than the shadows of the wood. A veil had fallen between him and these living men he loved. He was no longer the man who had commanded them. He was a vampire.

Simon leaned down from his horse to put a hand on his shoulder. "Tristan?" he said softly, his brother in cursed blood. "Are you certain?"

Tristan nodded, his jaw clenched tight. His course was set; he could not leave it now. Swinging easily into the saddle, he trotted out onto the road.

"My lord!" Sir William saw him first, and a smile of pure relief broke over his face. "You live!" He leapt down from his horse to kneel before Tristan, then rose to clasp his hand. "May Christ be praised!"

"Amen," Tristan answered with a smaller smile, the word burning his tongue.

"Where is Henry's clerk?" another of the knights, Sir Andrew, demanded, looking back at the caravan behind him. "And where is that damned baron?"

"The baron of Callard said he had heard you were murdered," Sir William explained. "He met us on the road with troops of his own, headed for your castle." His face fell as in shame. "Forgive us for believing him, my lord."

Tristan climbed down from his horse to embrace him. "I forgive you nothing, for you have done no wrong," he promised. "I was the victim of treachery, 'tis true." Simon and Orlando emerged from the wood. "But the duke came to my aid."

"The duke?" Sir Andrew echoed. He hastened to bend knee to Simon as well. "Your grace . . ."

"Simon, the duke of Lyan," Tristan explained. "And this is his wizard, Orlando." The caravan had stopped as shouts carried the news forward, and a crowd was gathering around them. "His healing arts preserved my life."

"But how were you attacked, my lord?" Andrew demanded. "Where is the villain now?"

"I know not," Tristan answered. "But we shall soon find out." A man dressed in a plain brown habit was galloping toward them on a palfrey, followed by an armored knight on an armored stallion. The clerk he recognized as one of Henry's favorites, a sour-faced young scholar named Nicholas who shared the king's love of history and figures. The knight was a stranger . . . but no. As he dismounted and lifted his visor, Tristan could have sworn he had seen him before.

"My lord DuMaine?" he asked, incredulous. "Verily, can it be you?" He was young, no older than Tristan himself, and he was nearly as handsome as Simon, his features so regular they might have been painted in a book. His armor was beautifully wrought—Italian-made, Tristan thought in passing, studying his face. But where had he seen this man before?

"I am Tristan DuMaine," he answered. "But who are you?"

"This is the baron of Callard," Nicholas answered, still sitting on his horse. " 'Twas he who gave us rumor of your death, my lord—if indeed, you are the man you say."

This was the baron? Tristan thought, barely hearing more. This pleasant-faced young fellow was the monster who had so terrified the servant of Gaston? This was the man who had murdered his guard, his mistress, and a coachman all in the same night? It hardly seemed possible. Simon had told him what he had heard from the peasants on the road, and they had agreed that some demon was surely in residence on the baron's lands. But this could not be him.

"Of course he is, idiot," Sir Andrew scolded. "You've seen him yourself a hundred times; surely you must recognize him."

"It has been my misfortune to learn that my eyes and memory cannot always be trusted," the scholar retorted. "The king sent me in search of one man only, a man he loves as friend and kinsman. Why have you ignored your king's correspondence, my lord, if you truly are his cousin?"

"Because I have been injured near to death for this

month past," Tristan answered, tearing his gaze from the baron's face. "While riding in this wood, I was set upon by brigands—"

"Lebuin!" Sir William cried, incensed. "The bastard!"

"The same," Tristan nodded. "Or so I do believe—in truth, I never saw my attackers. I was left for dead and knew nothing for days. When I awoke, I was with Simon and Orlando, and they have nursed me back to health."

"May heaven bless you, my lords," Callard said, bowing his head to Simon and Orlando. But Tristan could have sworn he saw him smile, a wicked gleam passing through his eyes before his face was hidden.

"Indeed," he said. He glanced over at Simon and saw him watching the baron as well, the look in his eyes impossible to read. "But how is it you were moved to come here, Baron?"

"My lands are close by yours, my lord," Callard said easily. "I heard rumor you had disappeared." Again, his expression was somber, but his wide blue eyes danced with amusement. "And other things as well."

"No doubt," Simon said, the first time he had spoken. "I hear tell you have troubles of your own, my lord."

"Of course," Nicholas said, smiling for the first time at the lilt in Simon's voice. "Lyan is in Ireland."

"What troubles?" Sir William asked, curious, looking to Callard.

"The duke must have heard of the supposed sickness that struck some of my peasants," Callard answered. The laughter in his eyes was gone, replaced by sadness.

Could Gaston's servant have been mistaken? Could the baron be innocent? "But the true culprit has been found, a murderer possessed by demons, or so it seemed to the priest. He has been hanged, and the deaths have stopped." He turned back to Tristan. "Perhaps this lunatic attacked you as well, my lord."

"Perhaps," Tristan said, more curious than ever. Simon seemed to think there was some connection between whatever had attacked the baron's lands and his own great enemy, Kivar. But Tristan was more concerned about the pact this man had apparently made with Lebuin. "But I doubt it. What other rumors did you hear of me, Callard?"

The young baron smiled, apparently unruffled by Tristan's tone. "It might be madness, my lord," he said. "But I heard that you were married."

Tristan returned his smile. "Madness indeed." He turned to Nicholas. "Well, sirrah? Are you convinced I am the man I say?"

"Aye, my lord." The scholar climbed down from his horse to make a deep, elegant bow. "I hope you will forgive me."

"Oh, I dare say he will," Simon said with a grin. "If you escort him to his castle."

Siobhan waited on the wide stone steps of the manor house as the courtyard filled with Normans, every bit of will she could muster focused on standing still. *I am not a little girl,* she told herself sternly, her heart pounding so hard she thought surely everyone around her must hear it. I am a woman, a warrior, a brigand. I will not be afraid.

Clare stood beside her, and she gave a little dancing hop of excitement. "He is coming," the child confided, putting her hand into Siobhan's.

Before she could answer, a small brown palfrey trotted to the head of the procession, and a small brown clerk climbed down from its back. "And who are you, my lady?" he said, making her a bow.

"Better I should ask that of you, sirrah," she answered, surprised to hear her voice was steady. "You ride beneath the banner of our sovereign king, but I do not know your face."

"I am Master Nicholas," he answered with a small smile that told her she had spoken right. Behind her, she heard Silas let out a relieved little sigh. "I do come on behalf of His Majesty, the king."

"Then you are welcome, Master Nicholas," she said with the graceful nod Silas had taught her. "I am Siobhan, Lady DuMaine."

His eyes widened for a moment, but his smile did not waver. "Then you spoke aright, my lord," he said, looking back at another knight, still mounted behind him. "The baron of Callard told us he had heard tell of your marriage."

"Did he indeed?" The knight raised his visor to show a handsome face. "'Tis fitting, I suppose." She made herself smile for a moment, the best she could manage. "I have heard tell much of him."

The baron smiled as well, swinging down from his horse to make her an elaborate bow. "Then I am blessed, my lady," he said, coming closer. "To be known by such a beauty is a boon indeed."

"I never said I knew you, sir," she answered, offering her hand. "I have only heard gossip." He took her hand and kissed it, and a queer, unpleasant tremor passed through her, but she would not let it show on her face. If Sean were right about this man, he might be her last hope. "I have yet to form my own opinion."

The last of the procession was inside, and the gates were being closed and barred again, a sound to make her shiver. "Not to worry, my lady," Callard said as he let her go, and his wide blue eyes were serious behind his easy smile. "I mean you should think well of me."

"Be careful, baron." The voice came from a hooded figure just inside the gates. "The lady's favor is hard won and bought at a terrible price."

Tristan had watched in shock as Siobhan greeted Henry's clerk, hardly believing his eyes. His wicked little demon was transformed to a lady of fashion, every detail perfect from the veil that covered her wild mass of black hair to the hem of the gown that matched her eyes. Even her manner was perfect, as cold and condescending as that of any highborn bitch at court. She had already marked Callard as her salvation, flirting with him shamelessly, and the poor man was apparently undone. "Trust me," he finished, pushing back his hood. "I know her well."

Siobhan should have been frightened. In truth, no fate could have been worse than this, her vampire husband appearing with a royal Norman army at his back to help him carry out his vengeance. But as soon as she heard his voice, her heart sang out inside her breast, "He lives!" As soon as he revealed his face, she could not help but smile, not the feigned, pretty expression she had practiced with Silas before the mirror but her own true, joyful smile. "Tristan!" Forgetting everything, she ran to him, tearing off her veil and kicking off her slippers as she went.

She stopped just in front of him as he climbed down from his horse, frozen by the fury in his eyes as he looked down on her. The last time they had met, she had tried to destroy him. He had tried to comfort her, had sworn to protect her, and she had repaid him by trying to slash his throat. How could she expect him not to hate her? "My lord," she whispered, reaching out to touch his face. "You have returned."

Tristan shuddered at her touch, his fury dissolving in the face of the hope in her eyes. Looking down on her, he found his reason lost. In spite of everything, she wanted him; she welcomed him, vampire, Norman, and enemy all. "Yes," he nodded, the word catching for a moment in his throat. "I have."

She smiled. "Thank God," she said, laughing as he caught her in his arms.

"Tristan, I'm so sorry." He kissed her before the words were out, crushing her mouth with his, and she wrapped her arms around his neck, oblivious to anything but him. He lifted her off of her feet, and she laughed, faint with passion and relief. "I did not want to hurt you." She kissed his jaw, his nose, his cheek, clumsy with happiness and love like nothing she had ever felt before. "I was so afraid . . ."

"Hush, love." He kissed her sweetly, drunk on the taste of her tongue. He did not want to hear her explanation, didn't want to think. All he wanted was to revel in her welcome, the warmth of her embrace. As for all the rest, the walls of pain the world had built between them, later would be soon enough to see them. For now, he would make them be gone. "Simon," he said, turning to his vampire brother who still waited, bemused, behind them. "Will you see my castle secured?"

"Oh, aye," Simon answered with a grin. "I can see you've more pressing matters to attend."

"I do indeed." He looked down at his brigand love, still curled against his chest, clinging to him as if for shelter from some dreaded storm. "My love," he repeated, a kiss against her ear. "My sweet Siobhan . . ." He swept her off her feet into his arms, and she kissed him, her hand against his cheek as he carried her into the manor.

"Aye me," Master Nicholas laughed, pressing a hand to his chest as the happy couple passed him by. "I would say Lord DuMaine is quite married indeed."

"Yea, verily," the baron agreed, his charming smile belied by the look of pure calculation in his eyes. "I say they are well matched."

14

The servants stared in shock as Tristan carried his wife through his own hall, their dead lord returned. One housemaid screamed in terror and fell into a faint. But the vampire himself barely noticed. Let Andrew and Sebastian explain where he had been. Let Simon secure the castle, at least for these few hours—he was a duke and a Crusader; surely he could manage. For now, Tristan would be with Siobhan. He paused at the archway to kiss her again, capturing her mouth with his.

Only one other soul could have distracted him. "Papa!" Clare cried from the doorway, running to catch up. "Papa, wait!"

"Clare," Siobhan said, tugging her kiss away. "Poor baby—Tristan, wait—"

Before the words were out, he had set her on her feet again and knelt to catch his child. "Papa," she wept, running to him.

"Hush, love, all is well," he promised as he hugged her. "Please don't cry."

"My lord Tristan," Silas said, coming to join them, wearing his enigmatic smile. "Welcome home."

Siobhan watched her vampire husband as he kissed his child, her heart aching with love she didn't dare let show. He meant to pretend she was his wife indeed; he had let his knights believe it. The last time they had stood together in this hall, she had forced him to pretend to marry her, the two of them cursing one another with the worst oaths they could make, oaths that had come true. But now he pretended to love her.

"Yes, my lord," she said, caressing his hair as he knelt beside her with Clare in his arms. "We have missed you." He looked up at her, a question in his eyes. Yes, love, she longed to tell him; it is true. But she could not. They had an audience. She must play her part. What would his true wife say to him, if such a creature could be real? "Where have you been all this time?"

He caught her hand in his. "Sorely wounded, lady." The last time he had been with her, she had tried to kill him with a sword Orlando believed was enchanted. The little wizard said she must know what he was and how to destroy him. "In faith, I am not mended now." What could she be thinking? He could not doubt she wanted him. Devil and brigand she might be, but she could never have hidden her feelings this well, could never have feigned the desire he had tasted in her kiss. But did she want him dead almost as much? He thought of her confession the night before, the heartbreaking pain he had seen in her eyes as she told him of her father's death. Such pain could drive any warrior to evil. And she was a warrior, his love. "But Simon has healed me well enough," he finished. He brushed a kiss across her palm before he stood. "Well enough to come home."

"I told you," Clare said happily, hanging on Siobhan's free hand. "I told you Papa was not dead."

"And I believed you." She smiled down on his child with genuine affection, and a fist of longing clenched around his heart. For a moment he let himself imagine that this play was real, that he was a true man again, and she was his true wife. In his life before, he had known he must marry, but he had never thought that he would love. Love was for squires and poets, half-girlish creatures with nothing else of consequence to do. He could never have dreamed that somewhere in the world there was Siobhan. She cursed him, fought him, challenged him at every turn. Her beauty was a burden to her; her feminine wiles she used as nothing but a joke. But she bewitched him like no gentle lady ever could have done.

"Siobhan," he said, his voice brusque with the feeling he dared not let her see. "Where is your brother?

Must we come to this so quickly? she thought, meeting his gaze with her own. Couldn't they pretend a little longer? "He is gone, my lord," she answered, only truth.

He brushed her jaw with the back of his hand, searching her eyes for a lie. " 'Tis well," he said at last. "I will not miss him." Turning away from her, he lifted

Clare up in his arms and kissed her. "You, my lady, ought to be in bed." The little girl twisted a lock of his hair around her tiny fist, frowning in protest. "I will come and kiss you before I go to sleep."

"Will you stay now, Papa?" she asked. "Will I see you in the morning?"

Simon's words came back to him. *Will you take this child into darkness?* he had asked. *Will you play lord of the castle as a demon?* "You will not see me in the morning, only at night," he answered, cuddling her close. "But I will still be here." He handed her to Silas. "Bring Sir Sebastian, Master Nicholas, and the duke of Lyan to the tower at matins," he told the scholar quietly. Siobhan was watching, obviously curious but silent, one eyebrow arched in question. "We will have much to discuss." The hall was beginning to fill with knights and soldiers, and the servants were serving the evening meal. The baron of Callard was still standing with Master Nicholas, the two of them deep in conversation. But as Tristan watched, Callard looked up at him and smiled, and the vampire was seized again with the feeling they had met before. He looked over at Simon, his vampire brother, talking with Andrew and Sebastian like any other visiting knight with a tale of distant lands to tell.

"My lord, are you weary?" Siobhan laid a hand on his arm. "Will you come to bed?" She knew he was not hungry, not for food, he thought. She knew he was a vampire.

"Aye, brigand." He cradled her cheek in his palm, and she smiled, the longing in her eyes impossible to miss or to ignore. Looking on her so, he could think of nothing else. He bent and kissed her tenderly. "I will."

She lifted her chin to catch his kiss again when he would pull away, catching his lip in her teeth. "Then come." She felt his arms enfold her, the powerful embrace she had longed for all her life and never known before him. Demon he might be, but she was his, just as he promised, at least for tonight. "Tristan," she whispered, pressing her cheek to his.

"Come," he echoed, a rumbling growl in his throat. Taking her hand, he led her to the stairs.

Gaston approached his master as the king's clerk finally moved away. "I swear, my lord, 'tis not my fault," he said softly for the baron's ears alone, a pointless plea for mercy. Callard was watching with his beautiful, blood-chilling smile as DuMaine and Siobhan left the hall. "Lebuin did swear to me the man was dead."

"Calm yourself, Gaston." The baron turned his eyes to him, still smiling, looking him over like he might have never seen his most faithful slave before. Then he looked over at the strange knight who had supposedly healed DuMaine, this Simon of Lyan, and his smile grew even wider. "All is well," he promised. The look in his eyes made Gaston remember what his own frightened servant had told him. *The baron has gone mad.* "Indeed, Gaston," he continued, putting a hand on his shoulder and making him flinch. "Things have fallen out far better than we ever could have dreamed."

Siobhan drew Tristan to her as soon as the door to the bedroom closed behind them. Don't think, she told herself again, clasping her hands at the nape of his neck as she drew him down into her kiss. He obliged her with a twisted smile, teasing the seam of her lips with his tongue before plunging it sweetly inside.

She raised up on tiptoe to reach him, sighing as she felt his arms around her. Before, in the stable, she had been entranced, powerless to resist him. Now she had her wits intact but no will to resist. "Why have you not accused me?" she asked him as she gazed up into his warm green eyes. How could she have ever found him cold? "Why did you not tell your knights and the others what I am?"

"I did." He brushed the hair back from her face. "You are my wife." His kiss this time was harder as he pressed his thumb against her chin and forced her mouth to open under his. Her legs went weak beneath her, and she swayed against him, clutching at his shirt. He was still dressed like a brigand and smelled of the forest, the warm, deliciously masculine smell she knew and loved in a consciousness deeper than thought. But his touch was commanding, a nobleman's touch of possession. No brigand, no matter how handsome or brash he might have been, could ever have dared to touch her so. She ran her hands over his shoulders and arms as he kissed her, his muscles contracting beneath her caress as he held her. But she could not forget for even this moment what he was. When her hands slipped around his tapered waist under his tunic to caress his back, she felt his flesh was cold.

"Vampire," she whispered as he scooped her off her feet. The wife in the book had been stoned for a witch when her dead husband came back to her from his grave. "Did I conjure you?"

"Aye," Tristan answered with a smile. She gazed up at him so sweetly, he could drown in her blue eyes. But last night she had struck him with her sword, a demon killer's blade. "Do you not remember?" Even now with her helpless in his arms, he could feel the sword strapped to her leg beneath her skirts. Did she mean to strike at him again? Why should he believe she did not? He kissed her, pushing the question aside as he carried her to the bed.

"I wished for you," she said as he lay her before him. "I knew it was wrong, but I dreamed you would come back." She touched his face as he bent over her, tracing the shape of his mouth. "No one had ever wanted me before."

"Nay, brigand," he said, laughing at her innocence. "I swear that is not true." This was the bed where she had ordered he be bound; the cut and broken bindings that had held him still hung from the bedposts. "But I will confess, I am pleased to imagine you believed it." He held her hand against his cheek, kissing her delicate wrist. She had told him she was a virgin that night, and he had laughed at her, enraged and inflamed by her artless, unladylike seduction. But she was a nobleman's daughter. If her father had lived, if she had been brought up gently in a manor on these lands, she would have been a perfect match for him, a most suitable bride. Looking down on her now as she smiled up at him, guileless, fearless yearning in her eyes, he tried to imagine the lady she would have been, but it was impossible. She could be no one but herself, and try as he might, he could not help but love her for it. "In faith, Siobhan, I am a fool," he said with a wry smile as he bent closer to kiss her.

"Aye, my lord." She fed upon his mouth, savoring his weight as he covered her, pressing her down to the bed. "And a blackguard besides." His kisses trailed along her jaw, and she bent her head back with a sigh, offering her throat. He kissed her pulse, and she felt the cool threat of his fangs against her skin. But he did not bite her. Moving back up to quickly kiss her mouth, he backed away, rising from the bed.

"Alas," he said, smiling as he held her hand, her fingers laced with his. "I cannot trust you." He broke the silken cord that held back the bed hangings on one side and looped it tight around her wrist, binding her to the bedpost.

"No!" she protested, instantly alert. "You will not!"

"How will you stop me?" He caught her other wrist with careless ease as she drew back to strike him. "I came back home to be avenged, remember?" He bound her to the other post with the cord from the other side, lying across her to do it, ignoring her struggles.

"Tristan, please . . ." He saw fury in her eyes but fear as well. He had hurt her as much in the past as she had hurt him, and she knew he was a demon. She had every cause to be afraid.

"No, my love." He caught her writhing hips between his hands and held her gently still, pressing a kiss to her stomach through her gown. "Trust me." He caressed her curves, nuzzling her softness, the hollow of her hip and lower still. The warm, sweet scent of her made him feel drunk, made him want her even more. "I won't hurt you, I promise." He drew her skirt up slowly, gathering it in his fist until the blade was revealed, strapped to her thigh. "But I cannot leave you free to hurt me, either." He pressed a fervent lover's kiss to the inside of her knee, her skin soft as velvet, as he drew the blade, and a strange shiver raced through him, echoed in her sigh. Tossing the weapon aside, he took the sheath as well, unbuckling the leather to nuzzle the skin underneath.

"Tristan," she protested, twisting beneath his touch, no longer certain if she hated or savored her bonds. She hated feeling helpless; she needed control, the comfort of her reason and her sword. But this demon whispered, "Trust me," and her soul longed to obey. He promised not to hurt her, and in spite of everything she knew, her heart longed to believe. Closing her eyes, she heard the ripping of her stolen gown, felt the cool night air against her skin as her lover/captor tore the silk that covered her away.

"Beautiful," he whispered. This time, he kissed her bare stomach, and molten desire rushed through her, burning hot and sweet. "So beautiful." His shadowed beard was rough against her skin, but his voice and his touch were so tender, she thought she might cry. His tongue flickered inside her navel; his teeth grazed the edge, and she whimpered, tugging at the cords that held her. She wanted to hold him, to touch him. His hands kneaded the curve of her hips, lifting her up as his kiss found her sex, and she screamed, wordless longing.

"I want to see you," she begged him, trembling all over. "All of you . . . Tristan, please." But he was relentless, his tongue delving inside of her, driving her mad. He drew the deepest heart of her desire gently through his teeth, and she cried out again in blissful agony, oblivious to shame. "You bastard, come inside of me," she cursed him as he tenderly suckled her flesh and a wave of want broke hot inside of her, teasing the edge of release. "Now . . . I need you now."

With a groan, he moved away from her, tearing off his clothes only slightly more carefully than he had torn away Siobhan's. "Shut up," he ordered her, rough with tenderness and want. "Do you know how much I want you?" He moved over her, framing her face in his hands, his beautiful brigand. "Do you want to drive me mad?"

"Yes," she answered, smiling up in triumph. "Always, every moment." Her hips arched up beneath him, and her hot little sex brushed his cock, burning his flesh like a brand. "Love me, Tristan."

"Dear God, yes . . ." He kissed her for barely a moment, crushing her beneath him as he drove his cock inside.

She gasped, complete at last. "My love . . ." Even bound and fighting, she felt safe with him, twisting her wrists in their cords to be free. He was here, her beloved. He was hers. She wrapped her legs around him, rising up to meet his thrust, and release tore through her, making the world go black. Her grip weakened as she shuddered, and he kissed her, bringing her back to the world, to herself, to his arms. Her climax rose again as his tongue battled hers, and she moaned into his mouth, feeling him spill inside her.

"Siobhan," he murmured, kissing her cheek, and she whimpered something in response, wordless pleading as her tears spilled on his lips. He reached up and broke the cords that held her wrists, and she twined her arms around him, pressing closer, not trying to fight or to flee. "My sweet Siobhan." He drew her hands against his chest and rolled to his side, and she snuggled against him, warm and soft. I love you, he thought but could not tell her even now.

He thought again of her tears the night before, the terror and hurt he had seen in her eyes. "You are safe, little brigand," he swore to her instead, pressing a kiss to her hair. He would have his revenge on her brother, would make his castle safe. But he would leave her there. He would go with Simon and Orlando in their quest, take up the burden of his curse. But Siobhan would have the castle, the lands that by blood should be hers. "I will keep you safe." She mumbled something more he could not understand, and he smiled, tears of blood in his eyes. Stroking her hair, he held her close until she fell asleep.

At the last bell before dawn, he found Simon and the others in the solar, just as he had ordered. "Well met," his vampire brother said, offering his hand as he came in. Andrew and Sebastian were sitting before the fire, playing chess, but they still wore their armor, he noticed. "How fares your lady?"

"Well enough," Tristan said brusquely, unwilling to say more. Orlando and Silas were sitting together over a book, discussing some sort of alchemical equation as if the fate of the God's heaven depended upon it, in obvious enjoyment. But Silas wore a dagger at his hip. "I thought they might get on," Tristan said, indicating the two scholars with a nod.

"Like pups of a litter," Simon agreed with a grin. "Would that my lady were here to join into their debate. She has strong opinions on the subject."

Tristan looked at him, surprised. The other vampire had spoken of a true love but with such sadness, he had assumed the lady was long dead. "Your lady is a scholar?"

Simon's grin widened, but his eyes were sad. "You cannot imagine." He shook his head as if to shake away a thought. "I have spoken to some of your servants," he said, changing the subject. "The young man we captured is a suitor of your daughter's nurse and a follower of Lebuin. He remembers nothing beyond what we put into his mind, at least not yet." He frowned. "Such magicks often do not last."

"It doesn't have to last," Tristan promised. In truth, he was no more comfortable manipulating men's minds than Simon, for all it could be useful. "What have you learned?"

"Lebuin and some of his men slipped out of the castle late this afternoon," he said. "The general feeling is that either he is the worst sort of coward for abandoning his sister or that he will return. Either way, the common folk no longer hold him in such high regard." The corner of his mouth quirked up. "It seems there have been murders within the castle walls that Lebuin could neither explain nor avenge. I have overheard many say that though they fear your wrath, at least you will bring safety to those you choose to spare."

"I ought to hang the lot of them," Tristan muttered, remembering his shock when Richard had told him the gates were breached with peasant help. Poor Richard, fallen in his first real battle. "But I will not," he finished. A wholesale slaughter would not bring back Richard or his knights. He would save his fury for those who most deserved it. "What of the soldiers?"

"Your lieutenants are still imprisoned in the dungeon," Simon answered. "The others are mixed in with the rest of the guard, I suppose."

"How many of the guards are brigands?" Andrew had noticed his presence and moved to rise, but Tristan waved him back into his chair.

"How should I know?" Simon laughed. "I do not know your men."

For a moment, Tristan couldn't understand what he meant—surely any fool could tell the difference between a Norman soldier and a Saxon thief. "They look just alike," he realized with a wry smile. "Fine, then—I will sort them out tomorrow. Or not." Lebuin had won Tristan's soldiers' friendship with mercy; perhaps Tristan could do the same to his. "In any case, will you go to my lieutenants? Tell them I would see them hanged, but you have interceded for them and asked me to show mercy."

"What will that accomplish?" Simon asked, puzzled.

"They will fear me too much to serve me as they once did, at least for a while," he answered. "But if they think that you have saved their lives now, when they are certain of death and dishonor, they will serve you, no matter what comes."

Simon raised an eyebrow. "And you would trust me to do this?"

He looked at the two knights playing chess by the hearth, once as close to him as kin. He thought of his true cousin, the king, so engrossed in dark affairs of state so far from here he had never known Tristan was attacked. "I have no choice," he answered, meeting his new brother's eyes. "In truth, you are the only friend I have."

"My lord," Andrew said, getting up as if unable to contain himself any longer. "What goes on here? The groom who took my horse told me tales to make my hair turn white, and Sebastian's servant told him he has heard the same."

"I am surprised at both of you, paying heed to gossip," Tristan said with a wry smile, secretly pleased. They were both of them so young, and they seemed ready to challenge Satan himself on his behalf.

"We are in earnest, my lord," Sebastian said as if to emphasize the point.

"I know, sir knight," he answered, sobering. "'Tis true, I fear. Things at this castle have gone ill indeed while you've been away, and we are not safe yet."

"Lebuin," Andrew said, speaking the name as a curse.

"The same," Tristan answered. "His sister is my wife, and I do mean to keep her. But for the man himself, there will be no pity."

"Do you think that wise, Lord Tristan?" Orlando said in the tone that seemed to always bring Simon to heel and made Tristan want to pick up the little wizard and shake him like a rat.

"Aye, sirrah," Tristan answered, giving him a glare to grind a stone to dust.

"I have to agree with Tristan in this." Silas nodded. "If Lebuin is not found, he will return."

"Let him come," Sebastian said with a laugh. "Your knights are returned to you, my lord. We need have no fear of common bandits."

"Lebuin is no common bandit," Tristan answered. "And the people we would keep within these walls do love him well." He thought of Siobhan, weeping before she struck him. "I couldn't let you kill him," she had said of Sean. "He loves me . . . he's all I have left." No more, my love, he silently promised, refusing to try to imagine how he would comfort her after the deed was done. "I am still not strong," he said aloud. "I have joined the duke in a program of abstinence and prayer in hopes of regaining my health."

"My lord?" Andrew said, looking back and forth between the vampires in obvious confusion.

"You will not see me in the daylight," Tristan explained. Simon had doubted the wisdom of his returning for just this reason—he couldn't imagine Tristan could make men who had known him so long and so well believe such a wagonload of nonsense. But these were Tristan's knights, sworn to him since boyhood. They would believe whatever he told them. "Nor will I take meat in company. In the daylight hours, you must report to these two men." He pointed to Silas and Orlando.

"A scholar and a dwarf?" Sebastian said, appalled. "No offense intended, sirrahs, but . . ." He looked helplessly at Tristan as if waiting for the finish of the jest.

"Silas has held this castle faithful to the crown in my

absence with no help but his wits," Tristan said sternly. "And Orlando is a wizard; I dare say his wisdom will more than make up for his size."

"If they are your men, we will serve them, my lord," Andrew promised, giving his friend a scornful look.

"Aye, my lord," Sebastian hastened to agree. "Of course."

Orlando watched the knights give in to Tristan's will like scolded puppies, and a chill shivered through him. This man had no business being a vampire. He thought of the signs he had seen in his portents for days, the harbingers of some great shadow moving over them, ready to strike. Kivar was close; he could feel his evil presence. Would Tristan be his vessel? He did not like to think so. He liked the young lordling; there was great nobility in him far deeper than his blood. But he would not risk their quest for him, could not risk Kivar's return in a shape of such power. Tristan must be watched.

"My bride must be watched," Tristan was saying to his knights. "She is not a prisoner; she is not to be molested or abused. But she must not be allowed to leave the castle."

"We will keep her safe, my lord," Sebastian promised. "And Lady Clare as well."

"I have no doubt." Tristan nodded with a smile. "Now leave us. I would speak to my healers and Silas alone."

"As you will, my lord," Andrew said, obviously disappointed.

"I will be with you again tomorrow night." He clasped each of their hands in turn. "And when I am healed, I will give you thanks."

"No need, my lord," Sebastian said with a smile of relief.

"They serve you well," Orlando said when they were gone. "You must be a good master."

"Not good enough," Tristan said grimly, turning back to him. "But even so, here is my plan."

15

Siobhan was not surprised to find Tristan gone when she awoke the next morning. But when she discovered he had taken her sword, she cursed herself for her own stupidity. "Stupid girl," she muttered, tossing through the pretty rags that had been her gown in hopes she might have missed it. "Lazy cow . . . sleeping so long." In truth, she had slept better than she had in months, curled against her husband's side, demon that he was. But that in itself was enough to make her think herself a fool.

She put on another borrowed gown, tossing the remains of the one he had ruined into the rag bag at the bottom of her wardrobe. For all she knew, her slippers were still in the courtyard where she'd kicked them off, and in truth, she did not miss them. She briefly considered a second pair with long, curled toes before pulling on her own boots, the dictates of womanly fashion be damned.

The hall downstairs looked almost just the same as always, just a bit more crowded. Tristan was not present, of course, but neither was his friend the duke, or the baron of Callard. The king's clerk was sitting in the corner near the stairway, poring over a book. He glanced up as she passed and nodded, mumbling, "My lady," before going back to his reading. The knights having their breakfast at the dais rose from their seats just as her father's men had done when her mother appeared. She managed a sickly smile before hurrying past them and out through the arch. Yes, her mother had been a lady, worthy of such courtesies. And think what had happened to her.

She hurried across the courtyard toward the stables. She wanted to find Sean and the others quickly, form some plan of action before she was any more confused. Obviously she was not to be trusted; her mind was in a stupid woman's whirl of kisses and horrors combined. But perhaps a night spent in the forest had cleared her brother's head.

In truth, she couldn't imagine what she meant to do any more. With Master Nicholas and a full battalion of knights in residence again, her and Sean's great dream of driving the Normans out was surely dead. She couldn't abandon the people who had trusted them to the rule of a vampire, or Sean to a vampire's revenge. But how could she save them without destroying Tristan? And now that she knew she loved him, how could she do that? Even assuming she ever found her sword again . . . a pretty muddle, to be certain. "Good morning, my lady," another knight called out pleasantly, coming quickly to meet her.

"Good morning," she answered, barely noticing. She had to talk to Tristan, not let him sweep her off her feet but talk to him. She could plead for Sean's life, perhaps even make him tell her his intentions now that he had returned to be lord of his castle. But first she had to find Sean and make certain he tried nothing foolish in the nonce.

"A fine morning, isn't it?" the knight said as he reached her.

"Yes," she said, hiding her annoyance with a pleasant expression that she hoped made her look as if birdsong and sunshine concerned her in the slightest. "It's lovely." She started to walk past him, and he sidestepped in front of her.

"I am Sir Sebastian, by the way," he said, still smiling. He was a handsome fellow with an open, honest face, but he wore his full armor on this fine summer morning, and he stood a head and shoulders taller than she herself. "I have served your husband since first he came to England."

"Have you?" she said, trying to imagine what a real lady would say to such a statement. "Then you have known him far longer than I have myself."

"Indeed." His smile never wavered, but his blue eyes, she now noticed, were sharp with suspicion. "Where are you going, my lady?"

"Nowhere in particular," she answered. "I thought I

might take a ride." She gave him her most dazzling smile. "It being such a lovely morning."

"I'm sorry, my lady," he said. "I'm afraid I can't allow that."

"Pardon me?" she asked, arching a brow. "You cannot allow?"

"Things are still rather chaotic," he explained with an apologetic smile that didn't fool her in the least. "With all the excitement of our returning on the same night as Lord Tristan, every knight in the garrison is engaged. But perhaps this afternoon someone will be free to escort you."

"Sir Sebastian, I can certainly imagine how busy you all must be," she said, struggling to maintain her ladylike tone. "But I assure you, I have been riding on my own with no escort for quite some time now—"

"Lord Tristan has left strict orders that you are to be protected at all times," he cut her off again. "Nothing is more important to him than your safety and that of Lady Clare." His voice took on a definite edge as his smile faded a notch. "And I assure you, there is not a man in this castle who would betray your husband's trust."

His warning was impossible to miss. "How very reassuring," she said, her cheeks warming slightly but her smile intact. "I will wait, of course." Damn Tristan's eyes—he might as well have thrown her in the dungeon. "Tell me, Sir Sebastian; do you happen to know where my husband is now?"

"As a matter of fact . . . he has taken up residence in the dungeons," he admitted with a more genuine smile. "Apparently he and the duke are . . . well, to be honest, my lady, he said they would be praying."

"Praying?" she echoed.

"Aye, my lady," he said, sounding rather dubious himself. "Apparently the duke is a member of some sort of Crusader's order that forsakes both the daylight and company for prayer and meditation."

"And Tristan has joined him in this?" So Lyan was a vampire, too, she thought with a shiver. The demon in Silas's book had held off an entire garrison of Roman soldiers on his own; how was she supposed to deal with two at once?

"In faith, my lady, I was as surprised as you are to hear it," Sebastian admitted. "As I said, I have known Lord Tristan for years, and nothing . . ." His voice trailed off as if he weren't quite certain how to finish.

"I know just what you mean," she said with a smile he returned.

"He said he would join us in the manor at sunset," he said. She started toward the tower, and he hurried after her. "My lady, if you will only wait—"

"Must I wait for everything?" she cut him off, turning to face him halfway across the bridge.

"I know it seems hard," he said. "In faith, I don't . . . my lady, please." He caught her gently by the arm, and she should have bristled, should have been appalled. But something in his eyes touched her in spite of her better judgment. This Norman knight was as confused and worried as she was herself. "Lord Tristan is obviously fond of you, and he would very likely forgive your intrusion."

"Fond of me?" she echoed with a laugh.

"An understatement, obviously." In truth, she had thought he'd overshot the mark. Tristan wanted her, but she had never imagined his feelings could be described as fond. "You are his true love." He was serious, she realized. "But he left most careful instructions that he was not to be disturbed by anyone, not even his most loyal knights. If you were to interrupt his prayers, he would certainly blame us for it." His smile was charming enough to call down the birds from the trees. If she had been the creature she pretended to be, she would surely have been dazzled. "You don't want that, do you?"

"Of course not." She laid a hand over his on her arm. "The last thing I would wish is for you or any of your brother knights to come to harm." *I have no mercy for you,* her own voice echoed deep inside her head. *I will not watch you die.* Not so very long ago, she had stood very near this spot and helped condemn four of this man's comrades to the axe. Just thinking of it made her dizzy now. How could she have come so far so quickly?

As if to answer her thoughts, the portcullis opened, and the baron of Callard rode in, followed by Gaston. He turned his handsome face up to the sunlight as the dogs circled his horse and barked, smiling as if from pure joy. "Thank you, my lady," Sir Sebastian was saying. "I feel certain that my lord will seek you out the moment he emerges."

"Yes," she answered, barely listening. "I'm sure he will." She could not leave the castle, but Callard could. If she could not get to Sean herself or talk to Tristan until sundown, perhaps she should pass the time of day with him. "Thank you, sir knight." Sean trusted this man, and he seemed clever enough to keep a foot in either camp more efficiently that she was managing to do. Perhaps he could help her after all. With a final smile at Sir Sebastian, she started back across the bridge to follow the baron to the manor.

Tristan was sleeping peacefully in one of the beds he had ordered assembled in the dungeons, but Simon was struggling to stay awake, watching Orlando examine Siobhan's sword. "Is it the same weapon?" he asked.

"It could be," the wizard said, comparing the short, thick-handled blade to the ancient drawing of the Chalice with its cross of stake and sword below. "Tristan said he felt a frisson of some kind when he first touched it. Here." He held it out to Simon by the blade. "You try."

Simon took the handle cautiously. "Nothing," he answered. "But I didn't feel anything special when I picked up Joseph's stake, either." He examined the blade as well. "It looks old."

"It is ancient," Orlando nodded. "That much I'm certain of. The metal is neither steel nor bronze, but it's much too sharp for iron." He consulted another scroll, then shook his head. "Some Roman could have dropped it in the days of Julius Caesar," he said. "Or it could be as old as Kivar."

"Where do you suppose she found it?" Simon said, handing it back to the dwarf.

Orlando smiled. "That would be the question." He gave it an experimental swing, and Simon smiled back.

"It suits you," he said. "It's just your size."

"Not quite," the wizard said, setting it aside. He left the cell to pace the narrow passageway outside for at least the tenth time that morning.

"These are the dungeons, Orlando," Simon pointed out. "I doubt you'll find any secret passageways out."

"It's here," the wizard insisted. "I can feel it." He pressed his hands against the hard-packed earthen wall. "DuMaine's tower is new, but these caverns are ancient, as old as the catacombs at Charmot. They must lead out to the caves we found in the wood."

"There is a cave at Charmot as well," Simon said, the memory of the horror he had suffered there like a waking nightmare in his current drowsy state. Lucan Kivar had chained him to the wall with the sunlight creeping closer through a hole in the roof and an innocent bleeding in his arms. Only his love's intervention had saved him. "Perhaps it was connected to the catacombs as well."

"It makes sense," Orlando agreed. "The ancient ones would have wanted a hidden escape." His expression clouded as if at some memory of his own, and Simon tried to ask him what it was. But when he opened his mouth, all that came out was a yawn. "You should sleep," the wizard said with a smile. "Tonight we will all have much to do."

Siobhan found the baron in the manor's hall. "My lord," she said softly, laying a hand on his arm. "Will you join me in the solar?"

He turned with a look that took her in from head to toes, a strange, speculative smile teasing the corners of his mouth. "Of course." He took her hand and tucked it into the crook of his elbow, and the same shiver she had felt when he touched her the day before passed through her. "Please, lead on."

It's because Sean wanted us to marry, she decided as they moved discreetly through the crowded hall. That is why he makes me feel so odd. Silas had joined Master Nicholas over his books, and he met her eyes as they passed, frowning slightly. But Silas was Tristan's friend more than hers, she knew. She needed an ally of her own.

She closed the solar door behind them and slid the bolt home. "Don't," Callard warned, reaching past her to open it again. "Your husband's castle has eyes, my lady. Have you not noticed?" He pulled the door ajar, smiling at her before he moved away. "If we are to hide, we must do so in plain sight."

"As you will," she murmured, glancing through the crack before she followed him to the far side of the room. Obviously he was far more skilled in such intrigues than she was. "Are we hiding?"

"Are we not?" His smile was friendly, but she still didn't trust him. Such a pretty face could hide a multitude of sins, and despite what Sean might think, she had seen very little evidence of his honor. "Where is your brother, my lady?"

"What makes you think I know?" she said lightly, moving past him to open the shutters. He flinched slightly from the light as if it hurt his eyes, but he did not move away. "And if I did know, why should I tell you?"

"Because I can still save him." She turned to find his expression more serious. "Is that not what you want?"

"Why should I trust you?" she countered. "You called yourself my brother's friend, yet you arrive here in procession with his enemy."

"So I look like a traitor," he answered, his smile slowly returning. "But I only rode in with DuMaine. What shall we call you?"

"His wife," she retorted without a moment's pause. He could not hurt her by suggesting she had betrayed her brother and her cause to be her demon's whore; she thought the same herself. "Tell me, my lord baron, what should I be instead?"

"That is still to be decided." He took a half-step back from her as if surrendering the field. "You should not fear me, Siobhan." He waited for a moment as if he expected her to answer, but she only looked at him, waiting for him to go on. "I met Master Nicholas on the road on my way here," he said at last, taking a seat on a bench. "When I realized he knew nothing of Tristan DuMaine's death, I thought it best not to enlighten him." He smiled. "Good thing, too."

"What did you tell him?" she said, not returning his smile. "Why did you tell him you were coming here?"

"I told him I had heard rumors of changes here at Castle DuMaine, conflicting rumors of war and marriage," he answered. "The question is, why did we meet DuMaine himself less than a day's ride away, accompanied by an Irish duke, no less?"

His manner was still easy, but his eyes were searching hers, suddenly intent. "I could not say," she answered, forcing herself not to look away. "Like you, I assumed he was dead."

"Really?" he asked. "Did you see his body?"

"I saw him all but dead, carried away from here by men who would not hesitate to murder him at my brother's order," she said. "Did your man Gaston not tell you as much himself?"

"He did," he nodded. "Gaston has told me many things, my lady." He looked down at the dagger in his belt, his handsome face drawn slightly in a frown. "But some of it I choose not to believe."

Nothing else he could have said would have swayed

her so much to his favor as this. "You do not trust your own servant?" she asked him.

He smiled. "Do you?" She smiled back slightly, and he shook his head. "Gaston has his uses, Siobhan. But he does not have my trust." He reached out and lightly took her hand. "And I do not have yours."

Again, her flesh prickled with revulsion. His hand was clean and warm, perfectly formed. Why should she be so loath to let him touch her? Was she doomed now to crave only demons? "I do not give my trust so easily, my lord," she said, withdrawing her hand.

"Not even to your brother?" he countered. "Did he not tell you to confide in me?"

"He also told me to marry DuMaine," she pointed out with a wry smile. "Aye, my lord, Sean does believe in your friendship." If she did not mean to trust in him even a little, why had she brought him here? "And I do need your help." She sat down beside him on the bench, carefully keeping her skirts from touching his knees. "Forgive me for being so cautious."

"There's nothing to forgive, Siobhan," he promised with his winning smile. "I admire your caution and your courage." He touched a lock of her hair, brushing it back from her cheek without touching her skin. "You have been wounded many times, and it has made you stronger." The look in his eyes subtly changed, his smile turning sadder and more real. "We have that in common, you and I."

"Sean fled into the forest, just as I told DuMaine,"

she answered. "But I told him to do it. He promised to return, but I don't see how he can. I can't even leave the castle—Tristan has me under guard. And I'm afraid Sean will try to rescue me or—" She broke off before she could say "destroy Tristan." She would not tell this stranger the truth of Tristan's nature, not yet. If he did not believe her, he would think her mad. And if he did . . . she did not even want to think what that could mean.

"I have no doubt Sean means to rescue you," he answered. "But I doubt even he would attempt another open siege. But there may be another way." He got up from the bench and walked over to the door, glancing casually outside. "Did Sean tell you anything about the passages under the castle?"

"What? No . . ." She shook her head, confused. "What passages?"

"He said he remembered as a boy his mother speaking of catacombs under the hill where DuMaine's motte now stands," he answered. "Apparently they led to a cavern in the forest, a place he had already found."

"The druid's hill?" Could Sean have found something related to the ancient places and not told her about it? After his amused reaction to Tristan's destroying the tower, she supposed it was possible. "My mother did speak of the ancient ones living in a tower on that hill, but I never remember her mentioning any caves underneath it," she said aloud. "And I know nothing of any cave Sean found in the forest."

"I assure you, my lady, he did," he answered. "His original intention before I agreed to supply him with siege engines and troops was to use the caves to enter the castle. If we could find the entrance under Du-Maine's tower, you could escape with your husband none the wiser." The intense light she had seen in his eyes before had returned, a kind of piercing gleam quite at odds with his usual demeanor. "Sean might even be able to lead more men inside and take the castle back again. We might still rescue your people before DuMaine takes his revenge."

"Tristan doesn't mean to hurt the people," she said before she thought.

"Are you certain?" he asked gently. "From what I've heard of him, he is not the sort to easily forgive."

She didn't answer, but in her heart, she had to admit he was right. But he had said nothing to the king's man or his own knights of what he had suffered. He had let her live, had kissed her, not clapped her in irons. "I know nothing of these passages," she said at last. "But I suppose we could look."

"We will have to be cautious," he warned her. "If DuMaine suspects—"

"He won't," she cut him off. Tristan had to leave his dungeon sanctuary sometime. She would talk to him, discover his plans if she could. But if there was a secret way out of the castle, she would escape with any of the people who wanted to come with her. Somehow she would convince Sean to flee, to give up their cause for good. But could she give up Tristan? "Thank you, Baron," she said, smiling at him. "I am in your debt."

"Not at all." He made her a small bow. "Now come. We have been in private long enough."

"Yes." If Tristan's knights were all watching her as closely as Sir Sebastian, one of them would have taken note of where she was by now. "Tell me, my lord," she said as they started out, raising her voice to be heard in the corridor beyond. "What is your Christian name?"

"My Christian name?" he echoed with a queer, barking laugh that made her turn to look at him again. "Lucan," he said with the same sad smile as before, when he had spoken of how they had both suffered. "You may call me Lucan."

"As you will." This time she made herself take hold of his arm before he offered it. "Lucan."

"Siobhan!" Clare came running up the stairs, her little slippers ringing on the stones. "The guards won't let me see my papa," she said, her little girl's face drawn into a perfect miniature of Tristan's scowl of fury. She gave the baron a glance as Siobhan knelt down before her. "Tell them I must speak to him."

"I would, love, but they won't listen to me." She smiled at Callard as she picked the child up in her arms. He smiled back but only slightly, and his eyes were cold. Lucan of Callard apparently did not care for children. "They would not let me go in, either," Siobhan said, kissing Clare's cheek. "They are being very naughty."

"Yes." She kissed her back. "We will tell Papa."

"Yes, we will," Siobhan agreed. "Come . . . you shall stay with me." Nodding one last time to the baron, she carried the child away.

Tristan awoke at sunset, haunted by dreams he could barely remember, images of his castle in flames once again and of Siobhan in peril, her beautiful face smeared with blood and soot. "No," he muttered, turning his face into the pillow. "Not real."

"I beg your pardon?" Simon said with his accustomed humor, watching him from the other bed, already wide awake.

"Nothing." He got up and went to the door. "You there!" he called to the guards at the end of the passage. "Somebody fetch me some water."

"Orlando has gone to find Silas," Simon said when he came back. "He wants to start digging through your dungeon wall."

"Why?" Tristan asked, annoyed. Hunger gnawed inside him, inconvenient but impossible to ignore. He would have to hunt soon.

"He thinks there is a way into the catacombs from here," his vampire brother answered. If he suffered similar pangs, he hid them well.

"There might be, I suppose." The guardsman carried in a wooden bucket of water with a pewter basin and clean towels, and the sound of his heartbeat echoed in the vampire's ears, almost too tempting to resist. He set his burden down on the table, and Tristan dismissed him with a wave. "We built this tower on the foundation of an ancient structure that the peasants treated like a shrine," he said, filling the basin. "They made quite a ruckus when we took it down." He ducked his face into the water, trying to clear his head as he washed.

"My lord!" Sir Andrew was coming down the passage, ready to report. "Forgive me for disturbing you," he said, quaking a bit at Tristan's scowl. "I heard you were awake."

"Who else is coming, sir knight?" Simon said with a grin as he got up himself. "Should we make ready for a procession?"

"None else but me, your grace," the knight said, returning his smile. "Though I do believe Lady Siobhan and Lady Clare would both have visited long since if the guards had allowed it."

"Siobhan was here?" Tristan asked. "Where is she now?"

"She was not here in the dungeons, my lord," Andrew answered. "Sebastian stopped her on the bridge and explained you had asked not to be disturbed. She did not like it, but she did not press him, either."

"I will go and find Orlando," Simon said, clapping him briefly on the shoulder as he left.

"Meet me later in the stables," Tristan told him. "We will ride out."

Simon nodded. "As you will."

"So Sebastian spoke to my wife," Tristan said when his vampire brother was gone.

"This morning," Andrew nodded. "She meant to ride out, but he would not allow it. Then she said she would come and speak to you, but he persuaded her not to try."

The young knight's eyes were troubled. "What is it?" Tristan asked.

He looked back down the passage toward the guards as if to make certain they weren't listening. "My lord, we have questioned the lieutenants," he said more softly. "They told us . . . if it isn't true, you can hardly imagine what they said."

"It is true," Tristan answered. "Lebuin and his brigands took the castle."

"Sweet Christ." Andrew's heart stepped up its pace, and Tristan closed his eyes, trying to shut out the sound, to focus on the conversation. "And Lady Siobhan—"

"Lady Siobhan is my wife," Tristan cut him off. "That is all you need know."

"Yes, my lord." The young knight dropped his head to hide his expression as Tristan opened his eyes, properly chastened but obviously unconvinced.

"Assemble the knights and lieutenants in the tower hall," Tristan said more gently. "Remove anyone you do not know yourself, anyone not of our original garrison— send them across the bridge to the manor. I will meet you there before midnight and explain my plan."

Andrew smiled, relieved. "Yes, my lord." He started out, then stopped. "My lord, what do you know of this baron of Callard?"

Tristan frowned. "Why do you ask?"

"No just reason, I hope." In the past, Andrew had always been his least diplomatic, most plainspoken knight; if he was hedging, something was amiss. "But when Sebastian refused to allow your lady to leave the castle or come to you, she sought out the baron of Callard."

"Sought him out?" Tristan repeated. Jealousy sparked inside him, fed by his demonic hunger. Lebuin had spoken of Callard as Siobhan's future husband after he himself was dead. He had told Callard's man that Siobhan was against the plan. But since then, had she changed her mind? "Are you certain it was not the baron who sought her?"

"He seemed none too displeased to see her," Andrew allowed. "But she approached him first. They spent some half an hour alone in the solar together." He frowned. "If I had been there, I would have interrupted, or at least sent a servant to eavesdrop on their conversation."

"I'm sure it was nothing," Tristan said. "Now leave me." The young knight nodded, leaving him alone to dress and sort his thoughts. He put on his own clothes for the first time in weeks, but it gave him little pleasure. Somehow he had to leave the castle, hunt, and feed without causing a stir, then return and make his garrison believe he was still their lord, all while satisfying Simon and Orlando in their mythic and, to his mind, mostly pointless quest.

But first he must see to Siobhan.

16

Siobhan sat on the hearth of the tower hall, smiling at her stepdaughter over the chessboard. "This is the queen," she explained, holding up the piece. "She is your most powerful soldier, the only one you can move in any direction for as many squares as you wish."

"More powerful than the king?" Clare said.

"Much more powerful." She set down the queen and picked up her ivory mate. "The king can move in any direction, but only one square at a time, thus."

"But the king is the one who must be captured," Clare said.

"Just so." She put the king back down in his place and picked up the queen again. "All the other pieces protect the king from the enemy. But none so well as the queen."

"So she loves him," Clare decided.

"I suppose," Siobhan allowed, smiling at the child's whimsical turn of mind. "Perhaps she only loves to win."

"Excuse me, my lady," the knight Sir Sebastian said, making a bow as he reached them. "Your lord has asked that we assemble his soldiers in this hall. May I escort you and Lady Clare back to the manor?"

"You have spoken to Tristan?" she said, instantly alert. "He has come out of his hole?"

"He is awake," the knight nodded, blushing slightly.

"Lovely." She got up from the hearth with a warrior's grace, mindless of her skirts. "Come, Clare."

"Wait, my lady," Sebastian protested.

"No, sirrah. I will not." She took Clare's hand and brushed past him, headed for the door.

Tristan emerged through the archway just as his brigand bride was stalking past his poor knight like he might have been a statue, his daughter's hand clasped in her own. They seemed so comfortable together, these two that he loved. Clare had even taken on Siobhan's style of walking, long, boyish strides with her shoulders thrown back. Instead of silk or velvet, she wore a plain wool kirtle with telltale smudges of dirt smeared on the knees. His cherub had become a wild thing, too. "Never mind, Sebastian," he called, fierce, jealous love for both of them clenched like a fist around his heart.

"Papa!" Clare broke free of Siobhan to race to her father, coming through the arch. He scooped her up as always, and she wrapped her arms around his neck, kissing his cheek. But before he could answer or kiss her back, a wave of hunger swept over him, the sweet smell of her skin and the sound of her heartbeat inciting the demon that possessed him.

"Take her!" he ordered, sick with revulsion as he shoved her into Siobhan's arms.

Siobhan saw the sudden, golden glow in his green eyes and clutched the child close to her, backing away. "It's all right, kitten," she soothed, turning Clare's face away from the vampire to her own shoulder. "Your papa is still sick." Even if she had not loved him, she would have felt pity for her demon lover, seeing the horrified expression on his face. But she was afraid of him, too. Whenever she had seen him before, he had always seemed completely in control of the power inside of him. Now it was obvious that he was not.

"Take her upstairs," he ordered, his voice more natural as his eyes faded back to simple green. "Wait for me there in your room."

"No," Siobhan answered, shaking her head. "I have to speak with you."

"I have to go out," he said brusquely. "I will speak with you later when I return."

"Take me with you—"

"No!" Clare had turned back to him, her own green eyes wide with confusion, and he smiled, touching her cheek. "Do as I tell you, Siobhan. Go to your room and wait for me."

"I have been waiting for you all day," she pointed out, fear quickly giving way to fury. Was she a child, too, that he could order her to bed?

"Then another hour will hardly make a difference." He touched her cheek as well, and though she knew he would sooner die than say the words, she saw pleading in his eyes. His hands are cold, she thought. She reached up and clasped his hand in hers, and the flesh was chill, like a statue come to life. Or a corpse, she could not help but think, her own flesh tingling with horror.

"Another hour," she echoed, her blue eyes focused hard and searching on his face. She pressed a kiss to the heel of his hand, making him shiver with ravenous desire. If she did not let him go, he would take her here before Clare and the household and probably murder her besides. "Fine, then. We will wait."

"I'm sorry, Papa," Clare said solemnly. "I did not mean to make you sick."

"You didn't, kitten," Siobhan said before he could answer. "I did. But he will be well soon." She let go of his hand, trailing a caress across his cheek that burned him like a brand before she started up the stairs.

As soon as they rounded the curve of the staircase, Clare lay her head against Siobhan's shoulder and began to cry, quiet and shaking in her arms. "Sweeting, what is it?" Siobhan said, pressing her closer. "All is well, love, I promise." She kissed the little one's cheek, stroking her hair.

"Why are you and Papa still so cross?" she demanded.

"We're not, love." She carried her into her bedroom, kicking the door shut behind them.

"You are," she insisted, curling against her as Siobhan sat down on the bed and held her on her lap. "Both of you are angry; I can tell."

"No, Clare, not angry." She kissed her again, desperate to comfort her. She had never been close to a child in her life, but Clare was different, so serious and brave.

"Siobhan, what is wrong with him?" She looked up with her father's eyes. "He felt so cold."

"I know." She drew her close again to hide from those eyes. "He's ill, sweeting. Did he not tell you so?"

"He cries tears of blood." Her voice was barely louder than a whisper, as if she were afraid to speak the words aloud. "I saw it. And when he touched me . . ." She touched her own cheek. "He felt like ice."

"He has a strange sort of fever, I think." He cried? she thought, grief and guilt twisting her heart. "But he is getting better every day."

"Tell him you are not cross with him anymore." The child drew back to look at her again. "Tell him you are sorry for what Sean Lebuin did, and he will be better."

"Clare . . ." She laid a hand against her cheek.

"He will," she insisted. "You have to, Siobhan. If he isn't better soon, he will go away." Her cherub's bow of a mouth quivered as fresh tears spilled down her cheeks.

"No, Clare," Siobhan said. "Listen to me. No matter what else might happen, your father would never willingly leave you." As abhorrent as the thought might be, she might somehow find the courage to destroy Tristan to save her people. But she would not let his child lose faith in him, not when he loved her so. "Remember the night I came here with Sean? Remember how I held the knife to your throat and threatened to hurt you?"

"Yes." A new sort of horror dawned in the little one's eyes at the thought.

"He did not know me then, and he believed that I would do it." All the trust that had grown up between them might be dissolving in an instant as she spoke, but she could not stop. "He gave up everything—his castle, his men, his mission, even his own life—to stop me. He would not let you be hurt, not for the whole wide world. Do you remember?"

"Yes." She seemed calmer. "But you would not have hurt me, would you, Siobhan?"

"No, love, I would not." She smiled, brushing a tear from Clare's cheek. "Your papa and I might be cross with one another, but we both love you very much. Whatever else might happen, we will keep you safe."

Clare's answer was to cuddle close again, her little arms around Siobhan's waist. Not for the first time, Siobhan thought of this child's mother. What must she have been like? What could have happened to her? Did Clare and Tristan mourn her? "I love you, too," she murmured, catching the end of Siobhan's braid and holding it against her cheek.

She held the child until she felt her grow heavy with sleep in her arms. Then she tucked her gently into bed and tried to decide what to do next.

Tristan had told her to wait for him. But where could he have gone? She went to the door and looked out to find a pair of guardsmen loitering in the hallway, not quite on alert but obviously present. Smiling at them weakly, she closed the door again. "God's bloody feet," she muttered, chewing her lip. Was she to spend the rest of her life shut up in this tower, waiting for disaster?

She looked out the window toward the wood. Tristan had said he was going to ride out. Had the duke gone with him? She ran a hand along the stones that edged the window frame, tracing the mortared cracks. Ever since the night she had climbed the cliff to escape her first Norman soldier, she had hated heights. But the wall was new, and the cracks were deep. With a stifled sigh, she started changing clothes.

Tristan watched the stag struggle to its feet and bound away into the forest. "We should keep cows," he grumbled.

Simon just stared at him for a moment, aghast, then smiled. "It might be easier." He wiped his mouth on the back of his hand. "You think little of the blood we take, don't you, brother?"

"What is there to think of?" The animal's blood was not entirely satisfying, but it had taken the edge off his hunger.

"We feed on life," Simon pointed out as they made their way through the trees.

"What man does not?" he countered. "If I were as I was, I would have killed the stag and fed it to my household. As I am, I feed and set it free. I call that merciful." They had reached the horses tethered in a thicket, and he untied Daimon's reins. "'Tis likely the stag would agree."

"But not all of your prey receives such mercy." Simon's horse, Malachi, tossed his head and snorted, restless as always in the presence of a demon other than his master. "Do you not regret the men you have killed?"

"Some of them, I suppose." He stroked Daimon's neck, considering. "I regret some of the men I killed as a soldier, too. Were you not a soldier once?"

"Yes," Simon allowed. "But that was very different."

"Aye, it was." He swung up into the saddle. "Then you had a choice. You did not need to kill those men to survive; you could have been a shepherd." His Irish brother's sudden look of remorse made him smile. "Satan's horns, Simon. You cannot take yourself to task for every evil in the world."

"No, not every one." He mounted as well. "Just my own."

"Absolve yourself a little," Tristan advised. "You have done penance enough."

"Not nearly," he retorted. "You, for example. Your death is on my head."

"I forgive you," Tristan said. "There, that settles one."

"Not much progress," Simon muttered, but he smiled. "Are you going back to the castle?"

"Are you not?" Daimon trotted in a circle, eager to be off.

"Only to collect Orlando," he answered. "He has Silas digging, but he wants to start exploring the catacombs from the other end in the meantime. We're coming back to the forest." Malachi shied to one side, but he easily turned him back. "I don't suppose I could convince you to help."

"I almost wish I could," Tristan said with a wry smile. "But I still have a quest of my own."

"Revenge," Simon said, shaking his head.

"No." His friend looked up, surprised. "If Lebuin has fled, I will not chase him. But I have to make certain my castle is safe—my daughter and Siobhan."

"I thought Siobhan was the enemy," Simon said gently, raising an eyebrow.

"That is my other task," Tristan admitted. "I have to find out if she is." He thought again of what Andrew had said, that Siobhan had spent time in private conference with Callard. "I have much to do yet, brother," he said. "But when I am done, I will keep my word." He pulled up on the reins. "We will find your chalice."

Gaston stood at the window of his master's rooms in the manor, watching as Tristan DuMaine and his friend, the Irish duke, rode out through the gates. "I can't believe he lives," he said again, shaking his head. "I saw him, my lord. No man could have survived such a beating."

"And yet it seems he did." Callard was lounging at

his ease before the fire, a lady's linen handkerchief dangling from his hand. Gaston had rarely seen him in so fine a humor.

"So it would seem," he agreed. "And Lady Siobhan ran to him as if he were her long-lost love."

"Perhaps he is." The baron stared into the fire, the strange new smile he had acquired teasing the corners of his mouth. "She knows what he is," he mused. "The marks on her throat . . . he has drunk from her."

"My lord?" Gaston said, confused.

"And yet she runs to him." He lifted the handkerchief to his face and breathed in deeply. "She has my blood, Gaston."

"My lord Baron," Gaston began again, his scalp beginning to prickle. "You make no sense."

"Do I not?" He looked up and mildly met his gaze. "In truth, Gaston, I find it harder and harder to remember who I am." He twisted the bit of cloth around his fingers, his brow drawn in thought. "I am stronger in body and spirit, but I begin to lose myself. This baron of yours . . . I forget where he ends and I begin."

He is mad, Gaston thought, feeling sick. "You are the baron, my lord."

"Of course I am." He frowned. "Merlin's blood . . . here. There must be a reason. Too dilute, of course— the girl is nothing, really. It is the other one who is the key. Her blood is pure." He looked up again as if he expected Gaston to be someone else. "And Simon." He smiled, the angel's smile. "My Simon."

"My lord, what is in your head?" Gaston demanded. "Why do you say such things? Explain your plan to me, and I will do all that you wish."

The baron rose from his chair. "Do I disappoint you, Gaston?"

"Never, my lord." He sank to his knees before him. "Am I not faithful?"

"Yes." He smiled. "It seems you are."

"Not seems, my lord. I swear it." He reached for his master's hand and kissed it. "I beg you to give me a task."

Callard stroked his hair in a fatherly caress. "There is something you can do for me," he said. "Something that will make me strong again."

"Yes," Gaston said, entranced by the love he saw reflected in his master's eyes. "Anything."

The baron knelt as well to face him, framing his face in his hands, smiling his beautiful smile. He kissed him tenderly on either cheek. Then his head fell back, his lips drawn back to reveal long, curved, white fangs. "Master," Gaston whispered in horror, frozen with fear, then the fangs were clamping hard upon his throat. He barely struggled as his life's blood drained away, his body going cold. But just when it seemed he was dying, just as his heart was slowing to a crawl, he felt the baron's embrace give way. A great, black cloud rose up around them like blood dropped in water, engulfing them both. Gaston opened his mouth to scream, and the cloud rushed inside of him, filling him up. His consciousness fought as with a demon, pummeled and torn until he no longer knew who he was. Dying, he thought. I am damned . . . then cold, black silence.

Lucan Kivar opened his eyes, rising inside his new form. The world was bright and sharp again; his purpose clear and strong. The mind that had been this man Gaston was nothing but a shadow. He looked down at the body of the baron, the vessel that had brought him to this place. He had been strong, his will and evil extraordinary for a mortal. Gaston had been weak. He would not last for long. "Soon," he murmured, turning to the mirror to learn his new face, his mind paging through this body's memories like a scholar paging through a book. He saw the image of Siobhan, this child of his son Merlin's blood who feared no demon, and he smiled. "Soon I will be someone else."

Siobhan crawled slowly like a spider down the rough stone wall, praying the prayer of a brigand as she went. "Remember me in hell, my God," she whispered, stretching for the next toehold. "You know I did my best as best I could."

The tower was the latest in Norman defenses, not a plain square but a sort of squatty cross with a deep, slitted crevice at each corner where archers could fire down on anyone agile or foolish enough to try to climb the motte. She worked her way into the nearest of these corners in hopes of hiding from the guards below.

She could hear their voices from where they stood in the arch around the corner, but directly below her were the kennels. If she could make it to the bottom, she might gain entrance to the tower there and the dungeons beyond—Tristan's lair.

Just below the halfway mark, her boot struck a deeper, wider crack, too big to hold her foot, and she almost slipped and fell. "Bloody hell," she muttered breathlessly, heart pounding. Resisting the urge to look down, she felt her way with her foot again, clinging harder with her fingers. Too wide to be an arrow slit, the opening was hidden in the very point of the corner. Skirting around it, she inched slowly downward, reaching out now with her hand to feel the edge—a doorway. She stepped onto the ledge and found the wooden door, its iron handle tucked sideways into a niche in the wood. To her surprise, it turned easily, and the door opened before her.

Crouching low, she slipped inside and found herself on a gallery above the tower hall. Tristan's knights and soldiers had already begun to gather there—she saw Sir Sebastian sitting by the hearth, studying her chess game. A narrow door at the end of the gallery opened on a tight spiral stair, and she slipped down it, careful to make no sound. But the door at the bottom opened directly into the hall, probably behind a tapestry. She could hear voices just outside, too close to avoid if she passed through. "Lord Tristan rode out with the duke," a man was saying. "But he told Sir

Andrew he would return and reveal to us his plan."

Siobhan chewed her lip. She could wait and eavesdrop in relative safety—Tristan's plan was something she would very much like to hear. But now might be her only chance to explore the dungeons with Tristan and his friend gone out. Biting back an oath, she climbed the stairs again.

At least the rest of her climb down the tower was simple—an iron ladder led from the door almost to the ground. She dropped the last few feet into the turf below, breathing a sigh of relief. The great wolfhound bitch that she had rescued from the brigands' mutts her first morning at the castle walked up and sniffed her curiously, nuzzling her hand for a caress. "Fair e'en, milady," she murmured, scratching between the dog's ears. "Where has your master gone?"

The boy who kept the kennels was a particular pet of hers, and had been since Sean had taken the castle. He stood up, surprised, as she came in, but grinned when she put a finger to her lips. She motioned him closer and put a hand on his shoulder. "How do I get to the dungeons?"

"Careful, my lady," he answered, matching her near-whisper. "The master of works has a crew of diggers there."

"Diggers?" Callard had spoken of tunnels under the castle, tunnels Sean had known of and never mentioned to her. Could Silas or Tristan know about them as well? "Why do they dig?"

"I couldn't say," the boy shrugged. " 'Twas the little one's idea, the duke's jester."

She had barely noticed the dwarf the day before, so intent had she been on reaching Tristan, but she remembered him even so, a bearded little man in motley clothes. "The jester says to dig up the dungeons, so Silas obeys him?"

"They're mad, the lot of them." The boy nodded. "They're on the far end, away from the door I will show you. But you must be careful."

She smiled. "I will."

The door was little more than a hatchway, built to pass trash out of both the dungeon and the kennels into the ditch around the motte, so low she had to crawl through on her hands and knees. Once inside, she climbed into a crouch and crept through the darkness, listening intently. At the far end of the dungeon was indeed a crew of men digging a hole in the floor. Silas stood over them, his chin in his hand as if he were deep in thought. But she saw no sign of the dwarf. Just across from where she crouched in the shadows was an open cell with two large beds and some chairs inside— Tristan's underground chamber. Giving the diggers a long look to make certain they were engrossed in their task, she darted across the torchlit corridor.

Some scrolls were spread across a chest—a map and some others covered in gibberish, writing she could not decipher. Both beds were neatly made, and Tristan's peasant clothes were folded on the foot of one. Glanc-

ing again at the group working just a few feet away, she
lifted the papers away and opened the chest.

Inside were more clothes that smelled like Tristan,
and she smiled without thinking, lifting them away.
Under these was the castle's accounting book; she had
seen Sean studying it many times. She flipped it open
and saw new accounts written in Tristan's hand—the
numbers of his men returned from war and a list of the
stores sent from the king. The vampire truly meant to
be lord of his manor again.

"You must be Lady Siobhan." She turned to find the
dwarf standing behind her. "I must admit, I did not see
your face very clearly yesterday."

"I did not see you either." She could flee, she supposed, but what would be the point? "But yes, I am
Siobhan." She closed the book but made no move to
put it away. "Are you the duke's jester?"

He smiled. "I fear I do not amuse him very well. Nay,
lady." He came closer, his manner relaxed. "I am a wizard. My name is Orlando."

"Well met, Orlando." He was studying her, and his
eyes lingered pointedly on her throat.

"Well met indeed." He offered his hand, and she took
it. "We have much to talk about, I think."

"Do we?" She dropped the book back into the chest
and went back to her search, emerging with her sword
that Tristan had taken. "Why would you say that?"

"Because you know your husband is a vampire," he
answered. "And you tried to kill him with that sword."

"What is that to you?" She tucked the sword into her belt. "You speak of vampires as if you might know much of them. I know very little at all."

"You know more than any woman I have met yet in this Britain," he answered. "How is that, my lady?"

"I married one," she retorted. Under the sword was a wooden stake, old and dry as bones from a grave. "And he married a thief." She took this as well, tucking it beside the sword.

"Do you still mean to slay him?" He asked as if he were merely curious, as if it mattered very little to him what her answer might be.

"No," she answered. "Not unless I have to."

To her surprise, he smiled. "Good," he nodded. "If it comes to that, I wish you well, Siobhan."

She frowned, confused. "Thanks . . ." Still watching him, trying to interpret his smile, she backed out again and headed for the door.

Orlando watched the girl disappear into the shadows, silent and graceful as a cat in the dark. "Good fortune, little warrior," he mumbled. "May your gods protect you." He reached into the pocket closest to his heart and drew out the ruby-colored bottle he kept there.

"My friend, there is nothing here," Silas called back to him, sounding tired and impatient but completely oblivious to the girl's ever having been there. "If there are caves in this hill, this is not the source."

Orlando pressed a kiss to the bottle, the glass like ice

against his lips. "She is strong, beloved," he whispered, knowing the vampire sleeping as a vapor inside could not hear him, but needing to tell her even so. "If Kivar should take this Tristan, I believe she can destroy him." Simon was fond of his vampire brother; he would not understand. But in so many ways, Simon was still little more than a child. "You will be free, my love." Tucking the bottle back into his pocket, he went to join the scholar.

Tristan stood before his assembled men with the fire behind him, a familiar posture that should have pleased him. This was what he had wanted, after all, the vengeance his soul had bought for him when he became a demon. But looking out at them, his mortal friends and comrades, he felt empty and sad.

"Why did you not tell us straightaway, my lord?" Sir Andrew demanded. "Why did we not lay waste to these villains yesterday when we arrived?"

"Because many in this castle are not villains," he answered. He had told them almost all of the truth, how Lebuin and his brigands had taken the castle and murdered their friends, how he himself had been married to Siobhan, then taken far away to die alone in shame. "And the true villain has fled."

"Lebuin," Andrew nodded, speaking the word like a curse.

"But what of the lady, my lord?" Sir Sebastian said.

"The lady is noble at heart," one of the recently rescued lieutenants said before Tristan could answer. "'Twas she who pled for young Richard's life, and she nursed him herself, did all she could to save him. She has interceded for the common folk and for our soldiers many times with her brother and his men. You are right to spare her, Lord DuMaine." He seemed to feel too many eyes on him and blushed. "Or so I do believe."

"So do I," Tristan said. Silas was standing at the back of the hall, his arms crossed on his chest, and he nodded as Tristan looked his way. He had told the scholar his plan before coming into the hall; this soldier's speech made it seem that it might work. "Lady Siobhan has been at the mercy of her brother since her father's death. She had no choice but to follow him. But now she is my wife, and I will protect her, if I can." For a moment, he thought he heard a small sound from above, like a bird in the rafters, and he looked up. But he saw nothing. "Lebuin seems to have great affection for his sister," he went on. "He may be a coward, but I cannot believe he means to abandon her completely." Andrew smiled, already understanding, and Tristan smiled back. "He will return to rescue her, particularly if he thinks I am still weak," he finished. "And when he does, we will have him."

The rest of the conference passed quickly, with orders for watches and fresh oaths of loyalty from the traitorous lieutenants. But as the men were dispersing, Tristan saw movement in the gallery above. "God's arse," he muttered, catching Silas by the arm. "Tell Simon and Orlando I will see them before dawn." Without waiting to hear the scholar's answer, he sprinted for the hidden stairs.

He opened the door at the top and looked down, expecting to see some brigand making his way down the iron ladder to the ground, but there was no one. He sniffed the air, his vampire senses picking up a heartbeat.

Siobhan froze, clinging to the stones above, her heart pounding with fury from what she had heard and fear that she would be discovered. Bait . . . he meant to use her as bait.

Above, Tristan suddenly realized. The spy was above him. Catching hold of the doorframe with his left hand, he reached up with his right and caught a booted foot. Yanking hard, he meant to fling the brigand to his death in the rocky ditch below. Then he heard her scream. "Siobhan!" Letting go of the doorway, he lunged after her, nearly losing his own balance as he caught her by the wrist. "Holy Christ!" The name burned his mouth, but he barely felt it.

Siobhan gasped as he snatched her back from the void into his arms. "Are you mad?" he was demanding, holding her close, and for a moment, she let him, weak with relief. "Holy Christ," he repeated, kissing her hair.

"Let me go." She felt like crying, but her voice was flat and cold. "Let go of me now."

Tristan drew back to hold her by the shoulders. She was looking up at him with no expression, her beautiful blue eyes like ice. "No," he answered, his heart twisting with pain as he matched her tone. "Not a chance." Catching her wrist again, he started for the stairs, dragging her behind him.

17

He dragged her up the stairs, past the guards, who stared in shock as they passed. "Are you mad?" he repeated as he flung her into the bedroom and slammed the door shut behind them. "You could have been killed—I could have killed you—"

"And why not?" she retorted. "You've promised to kill me since the first night we met, remember? Why not let me fall?" All this time, even when she had hated him, she had thought that Tristan understood her, that he knew she was more than some prize to be protected or burden to be borne. But he was just the same as all the others, just the same as the first man she had killed, just the same as Sean. "But you can't, not yet," she went on bitterly, turning on him. "You still need me for bait."

"What?" He could barely hear what she was saying; he still felt sick every time he thought of what might have happened a few moments before. He could have thrown her to her death, could have lost her forever. "What are you—?"

"I heard you, Tristan!" She was still trembling from her brush with death; she could still hear the roar of the wind in her ears as she started to fall. "I heard you tell your men that Sean would come for me, that you would use me to capture him."

"What should I have told them, Siobhan?" he demanded. "That you have bewitched me? That I don't care anymore what part you played in my destruction? That the lives of the knights you and your brother killed are nothing to me compared to you? They saw me yesterday; they saw me come into my castle wanting nothing but to have you in my arms."

"They would understand. They know you." She felt as if her heart were dying inside her as she remembered the words he had spoken the first night they met. "You are a soldier. You can fuck anything if you must."

He caught her by the shoulders and shoved her hard against the wall. "Idiot," he snarled, his face scant inches from her own, so close she could see the demon fangs inside his mouth, the fire burning in his eyes. "Can you believe that? Can you still be such a fool?" Tears welled in her eyes, clouding her vision, but she saw his expression soften. "Siobhan . . ." He cradled her face in his hands. "No . . ." He kissed her tears away, his voice the tender lion's growl. "My love . . ." He kissed her mouth. "I love you."

"Liar." She stiffened in his grasp, desperate to shut him out, to not believe him. He brushed his lips over her cheek, and a sigh she could barely suppress rose in her throat, a sound of perfect longing. "You lie."

"I do not." She tried to look away from him, but he wouldn't allow it, holding her by the chin. "Why should I lie? If I truly wanted you to die, could I not kill you and be done?"

"No." She drew her sword as she broke free, holding the point to his throat. "I will not let you." She drew the stake from her belt with her free hand, raising it over his heart. "I will not let you break me."

He smiled, shaking his head. Fate had truly given him his match. "How could I not love you?" He caught hold of the stake as well, pressing the point more closely to his breast. "Slay me, Siobhan," he ordered. "If you can't believe me, drive the stake into my heart; cut my head off with the sword. I will not try to stop you."

"You think I can't do it," she said, trembling. "You think I am weak—"

"Never, my love," he promised. "How could you be weak when you have mastered me completely from the first moment we met?" Her breath caught short with unshed tears, and his heart ached for her. But he knew she must choose for herself. "But if you kill me, you must face my knights alone. How will you explain what has happened to me?" Her lower lip trembled, and her lashes were dark and spiked with tears. "If you tell them I am a vampire, Silas will confirm the tale. Do you think the two of you together can make them believe it?"

"I will run away," she insisted. "I will escape."

"You might," he said. In truth, he had no idea what she might do next. He had no doubt she could destroy him. Even now, the blade burned at his throat, its strange magic making him feel weak. But he could not bribe her, could not tell her he meant to give her rule of the lands her father had lost. Fool that he was, he wanted her to spare him for his sake alone. "So do it, then." He caught her by the wrist and drew the sword closer to his throat, its point piercing his skin. "Slay me and be free."

Her tears spilled down her cheeks. "I cannot be free," she admitted, letting her weapons fall. "Not of you." She touched his face, looking deep into his eyes before she fell against him, pressing her cheek against his throat. "May God help me, I love you."

He held her to him, weak with relief. "Siobhan . . ." He turned her face up to his and kissed her, devouring her mouth. She sighed in surrender, his brigand soft and yielding in his arms at last.

She ran her hands over his arms, drawing back to clasp his wrists and pull him toward the bed, her mouth still brushing over his. "Tell me again," she pleaded, reaching up for him as she sat back on the bed. "Tell me you love me."

"I love you," he promised. He bent over her, kissing her, laying her back on the bed. "I love you I love you I love you." The sheer surrender of it made him dizzy— he loved no one. To love was to be weak. But she needed him; he saw it in her eyes as she gazed up at him now. She needed the words to believe him, to feel safe. "I love you," he whispered, brushing the hair back from her brow. Her lips parted in a sigh, her sapphire eyes soft with longing, and he kissed her, unable to resist.

He made love to her slowly, lingering on every touch until she arched beneath him, crying out his name. He brought her to climax again and again, cuddling her close, then teasing her to madness. Only when he felt all trace of tension leave her precious body did he seek his own release, thrusting deep into her warmth to join with her completely. "Tristan," she murmured as he fell at last, crushing her beneath his weight and sheltering her in his arms. "Please don't leave me."

"Shhh," he whispered, exhausted, as he kissed her cheek. The dawn was coming quickly; he could feel it.

"Take me with you, please," she begged. Never in her life had she felt so safe, so loved. She could not give it up. "I want to be with you."

"You don't know what you ask, my love." Still holding her, he rolled onto his back, cradling her against his chest. "I want to be with you as well, every moment." He lifted her hand to his lips, kissing the palm. "But I am a demon, not a man."

"Tell me." She nestled close against his shoulder, her hand entwined with his. "How did it happen? Were you always a vampire?"

"Of course not." He kissed the top of her head, too weary and relieved to hold back any more. "Sean and his men all but murdered me, just as you saw." She turned her face into his chest for a moment, and he smiled to feel her tears hot on his skin. "But before I died, Simon of Lyan found me."

"And he is a vampire," she said, struggling to find her voice again.

"Yes, but not by choice." He trailed his fingers through her hair. "He killed the two men Sean sent to dispose of my body."

"Bruce and Callum," she murmured.

"He attacked them in the shape of a wolf and drained them of blood," he went on. "When he saw I was still alive, he only meant to end my pain. But when he drank from me, I bit him. I drank his demon's blood, and it made me a vampire, too."

"God's love," she said softly, picturing it in her mind. She should have been appalled, repulsed not only by this sacrilege but by the image of her love and the handsome duke so intertwined, but she was not. Frightened, perhaps, but not appalled. "So now you feed on living blood as well," she said. "You killed Angus and the others—"

"No," he interrupted. "One of those killings was not mine. The night I swore to you no one would die, I kept my promise." She kissed his shoulder for an answer, silent thanks. "And I can feed without killing my prey." He touched the wound still healing on her throat, and she smiled. "But I cannot speak the name of Our Lord without pain or touch a cross." He traced the shape of her mouth with his fingertips. "I cannot face the sun—the slightest touch will burn me. In daylight, I am all but pure demon and must sleep. Any creature that awakens me I could kill and never know it." He caressed her silken cheek. "That is why you can only be with me in darkness."

"And before, with Clare?" she asked gently. "Why could you not hold her?"

For a moment, she thought he would refuse to answer. "I had not fed for more than one full day," he said at last. "I heard her heart and smelled her blood . . ." His voice trailed off as he buried his face in her hair.

She kissed his throat. "I see." The wound he had forced her to make in his flesh with her sword still had not healed, and she touched the smear of blood there with her mouth, tasting it with her tongue. A chill like ice in fire shivered through her. Everything he had told her should make her want to turn away from him. But in faith, she loved him even more, knowing all of what he was, hearing him tell her the truth. He trusted her. He loved her, demon that he was, and that was everything. But there was still something more, one more barrier between them. "Tristan," she said softly, curled safe in his arms. "What of Sean?"

He breathed in the scent of her again, closing his eyes. No matter how dearly she loved him, her heart would always be divided. Her brother would always be there. "You asked me once why I could not leave you and your people in peace," he said. "I mean to do just that." She sat up to look at him in shock, and he smiled. "I will leave you lady of this castle to rule in my stead." He twisted a lock of her hair around his fingers. "You will take your father's place, protect your people just as you always wanted, with my royal favor and my knights to guard your claim." She opened her mouth to answer, and he shook his head. "But not Sean." He sat up as well, putting a hand softly to her mouth to stop her protest. "Do not ask me to forgive him." He thought again of his knights, the look of helpless reproach in their eyes as they watched him, their lord, watch them die. "I love you with all my heart, Siobhan. But I cannot."

She laced her fingers with his to take his hand away. "I know." She pressed a kiss into his palm. He could forgive her because she was a woman, and he loved her. He could pretend she had changed or that she had never been his enemy at all, and that could make her angry. But she loved him as he was, and she understood. "But what if he never comes back?"

"He will," he answered. "You know it as surely as I do. He will wait however long it takes to seize his moment, but he will come again. He will try to take this castle." He touched her cheek. "And you, my love, will let him."

No, she thought but did not say, knowing she could never make him believe it. She smiled instead, looking down through a fresh veil of tears. "So I am to be bait after all."

"He must be punished, Siobhan—"

"You mean killed—"

"I hope not." She looked up at him, an accusation in her eyes. "But yes," he admitted. "Probably so." She shook her head, looking away, but not before he saw her tears again. He asked too much of her, he knew. But he had no choice. "Siobhan, who is the baron of Callard?" he asked gently, meaning, Who is he to you?

"How should I know?" she said lightly, forcing a smile. "Did you not bring him here with you?" But she could not meet his eyes, could not lie to him anymore. "He was Sean's ally, Tristan," she answered. "At least he pretended to be." She splayed a hand against his chest where his heartbeat should have been. "Sean is my brother, Tristan." She looked up into his eyes at last. "But you are my husband."

When he had first met her, he had mistrusted every word she spoke, certain that she was born a liar. But now, in spite of all his better judgment, he had no choice but to believe her. He kissed her brow, closing his eyes. "I must go," he said aloud, letting the matter drop. "It's nearly dawn." The distress in her eyes made him smile, and he pulled her close again. "I cannot let you leave the castle. Not until Sean is caught."

"But then you will trust me." She wrapped her arms around his waist, swallowing the sobs that threatened to rise in her throat. "When Sean is dead, you will leave me."

"Not for long, I hope." He turned her face up to his. "Will you want me to return?"

The pain in her eyes was proof enough even without her words. "How can you ask me that?" He kissed her, and she clung to him, their passion igniting again.

When he was gone, Siobhan stood at the window, watching the first streaks of dawn appearing in the sky. She was tired, but she would not sleep. Somehow she must find this passageway out of the castle. "Forgive me, love," she whispered to the shadows. "I have to send him away."

After he left Siobhan and just before the dawn, Tristan knelt at his daughter's bedside, stroking her golden hair. "Papa," she murmured, smiling through a yawn.

He kissed her forehead. "Do you remember when I went away to Scotland?" he asked her. "You were a very little girl."

"I do remember." She touched his cheek. "You had to go to war."

"Yes." He smiled at her, his precious little child. "But I came home again. Remember?"

"I remember." Her eyes were serious, too wise for such a cherub's face. "I do not wish for you to go."

"I do not wish it, either." He opened his arms, and she sat up to hug him. "But if I go, I will always come back to you, I promise." He pressed her close and kissed her. "Do you believe me?"

"Yes, Papa." Her little heartbeat throbbed between

them, so strong, a comfort to him now rather than torture. He was a horrible father, but she was strong enough to survive. "Are you going now?"

"No," he promised. "Not now." He drew back and kissed her cheek. "I will see you tomorrow night."

Siobhan returned to the manor just after dawn to find chaos. "What is it?" she asked, catching hold of a weeping maid as she came down the stairs. "What has happened?"

"The baron, my lady," the girl said, her eyes wide with horror. "The monster has killed him."

"No . . ." She started up the stairs. "It can't be." Tristan had left her only minutes before sunrise. How could he have returned to the manor and murdered Callard? But then he had been hungry when he left her the first time, so hungry his own precious child had been in danger. Who is the baron of Callard? he had asked her, and she had pretended not to care.

Gaston was standing over his master's shrouded body, looking down at the corpse with no expression on his face. "What happened?" she asked him.

He looked up, a strange light in his eyes. "See for yourself." He threw back the shroud, and she had to put a hand to her face to keep from being sick. The baron's face had already begun to swell with decay, and the stench was unbearable. But even so, the marks on his throat were impossible to miss. "Enough?" Gaston said, raising a brow.

She nodded, turning away as he covered the body again. "Holy Christ," she murmured, her legs weak beneath her. "How did we come to this?"

"Do you not know, my lady?" he asked. "Is this not your work?"

"My work?" She turned back to him, appalled. Gaston was the one who had convinced Sean she had murdered Angus with a dog. "Can you still believe these murders are mine?"

"Why not?" He sounded strange, not like himself, but this new tone was no improvement. "Perhaps your creature is something more vicious than a dog."

Before she could answer, Master Nicholas came in, followed closely by Silas. "My lady, come away from there," he ordered, putting an arm around her shoulders.

"Yes, Lady Siobhan, by all means," the king's clerk agreed, holding a handkerchief over his face. "I have questioned the baron's household." He fixed Gaston with an angry glare. "It seems there was a plague already with them."

"A plague?" she repeated. He knows, she thought, still looking at Gaston. Somehow he knows Tristan is a vampire.

"So it would seem," Silas said, his voice low and even. "Come away now. All will be well."

"Take this corpse away from here at once," Master Nicholas ordered Gaston. "All who served the baron will go with you."

"As you wish, of course," Gaston said with a bow.

He looked at Siobhan. "Let us all pray that will help."

"Now, my lady," Silas said more sharply. "Please."

"Yes." She met Gaston's eyes with her own. "I am sorry for your loss, Gaston. May you find better fortune at home." The corner of his mouth curled in a smile that was familiar but strange on his face, as if it belonged to someone else. "You know well how dearly I will miss you."

"Aye, my lady," he answered. "I do."

"Come," Silas ordered, leading her out.

She took hold of his arm on the stairs. "You have to help me, Silas," she said, her mind racing. Michael was coming across the hall, and when he saw her, he hurried to embrace her.

"Are you all right?" he demanded.

"Yes, I'm fine," she promised, grateful for his hug. Ever since Tristan had returned, Michael had seemed distant, not himself. "Callard is dead."

"I know," he nodded.

"Do you know I didn't kill him?" She looked back to include Silas in the question.

"Of course," Silas nodded.

"I do, yes," Michael agreed. "Siobhan, I'm so sorry—"

"It's all right," she cut him off, softening her words with a touch to his cheek. "But you must tell me the truth. Did Sean say aught to you of passages underneath this castle?"

He hesitated for barely more than a moment. "Aye, love," he answered. "He said your mother told him some druid's tale of a battle on these lands, of passages dug to hide some treasure being used to escape." He glanced at Silas. "We found tunnels underneath one of the shelters in the wood with queer pictures painted on the walls. He thought they might lead to the castle, but he was afraid to tell you. He thought you might be frightened of them, that you might refuse to use them."

"He was probably right," she admitted. "Silas, what does Tristan know of this?"

"I don't—"

"I know you were digging," she interrupted. "I saw you. I spoke to Lyan's wizard, Orlando."

"And what did he tell you?" he asked.

"Nothing," she admitted. "But he is a stranger. You are my friend."

After a moment, he nodded. "They found the entrance in the forest as well." He glanced at Michael for a moment. "Orlando thought there might be an opening here in the castle underneath the motte."

"The druid's hill," she said, looking away. In her mind, she could see it as it had been, surrounded by the forest. Memories that seemed to belong to someone else flashed through her head, another village burning, not her own.

"But there's nothing there, my lady," the scholar continued. "We dug in the dungeons, the kennels—the motte is solid."

"No." Her hand strayed to the pocket of her gown and the hilt of the sword she had concealed against her leg again. The night she had found it, the earth around it had crumbled underneath her hand. "I don't have to dig." She looked up at Silas. "Stay here. If anyone asks for me, tell them I am overcome with grief, that I have gone back to the tower to my room." She caught Michael's hand. "You come with me."

"Siobhan, wait," Silas said, catching her arm. "If we are friends—"

"You are Tristan's friend as well," she cut him off. "I do not ask you to betray him." She took both of his hands in hers. "Nor will I, I swear. Whatever happens, wherever I may go, I will come back." She smiled. "I will not allow your castle to be hurt again."

"Wait for Tristan," he urged her. "Wait until tonight, tell him what is in your mind—"

"I can't." Framing his face in her hands, she kissed his cheek. "All will be well. I promise."

She crossed the courtyard quickly, trying not to run, with Michael following behind her. All around them, the baron's servants were loading their wagons with an air of desperation, but she barely saw them. In her mind, she was a child again, running for her life through a patch of woods long gone.

She half-walked, half-slid down the rocky slope into the ditch, catching Michael as he almost fell. "This is madness," he muttered, straightening up again.

"Yes," she admitted. "But it's our only hope." She skirted the edge of the hill, looking up at the sun, half-risen in the east. "My father's house would have been there," she said, pointing. "So I would have come from this side . . ." The briars were still there, blocking their path. "This is it." Shrugging an apology to Michael, she dropped to her stomach and crawled.

"You can't be serious . . ." He did the same, cursing as he came.

She straightened up against the rocky cliff. "This is definitely it." Her stomach twisted with remembered fear; she could almost hear the voice of the Norman behind her. *I will catch you, poppet!* But that man was dead, and she was a woman grown. She ran a hand over the wall as Michael scrambled to his feet beside her. "Give me a boost."

He looked up at the sheer cliff with the tower high above. "A boost?"

"It's not far," she promised. Somehow she knew exactly where to find the entrance, as if she had always known. Shaking his head, Michael bent and put a shoulder underneath her rump, heaving her up the wall.

Before, when she was a child, she had climbed high enough on solid rock to be out of reach of her pursuer. But this time, the cliff opened before her, her hands breaking through the crumbling earth so quickly, she almost tumbled through.

"God's bloody feet," Michael breathed.

"Aye," she answered, crawling through the hole.

The passage dipped down sharply but was tall

enough for her to stand almost at once. The morning light beamed down from the hall to illuminate a narrow cave, its walls painted with figures. "Come in," she called back to Michael.

He swore another oath as he reached her, more blasphemous than the first. "What is this place?"

"I don't know." The floor was littered with piles of trash that gave her a shiver of foreboding. "Do you have a flint?" she said, taking a dusty torch down from the wall. He struck a spark and lit it, confirming her fears. The trash was bones, the long-dead skeletons of the fallen.

"Does this lead to the forest, do you think?" Michael asked, following her deeper.

"I know it does." Somehow she knew exactly where to go. A great, smothering sadness overwhelmed her, as if she had known these people who were dead, had lived among them. Her mother had said they were descended from Merlin, though Sean had said it was not so. But Sean had been wrong often enough. The day after Tristan's return, she had dreamed of the druid's tower, of living inside. *The wolf has found us,* a voice had spoken, and she had been afraid.

Farther along the passage were more skeletons, and a great section of the cave seemed to have collapsed. But the narrow passage led on. "Bring the others here," she said aloud. "All of our men, one by one so we won't be noticed—we're brigands, we can manage it. I will be in the manor house playing lady—come and get me when you're done."

"And then what?" he asked, still looking aghast at the bones that littered the floor.

"I have to find Sean," she answered. "You have to help me convince him to go away, to France or to Scotland—"

"He won't," he cut her off. "You know he won't give up your father's people."

"I will protect my father's people." She met his sudden stare of shock without flinching. "I am coming back, Michael. I mean to stay with Tristan."

"Stay with . . . Siobhan, are you mad?" he demanded. "You said yourself, he is a demon—"

"And he loves me," she said. "And I love him. I cannot betray him, and I cannot leave him." She put a hand on his arm, pleading with her eyes. "But I cannot let him murder Sean, either. So Sean must go away."

The day wore slowly on. Siobhan sat in the solar with Master Nicholas and Silas, barely listening to their talk, her spinning in her lap. 'Twas odd, she thought, trying to occupy her mind with something more benign than her plan to find her brother or what might follow after—in truth, every time she tried to imagine what she would say to Sean, she felt sick. She had not picked up a spindle for years after her mother's death, but in the past few days, she had discovered she still had the knack. Twisting the thread, she could almost imagine her mother was beside her, that her life had been what it was meant to be and she was the lady she pretended. She found it strangely relaxing.

"What can that be?" Master Nicholas complained as shouts were heard from the guardsmen on the wall. The king's clerk was still obviously shaken from the baron's death; he was nervous as a cat.

"Nothing dire, I hope," Siobhan said with a smile as she stood up. "I will go and see."

"Are you certain, my lady?" Silas said, standing up as well.

"Of course." Giving them each a gracious nod, she made herself walk slowly to the door.

She quickened her pace as she crossed the courtyard and climbed the steps to the top of the wall with a pounding heart. What now? her mind kept repeating. Dear God, what now?

The riders, hooded and cloaked, were waiting on the other side of the moat. "They've only just reached us," Sir Sebastian said, standing beside her. "Hail there!" he called. "Who comes?"

The larger of the riders threw back his hood to reveal a black helmet crowned with a demon's horns. "Brautus of Charmot!" he called back. The second rider lowered her hood as well—a woman with striking red hair. "And this is the duchess of Lyan."

18

Master Nicholas was in danger of tripping over his own clever tongue, he was so eager to fawn over the duchess. "Your Grace, you honor this house," he said, ushering her to a chair. "But I fear for your safety. The plague the guardsmen warned you and your man of at the gates is no joke."

"I have no fear of plague, master," the duchess answered. She glanced over his shoulder at Siobhan and smiled as if they had a secret. "They say it only afflicts the unrighteous, do they not?"

"Aye, Your Grace," he agreed with a laugh that sounded rather forced. "They do indeed." He turned back to Siobhan. "Lord Tristan should be here, my lady," he said, an edge of reproach in his tone. "Surely he can be disturbed—"

"No, master," the duchess interrupted. "Lord Tristan and my husband are of the same order, and I can assure you, he cannot." She was beautiful, the most delicate, feminine creature Siobhan had ever laid eyes on her life. Beside this vision, her own disguise was a joke.

"But if you would fetch me my servant, Orlando, I would be most grateful."

"Me, my lady?" Master Nicholas said, surprised.

"Yes, please." She smiled at Siobhan again. "I would speak to Lady Siobhan in private." She maintained her gracious smile as he bowed and murmured, "Of course." But as soon as he was gone, she was out of her chair and closing the door behind him.

"Are they well?" she asked, turning back to Siobhan. "Your Tristan and Simon, are they all right?"

"Yes," Siobhan answered, still rather stunned by the change. "They . . . I suppose they are fine."

"And Kivar?" she demanded. "Has he appeared?"

"I . . . I don't think so." Everything about this strange woman, from her perfectly coiffed red hair to the tips of her fine-tooled little boots, made Siobhan feel like a mule in a palfrey's harness. Yet here she was addressing her like they might have been old friends. "I don't know who that is," she admitted.

"Don't know . . . ?" The duchess sat down on a chair as if her legs had given way beneath her. "But don't you . . . ? Lady Siobhan, how did you come by those marks on your throat?"

"Tristan bit me," she admitted. "I know he is a vampire." She sat down as well. "And your husband, too, I suppose, though he has never told me. Indeed, I don't believe I have spoken with him at all." Too late, she remembered Silas's lessons. "Your Grace," she added.

"Please, for pity," the other woman laughed, obviously relieved. "We have the same problems, my lady. Do call me Isabel."

"Isabel," she repeated, smiling back. "I am just Siobhan." She found herself liking this duchess in spite of herself, and a strange sort of longing seized her. She had never had a woman friend in her life, and Isabel was right; they did have some of the same problems. How lovely it would have been to blurt out all her troubles and compare, to hear what this clever, pretty creature thought she ought to do. But of course she could not. "To answer your question, Isabel, I think both our demons are well," she said instead. "Are they in some sort of danger?"

For a fleeting moment, she saw a guarded look flicker through the other woman's hazel eyes, but her smile never dimmed. "I certainly hope not," she laughed. "But their position is rather precarious, wouldn't you say?"

"I suppose," Siobhan allowed. "Though I must say I'm more worried about the rest of us."

The pretty smile faded into an equally beautiful look of concern. "Are you truly?" she asked.

Before Siobhan could answer, the door opened, and Orlando came rushing in. "My lady," he demanded. "What are you doing here?" He embraced Isabel like he might have been her father, not her servant. "What has possessed you?"

"I missed my husband, of course," Isabel said lightly, but there was an unmistakable edge to her tone. She extricated herself from his arms. "We are very newly wed," she explained to Siobhan over his head.

"He is very handsome," Siobhan said, the only reply she could think of. "I will leave you to speak with Orlando alone." Making a curtsey, she left them, curious but too engrossed in her own troubles to scheme to find out more.

When she was gone, Orlando bolted the door behind her. "My lady, truly, what is wrong?" he asked Isabel. "Why have you come?"

"You never learn anything, do you, Orlando?" she said, letting her full fury show. "That poor girl . . . none of you has told her anything." She opened the pouch she would let no servant touch and took out the sheaf of scrolls inside. "Fools, the lot of you," she muttered, spreading them on the table.

"That poor girl, as you call her, is a brigand and a thief who had tried on more than one occasion to murder her husband," Orlando pointed out. "You should not have come, Isabel. You have no idea—"

"I know more than you think," she cut him off. Her expression softened somewhat, and she reached for his hand. "When Simon awakes, I will show you both."

"But why—"

"Orlando, please." She let him go, her hazel eyes troubled. "Please, just let me wait."

Siobhan walked out into the hall where the servants were setting up the trestle tables for dinner. The long afternoon was almost over; soon it would be night.

Michael was coming toward her. "It's done," he said

softly when he reached her side. "Everyone is in the caves."

"Were you noticed?" she asked. Silas was playing chess at the hearth with Master Nicholas, but his eyes were on her.

"I don't think so," Michael answered. "Old Jack told that knight, Sebastian, that you had ordered the brush cleared from a section of the ditch for drainage. Some of the peasants are still clearing; the soldiers disappeared into the hole."

"Well done," she said with a smile. Any moment now, the sun would be down, and Tristan might appear. If she waited just a little longer, she would see him again before she fled. But if she saw him, she might never go at all.

"Siobhan!" Clare was running down the steps. "I took a long nap," she announced, smiling up at Michael as Siobhan bent down to greet her. "So I can stay up late with Papa."

"I think you should," Siobhan agreed, hugging her tight.

"Don't tarry," Michael warned, giving Clare's braid a friendly tug as he left.

She sat down on the step to the dais and drew the child into her lap. "I'm glad that man is gone," Clare said, taking her hand.

"Who? Michael?" Siobhan said, surprised.

"No, Michael is good." She traced the lines in her stepmother's palm. "The other one. Gaston." She didn't look up, but she frowned. "He is very, very bad."

"Do you think so?" She kissed the top of the little one's head. She had always heard it said that children could see such things more clearly than adults. "I think so, too." She turned the child's face up to hers. "Do you know I love you very much?"

"Yes." She looked so solemn, Siobhan could not help but smile. Clare would someday be a scholar, she predicted.

"I will always keep my promise," she said aloud. "No matter what might happen or where I might go, I will always come back to take care of you, just as I promised your papa. And when you are old enough and strong enough, I will teach you how to fight. Do you believe me?"

She nodded. "I will have your sword."

"Yes," she promised, kissing her cheek. "You will have my sword."

The door to the hall burst open. "Where is she?" the duke demanded, coming in.

"Upstairs, Your Grace," Siobhan said, standing up. "In the solar." Vampire he might be, but the look in his eyes and his smile as she pointed the way to his bride made him seem very human indeed.

"Thanks, my lady," he said with a grin, sprinting for the stairs.

Tristan was coming more slowly behind him. He paused to scoop Clare up to his shoulder. "Let us see this duchess," he said with a wink at Siobhan. Before

she could answer, he had taken her hand to lead her to
the stairs.

The duchess in question was being kissed senseless
by her demon duke. "I told you to stay at Charmot and
be safe," he was scolding between kisses, her face
framed in his hands. "I told you not to come."

"I had to," Isabel answered, crystal tears gleaming
on her cheeks. "I had to come." She touched Simon's
face as if to prove to herself he was real. "I had to see
you." She laced her hands behind his neck and raised
up to kiss his mouth again. "Angel," she murmured as
he crushed her close.

Watching them, Siobhan felt tears of her own stinging her eyes. Isabel seemed to understand so much
more of what her lover was than Siobhan did Tristan,
yet still they were parted. Still they were in pain.

Tristan cleared his throat, and his vampire brother
looked up. "Shall we leave you, then?" he asked him
with a smile.

"No," Orlando said quickly.

"No," Simon agreed, but he sounded far less certain.
He traced the shape of his beloved's kiss-stung mouth.
"Later," he promised in a whisper.

Isabel smiled. "Always."

"We have much to discuss," Orlando went on, giving
Siobhan a pointed glance.

Siobhan clasped Tristan's hand in both of hers. "I
want to stay," she said, meeting his gaze. Let me stay
with you, she pleaded silently inside her mind. Let

me know everything, and nothing else will matter.

"Forgive me, brigand," he answered, his sweetest endearment. "Wait for me, please."

She took Clare from his arms and smiled. "Go find Master Silas," she told the child, kissing her cheek before she set her on her feet. Then she turned back to Tristan. Without a word, she raised up on tiptoe to kiss him, her arms around his neck. Smiling, she brushed a final kiss across the corner of his mouth before she let him go.

"Orlando tells me that girl tried to kill you, my lord," Isabel said when she was gone. "I must say, I cannot believe it."

"I fear 'tis true, Your Grace," he answered with a smile. Simon's lady was a beauty, no question, with a saucy manner and a scholar's intelligence clear in her eyes. But beside Siobhan, she seemed almost like a doll to him, too delicate to really be alive. "But I do not hold it against her."

"Do you not?" she countered. "Then why is she not here?"

"Isabel believes we do Siobhan an injustice by not telling her all that we know of your quest," Orlando explained to Simon.

"I do indeed," the duchess said. "Lord Tristan may be forgiven, I suppose; he is newly made. But after what happened at Charmot, you two should know better." Tristan smiled inside to see both vampire and wizard look chastened as children by her wrath. "Think how much pain might have been avoided if you had only told me the truth."

"This is very different, love," Simon said, taking her hand. "I told you, Siobhan was part of the rebel force that took Tristan's castle. And there's something else." He led her to a chair. "She has the sword, the one from the drawing of the Chalice."

"Siobhan has it?" Isabel said, her eyes going wide. "Are you certain?"

"Had it," Tristan corrected. "I took it from her . . ." He stopped, seeing Orlando's face. "What is it?"

"She took it back," the wizard said. "Last night, while the two of you were hunting. She came into the dungeons and rifled through your things until she found it. She took the stake as well."

"And you saw her?" Simon said, appalled. "You did not stop her?"

Orlando looked at Tristan. "I could not."

"But you're certain the sword is the same?" Isabel interrupted. "You know it's the one from the drawing?"

"Siobhan struck Tristan with it," Simon explained, putting a hand on her shoulder, not caring for the look he saw passing between the wizard and the other vampire. "In truth, she almost destroyed him."

"His wounds did not heal for hours," Orlando agreed. "If he had not been able to reach shelter, the sunrise would have consumed him. Do you still think we should confide in Siobhan?"

"More than ever," she answered. "We need her." She

reached for her scrolls. "When I'm done, I suspect you will agree."

"You found something," Simon said. He grinned. "So you didn't just come to see me after all."

"Not just," she admitted, smiling back for a moment before she looked at Orlando. "Four days ago, I found more text in the catacombs at Charmot, hidden in plain sight." She opened a scroll on the table. "Remember the paintings on the walls?"

"That's impossible," Orlando insisted. "We searched them thoroughly; there was no text—"

"No painted text, no; there was not," she agreed. "It was carved into the stone." She showed them a mostly black parchment covered in white lettering of a kind Tristan had never seen. "I put the parchment over the stone and rubbed it with a bit of charcoal," she explained. "And I discovered much." She reached back for her husband's hand. "Orlando has lied to you, Simon," she said. "From the very beginning."

"No," the wizard insisted, but Tristan noticed he went pale. "I did not—"

"You told Simon you were a servant of the caliph murdered by Kivar," she cut him off.

"No," Orlando said, shaking his head. "He may have believed that, but I never—"

"You told him the Chalice would save him," she interrupted again. "That if he found it, he could be mortal again."

"And so he will," the wizard insisted.

"Will he?" she countered. All the sweetness was gone from her manner, and seeing the fury in her eyes, Tristan thought that perhaps she and Siobhan were not so different after all. "Listen to this," she said, reading from the scroll.

"And thus was Lucan Kivar banished from the realm of gods and mortal men, his cursed body flung into the night to burn across the sky until it came to rest in a far land over the mountains. All of his children were destroyed save the two sons born of mortal women before he touched the Chalice. The younger of these was Merlin, mortal but blessed with the love and the beauty of the gods. 'Twas he who led his mortal kin across the frozen wastes to scatter over the islands they found, teaching them the old ways to pass on to their children in the time to come. 'Tis said he died at last on Eire, the furthest of these islands."

She looked up at the wizard again as if daring him to speak, but he said nothing. She went on.

"The older was Orlando. Misshapen and stunted in body, he possessed the wisdom of the gods and immortality. Most loathed by his father, 'twas he who betrayed Kivar to save his mother's kin. Beloved of his brother and all mortals for his sacrifice, he still would not join them in their journey. He swore to

*cross the mountains and find the resting place of the
Cursed One, to find a way to destroy him forever."*

"And so I did," Orlando said at last. "I found him,
and I found the way to destroy him."

"Yes, but at what cost?" Isabel asked. "When I read
that story, I was shocked, but I came to believe it did not
matter, that I had always known you had a power beyond any mortal conjurer. In truth, I felt better, knowing Simon had you to protect him." She opened
another scroll. "Then I found this."

"Wait—you mean to say this tale is true?" Tristan
demanded. "That all that you just read actually happened?"

"You are a vampire, brother," Simon said, his tone
flat and even. "Can you not believe it?" He touched Isabel's cheek. "What is written there?"

"The true power of this chalice Orlando so wants
you to find." She read from the parchment, " 'The
Chalice was hidden in the realm of the gods, to be safe
from all save those who know its secrets and share the
blood it held once at their table. Only the Chalice can
destroy Kivar, and only one of mortal blood can wield
it.' " She looked up. "I take that to mean not a vampire,
but perhaps I am mistaken," she said acidly before she
read on. "If a warrior of noble heart and mortal blood
should wield the power of the Chalice against him,
Kivar would be destroyed, and all his demon spawn
must perish in his flame.' " She looked up again. "His

demon spawn," she repeated. "Simon. Tristan. If you find this chalice and use it against Lucan Kivar, they will die."

"No," Orlando insisted. "I swear that is not so. At least . . . I do not believe it." He paced the room in agitation. "There was so much to remember, so much . . . I tried to write everything down, but so many fragments were lost." He smiled bitterly at Simon. "May you never truly know the curse of immortality."

"So you're saying this writing the duchess found is all a lie?" Tristan said.

"No, it is true," the wizard admitted. "The most important truth we had—that is why Merlin would have taught his children to keep it. But it is not the whole truth." He looked at Simon again then looked back at Tristan. "I cannot bear it," he mumbled. "It has been so long, and there is so much I have forgotten without ever knowing I forgot. When I found the drawing of the Chalice, I realized how much I had lost." He turned back to the others. "Isabel, you found no mention of Joseph or his stake, did you?" he asked. "Yet we know the stake drove Kivar from his mortal form into his true, immortal shape, if only for a moment. If Simon had possessed the sword, he might have killed him then."

"Wait," Tristan said. "I am confused." His pragmatic warrior's mind had been turning this story over and over, trying to find a way to believe this dwarf before him was immortal, the offspring of some evil demigod.

"The Chalice is good, because it destroys this Kivar, yes? Then why should Kivar want it? I would think he would want to put himself as far away from it as possible."

"It doesn't have to destroy him," Orlando explained. "That is something Merlin would never have carved into a wall, for fear Kivar would find it. Kivar has forgotten many things as well, more than I have, I think. Every time he changes form, he loses some part of himself. All he remembers is that the Chalice gave him power before he was cursed, that when he possessed it, not even the gods could touch him."

"He said it could heal him." Simon was staring into the fire. "He told me you were wrong, that the Chalice was not salvation, but healing."

"And so he believes," Orlando said. "And so it may be, for him. If he drank from the Chalice again, the curse that damns him to darkness might be broken."

"So he would possess all of the powers of a vampire with none of the weaknesses," Tristan said.

"Much more than that," Orlando said. "He could remake himself as he believes he should have been, an all-powerful god." He looked back at Isabel. "Having made his acquaintance firsthand, my lady, can you say we should not do whatever we must to stop him?"

"But what is that exactly?" she countered. "What must we do? Everything we think we know could be wrong; isn't that what you said? And everything you say could be a lie."

"Are we certain Kivar still lives?" Tristan said as Simon put his arms around his love.

"Unfortunately, yes," Simon answered. "His spirit escaped me when I met him last. And there is evidence that he has followed you. The voice you spoke of hearing on your way back here—that was almost certainly Kivar. And you said you dreamed of his hall, of his saying he would come to you."

"Yes." Suddenly the dream that his mind had all but lost came back to him with shocking clarity, the golden hall and the long, lean figure in the golden robe changing into someone else, a smaller, stockier man with a handsome, open face. A face he had seen somewhere else. "Bloody hell," he muttered. "Callard." He stormed out into the corridor and down the stairs to the hall. "Siobhan!" Andrew was coming toward him, looking worried, and he caught him by the arm. "Where is my lady?" he demanded.

"In her room, I would guess," the knight answered. "She was much shaken by the baron's death."

"The baron's death?" Tristan echoed. "What—?"

"Forgive me, my lord," Andrew said quickly. "I forgot you had not heard. The baron was found in his rooms this morning, dead. Some of his servants confessed to Master Nicholas they had suffered a plague at his own house before they came here, but in truth, this looked like no illness I have ever seen. His throat was torn out."

Simon had come after him. "Did you tear the baron's throat out?" Tristan asked him.

"No," he answered with a bitter smile.

"My lord?" Andrew said weakly, obviously shocked.

"Find my daughter," Tristan ordered. "Take her to the priest in the chapel—stay near the cross, and surround her with knights. If any man other than myself or the duke should try to come near her, cut off his head." He thought of what Simon had told him of how Kivar had changed his shape to fool Isabel. "And if the man who comes is the duke or myself, question him closely," he finished. "Make him tell you Clare's mother's name."

"What was Clare's mother's name?" Simon asked as they pushed their way out of the hall.

"Alisande." As soon as he reached the courtyard, he broke into a run. "Her name was Alisande."

He sprinted across the bridge to the tower and up the winding stairs. "Siobhan!" He threw open the door to her room, but it was empty. "Siobhan!"

"Please, my lord." Emma came in behind him, wringing her hands. "They've gone."

He forced himself not to grab her. "Who is gone?" he asked.

"Lady Siobhan and the others," she answered. "All the ones who served Lebuin. They have escaped."

"Oh, no," Simon muttered, shaking his head.

"How, Emma?" Tristan said, putting his hands on her shoulders but keeping his tone calm. "How did they escape?"

"Some sort of tunnel, my lord," she answered.

"Michael didn't want to tell me, but I made him. I begged him not to go."

"Where is this tunnel, sweeting?" Simon said. "Do you know?"

"Here," she said, meeting his gaze. "Under the druid's hill."

19

Siobhan raised her torch as she rounded another sharp curve in the tunnel. "Siobhan?" Michael touched her arm. "Do you hear that?"

She listened—voices from the passageway ahead. "DuMaine," one of the men said woefully. "We're dead."

"No one is dead," she snapped. None of the voices was Tristan, she was certain. But at least one of them was familiar. "Sean . . ." She smiled just as her brother emerged from the dark, carrying a torch. "Sean!" Handing her own torch to Michael, she ran to his arms.

"Here she is," Sean laughed, scooping her up and swinging her around. "You see, Gaston? I told you she would find it."

The man she had thought herself rid of emerged from the shadows as well. "So you did," he agreed with a smile.

"Gaston found me and told me what happened to the baron," Sean explained. "My poor lamb . . ." He hugged her close again, kissing her hair. "Thank God you escaped."

"Sean, listen to me," she insisted, breaking free. "I have to go back."

"Are you mad?" he said, laughing. "Not this time, Siobhan. I will come back and deal with DuMaine after I know you are safe."

"I am safe with DuMaine," she said. "You and the men are not; he still means to take revenge on you. I tried to convince him you were gone, but he didn't believe me." Once again, he was staring at her as if she might have sprouted horns and started chanting the Black Mass. "But I cannot leave him. If you go, I can stop his coming after you, I know it, but even if I couldn't . . ." Gaston looked ready to laugh out loud. "Please, Sean," she said, catching hold of her brother's tunic and trying to ignore him. "Please, just let me go."

"What did I tell you, Lebuin?" Gaston said. "The demon has bewitched her."

"Be quiet!" she ordered, drawing her sword and lunging for him.

"Siobhan, stop!" Sean said, catching her as Gaston sprang back, his eyes wide with shock.

"Don't listen to him, Sean," she said, struggling to break her brother's grip. "The man is poison—even Callard himself did not trust him!"

"It may be too late for her, Sean," Gaston said, an edge of true fear in his tone. "She may be a demon herself."

"Don't be ridiculous," Sean scoffed. "Siobhan, be still—"

"Don't you see?" she demanded. "He is trying to turn you against me—"

"So what if he is?" Sean said, catching her hard by the shoulders. "You are my sister, remember?" She stopped fighting as he made her face him. "No one can turn me against you or you against me." He framed her face in his hands. "Is that not so?"

He means Tristan, she thought, her heart twisting with pain. Even if he doesn't know it, that is who he means. "Yes," she answered, barely louder than a whisper.

"Come with me now, Siobhan," he said. "I am not leaving without you."

"Yes." She looked over his shoulder to Gaston. "I will come with you."

Michael hung back to guard the rear without a torch, so he was the only one who saw Gaston stop to look around the chamber. "Of course," the courtier muttered, a strange light in his eyes. "How can I have forgotten? This way is already shut." He stepped on the skull of one of the skeletons, crushing it under his boot. "But no matter. There is another." He looked back to find Michael watching and smiled. Without a word, he turned to follow the rest.

Siobhan stood in the moonlit grove, watching the men load the last of her brother's stolen treasure from the stash in the caves onto horses. "This is a mistake," she said softly to Michael, standing beside her. "You should go, all of you, now." She thought of Tristan discovering her gone. He would think she had betrayed him, that all her words of love had been nothing but lies. "Holy Christ," she whispered, raising a hand to her eyes.

"Aye, love," Michael answered grimly. "We should be gone, and we should leave that lunatic behind." Gaston was now standing in the middle of the circle of trees, gazing up at the moon with his strange little smile on his face. "His master dying has cracked his wits at last."

"Sean," she said, going to her brother. "Why do we need this now? We should be gone."

"I will need gold to hire mercenaries," he answered as if he thought her own wits had gone dim. "We will need twice as many troops to take the castle a second time; DuMaine will be prepared."

"Sean . . ." Before she could form an argument to this madness, a strange sound made both of them turn. Gaston had begun to sing, a kind of tuneless chant in a language she didn't understand. "What in the name of hell . . . ?"

His voice grew louder, filling the grove, and all of the men stopped what they were doing to watch him as if spellbound. "Gaston, stop it," she said, moving forward. "Sean, make him stop." A queer, milky light rose up in pillars from the ground in a circle around them, a pillar before every tree. "You bastard, what are you doing?" He looked back at her and smiled, but his song went on. She staggered as the ground beneath her feet began to shake. "Sean!" She turned to find her brother looking back at her, eyes wide, but the others were smiling or had no expression at all.

"What is it?" Sean demanded as if she should know. Inside each pillar of light, the ground broke open, and a thicker, greener light in the shape of a man shot out. "Holy Christ!"

"Draw your sword!" she called to him as she did the same, and he obeyed as if breaking out of a trance. The men were moving toward the lights as if walking in a dream. "Stop them!" She reached out and caught hold of Michael's arm, and he flung her away hard enough to knock her to the ground. "Michael, stop!" She flung her dagger at him, stabbing him through the thigh, and he fell, howling in pain. "What are you doing?"

He looked at her as if waking from a nightmare. "God's truth, I don't know." The others had reached the writhing lights and stepped inside, swords and daggers drawn. With a flash like lightning, each one changed, growing taller, with short, thick swords like Siobhan's.

"Behold our army, children!" Gaston laughed, but the voice was not Gaston's. "Now we will take your castle."

As if in answer, three great horses galloped into the circle. "Siobhan!" Tristan shouted, striking as one of the ghost warriors attacked. "Get back!" He lopped the man's head from his shoulders. Then in an instant, he was sitting up, putting his head back on his shoulders to become the ghost warrior again.

"Tristan, look out!" she screamed as he attacked again, knocking her love from his horse.

"Take the woman!" Gaston shouted, laughing with delight as he pointed toward Isabel's horse. "Bring her to me!"

"No!" Siobhan screamed, not certain where to attack first. "Sean, fight them!"

"We can't!" he shouted back. "They are our men!"

"We have to!" She plunged her sword into the back of one of the half-dozen creatures attacking Tristan, and this time when he fell, he stayed down, a mortal man writhing in pain. "We can hurt them, but Tristan cannot!"

"Good!" Sean said, still standing back with his sword in his hand.

"Idiot!" More ghosts were rising from the cracks in the earth, ethereal but armed with swords. Simon was trying to fight his way to Isabel, but the ghosts swarmed over him like locusts, dragging him off his horse. "Sean, please!"

"Oh, bloody hell," he grumbled, plunging into the throng around Isabel's horse.

Tristan saw Lebuin going after Isabel. With an oath, he drew his dagger, ready to fling it through the brigand's throat. Then he realized he meant to save her.

"Tristan!" Siobhan was still trying to reach him, fighting like she might have been a demon herself. One of the ghosts tried to lunge past her, and she ducked, driving her shoulder hard into his chest to knock him backward to the ground before stabbing him through the thigh. Behind her, he saw one of the ghosts strike Orlando from his horse, knocking him unconscious to the ground.

"Be careful!" Tristan tried to shout, but before the words were out, a blade had slashed across his throat. The same freezing fire he had felt when Siobhan struck him with her enchanted sword engulfed him as blood poured from the wound. He staggered to his knees, and more ghosts swarmed over him, stabbing him from every side.

"No!" Siobhan screamed, seeing him fall. The man she had struck was a human at heart, and her blow had brought him back to himself, clutching his gushing wound. But the cracks were still pouring out more ghosts by the moment, more than she could have cut down in a year. Simon's horse was rearing and screaming, striking at a teeming pile of greenish bodies writhing like snakes at his feet.

"Simon!" she heard Isabel sob. Sean was still trying to reach her, but the ghosts were fighting him back, and his sword was not enchanted. They dragged Isabel to Gaston, waiting with his dagger drawn. Meeting Siobhan's gaze with an evil smile, he grabbed Isabel's arm and slashed the blade across her wrist, driving her bleeding to the ground. Immediately the ghosts seemed to grow stronger, more solid, and the milky light in the clearing grew brighter, more like daylight.

"No!" Siobhan screamed, running forward. Without thinking, she drew the stake from her belt with her free hand. Gaston turned just as she reached him, and she drove the stake with all her strength into his heart.

"Good girl," he gasped, laughing, as she raised the sword. "Now finish me."

"My pleasure," she snarled, striking off his head.

The corpse fell backward, the head rolling away. Isabel screamed as a cloud of thick black mist poured out of the severed neck and gathered around Siobhan.

Tristan drove his hand through the spongy breast of the ghost bending closest over him, clutching at what felt like the heart and yanking it out in his fist. As the creature screamed and reared away, he saw Siobhan engulfed in a cloud of black. "No!" he roared, trying to stand.

"No!" Sean echoed, rushing forward. Siobhan could barely see him, could barely breathe. The mist was in her nose and mouth, drowning her, worming its way inside. She staggered, dropping her sword.

Suddenly Sean tackled her, shoving her aside. In a moment, the mist had released her, rushing into him instead. His eyes went wide, but he did not make a sound.

"Sean?" She touched his arm. "Sean, dear God, are you all right?"

"Enough!" he shouted, and the ghosts began to fade. The light was fading from the grove, and the cracks in the earth were closing up.

"It's all right," Siobhan said, falling to her knees beside Isabel, still bleeding on the ground. "It will be all right now." The green light was bleeding into the ground and disappearing, leaving the men looking as they had before, only dazed.

"Bring the girl," Sean ordered. "Tie the wizard to his horse." Tristan and Simon were both lying prone on their backs, the ground around them soaked with blood.

"Sean, we have to help them." She rushed to Tristan's side, and he looked up at her, his eyes clouded. "Tristan . . ." She laid a hand against his cheek, her throat thick with tears. "You are a demon," she reminded him. "You cannot die."

"Sean . . ." His throat had been cut, and his voice came out a strangled growl. "Not Sean . . ."

"What?" She turned to find her brother standing over her, holding his sword.

"I would have spared you." His voice was cold, the voice of a stranger. "You did not have to die."

She lunged for her sword, and he stabbed her through the stomach. "Sean," she whispered, falling to the ground. This can't be happening, she thought, her body going cold. This can't be real. He picked Isabel up by one arm and flung her over his shoulder. "Sean, please . . ." Pain was spreading from her stomach like a freezing fire, making her feel sick. She spit out her own blood as Sean mounted his horse, Isabel flung over the saddle before him, limp as a corpse herself.

Not dead, Tristan thought, fighting with all his will to move. Not dead yet. If he had been Simon, he supposed he would have stopped to think about the consequences of what he meant to do, sift through the layers of heaven and hell. But for himself, he did not have the time. Siobhan collapsed beside him, coughing blood, and he reached for her, closing his fist around her arm.

"Fight," he ordered. His voice was clearer now; he was slowly healing. But not fast enough, not if she did not fight to stay alive. "Fight, Siobhan."

She pressed her cheek against his arm, wishing he would hold her, make her warm. "So cold," she whispered, tasting blood.

He rolled to his side, the pain in his own stomach making him feel faint. But his body obeyed him now; he could move. "Fight, brigand," he ordered again, making himself sit up. Rolling her onto her back, he drew her up into his arms.

"Yes," she murmured, clinging to him. The pain was less now, but the cold was terrible. "So good . . ." His arms were warm around her . . . how could a vampire feel warm? "Dying," she realized. "I'm dying, Tristan."

"No, you're not." He turned her face up to his, making her look at him. "You will not leave me," he promised, smiling down on her. "I will not let you go." He lifted her wrist to his mouth, sinking his fangs into the vein, and she cried out, struggling against the pain. But he held her fast, feeding until her heartbeat was no more than a flutter, his own strength returning with the blood. "Time to fight now, brigand," he said, his voice rough with love as he touched her cheek. "Time to live." He cut a gash over his own heart with his dagger and gathered her close, pressing her mouth to the wound. She made a sort of kitten's sound of protest, trying to push him, to turn her face away. Then he felt her taste the blood. Her teeth sank into his flesh, and a jolt of power like nothing he had ever felt raced through him, making him dizzy with love. Mine, he thought, cradling her close. Forever . . .

She lifted her head at last, the terrible power pulsing through her, making her feel drunk. Tristan was looking down on her, smiling but with tears of blood glistening red on his cheeks. "My love," she said, touching a crimson trail. "You always promised you would kill me in the end."

"Yes." He kissed her lightly on the mouth, and her arms came around him, wrapped around his neck as she wept on his shoulder. He held her close with all his strength, his beautiful vampire love. "Now I have."

Epilogue

Silas raised his wine cup. "To your marriage," he said, smiling on Tristan and Siobhan. "At last I may wish you happiness."

"And long life?" Tristan added, raising an eyebrow.

"And that," the scholar said, laughing.

Siobhan wrapped her arms around her husband's waist, cleaving to his side. "Very long indeed." She had wept for Sean, and she was still afraid of what would happen when they caught up with her brother again, as she knew they must. But she hadn't shed a tear for her mortality. Tristan was her heart's true mate, the only man who could ever have known her for exactly the brigand she was and loved her even so. At the moment of her body's death, she had looked into his eyes and known he would always be with her, would always protect her. The devil's knight was hers.

Tristan kissed her hair. "Sebastian and Andrew can manage the castle until we return," he said to Silas as he held her close, his arm around her shoulders. "Master

Nicholas will help them whether they want him or not. But Silas, will you watch over my daughter?"

"Emma will help you," Siobhan added. "Clare seems to understand that we must go away . . ." Her voice trailed off for a moment as she thought of exactly what the little girl had said. "That we must go away to war," she finished. Less than two days before, she had been desperate to save her brother. Now she must go to war against him. "But she will need both of you to reassure her we are coming back."

"And so we will," Silas promised. "Will you leave tonight?"

"We must," Tristan answered. "Lebuin . . ." He hesitated as well before he corrected himself. "Lucan Kivar already has a day's head start. We will leave as soon as Simon is ready."

"Is he still hurt?" Silas asked, concerned. Both Tristan and Simon had been badly wounded when Siobhan had led guards back into the woods to find them, mortally so, Silas would have said if he hadn't known they were vampires. Tristan seemed to be mostly healed after his day's rest, but he still bore a dark pink scar slashed across his cheek.

"His body is well enough," Tristan said. "But he fears for his soul." In truth, Simon had insisted on going to the castle's chapel as soon as the sun was down to pray for help and guidance in spite of the pain it must surely have caused him to do it.

"He fears for his wife," Siobhan corrected. "He thinks it was his fault she was taken."

"He thinks everything is his fault." He turned her face up to his, scowling down on her with a grim determination she knew now as love. "But the fault lies with Kivar," he finished, his green eyes haunted by what she knew was the memory of the grove. "And we will see he pays for it."

"Yes," she promised him, touching his cheek. "We will."

"I will leave you, my lord," Silas said. "I know you will wish to be alone for some time before you go."

"Thank you, Silas," Siobhan said, leaving Tristan for a moment to embrace the scholar. "I know we ask too much of your friendship."

"Not at all," he promised, hugging her back. "I will see you both downstairs."

Tristan pulled her close again as soon as he was gone. "You do not have to go with us," he said softly, caressing her hair. "You could stay here and manage the castle." She drew back to look at him, one eyebrow raised. "You would be safe."

"I would not." She pressed her cheek against his chest. "I am only safe with you." She smiled. "Are you so eager to be rid of me?"

"Yes," he said, wrapping his arms around her. "I can't abide the sight of you; can you not tell? 'Tis why I've fought so hard to keep you."

"And fool that I am, I have fought so hard to escape."

The night before, still wounded, he had taught her how to hunt, had fed her blood from his own wrist until the terrible hunger of her first night as a vampire abated. "I cannot be worth the trouble I have caused you. How could you not give me up?"

"In faith, my love, I tried." He turned her face up to his and smiled, feeling rather dizzy. She had been beautiful before, but as a vampire, she barely seemed real. "But you bewitched me." He kissed her tenderly. "My little demon."

"Now in truth," she agreed with a smile of her own. "I did not mean to leave you . . . last night, I meant to return." She moved slowly from his arms, holding his hand. "I only wanted Sean to go away, to leave us and be safe. I never meant to leave you ever again."

"And so you will not." He lifted her hand to his lips, remembering their marriage vows. His curse was now their blessing, eternity bound to his love. Nothing could ever part them now; at last he felt certain. "We will find your brother," he promised. "We will save him if it can be done."

"Do you think he lives?" Her fingers curled more tightly around his as if for comfort.

"I did not see him die." During the day while she slept, he and Simon had talked, the two of them now joined in their quest as if they were brothers indeed. "Simon said Kivar has always possessed men already dead in the past, or so he believes. But without Orlando . . ." He let his voice trail off.

"Orlando was alive when Sean took him," she said. "And Isabel as well."

"Simon believes Kivar will wait to murder Isabel until he finds a pathway to the Chalice, that he needs her blood to open up the door." He drew her close to him again, shuddering to imagine the pain his brother felt.

"Then we must find her first." She raised up on tiptoe to kiss him as if to remind him she was there, safely in his grasp. "Kivar may have Sean's body and his ghosts may have his men, but they are all still mine as well. I know I can track them." Caressing his cheek, she moved away. "But you must tell me of this chalice that we seek."

"I will," he promised. "You will know all." He caught her hand. "But you know the most important truth already." She smiled as if she knew what he would say. "Chalice or not, we are one."

"Forever," she answered.

He kissed her again, pressing her close as the passion they had known from their first meeting flashed between them like a flame. "Forever."

Pocket Books
proudly presents

DARK ANGEL

Lucy Blue

Coming soon in paperback
from Pocket Books

Turn the page for a preview of *Dark Angel*. . . .

Roxanna climbed naked from the icy lake, her face turned up to the moonlight. The Highlands rose around her like the Urals of her birth, and for a moment, she let herself imagine she was back there, back home, a mortal princess with a life of light before her who had never heard of such a cursed creature as a vampire. She would bring her people peace, would fill her golden palace with the laughter of children, heirs to a land of prosperity for all. She thought of Gareth, and a sob rose in her throat. If she had met him then, if he had come to her before Kivar, she would have given him her soul, would have loved him all her mortal life.

"Roxanna." She opened her eyes to find him standing on the bank as if her wish had conjured him, the mortal knight who held her heart. He was dressed now like his Highland kin in a woven woolen kilt, the bruises and cuts she had tended on his face healed and gone. His light brown hair glowed golden in the moonlight, and his blue eyes broke her heart with yearning. He was what his fate meant him to be, a prince in his own right. He should not yearn for her, should not know her at all. She was a demon, a monster, cursed to an eternity alone. "Why did you leave me?" he demanded, coming closer, and she took a step back along the sandy shore.

"Your kin had come for you," she answered. "You did not need me anymore."

"You know that isn't true." He looked her up and down, incredulous, as if he'd only just realized she was naked. "My God, you must be freezing!" He moved closer, taking off his mantle.

"Stay back!" She bent down and picked up the rough wool gown she had discarded. "You must not think of me, Gareth." She held it before her to cover her nakedness, trying not to hear the way his heart beat faster. He thought she was an angel, his rescuer, a mortal maid. "Go back to your grandfather's castle and forget me."

"Oh, for pity's sake . . ." Losing patience, he reached out for her, and she broke from him and fled into the forest, dropping the gown behind her. "Roxanna!"

She should have outpaced him easily, but she could hear him gaining on her, crashing through the trees. She should transform into a cat and disappear, leave these mountains, go after Kivar. The very fact that she wanted to stay was proof enough she could not. "Stop!" he ordered, catching her wrist before she could decide to flee indeed and yanking her back to face him.

"Let me go!" She twisted in his grasp like she might have been the helpless woman she appeared.

"I will not." He frowned, not angry, just perturbed. "God's grace, girl," he muttered, holding her fast with one hand as he draped the mantle over her shoulders with the other. "Madness is one thing, but this is ridiculous." He was teasing her now, his blue eyes twinkling with mischief, and her heart clenched like a fist. He was her perfect opposite—blithe while she was melancholy, light while she was dark. Good while she was evil. Mortal while she was undead.

"I am not mad." She tried to shrug out of his grasp, but he wouldn't allow it, holding her fast by the shoulders.

"Oh no, I forgot," he said, still teasing. "You are a princess from a distant land, traveling under a curse. And running naked through the forest in October."

"Gareth—"

"My grandfather wants to thank you." He let her go to brush her hair back from her cheek, his smile like the sun she had lost. "In truth, I'm not certain he would believe you exist except for the stitches you put in my back. He thinks you are really an old crone, and I was delirious."

"Perhaps you were." She smiled back just a little, unable to help herself. How could she feel so happy and so miserable at once?

"I still am." She felt some of the tension leave him, heard his heartbeat slow again. He brushed the pad of his thumb across her lower lip, a lover's caress, and she stiffened, desperate not to want him, helpless to resist. His touch was like a drug to her, all the warmth and tenderness Kivar had stolen from her brought back in this single, beautiful mortal. But she could not have him. "My uncle would like to get a good, long look at you, too, I suspect," he went on. "No doubt he takes it ill, you're not leaving me to die as he wanted. It isn't safe for you alone here anymore."

"I do not fear your uncle." His enemy still lived; he could still be hurt or murdered, even. If she left him, she could not protect him . . . but that was madness. He was a man, able to protect himself from other men. She could only protect him from herself.

"You fear no one," he answered, amusement and admiration mixed equally in his tone. "But I fear for you."

"You shouldn't." She braced her hands against his chest to push him to arm's length. "I can take care of myself far better than you know."

"Then come take care of me." He took her hand and raised it to his lips. "I might even give you a dress."

"Stop it!" If she were kind to him, he would never let her go. So long as he thought she was a gentle maid, he would try to protect her. "I don't want to go with you," she said, collecting all the hauteur her station had ever allowed her to possess, the daughter of the caliph addressing a slave at her feet. "I don't want you."

"Is that so?" he asked, quirking a brow.

"You were a lovely diversion." In her mind, she saw him bending over her before the cottage fire, remembered the sweetness of his kisses on her lips. "And I could hardly leave you to die in the woods or be eaten by wolves or . . ." Hurt and anger were dawning in his eyes, and she made herself turn away, refusing to see it. "But I hardly meant to make a career as your nursemaid."

"Nursemaid?" he repeated, the edge in his tone making her shudder inside. "Is that what you called the last night we spent together? Nursing?"

"What else?" she said with a laugh.

"Your physic is quite unique, my lady," he said sarcastically. "Not that I'm complaining, of course."

"It has always served me well enough." She ventured a look back over her shoulder, smiling the deadly, bitter smile that Kivar had always found so charming, expecting to find him wounded to the core, bracing herself against it. "You are living, are you not?" But he was smiling again.

"Roxanna, stop it." He touched her cheek. "Tell me the truth. Why are you running away? Why are you afraid?"

"You think I am afraid of you?" she scoffed.

"Aye, love, I do." His manner softened even more, turning tender as he traced the shape of her jaw with his touch. "I don't know what has hurt you," he said. "I don't know why you cry in your sleep or hide from the sunlight or pretend to be some heathen caliph's daughter—I don't even know you."

"No," she answered, still and cold as a statue. "You do not."

"But I know that I owe you my life." She closed her eyes, as he moved closer, holding her shoulders as he bent and kissed her hair. "Let me help you now."

"You can't." She laid her palms against his chest to

push him back again, and his arms closed around her. "Gareth, you can't help me," she protested. "I am not afraid of you, I swear it."

"Liar," he said gently.

"It's true." Tears burned her eyes again as he kissed her brow. "I will hurt you, Gareth."

"You might drive me to distraction," he allowed. "But I will risk it."

"You don't understand." Still enfolded in his arms, she opened her eyes to see the marks her fangs had left on his throat when she'd fed from him. She had never imagined she could come to care for him, had barely seen him as a man at all. "I didn't save you because I am good; I saved you because I am evil."

"Love, that makes no sense." He turned her face up to his, smiling down on her, so innocent and strong. "How could you be evil?" Before she could answer, he kissed her, tenderly at first, then harder as she sighed against his mouth. She tried to turn her head away, her lips parting to protest, and his tongue pushed tenderly inside, sending shivers through her, making her melt in his embrace. His kiss was sweet as honey, warm as blood, and her need for him was like a fever, burning to the marrow of her bones.

"Gareth," she murmured, begging him for mercy as his kiss moved to her cheek, his arms crushing her closer.

"Come home with me." He nuzzled underneath the curtain of her hair, his words soft but intense against her ear.

"No, I won't." She was crying tears of blood, but his eyes were closed; he could not see, had never seen the truth. "Gareth, I can't—"

"You can." He wrapped his arms around her, cradling her head against his shoulder, her face still hidden as he tried to comfort her. "Whatever has happened, whatever has hurt you, I can keep you safe." A strangled sob escaped her, her heart twisting with grief. "Marry me, princess." The teasing endearment was more than she could bear; surely she must lose her mind indeed. How could she have let this happen? How could she have let them come to this? "I will even build you a castle," he promised. "More beautiful than the one you say you lost."

"No." She could not pretend anymore, for his sake or her own. Drawing back to look at him, she let the hunger come into her eyes, amber with the demon's glow. "Look at me, Gareth." He drew back a step, still holding her arms, and she snarled, baring her fangs.

"You . . ." Recognition dawned in the light of his blue eyes, and his face turned pale. "I dreamed . . . I thought it was a dream . . ."

"A nightmare," she corrected. She snapped at him like an animal, and he drew back at last, letting her go. "Will you take a demon for your bride?" His mouth worked as if he would answer, but no sound came out, his eyes still glazed with horror. She reached out to touch his cheek, and he recoiled, raising his hand as if to strike her back. "Forget me, Gareth." Her heart ached as she backed away, grief like she had thought she could never feel again. "You must not think of me."

"Roxanna!" he called as she reached the edge of the clearing. She turned back and looked at him, tears streaming down her cheeks. Then she transformed into the black mountain cat and disappeared into the forest.

FINALLY
A WEBSITE
YOU CAN GET
PASSIONATE
ABOUT...

Visit
www.SimonSaysLove.com
for the latest information
about Romance from Pocket Books!

READING SUGGESTIONS

LATEST RELEASES

AUTHOR APPEARANCES

ONLINE CHATS WITH YOUR
FAVORITE WRITERS

SPECIAL OFFERS

ORDER BOOKS ONLINE

AND MUCH, MUCH MORE!

POCKET BOOKS
A Division of Simon & Schuster
A VIACOM COMPANY

POCKET
STAR BOOKS
A Division of Simon & Schuster
A VIACOM COMPANY

Love is timeless...

Bestselling historical romance from Pocket Books

One Little Sin
Liz Carlyle
One sin leads to another...

First in an exciting new series!

Two Little Lies
Liz Carlyle
Because just once is never enough!

His Dark Desires
Jennifer St. Giles
Can she resist the passion in his eyes—or
the danger in his kiss?

Outlaw
Lisa Jackson
The only woman who can tempt him is the
one woman he swore to destroy...

The Lawman Said "I Do"
Ana Leigh
All he wanted was a night of pleasure. But
she wanted so much more...

13445

 POCKET BOOKS
A Division of Simon & Schuster
A VIACOM COMPANY

 POCKET STAR BOOKS
A Division of Simon & Schuster
A VIACOM COMPANY

Available wherever books are sold or at www.simonsayslove.com.